Amelia's Marriage

Amelia's Marriage

by Agnes Alexander

Cover Artist: Susan Krupp
Editor: Melanie Billings
Printed in the United States of America

Published by
WHISKEY CREEK PRESS LLC
Whiskeycreekpress.com

Print ISBN: 978-1-63355-740-6

Dedication

For my cousin, Elaine 'Lanie' Walsh who is my horse expert and my very dearest friend.

Chapter 1

Amelia Donahue sat atop her sleek, golden palomino, Rambler, and looked across the expanse of open range below the ridge. She'd chosen to come here to ponder what had happened in the last few days instead of going to the secluded spot beside the creek where she usually went when she was upset and needed to think. Today she wanted to be out on the ranch she loved. The ranch where her grandfather had created an empire and where her mother had been born and raised. And where Amelia had come into the world eighteen years ago. The ranch where her grandmother had died when Amelia was five and where her grandfather joined his wife in death four years ago. The Double D Ranch. The place she planned to spend the rest of her life. Her home.

She shifted her eyes from the open plains to the pit fire below the ridge. She couldn't miss the sound of the clanking irons, the stench of burning flesh, the bawling of cows as the hands burned the Double D brand into their sides, and the undercurrent of laughter and talking among the men. The sounds and the smells floated up to her now attesting to the fact that life on her beloved ranch was going on as normal. As if nothing of significance had happened. It was just another work day for everyone. That is, for everyone except her, it was as if only a minor interruption had occurred. A short pause. Not the shattering event that if pulled off would change, not only her life, but the life of everyone on the ranch forever.

She now knew nothing she said or did would change Rafe Donahue's mind about his plan. She'd finally accepted the fact that her father would never listen to her protests no matter how much she tried to convince him she couldn't go along with him. He didn't or wouldn't understand why she felt she had to buck his hideous plot. He was set on the idea and only laughed and then ignored her when she begged, fussed and flatly refused to fall in line and do what he expected. No amount of arguing had helped. After all, according to him, she was only a woman and there was no way she could know what was good for her. And in his way of thinking, no females knew enough about worldly things to make their own decisions about their futures. Especially not his headstrong daughter.

As Amelia thought back she realized it had been this way since she was a little girl. She'd rebel and her father would reel her in and insist she bend to his will. He'd convince her to comply with his wishes by reminding her she had the privilege of being the daughter of one of the richest ranchers in Wyoming. Nothing money could buy had been, or would ever be, denied her as long as she went by his rules. She was a Donahue and as such, could not be allowed to ruin his reputation. He'd always remind her that he'd worked too hard and sacrificed too much to establish the Donahue name in the area and nothing or nobody was going to besmirch it. Even the times when Amelia thought she'd pushed him too far, he'd cleaned up her messes and with strong lectures made her come around to his way of thinking. She was his daughter. His property. She was supposed to always obey him without question. It was like a business arrange-ment. She was never to question or refuse anything he demanded and in turn, he would see she was continually pampered and cared for and had every material thing she desired. But now that she was a grown woman, what he wanted wasn't what Amelia wanted or needed.

In the four years since Grandfather Downey's death she'd no-ticed how Rafe Donahue had become more unreasonable. He'd lost his temper often, not only with her, but with the cowhands. Many of those who had worked on the Double D for years dared not question any of his orders. And some of those who did were fired. Not only was he more demanding and stubborn where the hands and Amelia were concerned, but he'd become angry with her mother on more than one occasion, which was unusual. In fact, Amelia wondered if this was why her mother had chosen to visit her sister in St. Louis for the second time this year.

Even though Refe had argued with Amelia several times in the four weeks her mother had been gone, this time it was different. It had to be. There was no way she would give in and go along with his outrageous plan.

She wished her mother was home so she could talk things over with her, but that was impossible. Elizabeth Donahue wasn't expected back for another month. This time Amelia was on her own. She would somehow have to think of a way to convince her father she'd never bend to his will this time. She wasn't positive what she wanted for her future, but she knew it certainly wasn't what he'd decided for her. Some way, somehow she would come up with something to thwart the arrangements he'd made because he thought they were not only in her best interest, but in the best interest of the ranch. This time she had to stop him.

It all started three nights earlier when a thunderstorm woke her. She heard the big clock in the entry strike eleven, but no matter what she tried, she couldn't go back to sleep. Thunder and lightning had always made her jittery and for some reason it seemed especially bad tonight. Thinking a glass of milk might help her relax, she got out of her big four poster feather bed and grabbed her robe. Her bare feet made no noise on the colorful rug covering the polished wooden floor in the hallway and down the stairs. As she started across the Spanish-tiled entry, she frowned.

A light peeked out from under her father's study door and there was the sound of voices on the other side. This was unusual. Rafe didn't stay up late unless there was important business to handle or he and her mother were having a rendezvous out on his terrace as they used to do, though Amelia couldn't remember catching them there since she returned from school in Boston when her grandfather died.

Since her mother was away, tonight it had to be some kind of business. But with who? And why this late at night?

Amelia couldn't control her curiosity. She eased to the door and stood close so she could listen to what was being said.

Her father spoke. "I think it's the best thing for everyone, Vince. I know you fancy Amelia and I've decided you'll make her a fine husband."

"You're right," Vince Callahan's gravelly voice answered. "I've always cared for your daughter. In fact, I've told her when she was all grown up I was going to marry her. She thought I was kidding, and I was when she was younger, but not now. I've always known she'd grow into a beautiful young woman and become a wife any man would be proud to have."

"It relieves me to know she'll be married before Elizabeth and I take our trip abroad. My wife has always wanted to visit her English relatives. Though I don't care a damn about going, it could prove to be good financially. Some of her family there are wealthy. Therefore, I want the voyage to be a peaceful one so she won't wonder why I finally decided to take her." He chuckled. "Since Amelia won't be going, I don't want to be worrying about what my daughter is up to while we're gone. She can get into some messes and if she's married to you, I won't have to be concerned. I'm sure you can handle her. I also know everything on the ranch will be taken care of the same as if I were here."

"I appreciate you trusting your ranch and your daughter to me, Rafe. You've made me a happy man."

"I thought I would, but I'm sure there's going to be one hurtle to get over. Amelia probably won't like the idea at first, but give her time and she'll get used to it."

"Then it's settled. You convince Amelia to marry me and we'll have the wedding as soon as I get back from the cattle drive."

"Sounds good. I'll get it all arranged and we'll throw one big wedding party when you return." Rafe chuckled. "Then not only will I be your father-in-law, but your partner on this ranch as well."

Vince laughed. "You don't have to make me a partner, Rafe. I look forward to marrying Amelia. I'll make sure she's happy and well taken care of."

"If you don't make her happy, you know I'll have your head. Though she's been more trouble than a rampaging buffalo since the day she was born, that little girl means the world to her mother. I can't afford for Elizabeth not to be happy about the marriage. She still controls some things on my ranch."

"I'll make sure Miz Elizabeth comes around."

"Good." Amelia heard her father sigh then say, "Most everybody knows I'd have rather had a son when Amelia came along, but I didn't. So I made the best of it and no matter what anyone thinks, I love Amelia and I want her treated right."

Amelia could stand it no longer. She barged into the room. "If you love me so much then why are you trying to ruin my life and marry me off to this old man?"

Rafe jumped up from behind the desk and Vince came to his feet from the overstuffed pull-up chair. "Where did you come from?" Her father demanded.

"That doesn't matter. What's going on here?" Amelia's eyes blazed.

"Now, calm down, daughter. Vince and I are only making plans for your future."

"You have no right to discuss my future with him."

"Amelia…" Vince started.

"You shut-up!" she yelled. "This is between my father and me."

"I told you to calm down, Amelia." Rafe's voice was sharp as he came around the desk and took his daughter's arm. "I'm only arranging things so you'll be happy and safe when your mother and I go abroad."

"Do you think marrying me to your hired hand is going to make me happy or keep me safe?" She glared at him. "How dare you! He's been trying to bed me for years and you're making it easy for him."

"You're lying!" Vince yelled. His pale gray eyes couldn't disguise the anger. "No matter what I might've been thinking, I've always been a gentleman around you and you know it."

"Is he telling the truth?" Rafe turned sharp eyes to his daughter.

Amelia hesitated as both men stared at her. "Well, I can tell by the way he looks at me what he has on his mind. He's always saying he's going to marry me someday."

"I thought as much. Now calm down and let me explain…"

"I'll do no such thing. I'm not going to marry Vince Callahan. Not now. Now after the cattle drive. Not ever."

Rafe nodded toward the door. "You can leave, Vince. I'll make my daughter see things my way."

"You will not!"

Vince ignored her, picked up his hat and slapped it on his head. It didn't cover the long dingy blond hair which had touches of gray at the temples. "Good-night, boss."

After he closed the door, Rafe took Amelia's shoulders and sat her down in the chair Vince had vacated. "Now, be still and listen to reason, girl."

"I will not listen. What you're doing is barbaric. This is 1878 and women aren't slaves." She glared at her father. "Don't I have a say in who I marry?"

"Like the dandy you thought you loved while you were in school in Boston?" His deep blue eyes glared at her.

Amelia snorted. "So I made a mistake. It didn't last long and nothing ever happened between us."

"Of course it didn't. Not after I proved he was out for your money."

When she said nothing, he went on. "Since you can't handle your own life, I've decided I'll do it for you. Vince is a good man. He likes you and he'll do right by you. Besides, he'll keep this ranch running as it should be run while I'm gone."

"Yeah, since you're making him a partner."

"I'd make any man you married a partner, Amelia. Besides he deserves it. He's a good foreman."

"Vince has worked here less than five years, and he's been trying to get his hands on this ranch ever since Grandpa died. And you marrying me off to him will give him the way to do it."

"Vince doesn't want the ranch, honey. He cares for you. He told me so."

"He lied. He only wants to sleep with me and get the Double D. You'd see that if you'd open your eyes." She shuddered. "I can't stand the thought of having to go to bed with him."

"Don't be vulgar, child. Vince is a loyal employee and no matter what you say, he does care for you. I'd know it if he was lying." Rafe took a deep breath. "Besides, I won't have to worry about anything here with him in charge of things."

"Me, you mean?"

"I was also thinking of the ranch, but you're right. You're the main problem." He shook his head. "You can get into more trouble than any other young woman I know. Marriage to Vince will settle you down."

"I don't get into anything I can't get out of."

"How about last year when you and your friends, Grace and Wilma, decided to check out a saloon? It's no telling what would've happened if Wilma's brother hadn't walked in."

"We only wanted to see what the inside of a saloon was like." She flipped her long blonde hair back. "It sure appeals to a lot of you men."

"It's that sort of thing that has people saying Rafe Donahue should get his daughter married so she'll stay out of trouble. I've decided to do like they've suggested."

Amelia's shoulders dropped. "Daddy, I don't trust Vince. I know he wants your ranch and he's only marrying me to get it. Besides, I don't love him."

"Love has very little to do with most marriages, my dear."

"What about you and Mother? I think she loves you, and if I'm not mistaken, you love her, too. At least you used to love each other."

"Of course your mother loves me. We are one of the few lucky couples. Through the years we've learned what the other expected and we each know our places in the marriage. But most marriages are not like ours. It's the general rule that love usually comes after you get married."

"But I want to love my husband and have him love me before I say 'I do'."

"I'm sure in time you'll come to love Vince." He patted her hand and started back to his desk chair. He seemed ready to dismiss her.

She jumped up. "No I won't! He's almost as old as you. He could be my father."

Rafe laughed. "He's only forty-two. A good age for a man to settle down with a pretty young wife who can give him children. I want you to have me a grandson so I can leave this ranch to him."

"What about me? Grandpa Downey always told me the ranch would be mine someday. I thought you'd leave it to me."

"Amelia, your grandpa spoiled you so much he'd promise you anything. You should know since you're a woman, you have no business owning a ranch. Of course it'll be yours with Vince, but he'll be the one in charge."

"I don't want Vince to have any of this ranch."

"When you have children, you'll feel differently. Now relax and think about it. Wouldn't you like to have a couple of babies to make your mother happy?"

She stared at her father. "Even if I wanted children, which I don't, I sure don't want to have Vince Callahan's brats."

"That's unfair, Amelia."

"Unfair! What's unfair is the fact you're trying to marry me off to a man more than twice my age. You know I'm too young for him."

"I don't trust anyone else to marry you. Vince wants you and he'll make a fine husband. All you have to do is act like a wife should."

"Well, I don't care if he does want me, I don't want him! And I sure don't trust him. If he comes near me, I'll take a gun and castrate him just like he's doing to those young bulls out on the range."

"That wouldn't be a nice way to treat your husband." Rafe couldn't hide the smile her remark brought to his lips. "I'd never have grandchildren then."

"If I ever give you grandchildren it won't be with Vince Callahan. He's never going to be my husband."

"I don't care what you think, daughter. I've made up my mind and it's settled." Rafe picked up some papers on his desk. "I don't trust you to make the right decision which will affect the rest of your life, so I'm making it for you."

"You're not listening to me, Daddy. You never do anymore. What has happened to you?"

"I hear you, Amelia, but you have no say in this matter. You're going to marry Vince because it's the best thing for all of us. Now accept that and go back to bed."

"But, Daddy…"

"Hush, now, child." He smiled down at her as if she were six years old and they were discussing her playing with fire, not a woman who would be nineteen on her next birthday. "I've made the decision and set everything in motion, so you might as well get used to it. Tomorrow I'm going to wire your mother to come home because she has a wedding to plan."

Amelia wanted to scream, but she knew there was no use to argue with him any longer. Without another word, she got up and stomped back to her room. Though the storm still raged outside, it couldn't compare to the storm raging inside her.

Since that night, they fought every day about the coming wedding, but it was as if her father was deaf to her objections. He was determined to marry her off to Vince Callahan before he went abroad, no matter how much she objected.

Since Amelia found out what her father had mapped out for the rest of her life, she continually thought of ways to change his mind. Though she hadn't come up with anything that worked, she was still determined to find a way to foil his plan.

Today, as she sat atop Rambler and looked out on the ranch she loved, she knew, in spite of her father's hard-headed decision, she couldn't and wouldn't marry Vince. She'd as soon marry one of the cowboys who dropped by the ranch now and then asking for work. At least they weren't as old and as disgusting as her father's foreman.

Vince had been the foreman of the Double D ever since Grandpa Downey fell sick four years ago. Grandpa hadn't liked or trusted the man, but Rafe insisted he was the person for the job. Amelia agreed with her grandfather. Ever since, she'd tried to steer clear of Callahan. She didn't think he'd attack her, but she was sure he'd try to talk her into something she didn't want to do. But her father was blind to all the man's faults. It was if he'd somehow found the son he'd always wanted, though Vince Callahan was only five years younger than Rafe.

Why couldn't her father understand this wedding could never take place? Didn't he know she had a mind of her own? She didn't need him or any man to arrange her life, even if he did think he was doing it for her own good. If she only knew who she could ask to marry her before she was caught in her father's web. There had to be somebody. Somebody her father wouldn't be able to scare off.

A thought flitted across her mind and interrupted her musing. The hint of a smile crept across her full lips. Removing her hat, she felt the long braid tucked up inside fall down her back. She wiped her brow with the back of her sleeve as the thought began to seep in, take root and begin to solidify.

It was the perfect plan and he was the perfect man, if she could just pull it off. Her father would never demand she get a divorce or an annulment and Vince wouldn't think of trying to take her away from him. Everyone in town thought he was a man to be reckoned with. If she could only find him, and if she could make it happen in time, and if she could get her hands on enough money, she wouldn't have to marry Vince Callahan or anyone else her father picked out. She would marry the man of her choice even if she'd never met him. Then things would be as they should be in her world again, but she knew she had to move fast to get these "ifs" out of the way. It might take a little while to put this bold plot in action and time was running out. But if everything fell into place, she was sure she could make it work.

* * * *

Former US Marshall and now bounty hunter, Jed Wainwright, walked out of the jail in the small town of Settlers Ridge, Wyoming where he'd turned over his prisoners to Sheriff Lance Gentry and his deputy, Bryce Langston. He told them he'd come back to the office in a day or two and collect the reward because he didn't want to bother with the paperwork at the moment. After all, the gang had to wait to go on trial when the territorial judge came through again. He'd have to stick around here to testify against them when the judge arrived, which Lance said would be in three weeks. Jed didn't mind. He needed a little rest.

It had been a rough capture and at age thirty, he felt it was time to think about giving up this work and following his plan of becoming a ranch owner. This case had only served to make him sure of what he wanted to do with the rest of his life. It had taken three hard months to find and capture the four members of the McBride gang and bring them here to face trial. He'd slept in the rain, fought off rattlesnakes, eaten dust, lived on hardtack and jerky and at times went without coffee because building a campfire would give away his position. But in a year or so, with a few more good paying captures, he'd hang up his hat as a bounty hunter, and settle on a ranch somewhere in Arizona or Wyoming Territory with his friend, Curt Allison.

Once he closed the jailhouse door, Jed stretched his full six feet and four inches as he looked down the dusty street which dissected the town. Of course, he couldn't see the side streets, but everything he could see from this point was familiar. Besides the only stone structure, the two-cell jail, there were Brown's Mercantile, The Wildcat Saloon, which was connected to a house of pleasure, a livery stable, a feed and seed store, a blacksmith shop, a restaurant, Miss Purdy's Dress Making and Hat Shop, a funeral parlor, a trading post, Olsen's Hotel, Settlers Ridge Bank, a telegraph office, a barber, and a few businesses he couldn't see or read the signs on. On the edge of town was a school house, a boarding house and under construction was what looked like a church. Other than the new building, the town hadn't changed much since he'd come through six months ago. Of course, places like Settlers Ridge seldom changed unless the railroad was rumored to come through.

Shifting his saddlebags to his left shoulder, Jed wiped his forehead on his dirty shirt sleeve. He removed his black Stetson, ran his fingers through his hair, replaced his hat and headed toward the hotel where he knew his friend, Frank Olson, would have a room ready, and his wife, Henrietta would see that he had a good supper. The only other things he needed now were a good hot bath, a shave, a glass of good whiskey and a soft bed for the night. Though he hadn't had the satisfaction of a woman in three months and the lack of female companionship created a smoldering burn, he could control it for now. But soon he knew it would burst into a wildfire that would have to be put out. If he felt refreshed after his bath, maybe he'd stroll over to the Wildcat Saloon and check out the offerings. He kind of remembered a long-legged redhead, but right now food and a hot bath seemed to be the most important things in his immediate future. He was thinking about relaxing in a tub when he noticed a fancy black buggy in front of the hotel. He lifted an eyebrow as a small pretty woman dressed in a powder blue traveling suit was helped down by the driver. The young man followed her inside, carrying her valise. She turned to smile at the fellow and Jed saw beautiful golden hair peeking from under the matching blue hat topped with darker blue flowers.

"Wouldn't mind having her in my bed tonight," he mumbled as he drew closer. He then laughed at himself. "You're an idiot, Wainwright. She's a lady and you haven't had a lady in your bed since your wife died ten years ago."

He was so engrossed in his thoughts he didn't see the tiny older woman who stepped out of the ladies millinery and dress making shop until he almost knocked her down.

To break her fall, he grabbed her by the shoulders. "Ma'am, I beg your pardon."

She pulled away and looked up at him. There was a glint in her eyes. "Well, mercy sakes alive, you should be more careful, young man. If a fellow as big as you fell on an old woman my size you'd kill her for sure."

Jed grinned and tipped his hat to her. "I should've been watching where I was going. I'm really sorry."

"You should be, and I appreciate the apology." She smiled at him. "I guess I'm not used to cowboys yet, though I've got to admit, you're the biggest one I've met so far."

"Oh?"

"I arrived about a month ago from Savannah to live with my son and his wife, Eli and Margo. They came here last fall so he could be the new preacher. When the sister I lived with in Savannah up and died, my son insisted I come out here to live with them."

"I see." Jed wondered why this little woman was talking to him. Few decent women did, but she didn't seem to mind his appearance.

"By the way, my name is Gertrude Ellsworth."

"And I'm Jed Wainwright."

"I assume your full name is Jedidiah Wainwright."

"Yes, ma'am, but I'd appreciate it if you called me Jed."

"No, thank you. I'll call you Jedidiah. I bet your mother liked the name and I like it, too. It's a good old Bible name and you should be proud of it."

"As you wish, Mrs. Ellsworth." Jed figured it didn't matter what the woman called him. He'd probably never see her again. At the moment he was ready to move on toward the hotel and his bath. "If you'll excuse me, I need to rent a room and get myself cleaned up."

"Then I assume you're on your way to the hotel, Jedidiah?"

"Yes, ma'am."

"Good. Here." She handed him a hat box. "You can carry this for me. I'm going there, too. Margo and I are meeting Eli for supper in the hotel dining room."

The door to the shop opened again and a pretty auburn-haired woman, obviously big with child, stepped out. "Mother Ellsworth, why did you leave the store without me?"

"I figured if I didn't get out of there you and that Miss Purdy were going to talk all evening. I'm getting hungry and I want to go eat."

"Well, shall we head to the hotel?" The woman glanced at Jed, but said nothing.

"I'm on my way. I asked Jedidiah to carry my new hat for me." She looked at Jed. "This is my daughter-in-law, Margo Ellsworth. Margo, this is my new friend, Jedidiah Wainwright."

"Ma'am." Jed tipped his hat.

The woman nodded and reached for the hat box. "I'll carry this." She then took her mother-in-law by the elbow. "We should hurry. I'm sure Eli is waiting."

"Don't push me so hard. He won't mind waiting a little longer, Margo."

Jed suppressed a smile as he handed over the hat box and watched the two women head down the boarded sidewalk. He wasn't upset by Margo's reaction to him. He was used to it. Most ladies avoided rough-looking men. Especially if their Indian blood was as obvious as his. He followed them at a few paces behind.

In the lobby of Settlers Ridge Hotel, Jed said goodbye to Mrs. Ellsworth and again nodded at her daughter-in-law, who still didn't seem too happy the older woman insisted on befriending him.

"We sure would like for you come visit the church this Sunday," Mrs. Ellsworth said before Margo could lead her away. "Wouldn't we, Margo?"

"Of course." Margo didn't sound enthusiastic.

"I appreciate the invitation, but I'll probably leave town before Sunday." He tipped his hat again. "It was a pleasure meeting you, Mrs. Gertrude Ellsworth."

As Margo was ushering the older woman toward the dining room, Mrs. Ellsworth was saying, "And I enjoyed meeting you, Mr. Jedidiah Wainwright."

When the two women were out of sight, Frank Olsen, the man behind the counter, said, "Got an admirer haven't you, Jed?"

"Yeah, Frank. Old ladies like me." He picked up the pen. "How about room four? Is it vacant?"

"Sorry, it's not. Wasn't expecting you tonight and rented it a short time ago. How about room three? It's across the hall and looks about the same."

"Fine." Jed wrote his name. "Think I could get a bath brought up along with some food and a good bottle of whisky?"

"Not going to the saloon after your bath, like you usually do?"

"Don't think so. I'll head there after I get some rest under my belt."

"Must have been some tough outlaws this time."

"They sure were. Chased them through the Colorado Mountains then back to Wyoming. They ran me ragged for the last three weeks. I'm glad to get them behind bars."

"I see. I'm glad I have an easier job." Frank chuckled. "By the way, a friend of yours dropped by the other day and left a message for you."

Jed became alert. In his business you never knew who might be looking for you. "Do you know who it was?"

"He didn't say. Left this." Frank reached under the desk and pulled out a letter.

"Thanks." Jed stuck the missive in his pocket and took out some money, but as he always did, Frank shook his head and handed him a key. "You know your money's no good here. If you stay in this hotel every time you're in town for the rest of your life I'll not be able to repay you for what you did for me and my family."

Without argument, Jed grinned and picked up his saddle bags. "Thanks, Frank."

Nothing was said about why Frank was indebted to Jed. It had happened two years earlier when Jed had brought prisoners to drop off at the jail. As usual he rented a room in the hotel. It was about three in the morning when there was a sound outside his window. Getting up, he saw two drunken miners who had a young girl cornered on the street below. He couldn't tell who the girl was, but she was young and wearing a nightgown. He knew the men were dragging her away from the hotel for a no good purpose. Jed didn't stop to ask questions. He jerked on his pants and jumped from the second story window. Though the men fought with him, he managed to subdue the drunks with a few blows.

After getting the two men in jail, Jed learned later that they'd snuck in a window on the lower floor of the hotel where the Olsen family had their quarters and snatched Frank's thirteen-year-old daughter from her bed. Though Sophie was traumatized at the time, she recovered. The family hadn't quit thanking Jed for his intervention. Frank always gave him a room and anything else he wanted when he was in town. His wife, Henrietta, insisted Jed get the best food the kitchen provided and Sophie called him Uncle Jed and considered him her knight in shining armor. Even Teddy Olsen, Sophie's little brother looked to Jed as a hero.

Though he didn't think he'd done anything to merit it, Jed always tried to accept their offerings of gratitude without protest.

With a quick good-night to Frank, he headed up the stairs. He was going to read the letter from his friend then get out of his dirty clothes, shave, take his bath and get a good night's rest.

Chapter 2

After her revelation of what she needed to do to avoid the marriage to Vince, it took Amelia two days to work out her plan. First she told her daddy she'd thought it over and had decided marriage to Vince wouldn't be the worst thing that could happen to her. Though she knew it wouldn't be easy, she hoped she could keep her father fooled. To help convince him, she invited Vince to have supper with the two of them one night. Rafe seemed to be a little suspicious, but was pleased she was making an effort.

At the table, Rafe cut the big beef roast the cook served and said, "I knew you'd change your mind when you came to your senses, my dear. I've always known my daughter had respect for my opinion. Coming to this decision proves she has a good head on her shoulders as well."

"I've always valued your opinion, Daddy," she managed to say. Inside, she was seething because Vince had sat down beside her to eat.

"I'm happy you see how good this is going to be for both of us, Amelia." Vince held his plate for the meat Rafe was offering.

She forced herself to smile at him then quickly looked away when she saw the look in his eyes. She'd seen the look before and she didn't like it.

Though the meal was hard for her to get through without giving herself away, it got better when Rafe and Vince began talking about the upcoming cattle drive. She only said a few words now and then and hoped this evening wouldn't be a long one.

Finally the meal was over, and though it was hard, as he was leaving for the bunkhouse, she let Vince kiss her on the cheek.

"I'm really glad you came to your senses, daughter." Rafe put his arm around her shoulders as she started toward the stairs.

She sighed. "You're usually right, Daddy."

"I know I am." He leaned down and kissed her forehead. "Now go get a good night's sleep and I'll see you tomorrow."

When she reached her room, Amelia washed her cheek where Vince had kissed her. "Probably doesn't do any good, but at least I know I've washed it away," she said with a smirk as she prepared for bed.

The next day, she knew her father had swallowed her pretense of acceptance of the marriage when she convinced him she needed to go into Settlers Ridge for a few days so she could spend time with Miss Purdy in her shop. She assured him that it would be better for her to stay in town than to run back and forth from the ranch to have a wedding dress made. Fittings took time and she wanted her dress to be special for the nuptials. She told him she also needed some essentials for the honeymoon.

"I can't let you go alone, Amelia. I'm too busy to go with you and I can't spare Vince because of the roundup and branding for the cattle drive. I need him here in case we find out who is rustling the herds on the outer edges of the ranch."

"I'll be fine, Daddy. I'm a big girl."

"No, Amelia. I won't let you go alone."

"Then why not let Richard Malone, the stable boy, accompany me?"

He nodded. "How long will it take to get the kind of wedding dress you want made?"

"At least three or four days. Five at the most."

The next morning she dressed in her blue traveling outfit, saddled Rambler, hitched him to the back of her mother's buggy and let the teenage boy escort her to town. At first Rafe didn't want her to take her horse, but she insisted she rode Rambler every day and she wanted to board him in the livery stable so she could still go on her morning rides. To convince him she added, "If I get through at Miss Purdy's early, I'll be able to come home."

Her father looked as if he would refuse, but in the end he permitted her to take the horse. She knew it was because he thought she had completely accepted his marriage plans for her.

When they reached Settlers Ridge, they dropped Rambler at the livery stable and headed for the hotel. After she checked in and Richard helped carry her luggage to her room, she sent him back to the ranch. Up to this point her plan had worked perfectly.

Pleased with how things were going, she removed her hat, dropped it to the chair beside the window and stretched across the bed. As she was congratulating herself on the way she was fooling everyone, her stomach growled. She chuckled to realize she was hungry. She'd had an early lunch with her father, but was too excited about getting away to eat much.

"I'll have a good supper before I go to see Sheriff Lance," she said as she sprang to her feet.

Glancing into the mirror hanging over the small dressing table, she decided to leave off the jacket to her suit. The white blouse, with its ruffled sleeves and low neckline, was flattering and she wanted to look pretty tonight. Delores, their longtime cook and housekeeper, had helped her put her long hair on top of her head in a mass of blonde curls. It was holding well. She only had to refasten a couple of pins and it looked as pretty as it did when she left home.

Heading for the door, she decided she'd have a good meal, which would probably help her relax, then she'd visit Lance and put the next step of her plan in place.

Amelia had known Lance Gentry all her life. He was eight years older than she, but his younger sister, Nelda, was her age. Though she and Nelda were still friends, it had been hard to stay in touch since Nelda followed Major Spencer Barrington to Colorado where they were married at the fort he served in the area. Since Amelia and Lance were always friendly when they met, she didn't think there would any trouble getting the information from the sheriff about her target's whereabouts. If all went well, she'd be ready to leave early the next day to track him down. She knew her father would either come or send someone to get her in a few days, but it would be three or four more days before he'd learn she'd left the area. If her luck held out, by the time he found her, it would be too late for the marriage to Vince. At least she thought it would be.

Heading down the hall, she met Mr. Olsen's young son, Teddy carrying a bathtub. His sister, Sophie, followed with a bucket of steaming water in each hand. She stood aside and watched them as they paused and knocked on the room across the hall from hers. It crossed her mind that now Sophie was fifteen, she was turning into a beautiful young woman. Amelia smiled at them. Sophie returned the smile, but Teddy was too intent on his errand to respond.

Amelia turned and headed down the stairs and into the dining room. Pausing at the door, she looked around.

Grace Hunter, a pretty young woman with auburn hair up in a bun on the back of her head, and walking with a limp she'd had since a childhood accident, smiled at Amelia. "There's a vacant table near the window if you're interested, my friend."

"Sounds great." Amelia followed her. As she sat in one of the chairs at the round table, Amelia looked up at the girl she went to school with here in Settlers Ridge before her banishment to the Boston finishing school. She remembered well the day they were at recess and a violent storm arose. The teacher was gathering them to get back into the building when the fierce wind whipped a large limb from the only oak tree in the school yard. The limb was headed for the children and the teacher screamed for them to hurry. Everyone got out of the way except Grace. She stumbled and the tree limb fell across her right ankle. She almost lost her foot, but somehow the doctor was able to save it, though it left her with a permanent limp. Amelia never understood why some people shunned her because she limped.

After Amelia returned from school in Boston, she learned the Hunter's home had burned and Grace's mother and father both perished in the blaze. Her friend was the only one able to get outside. Because of the loss, Grace was left almost penniless and had taken a job in the hotel dining room to support herself, another reason for some people to shun her. She was a working woman, which was looked down upon if a girl was at the age she should marry. Such things didn't bother Amelia and on her return from the finishing school, the two young women resumed their friendship as if no time had passed.

Amelia glanced at Grace holding her pencil to write down the order and decided now was a good time to start spreading the news she wanted to get out in town. She hoped Grace would unknowingly help. "Guess what, Grace. I'm going to get married. I was supposed to meet my fiancé here tonight, but he couldn't get here in time for supper."

"Fiancé? When did this happen?" Grace looked flabbergasted. "Tell me about it."

"It's kind of a secret, but I'm sure it won't be long until everyone in town knows."

"Who is he? Do I know him?"

"I'm sure you've heard of him even if you haven't met." In case something went wrong, Amelia wasn't about to tell her his name.

"Please tell me who he is."

"I can't tell you right now, because as I said, it's kind of a secret. I don't want anyone to know who he is yet. If you tell anyone I'm engaged, just say you don't know the man. Can you do that?"

"I guess I can, but why in the world would you want to keep his name a secret?"

"I can't explain now." Amelia smiled at her and began playing with the silverware on the table. "I will tell you this. As soon as we have everything settled, you'll be the first person I introduce him to."

"Then I won't pry." Grace gave her a smile and changed the subject. "Our special tonight is steak, potatoes, and peas, or would you prefer something else?"

"The special sounds fine."

"It'll be right out with the tea I know you want."

"Thank you." Amelia smoothed her skirt and sat back. She was pleased with herself. She knew if she had fooled Grace, she could fool anyone. She began to watch the people in the restaurant. Three people were seated at a table near her. She recognized the minister and his wife, but she didn't know the older woman. She nodded at them and the older woman smiled at Amelia.

The preacher's wife grinned then turned back to her husband. Though she wasn't talking loud, Amelia could still hear when Margo said, "Eli, your mother was latched on to that rough-looking cowboy as if he were a long lost friend."

"I was no such thing." The older woman looked perplexed. "He was nice and I simply asked him to carry my hat box to the hotel. Of course Margo wouldn't let him, though I didn't see why not. He was on his way to check in and didn't seem to mind. I was only trying to be nice."

"It's always good to be nice to people, Mother, but you do have to watch it. Things are different here in the west than they were in Savannah. There are a lot of rough characters in Wyoming Territory, and they don't mind taking advantage of an innocent person like you."

"Eli Ellsworth, I'm not the fragile old lady you think I am. I lived through the war in Savannah with the Yankees burning and killing. I think I can manage to handle a cowboy."

"Well, at least nothing happened this time, but please be careful. Ivy would never forgive me if anything happened to you."

"Your sister knows you'll take care of me, son."

"Well, Mother Ellsworth, we need to make sure. You know when our baby comes I'm going to need you."

"And I'll be there for you, Margo." The little old lady shrugged her shoulders. "I don't see my talking to him hurt a thing. Jedidiah Wainwright was a perfect gentleman. I liked him."

"He didn't look much like a gentleman to me," Margo said.

"I've heard about him," Eli said. "I've never met the man, but some people around here think he's a hero. Others say he's the devil's spawn."

Amelia caught her breath. Though she recognized the Reverend and his wife, she didn't know his mother had come to town, but she realized the older woman meant Jed Wainwright, the bounty hunter. She'd never heard him called Jedidiah, but it had to be him. She was trying to work up her courage to speak when Grace brought her food.

Her friend didn't have time to question her about her fiancé any more. Two people came into the dining room and she hurried away to serve them.

Amelia tried to concentrate on the conversation between the Reverend and his family, but they began discussing the new church. She'd heard all she wanted to hear about the new church from her mother so she turned her attention to her meal and thought about what she'd heard. If Jed Wainwright was in town, it would solve one of her biggest problems. She wouldn't have to visit the sheriff's office to find out where she could find the bounty hunter. *It must be an omen. If he's in town, I know I'm doing the right thing.*

She finished her meal quickly and hurried out of the dining room. She didn't want to get tied up with the Ellsworths and she was glad they

were so involved in warning his mother about the Wild West that they
didn't notice her leave.

In the lobby, she paused to talk with Mr. Olsen for a few minutes
then hurried up the stairs.

* * * *

Jed read the letter Frank gave him and put it aside, then sat back
in the tub of soapy water to relax. The missive had brought good news
and he realized he was closer to his own ranch than he realized. Maybe
he wouldn't have to hunt outlaws much longer, if at all. Together they
already had enough money to buy a ranch. Now they only needed
money for stock. And if they could get the ranch at a good price, with
the little left over and the coming reward money they could get enough
stock to start ranching. Calling the McBride gang his last capture would
suit him fine. He decided he'd act on what his friend, Curt, had told
him tomorrow.

He was about to doze off when he realized his bath water was
almost cold, the whisky bottle was down a good third, and the back of
his neck was about to develop a crick because of the angle it had rested
on the back of the tin tub. He straightened and flexed his shoulders, but
before he could get out of the water, a light knock on his door brought
him fully aware of his surroundings.

He jumped up, wrapped a towel around his waist and grabbed the
pearl handled pistol from his holster. Though he figured it was the
expected supper, Jed didn't believe in taking chances. He learned early
in his business the most innocent event could be deadly.

He moved to the door. "Who is it?"

The only answer was another light knock.

"State your business," Jed demanded.

"I want to speak with you."

Jed didn't understand what the soft female voice said, but he knew
it was a woman. He grinned. Maybe Frank sent him a surprise. He

eased the door open, but kept his gun trained on the opening. "What did you say?"

"I said I want to speak with you."

He opened the door a little wider and looked at the small blonde standing there. If he could've had his choice, she would've had long black hair and come up to at least his chin, but he didn't let her know this. She would be fine even if she only came midway to his chest. His grin spread as he glanced down the hall. It was empty and he threw the door open. "Come on in, sweetheart. I'd love to have a talk, but I have a better idea of how to pass the time with you."

She gasped as her right hand flew to her breast. A blush started at the scooped neck of the lavender silk dress. "You're not dressed." Her eyes were wide with surprise and curiosity and he knew she'd noticed all the scars on his torso, but he had no intention of explaining to her how they got there.

"It'll be less complicated if I'm already undressed." He looked her up and down and though she was a tiny thing, he liked what he saw up close. He remembered she was the woman he'd seen get out the carriage earlier. At the time he'd thought she was some local lady, but right now he had no objections to a pretty lady. "Come on in and let's see how fast we can get you out of your fancy dress."

"How dare you!" she snapped. "I came to discuss a business deal with you, not take my clothes off."

He laughed when he saw the way her blue eyes lit up. Though he didn't like to play games with a potential bed partner, this woman was pretty enough to get away with teasing him. He'd go along with it for a short time. "Then, come in and let's discuss your business."

"I'll come in when you put some clothes on." She put her hands on her hips and glared at him.

"If I must." Without closing the door, he dropped the towel.

She let out a little scream and covered her face with her hands.

He laughed out loud after seeing her reaction to his naked body. Shaking his head, he slowly turned and moved toward the bed.

He took his time stepping into the clean pair of pants he'd laid out. He was buttoning the front when he said, "I'm decent, so you can uncover your eyes."

She dropped her hands. "Aren't you going to put on a shirt?"

"I can talk as well without a shirt." Jed was still sure this was a woman Frank had sent him and the fact that she seemed genuinely embarrassed intrigued him. He wasn't sure why and it probably wouldn't be happening if she wasn't so damn appealing.

She didn't answer and he walked to the door. "Well, are you going to come in to talk or are we having our discussion in the hall?"

She seemed to hesitate a few seconds then stepped quickly into the room. She still didn't say anything.

Jed decided to wait her out. He closed the door and walked to the bed where he plopped down and patted the feather mattress beside him. She ignored his gesture and took a seat in the only chair in the room.

She swallowed a couple of times. Finally she said, "I have a proposition for you, Mr. Wainwright."

"And what might your proposition be?" His dark eyes bored into hers. He couldn't help wondering what she was up to.

She looked away and whispered, "I want to hire you."

"I don't hire my services out to women, my dear. I'm free and easy with my loving."

"Mr. Wainwright, please control your tongue. I have no intention of hiring you for such a thing."

"I see. You don't want a man tonight, but you want to hire me anyway." He cocked his head to the right. "Well, I'm not adverse to money as long as I'm getting it lawfully, but I don't see why you'd need my services other than in bed. My regular kind of work is tracking people."

"I know. Your reputation is why I came to you."

He frowned. "You want me to find someone for you?"

"Not exactly."

Jed hated to admit the pretty little woman had him confused, but he couldn't help being curious. She was obviously nervous because she was clasping and unclasping her hands in her lap. Though he wondered what this was all about, he still wasn't ready to make it easy for her. "Well, what exactly do you mean?"

"Do you mind if I start at the beginning?"

He stood. "If we're going to tell a long story, I think I'll have a drink."

"I prefer to talk to you while you're sober." Her voice almost squeaked.

"I'm a long way from drunk, sweetheart." He picked up the whisky and poured a glass about half full. Turning to her, he held up the bottle. "Would you like one? It might help you to relax."

"No, thank you. I'm fine."

"Suit yourself." He sat the bottle on the dresser and moved back to the bed. He tried to keep his voice calm when he said, "I've had a rough couple of days, lady, and if you didn't come here to get naked with me, I'd sure like to know what you want so I can get some rest."

She took a big breath then blurted, "My name is Amelia Donahue and I want to hire you to marry me tonight."

Jed almost dropped the glass of whisky. What the hell was she saying? He must have heard her wrong. There's no way a woman would say what he thought she'd just said. He glared at her, but she wasn't looking at him. He turned up the glass and drank the contents without stopping. Still glaring at her, he rasped, "What the hell did you say?"

She cleared her throat. "I have to get married and I have to marry a man who my daddy can't intimidate. I want to marry you."

Jed stared at her. This must be Rafe Donahue's daughter. Though he'd never met the man, he knew Donahue owned the largest ranch in the area. He also knew he had a daughter who the town considered reckless, but he never dreamed she was crazy. He shook his head and started to get up. "You've got the wrong guy, honey. Pretty as you are, I have no intention of marrying you or anyone else."

"I'll pay you five thousand dollars."

"What?" Stunned, he dropped back to the bed.

"I said I'll pay you five thousand dollars."

"Why would a woman like you have to pay a man to marry her?"

"Because I have to get married."

There was a short pause while they eyed each other. Finally he said, "If you're so set on paying somebody to marry you, why don't you pay the father?"

She wrinkled her forehead. "What father?"

"The man who got you in a family way." He knew he was beginning to sound exasperated, but this woman, with all her appealing attributes had to be soft in the head.

"What gave you the idea I was going to have a baby?" She looked puzzled.

"You said you had to get married. That usually means a woman is going to have a baby."

"Look, Mr. Wainwright. This had nothing to do with babies. I want to marry you so I won't have to marry Vince Callahan."

He frowned. "Look, honey, I don't know what kind of game you're playing, but it needs to stop right now. Why don't you let me show you to your room and we'll forget this conversation ever took place."

"No!"

He raised an eyebrow at the sharpness in her voice, but she went on.

"I have to marry you, Mr. Wainwright. As I said, you're the type of man who isn't intimidated by anyone."

"That's true, but I don't think that has anything to do with marriage."

"Please. If I don't marry you, I'll have to marry Vince Callahan, and he's an awful man." She crinkled her nose and a tear slid down her cheek. "I don't trust him and he's old enough to be my father, and he makes my skin crawl when he tries to hold my hand or kiss my cheek."

"That bad, huh?"

She shuddered. "Yes. I can't imagine having to go to bed with…I mean… It would make me want to throw up because…you know what I mean."

Jed couldn't help himself. He laughed out loud at the woman's expression. She seemed to be really repulsed at the thoughts of this Vince fellow sharing her bed. He bit his lip and there was a teasing twinkle in his eyes when he said, "So you've decided sharing a bed with me would be better than being with old Vince."

The tears disappeared and she seemed to panic. "Of course not. All I want is a marriage paper signed by a preacher saying I'm your wife. Daddy couldn't make me marry Vince then."

He could tell she didn't think this conversation was going the way she wanted it to. He decided to push her a little further. "So there would no wedding night?"

"Of course not! Not in the way you're thinking." Amelia took a deep breath and looked into his eyes. "I have it all thought out. Will you please listen to the plan?"

"I'm waiting on my supper, so I guess I don't have anything better to do."

Amelia began pouring out the story to him. How her father had decided she was to marry Vince before her parents went to Europe. How he was forty-two years old and she didn't want to marry him because she didn't love or trust him. How she thought he was only after her because he wanted to own part of the Double D Ranch. And how she couldn't stand the thoughts of being a wife to him.

Jed said nothing during her story, but he studied the young woman before him. She was nothing like the women he usually found himself attracted to. No matter how the town branded her as wild and undisciplined, he could tell this woman wasn't the type to have a one night love affair with a man. She had the "wedding ring forever" look all about her. He figured if she ended up having to marry Callahan, she'd be a dutiful, if unhappy wife.

He couldn't help himself when he asked, "I'll be thirty years old this winter. Don't you think I'm too old for you, too?"

"Of course not."

Jed decided to try another tactic to reason with her. "I have no intentions of ever marrying, Miss Donahue, but let's say by some miracle you happened to talk me into this marriage, what would you expect of me?"

She smiled and her bright blue eyes grew brighter and bluer with excitement as she talked. "Oh, I wouldn't expect a thing, Mr. Wainwright. I even have the wedding ring. It was my grandmother's. Grandfather gave it to me before he died and said she…she'd want me to have it, and I'll wear it proudly."

"I see." He wondered if the grandmother was dead, too, but didn't ask.

Amelia went on. "As for us, this would be a marriage in name only, but you would have to squire me around town and pretend to be the attentive husband for a while. If Daddy didn't think we were really married, he'd have it annulled and I'd be right back where I started and he'd still force me to marry Vince."

"I don't think I'd be happy in a marriage that was in name only." Though he knew he'd never marry this woman, he couldn't fathom being with a wife he couldn't sleep with.

She shook her head and appeared to warm to her subject. "It wouldn't be forever. Six months, at most."

"Six months is a long time. I could track down a lot of outlaws in that length of time."

She bit her lip and then smiled at him. "Could you make ten thousand dollars in six months tracking down outlaws?"

"I thought you said five thousand."

"I will give you five thousand now and another five thousand when six months have passed."

Jed couldn't help thinking this would be easy money. In six months he might make a thousand dollars, fifteen hundred if he was lucky, but there was no way he could ever make ten thousand. And ten thousand dollars would more than set up the ranch he'd been dreaming about. With what he and Curt had already saved, they could buy a place and with the money from her they'd have plenty to hire hands and buy stock in the future. They would even be able to find men who would be good at rounding up wild ponies to break and breed to sell. He shook his head because he was shocked to realize what he was thinking. Could he seriously consider this preposterous proposal?

When he spoke it was slow and thoughtful. "So I'd be your husband to the outside world, but I'd still be free to pursue whatever work or pleasure I desired?"

"Yes, with a few exceptions." She gave him a brilliant smile.

He raised the dark eyebrow again. "And what are those few exceptions, Miss Donahue?"

"Well, we'd have to have some sort of home together. I guess when I'm married, Daddy would let us live at the ranch, but if he wouldn't let us live in his house we'd have to live on one of the places on the ranch. Of course we'd have two bedrooms, but only you and I would know."

"Anything else?"

"You'd have to stay away from the soiled doves in town." She lowered her head and almost whispered, "I've heard about your reputation with the fallen women, but I couldn't have you disgracing me. Everyone in town knows my family. I'm sure it wouldn't be long until somebody told Daddy you weren't honoring your marriage vows then he'd make me get an annulment or divorce."

"You expect me to go without a woman for six months?" Didn't this woman know anything about men?

"Yes, Mr. Wainwright, for ten thousand dollars, I'd require you to abide by my rules."

Before he could answer there was a knock on his door. A girl's voice said, "It's your supper, Uncle Jed."

He went to the door and spoke through it. "Thanks, Sophie. Put it there on the floor and I'll get it as soon as I'm dressed."

He turned back to Amelia. "Go on back to your room, and while I'm eating I'll mull over what you've proposed, Miss Donahue."

"Please. Let me explain…"

"I know everything I need to know." He stood and took her arm. "I'll knock on your door when I've made a decision."

Chapter 3

Am I really doing the right thing? Amelia paced the floor in her room. *What if Jed Wainwright doesn't take my offer? What if he does take it? Will he abide by the rules I set out? What if he doesn't? What if I marry him and…. No, I can't think like this. He has to accept. I can't marry Vince. I just can't. Not only is he a crook, he disgusts me.*

Her mind continued to race on. *What if Jed Wainwright demands more money? Can I get my hands on more?* She knew she had the five thousand available in the bank. Without telling her father, her mother had set up the account for her so she'd have it while her parents were in Europe. She could give it to Wainwright tomorrow. But what if he took her money and then refused to marry her?

No. That can't possibly happen. We'll be married tonight. I won't pay him until tomorrow and the marriage will have already taken place.

But what if he wouldn't go through with it without some sort of payment? The bank was closed. *How much money do I have with me? How much did Daddy give me to pay the dressmaker? Do I have enough for a down payment to satisfy Wainwright?*

She grabbed her drawstring purse and dumped the money on the bed. She counted a hundred and eighty dollars. Would that be enough? She stuffed the money back in the bag and resumed her pacing.

In a few minutes she paused and looked at the small gold watch which had belonged to her grandmother. It was pinned to the bodice of her gown. It told her only twenty minutes had passed since she made him the proposition though to her it seemed like at least an hour.

Has it been long enough to expect him to give me an answer? Maybe not. He probably wants to think it over to be sure. He could be thinking of all the options I offered him. Was I unreasonable with my demands? Are there places where I'm willing to compromise?

She paused in her pacing as another thought slipped into her mind. *What if he refuses to give up his whores? Can I live with him visiting the bordello occasionally? What would the people in town say if he were known to frequent such a place?* She knew the answer. They would laugh at her. Worse than that, her father would say he was worthless and demand she divorce him and marry Vince. She couldn't let it happen.

She muttered, "For the amount of money I'm offering, it wouldn't hurt him to forgo the pleasure of women. But will he agree to it?"

Amelia could certainly understand why he had a reputation with the women. He was good looking. She'd noticed how attractive he was right away. Those devastating ebony eyes were enough to set any woman's heart fluttering and besides that, there were the handsome chiseled facial features, wide-muscled shoulders, narrow waist line, and powerful legs. And without his clothes on…

"Stop thinking about him like that," she commanded herself. "You want the man's name, not his body."

But was the name all she wanted? He sure was a nice specimen of manhood. She realized how nice when he dropped the towel and stood before her like some Greek god. It was the first time she'd ever seen a living, breathing naked man. Were they all so well endowed? Even all the scarring didn't hide his muscles and near perfect physique. And where did all those scars come from, anyway? Were they from different fights he'd had while pursuing his bounty hunting?

She shook her head to change her thoughts. *A more important question to ask should be "is he reliable?" If he takes my offer, can I trust him to keep his word?*

What if he takes my money, marries me and leaves town tomorrow? If he does, will a marriage certificate suffice to prove to Daddy I can't marry Vince? She shook her head. *No. Daddy would never accept a piece of paper. He'd have the marriage annulled if there wasn't a man around to prove the marriage was legal.*

She paused again and looked at her watch. Thirty minutes had gone by. What was taking him so long? He was either going to marry her or he wasn't.

Amelia was tempted to go knock on his door and demand an answer. She got as far as her door and stopped. She couldn't do it. What if it only irritated him and made him refuse to marry her?

She whirled around and walked to the dresser. With a sigh she sat down and checked her appearance in the mirror. *Will he think I looked pretty enough to marry?* She'd tried her best to look nice for him, though she'd rather be in her riding skirt and have her waist long hair in a braid. She figured he was like most men. He'd want to see her in a dress and smelling good. After she'd been to the dining room, she'd changed into her prettiest dress, a lavender satin gown with the lace trim around the scooped neck. It showed off her tiny waist and the puffed short sleeves revealed her creamy arms. She hoped she looked as good as the women he usually spent time with. Did she?

She couldn't explain the little shudder she felt when she thought of him spending time with other women. Especially those painted ladies who made their money by sleeping with men. She didn't want to think about his long hands touching a woman or his sensuous lips against those of some whore. And the thoughts of his well-muscled chest pressing against…

"Stop it," she demanded aloud and stood. "Why are you thinking these things? It's none of your business what the man does as long as he marries you, and you can prove to your father you can't marry Vince."

She checked her watch again. Forty minutes.

"He's decided he's not going to do it," she muttered and dropped to the chair beside the window and looked out. "Now what am I going to do? I don't know anyone else who my father wouldn't scare away or pay to run off."

There was a sharp rap on the door. She jumped and her heart began to race.

Regaining her wits, she stood, smoothed her skirt and headed across the room. "Let it be him and let him say he'll do it," she said and opened the door.

Her heart raced when she looked at him. He was dressed in a beige collarless shirt, a black vest, and clean denims. There was a gun in a holster strapped below the wide belt and his worn boots looked as if they'd recently been cleaned. His black hat was pulled low on his forehead, but didn't hide his dark eyes. She'd noticed again how intriguing his eyes were. One second they seemed to be filled with amusement and the next they seemed to look into her soul. Was it because he had few feelings or was it because he refused to express the feelings he did have? She swallowed and whispered, "Come in."

"I usually stay in this room when I'm in this hotel," he said and stepped inside.

"You do?"

"Now I see why Frank said he'd already rented it." His eyes were slowly surveying her from the satin toes of her shoes sticking out from under her sweeping gown to the top of her head. When he finished, he began the same survey downward, pausing to look into her eyes and then stopping at the top of her gown where the lace barely hid the top of her breasts.

Finally he muttered, "There's not much of you, but what's there, isn't bad." He then turned and closed the door.

Amelia bit her lip. She wanted to ask him what he meant by the remark, but she didn't want to irritate him. She didn't say anything, though she couldn't help wondering what he'd do or say next. She wished he'd hurry, because if he didn't, her heart was going to beat right out of her chest.

He went to the bed, hung his hat on the post and sat down indicating she should sit in the chair facing him. He didn't waste time getting to the point. "You set out some pretty stiff rules for me to follow if I agree to marry you, Miss Donahue."

She nodded and muttered, "Maybe we could discuss…"

He held up his hand to stop her and said, "I've thought this over and I've come to present my rules to you."

"Your rules?" She was stunned. What rules could he have?

"Yes. My rules." He grinned at her, but there was still no indication in his eyes of what the smile meant. "Of course you know I want the money you're offering, but money isn't everything. Unless you'll abide by my rules, there'll be no marriage. I don't care how much money you offer me."

"All right." She bit her lip and hoped he couldn't see her heart begin beating even harder with excitement. "What are your rules, Mr. Wainwright?"

"First of all, you'll call me Jed and I'll call you Amelia. If two people marry they should at least be on a first name basis."

"I agree." If his rules were all this easy she would accept them and then he'd accept her proposal. She hoped the excitement she was beginning to feel didn't show.

He nodded. "Second, I want five thousand dollars put in my bank account tomorrow morning when the bank opens."

She nodded again. "I'll be happy to do that." She began to feel better and better. Maybe this was going to work out like she wanted it to.

"Third, I'll put the five thousand from you away for future use. A friend and I intend to buy a ranch with the money we already have.

There will be no living on your Daddy's place. You'll live on my ranch with me for the six months of our arrangement."

She hadn't counted on having to move, but if she had to, she would. "Where is this ranch, Mr. …Jed?"

"We haven't bought it yet. I hope we can settle in Wyoming, but we might have to go elsewhere to find what we're looking for."

"But I'd only have to live there for six months?"

"Yes."

"So far, I have no problem with going along with your rules." She wished he'd not look at her so intently. She was afraid he'd see how her heart was making her silk dress move with each beat.

"The fourth and last rule is the big one, Amelia, but the entire deal rests on it."

For the first time she saw expression in his eyes. They twinkled when he said her name. It made her feel funny inside, but she hoped her voice was calm when she asked, "What's rule four, Jed?"

He looked at her a moment, then said in his drawl, "You'll either share my bed as my wife, or you'll not open your mouth about my visiting whores or even bringing one to the ranch on occasion."

Amelia was shocked at his words and couldn't think or speak for a moment.

He didn't say anything, but waited for her answer.

Finally she stammered, "What…you mean…I can't…I mean…"

"I knew this one would throw you." His chuckle was deep and if she wasn't so obviously taken aback by his fourth rule, it would have been a pleasant sound to hear.

She finally composed herself. "What if I upped the money to…"

"As I said in the beginning, money isn't everything, Amelia. There's no way in hell I'm going without the comfort of a woman for six months. It will either be you as my wife or…you know the alternative. No amount of money will make me change my mind."

Is he serious? She glared at him. *What am I going to do now? There is no way I can give myself to a stranger, even if I am married to him. But if we marry, can I live with knowing he was sharing a bed with another woman or different women?*

Several minutes passed before anything else was said.

He spoke first. "I assume by your silence you can't go along with rule number four."

She didn't answer.

"Then, Miss Donahue, I'll head for the saloon. It was interesting meeting you." He stood, put on his hat and started for the door.

Seeing her future with Vince float before her eyes, she jumped up and quickly crossed the room. She put her hand on his arm. Her voice was barely a whisper when she said, "I accept rule number four."

He looked surprised, but only said, "You're positive?"

She wasn't at all positive, but she nodded anyway.

He grinned down at her. "Then which will it be for me? You or the whores?"

She was still whispering when she said, "I haven't decided yet."

He laughed out loud. "I guess that's fair enough."

When she said nothing, he asked, "Well, do you want to go find the preacher now, and put off telling me what your decision is after the wedding?"

She nodded.

* * * *

When Jed knocked on Amelia's door he thought he'd figured a way to push her into calling off her idiotic notion of marrying him. He didn't want to insult the beautiful young woman or tell her he had no intention of marrying her or anyone else. Even thoughts of getting her into his bed wasn't enough reason to marry. He felt confident she'd abide by his first three rules, but he was certain she'd refuse to go along with number four. It had been his ace in the hole. His way out of this ridiculous proposal of hers.

Then to his astonishment she said she'd accept rule four and he felt his heart almost fall to his feet from shock, but thanks to his training at hiding his feelings when he was in tight situations, he'd been able to conceal his reaction. It wasn't that he wouldn't like to get his hands on the pretty Amelia, he just didn't want to get married to do it. In the past ten years he'd been able to bed a lot of women without a mention of marriage.

Though not Miss Amelia Donahue. For some reason he felt he'd been outmaneuvered. If he hadn't been, why was he now sitting in this rented buggy with the lady and headed to preacher Eli Ellsworth's house to get married? Something he swore he'd never do again. Losing Marie had been heart wrenching and had changed his life. He never intended to love another woman, because he knew he couldn't go through the same kind of heartache again.

Of course he didn't love this pretty little blonde beside him, but he was physically attracted to her. In fact, more physically attracted to her than he had been to any woman since Marie, but it didn't mean he wanted to marry her. He only wanted to take her to bed, which he still might not be able to do. Even after saying those wedding words, he might be seeking his pleasure in the local whorehouse. Though he'd found comfort and relief in such establishments over the years, he couldn't help hoping Amelia would elect to choose the option of sleeping with him. It would be a pleasure to have someone like her in his bed instead of the kind of women who graced it most often now.

He glanced at her and a strange thought hit him. In an instant he knew no bordello woman could ever replace this beauty. A plan began to form in his mind and he made a silent vow. *No way in hell I'll settle for a whore when I'm married to this woman. It might take a little while for her to invite me to her bed, but she'll do it. I'll make sure it happens. Maybe not tonight, maybe not tomorrow, but in the near future.*

Jed pulled the buggy into the preacher's front yard. As the thought of seducing his soon-to-be wife took root in his soul, he was beginning to feel better about this whole marriage thing. With a grin he glanced at her and said, "Well, we're here."

She gave him a shy smile. "Thank you for doing this, Jed."

"I said if you'd agree to my rules, I'd marry you, Amelia. I'm a man of my word." He knew this was true, no matter how much marriage went against everything he thought he believed in.

"I've heard you always keep your word. It was one reason I knew I could trust you."

Good. You already trust me. Let's see how quick I can change your trust into caring enough to want to give yourself to me. He came to the other side and held his hand up to assist Amelia down. "You're still sure you want to do this?"

She nodded, took his hand and let him lead her to the door.

Preacher Ellsworth answered their knock. "Can I help you?"

"Yes, sir." Jed removed his hat. "My name's Jed Wainwright and this is Amelia Donahue. We've come to ask you to marry us."

"I know Miss Donahue, but I'm surprised about this." The minister's face didn't suppress his shock. He looked at Amelia and stammered, "Are you sure you want to get married?"

She nodded and Jed said, "Yes. We're sure."

Reverend Ellsworth took a deep breath and said, "Then, please step inside."

They followed him into the foyer and he showed them into the parlor. "Are your mother and father joining us as witnesses?"

"No, sir. My mother is visiting her sister in St. Louis. My father is busy with round up and trying to catch rustlers." She offered no further information.

"Then please have a seat and I'll see if my wife can join us."

"Thank you, Reverend Ellsworth." Amelia gave him her sweetest smile.

As soon as he was out of the room, Jed turned to her. "I'm not sure he wants to perform this ceremony."

"Whether he wants to or not, he will. He doesn't have a choice."

"He doesn't?" He raised an eyebrow at her.

She shook her head. "When he first came to town, he was trying to raise money to build a church. The church now has a sizable building fund and will be a reality in a few months because of my mother's influence. Of course I lent a hand occasionally and he knows me. He'd be afraid to refuse. He thinks it might upset my family and his building fund would dry up."

He eyed her. "You're more devious than I thought."

"What do you mean?"

"Nothing." He changed the subject. "Is your mother really in St. Louis?"

"Yes. She's visiting her sister, but Daddy said he was going to send her word to come home to plan my wedding to Vince."

"Does your mother want you to marry this Vince fellow, too?"

"She doesn't know anything about it unless Daddy has sent the telegraph, but she'll go along with whatever he says. She never crosses him."

Before they could talk further, the door opened and an older woman came in followed by the minister's wife.

"Why, Jedidiah, it's you," Gertrude Ellsworth exclaimed as her face broke into a wide grin. "I didn't know you were getting ready to marry this beautiful young lady."

Jed stood. "Yes, ma'am, I am." He smiled back and took her extended hand.

"No wonder you were in a hurry to get to the hotel and take a bath."

He winked at her. "You've got to admit, I needed it."

"That you did." She laughed and continued, "I hate to admit it, but this evening I overheard your lovely bride-to-be in the hotel restaurant tell the waitress she was there to meet her fiancé. I'm so glad it was you. You make such a handsome couple."

"Thank you." Jed glanced at Amelia. "I was sorry I couldn't meet her for supper."

"Jed and I have been keeping our engagement a secret, but it won't be long until everyone knows about us," Amelia said.

"Well, my dear, you're getting a nice young man. He was helpful to me in town today." She held her hand to Amelia. "My name is Gertrude Ellsworth. I'm Eli's mother."

"I'm delighted to meet you, Mrs. Ellsworth. I'm Amelia Donahue, soon to be Amelia Wainwright."

Margo finally spoke. "Hello, Amelia. Eli says you want to get married."

"Yes, Margo." She introduced Jed.

Margo nodded as Eli came into the room with some papers in his hand. He again asked the couple if they were sure they wanted to get married.

When they insisted they did, Gertrude announced she didn't think a bride should marry without flowers. "Why don't you go out back and pick some of those lovely blooms, Margo?"

"I'll be happy to, Mother Ellsworth," Margo said and glanced at Amelia. "I'll get something that will match Amelia's dress."

Jed decided probably few people would refuse to do Gertrude Ellsworth's bidding.

* * * *

It wasn't long until Jed was snapping the reins over the back of the horse and pulling the buggy out of the preacher's yard. Sitting next to him, Amelia was wearing her grandmother's wedding ring on her left hand and holding tightly to the bouquet of mixed flowers. In her right hand she had the signed official marriage certificate. The Ellsworths were all on the porch waving at them as they turned into the road and headed toward the hotel.

"I told Frank to move my things into your room while we were out, Amelia. I thought it would save confusion later on."

"Why?" She looked frightened.

"You're the one set on making your daddy think this marriage is real. It wouldn't look right if we spent our wedding night in separate rooms, would it?"

She looked perplexed. "I guess it wouldn't."

They rode a little further in silence. Then Jed said, "Have you decided if I spend our wedding night with you or with one of the saloon girls?"

"You can't stay with…" She glared at him. "I mean, it would get around town you spent our first night with a fallen woman. You can't shame me."

"Then I did the right thing having my things moved to your room, didn't I?"

Amelia gulped. "Yes, but…"

"But, what, Mrs. Wainwright?" He cocked an eye at her.

"Nothing," she whispered and looked away.

They rode the rest of the way in silence. When they pulled up to the hotel's front entrance, Teddy ran out to meet them.

"Daddy sent me to take the buggy back to the livery. He said you'd be too occupied to return it."

"Thanks, Teddy. He was right." Jed hopped out of the buggy, flipped him a coin and came around to help Amelia down.

"Thank you, Uncle Jed." The young boy's grin spread across his face. He climbed onto the buggy seat and took the reins.

Jed felt Amelia tremble as he took her arm and helped her up the steps. "Are you cold?"

"No. I'm fine."

"You must be nervous."

"A bit."

"I must admit, I'm a little nervous myself." He opened the door and followed her inside.

"Welcome, Mr. and Mrs. Wainwright," Frank said as they came in.

Henrietta stood beside him. "I'm delighted to have you spend your first night together in our hotel."

"Thank you," Jed said with a grin. Amelia nodded.

Grace came through the door. "Oh, Amelia, why didn't you tell me you were marrying Jed Wainwright?"

Amelia glanced at him as she submitted to Grace's hug.

"She wasn't sure I was going to make it to town, Grace," Jed said. "She knew I'd promised that when I captured the McBride gang, I'd give up bounty hunting and settle down. She just wasn't sure when that would be."

"Well, I'm happy for both of you."

"Thank you, Grace." Jed smiled at her.

"Yes, Grace. Thank you. I know you're always one friend I can count on." Amelia gave her hand a squeeze. "I'm sure my father is going to be a little upset when he hears I've eloped with Jed."

"Though we're all surprised, I think you've managed to get a wonderful husband," Henrietta said. "He's certainly special to our family."

"He sure is," Frank said and turned to Jed. "I moved your things into Miss Donahue...I mean Mrs. Wainwright's room, Jed. I hope everything is all right."

"I'm sure it will be, Frank. Thanks."

Frank grinned. "Congratulations to you both. I hope you'll be very happy."

"Yes, the heartiest of congratulations," Henrietta added.

"From me, too," Grace added.

"Thank all of you," Amelia mumbled.

Jed nodded, took hold of her elbow and ushered her toward the stairs. "Good night, all," he said when they started up the steps.

When they reached her room, she paused and looked at him. "I'll have to find the key."

"Of course." He stood by as she searched in her drawstring purse.

When she produced the key, her hand was shaking so she couldn't get it into the keyhole.

"Let me do it." Jed took it from her and opened the door.

Amelia stared into the room, but didn't step inside.

"Are you waiting for me to carry you in?" Jed looked down at her. She shook her head and he said, "I don't mind."

Before she could answer, he reached down and swooped her into his arms. She let out a little cry.

He ignored her and stepped inside, kicking the door closed behind them.

"You can put me down, now."

He put her down and looked around. "I don't think this room has ever looked this good."

Amelia glanced around. It did look better. There was a vase of flowers on the dressing table, a bottle of wine and two glasses on the table beside the bed along with a plate of sweets. The bed had been made with clean linens and a frilly lace spread. She knew this was

Grace and Henrietta's doing.

"It does look nice," she mumbled as she walked to the dresser and put her wedding bouquet in the vase with the other flowers.

Jed moved to the table and picked up the bottle. "Looks like a nice wine. Shall we drink a toast to our marriage, which is not really a marriage?"

"If you like." Amelia wasn't sure if she was doing the right thing by drinking alcohol, but a glass of wine might relax her, and she sure needed to relax. Of all the situations she'd gotten herself into, none had ever made her this nervous. Of course, she'd never been married before.

Jed poured the wine and handed her a glass. "To you, Mrs. Wainwright: May you never forget your wedding night."

Oh, Lord, now what am I going to do? I can't jump into bed with this man even if he is one of the most handsome men I've ever seen. He's still a stranger and one who I'm sure has had experience with a lot of women. What will he expect of me? Does he realize I know nothing about men? Of course, he doesn't. Maybe…should I tell him to go to the whorehouse? I'm sure he's well known there.

"You're not drinking," Jed said, breaking into her thoughts. "Don't you like wine?"

"It's fine." She took a sip. "I was thinking."

"Good. I've been thinking, too. I think we should get ready for bed. We've got some business to take care of in the morning then I have a surprise for you."

"What kind of surprise?"

"It concerns a message I got from a friend of mine, but I won't go into it now. Tomorrow will be soon enough." He drained his glass and set it down. "Now let's go to bed."

With a shaky hand, Amelia put her glass down beside his. She'd only drunk half her wine.

"Which side of the bed do you want?" he asked.

She looked at the bed. It seemed to be much smaller than it was when she checked into this room earlier. "Doesn't matter. I'm used to sleeping by myself."

"That was before you got married, Amelia." He lifted an eyebrow.

"I know." She began to fumble with the buttons on the back of her dress.

"Need my help?"

"No!" She backed away from him.

"I didn't think so." He laughed. "Though we're married, you don't want to do this do you?"

"I'm sorry, Jed. I thought I could…but…"

"It's okay." He turned toward her. "I guess that means I'll sleep elsewhere?" When she didn't answer, he headed for the door.

A million thoughts ran through her head. Tomorrow the word would spread about Amelia Donahue's new husband going to a prostitute because she denied him his right on their wedding night. Her father would come to town and with a smirk on his face and demand she get an annulment and then he'd make her marry Vince. She would face another wedding night and the man would be Vince Callahan. She knew in her heart Vince wouldn't think twice about demanding his right with her. She couldn't stand the thought. It would be awful if she had to marry him. Jed was by far the better choice.

"Please don't go." She moved to the door and put a hand on his arm. "I'll be all right if you'll give me a little time."

He stared into her eyes for what seemed a long time. Finally he took her by the arms and gently led her to the bed. He sat down and pulled her down beside him. "All right, Mrs. Wainwright." His voice was kind and seductive. "I'll make a deal with you."

"What kind of deal?"

"As you may or may not know, I'm back from a hard capture of a bunch of criminals. I've been two nights and three days without sleep. I'm not sure how I'm still standing on my two feet. Therefore, I won't make any demands on you tonight. All I ask is that you let folks see you as a happy and fulfilled bride tomorrow."

Is he telling me he wouldn't go to the whorehouse if I didn't… Oh, what a wonderful man.

"What do you think?" he asked.

"I think…I think you're a gentleman, Mr. Jed Wainwright. A wonderful gentleman. Thank you so much."

"Then it's a deal?"

"Of course. I thank you more than you'll ever know."

"Then, as I said earlier, let's get ready to go to sleep." He leaned down and kissed her forehead. "I'll lock the door and take the right side of the bed."

Almost in slow motion, Amelia slipped behind the screen in the corner, removed her dress then dropped her silk nightgown over her head. When she came back around the screen and sat down in the chair to remove her shoes and stockings, Jed was already in bed. By the time she hung her dress in the wardrobe and slipped into the other side of the bed, she knew her husband intended to keep his word. His deep, even breathing told her he was already asleep.

Chapter 4

Sunshine filled the room when Amelia opened her eyes. For a minute she didn't know where she was then it all came back. She married the bounty hunter, Jed Wainwright, last night and they had spent the night here in this room.

She turned her head to look at him, but the other side of the bed was empty. Where was he? Did he have a change of heart and run out on her? He probably didn't like it because they only lay in the bed together with nothing happening between them. Oh, Lord what would her father say when he learned she'd been such a fool? Would she have to get an annulment when she showed him the marriage certificate? Maybe not. At least she was still married as long as she had that piece of paper to prove it. Was it any good since she hadn't performed her wifely duty?

These thoughts came to an abrupt halt when a noise on the other side of the room drew her attention. Taking a deep breath, she turned her head.

Jed was sitting in the one chair in the room putting on his socks and boots. He nodded to her. "Good morning."

Now she felt guilty for not trusting him to keep his word. She nodded back and muttered, "What time is it?"

He took a gold watch from his black leather vest pocket. "Almost eight. I figured we've slept late enough that the folks in town will realize we had a wonderful wedding night. Now I think we ought to get our day started. We have some things to do, you know." He returned his watch and reached for his other boot.

Amelia didn't know what to say so she watched him.

In a few seconds he stood. He was wearing a clean shirt, and he'd shaved. "I tried to be quiet while I dressed. I wanted you to get as much rest as you could. I think it took you a long time to go to sleep."

She nodded again. Why couldn't she think of anything to say to this man? After all, he was her husband even if it was still in name only.

He walked toward the bed. "I'm going downstairs and get some coffee. Will thirty minutes give you long enough to get dressed?"

"It should be fine," she managed to whisper.

"Good. When I get back, we'll go down for breakfast together and let people see how happily married we are. Afterward, we'll take care of our business at the bank." Without waiting for her to reply, he walked to the door. "You might want to keep this locked while I'm gone. I'll knock when I return."

As soon as the door closed, Amelia bounded out of bed and turned the key. Without giving too much thought to his business-like attitude, she went to the wash stand and poured water in the bowl. Taking a quick sponge bath, she put on clean under garments and chose a blue muslin day dress decorated with colorful roses. The sleeves were below her elbows and had white lace gathered around the edges. There was matching lace encircling the lowered neck of the dress.

Sitting at the small dressing table, she tackled her hair. She wondered if she should try to put it in curls on top of her head, but she realized since it was down to her waist, it'd take some time for a fancy do. She opted to brush it smooth and twist it into one long braid. She wrapped it around her head so it would be neat and be in a style befitting a new bride.

She was putting the last pin in her hair when there was a knock. She moved to the door and hesitated. "Is that you, Jed?"

"Yes. It's me."

She opened the door and it flittered across her mind how handsome he was. He smiled at her, but his obsidian eyes showed little emotion, when he said, "You look nice."

"Thank you."

"Are you hungry?"

"Starving."

"Before we go down, let me warn you. Our marriage has caused a stir in this dusty little town."

"What do you mean?"

"It seems nobody can believe the daughter of the richest rancher in the area has married the no good, half-breed bounty hunter."

She frowned at him. "That's a terrible way to describe yourself, Mr. Wainwright. I'm sure there's a lot of good in you."

He raised an eyebrow. "I'm glad you think so, but don't you think you should refer to me as Jed?"

"Of course, Jed." She blushed.

He nodded and took her arm. "Now let's head to the dining room and see how the wagers are going."

"What wagers?"

"Some people are betting I've got you with child and this was a hurry-up marriage. They've marked down the date and they're already counting the time off on the calendar."

She gasped. "Surely not."

"It's the truth. Others are betting the marriage won't last three months. They say you'll tire of my ways and go running back to Daddy."

"I'm not going to do that and you know it."

"Still others are saying I'm marrying you to get my hands on your father's ranch."

"People can be so ridiculous. You don't want the Double-D."

"I know I don't, but let them have their fun. You and I are the only ones who will ever know you paid me to marry you."

She frowned again. "That sounds terrible, doesn't it?"

He kind of chuckled and opened the door. "Not as terrible as it would sound if people knew I accepted your money."

Amelia didn't answer, but followed him into the hall. At the top of the stairs, he took hold of her hand and whispered, "By the way, you do look pretty. Just like a new bride."

She smiled at him as he led her down into the lobby and toward the dining room.

Over a breakfast of steak, eggs and potatoes they continued looking at each other as newlyweds should. Only they knew it was playacting.

When they were half through, Jed said, "Last night, I told you I had a surprise, but actually it's something I wanted to talk to you about."

"Yes. What is it?"

"I had a message left here a few days ago from Curt Allison, a friend of mine. I used to work with him until a bullet shattered his knee beyond repair, leaving him with a bad limp. It ended his career, but not his ability to work with horses and cattle. Since his injury, we've stayed in touch and often talked about finding a nice little spread somewhere and becoming partners."

"So, he's the man you mentioned who is going to buy a ranch with you?"

"Yes. The note I got said he'd come across a place he thought would interest me. It's between here and Cheyenne. The man who owns it lost his wife and he doesn't want to stay in the area without her. He's thinking of moving to San Francisco to be with his daughter and her family and he wants to sell. Curt says the price is right."

"Are you telling me you want to buy this ranch?"

"Not without seeing it." He half smiled. "I want to go look it over."

"Are you going to leave me here alone?" she almost whispered.

"I hoped you'd go with me. If I buy it, it'll be your home for six months. I thought you might want to see it, too."

"Of course I do." Relief flooded her face.

"Good. After we go to the bank, I'll wire Curt and tell him we'll meet him in Swanson. It's the nearest town to the ranch."

"I went to Swanson with my grandfather one time. It isn't that far, is it?"

"It's about a day and a half from here. We can take the stage or ride horses. You can rent one at the livery if you like, but I'll let you decide how we travel."

"If it's all right with you, let's ride horses. My horse, Rambler, is stabled there and I'm sure he'd like a few days away from the livery stable."

For the first time Jed gave her a genuine grin. "I hoped you'd want to ride. I'm sure Devil wants to get away from the livery, too. Not only that, but these long legs of mine don't do so well on a stagecoach."

* * * *

"What the hell are you talking about, Elizabeth?" Rafe Donahue was trying to get straight the story his sobbing wife was telling him through her tears. "I told you Amelia went into town to have a wedding dress made."

"She didn't go anywhere near Miss Purdy's shop, Rafe. Our daughter married the bounty hunter, Jed Wainwright. He's the one who everybody says would as soon shoot his prey as bring them in alive."

"Here, Elizabeth, drink this. It'll calm you." He handed his wife a glass of wine. "Now start at the beginning."

Elizabeth took the glass and drank the wine in one gulp. She then dropped to the plush wine-colored velvet sofa and glared at her husband. "When I got your wire, I decided to come home the next day. I took the train then the stagecoach and I got into Settlers

Ridge about eleven this morning. I was tired and I decided to go to the hotel for some tea before sending for someone at the ranch to pick me up."

"You didn't do that. You hired a carriage and came home on your own. Why did you do that?"

"Do you want me to tell you the story or not, Rafe?" Her voice was a little sharp.

"Then get on with it."

"I was having tea when Margo Ellsworth came in. She joined me and we were having a delightful discussion about her coming baby. Then she says she guessed I'll like being a grandmother soon. Of course, I thought she was talking about Amelia and Vince and I told her not to start giving me grandchildren until after the wedding."

Elizabeth handed her husband her wine glass. He refilled it and she went on. "When Margo frowned, I asked her what was wrong. It was then she told me Amelia and the bounty hunter came to their house and got married last night. I was so surprised I didn't know what to say or do. When I finally gathered my wits, I asked her to tell me exactly what happened at the wedding."

Elizabeth took a sip of wine after relating a description of the wedding. She then added, "When Margo finished, I knew our daughter had married a man we've never met. A man everyone says is dangerous and mean."

"Elizabeth, I can't believe a word of this. Amelia has agreed to marry Vince. Oh, she had some reservations at first…"

"What do you mean, reservations?"

"To be truthful, she fought me like a cougar when she found out I'd arranged the marriage. She said she didn't like Vince and he was too old, but I knew when she thought about it, she'd come around, and she did just that. She was all excited about the wedding when she went into

Settlers Ridge to have some dresses made. I'm surprised you didn't run into her there."

"Listen to yourself, Rafe. I tell you our daughter is married and you go on as if it never happened."

"I'm sure nothing like that happened, my dear. Even Amelia wouldn't do something so stupid. Mrs. Ellsworth must have been mixed up."

Elizabeth yelled, "Rafe, get your head out of the sand."

"I think you're the one with your head in the sand."

"No, I'm not. Don't you understand? Amelia didn't want to marry the man you picked out for her so she went to town and married someone else. Someone who we know nothing about except by his reputation. I don't know how it all happened, but I sure know why. You're such a stubborn man when you get your mind set on something. You should have listened to your daughter when she said she didn't want to marry Vince. I have to say, I wasn't happy about the news either. He's much too old for her."

"My dear, marriage to Vince is the only answer for Amelia. We can't go off to Europe and leave her alone. It's no telling what she'd get into."

Elizabeth stood abruptly. "Rafe Donahue, you can be the most irritating man in the world. Not to mention mulish. I don't know how I've put up with your ways for over twenty years."

"You've put up with my ways because you know there's not another man around who can give you the things I can give you, Elizabeth Donahue. Not even Charles Fielding."

Elizabeth ignored his remark about Charles and said, "If you think a marriage between our daughter and Vince is ever going to take place, you're out of your mind. She's married already and to a man who…who…God only knows what he'll do to her." She put her wine glass on the table beside the sofa and turned toward him. Tears ran down her cheeks. "Your hard-headed inflexibility forced our daughter to marry a stranger and if it causes me to lose my daughter, I'll never forgive you, Rafe Donahue. Never!"

Elizabeth gathered the skirts of her green traveling dress and ran from the parlor.

Rafe frowned. Though his wife argued with him occasionally, she'd never talked to him like this. Not giving him an ultimatum. He shrugged. It must be because she was tired and upset. Of course she had to be wrong. Surely, Amelia wouldn't be foolish enough to marry some lowdown bounty hunter. *No*, Rafe picked up a cigar, *not even Amelia is that set against marrying Vince. There has to be some mix up. I'll get to the bottom of this. Elizabeth needs to calm down. She can't start bucking me when I make a decision this important to all of us.*

He walked out the back door and motioned for the first cowhand he saw. He'd send this man to town to get the real story then he and Elizabeth would have a big laugh about it over an early supper. Afterward they'd start planning the wedding of Amelia's dreams. They'd have it here at the ranch and invite everyone they knew. They might even invite Elizabeth's snooty sister and her daughter. Let them see how rich ranchers live.

* * * *

"Do you think we'll get there before dark, Jed?" Amelia stood by the creek where they'd stopped to rest and water the horses.

"No. We won't make it tonight." He looked at her. He couldn't help thinking she was a pretty sight in the buckskin riding skirt and crisp white blouse which fitted just right across her breasts. Looking away so his urges wouldn't get him in trouble, he said, "We might as well camp here tonight and go to town in the morning."

"You mean sleep on the ground?"

He almost snorted. "Yep. Right here on mother earth. I bet a fine lady like you has never slept on the ground have you, Mrs. Wainwright?"

She flipped her shoulder at him. "You'd lose your bet, Mr. Wainwright. I used to camp out a lot. When my grandfather was living, he even took me on a cattle drive. We not only slept on the ground, we ate from a chuck wagon and I helped the cook."

He raised his eyebrows in surprise. "That's impressive. I never knew you had such talents."

"Let's face it, we may have slept in the same bed last night, but we're strangers. There's a lot about me which might surprise you."

"Then I want you to prove what you've said is true. I suggest we test your camping skills right here and now."

"Fine by me."

An hour later a rabbit Jed had killed roasted on a makeshift spit. The coffee pot full of brewed coffee sat on the red-hot rocks surrounding the fire. Biscuits they'd brought from the hotel completed their meal. Jed hobbled the horses and Amelia leaned against a cottonwood tree.

He knew she was watching him walk back to the fire, but didn't know why the sight of her sitting there made his heart beat faster. He sat cross legged on the ground beside her, but didn't speak.

Amelia turned her head to the side and looked at him as she broke the silence. "Why did you become a bounty hunter, Jed?"

He glanced at her in surprise. Nobody had ever asked him that question. Of course he knew why he was hell bent on making guilty parties pay for their crimes, but he wasn't going to share the reason with anyone who didn't already know. Not even this new wife of his.

"Looked like easy money," he said and looked away.

"Is it the only job you've ever done?"

"No." He picked up a stick and began twirling it in his hand. "I've done some ranching and I was a US Marshall for a while. That's where I met Curt. He and I worked together on several cases."

"You were really a US Marshall?"

Jed nodded. "I sure was."

Amelia glared at him. "Why did you leave the job?"

"The law takes too long to find and punish guilty parties."

"But…"

"That's enough about me, Amelia." He threw the stick down and reached for one of the plates. "I think the rabbit is done. Let's eat."

When they finished their meal, she washed their tin dishes in the creek while Jed lay out their bedrolls near the fire. At first he thought he'd separate them, but decided against it. He wanted Amelia to get used to him being next to her. He had no intentions of bothering her tonight, but neither did he have any intention of letting her think he was not going to demand his right to her body at some time in the near future.

They were settled when the temperature dropped and the wind began to blow. Amelia shivered. "I hope it's not going to rain."

"I don't think it will, but you know springtime weather can be fickle. Are you cold?"

"A little."

"Move over closer to me."

"I don't think…"

"I'm not going to attack you, Amelia. It'll be more comfortable for both of us if we can generate a little body heat."

After she complied with his request and curled her small body close to him, he almost wished he hadn't asked her to share the blankets. She smelled good and her nearness was making his body hot all over. Even his toes. He didn't understand it. Though she was beautiful, Amelia wasn't the kind of woman he was usually attracted to. He liked his women tall, with long legs, dark hair and dark eyes. Women who looked like Marie. He always by-passed the blondes in the whorehouses unless they were the only ones available. Now here he was getting heated up over a tiny woman with blonde hair and blue eyes. He figured she wasn't more than an inch or two over five feet and she probably didn't weigh more than a hundred and ten pounds. Yet there was something about her which made him realize he was wading in water which would soon be over his head. He wished he'd walked out of her hotel room and never got involved in her marriage scheme, but he hadn't. Now here he was married to this snip of a woman and she was backed up in his arms with her firm, shapely bottom nestled against his groin. It was going to be a long night.

"Damn it to hell! I should have used my head instead of looking at the money and her pretty face."

"Did you say something?" Amelia mumbled in a sleepy voice.

"No. Go to sleep." His voice was sharper than he meant it to be. He cursed silently and tried to think of anything except how bad he wanted to make love to the woman who was now his wife.

Chapter 5

Rafe Donahue sat stiff backed in the buggy with his wife. Vince Callahan rode his horse beside them. Rafe wanted to yell at Elizabeth and demand she tell him why Amelia had pulled such a stunt, but he knew she blamed him for the incident. When Amelia became sweet and agreeable about the marriage to Vince, he should've known she was concocting a plan to get out of it. Why had he accepted her sweet acceptance as the truth? He knew his daughter was willful and wasn't easily pushed into doing something she didn't want to do. Yet, before this incident, she'd always eventually bent to his will as a good daughter should.

He expected her to do it this time, but for some reason this was different. Why couldn't the hard-headed girl see that marrying Vince was the right thing for them all? Sure he was a little older, all right a lot older, but she'd be safe with him. He'd protect her and give her a life many women could never hope to find. One day she'd inherit the Double-D and share it with her husband, as Elizabeth had done. Rafe had known the minute he met Elizabeth Downey he'd marry her because through her he'd eventually have control of the ranch. He'd even talked his father-in-law into changing the brand to the Double-D to include the Donahue name along with Downey. Elizabeth was attractive and he did care for her, but it wouldn't have mattered. He would've married her anyway. Too bad she'd never been able to birth him a son. If she had, he wouldn't be having this problem. Of course he was counting on Vince making a male child with Amelia. He was sure a boy from their union would be strong like Vince and daring and fearless like his daughter.

It was the prefect plan. Why did she put so much stock in the fact she wanted to love her husband? Weren't all women the same? Wasn't their main goal to have a home and children regardless of who they married? Why did Amelia have to be so different from other girls? Though he loved Amelia, nobody could ever know how many times through the years he'd wished she'd been a boy. He certainly wished it now.

He glanced at Elizabeth who looked straight ahead as the buggy bounced along the road. He realized she'd been a good wife. She'd taken her vows seriously and though there had been other suitors, once she agreed to marry him, she'd been faithful and true. She'd never refused him in bed and she still didn't. Nor had she ever questioned the facts when he made a decision. She didn't like what he did at times, but she always came to see he was right. It was the way the world was meant to operate. Men were smarter than women and they should make the decisions. A woman needed to keep her man happy in bed, raise the children and take care of the house. That was the extent of the responsibility most of them could handle. If a man loved the woman and she loved him, it was a bonus. If no love existed, there were always ways to satisfy a man's needs. Of course, Rafe loved Elizabeth in his way and was smart enough not to raise any questions about his faithfulness to her in Settlers Ridge. He'd only indulged in a few dalliances when he went to Cheyenne or some other distant city just for the change and the excitement of it. The good Lord knew there was no way he'd ever take a chance on Elizabeth finding out about these little indiscretions. The way her father's will was written, it would cost him dearly if she decided to turn on him.

He gritted his teeth. *If I can talk her into changing the will her father wrote, Amelia will never have that power over her husband. If she'll give me a male heir, there will never be a question. The boy will have it in his power to run the ranch any way he sees fit regardless of what any woman says, even if that woman is his mother.*

Again he glanced at Elizabeth. She was still a beautiful woman and it pleased him. He gave a slight smile and admitted to himself he loved her more than he wished he did. At least he loved her to the point he knew no other woman could ever take her place. *Like her mother, Amelia is a beautiful girl and she needs a man to love and take care of her as I do her mother. Vince swore to me he loved her and would always see she wanted for nothing. I'm convinced she'd eventually love him. Sometimes loves grows with a woman like it did for me. It's not always a first glance thing. Is it?*

"Rafe," Elizabeth's voice broke into his thoughts, "what do you plan to do when we find Amelia?"

"I plan to cart her home and lock her in her room until she gets some sense in her head."

"I don't think you can do that, dear."

"The hell I can't. She's my daughter and she'll do…"

"Rafe, she's a married woman. Don't you think her husband will have something to say about it?"

"I'll be damned if I'll allow my little girl to stay married to a lowlife like Jed Wainwright."

"I don't see what you can do if she chooses to stay with him."

"Don't be a fool, Elizabeth. I'll make her see she's made a mistake and she'll be happy to come home with us."

Elizabeth turned to her husband. "You have to promise me something, Rafe."

"What?"

"I want your word if Amelia agrees to give up this man and come home you won't push her into a marriage with Vince."

Rafe frowned. "I can't do that, Elizabeth. I intend to see this foolish marriage to the bounty hunter is annulled and that she marries the right man. I want the kind of life you've had for our daughter. Vince can give her that."

When Elizabeth didn't answer he said, "Now, don't worry, dear. I know what I'm doing."

"Like you did when you told her she was going to marry Vince?"

"You're not being fair." His voice was harsh. "She'll eventually see I'm doing this for her own good as well as ours."

Elizabeth took a deep breath. "I told you this before and I'm saying it one more time. If your actions cause me to lose my daughter, I'll never forgive you."

"You're talking nonsense, Elizabeth. You're not going to lose Amelia."

She didn't answer, but turned her head away and wouldn't look at him.

He shrugged and looked straight ahead.

They made the rest of the trip in silence.

* * * *

Pulling up in front of the hotel, Rafe climbed out. "Take care of the horses, Vince," he ordered and went around to help his wife down from the carriage. She took his hand and followed him to the door.

They stepped into the lobby. Frank Olsen looked surprised to see them.

"Mr. and Mrs. Donahue, it's good to see you. Did you come for our supper special?"

"No!" Rafe's voice dripped acid. "We're here to pick up our daughter."

Frank frowned. "What do you mean?"

"Just what I said, Olson. I was told Amelia was staying here."

"Mrs. Wainwright was here, but…"

"Her name is Miss Donahue to you!" Rafe glared at the man.

Elizabeth watched Frank's lip draw into a hard line. "As I was saying, she has checked out."

"What do you mean, checked out?"

"She's no longer staying in this hotel."

"Then where the hell is she?" Rafe's voice boomed and Elizabeth reached up and touched his arm. He shook her hand away.

"Mr. and Mrs. Wainwright didn't tell me where they were going, Mr. Donahue."

Rafe started to say something, but Elizabeth butted in. "Mr. Olson, did my daughter leave the hotel with her husband?"

"Yes, ma'am, she did."

"The son-of-a-bitch, I'll..."

"Mr. Donahue, will you please lower your voice. You're disturbing our guests."

"To hell with your guests." He turned as Vince Callahan came into the lobby. "He says she's not here."

"Where is she?"

"He won't say."

"I would tell you, Mr. Donahue, but I don't know where your daughter is. All I know is, she and her husband checked out and they haven't been back."

Rafe started to say something else, but Vince interrupted him. "Why don't we check out the saloon? If anyone in town knows where Wainwright is, it's those people."

Rafe nodded. "Elizabeth, you go have some tea or something. I'll be back as soon as I find Amelia."

Elizabeth nodded and watched the two men head down the plank sidewalk. She then turned to Frank. "Mr. Olsen, I'm sorry my husband was so rude, but he's upset about Amelia's marriage."

"It's fine, Mrs. Donahue, but I assure you, I don't know where the couple went."

"I understand." She gave him a smile. "I only have one question, Mr. Olsen. Was my daughter all right?"

"I think your daughter was more than all right, ma'am. If you could have seen her with her new husband, you'd say she was a very happy lady."

"Really? How could you tell?"

"Well, ma'am, they came down to breakfast and they were holding hands and looking into each other's eyes like there wasn't anyone else in the world except them. It was like that the whole time they were here this morning."

"I'm so glad. The only thing I want is for my daughter to be happy."

"Well, those two are happy. Any fool would know it if they saw the two of them together. They walked around town, talked to some people then came back here and went to their room for a while. When they came down, they were dressed for riding. Jed said they'd be gone a few days, but they planned to come back. They asked me to hold Mrs. Wainwright's luggage."

"I see." She took a deep breath. "Please do me a favor, Mr. Olsen."

"I will if I can, Mrs. Donahue."

"Don't tell my husband you're holding Amelia's luggage. I want him to calm down before he decides to confront Mr. Wainwright."

"I understand." Frank grinned. "I'm sure he doesn't think Jed is good enough for his daughter, but he's wrong. There's not a finer man in the territory. I hope my Sophie can find a man as good as him when she's old enough to get married."

"Really?"

"Yes, ma'am. Jed's been staying here for several years now and I've gotten to know him well."

"I've heard he's a ruthless man who kills for a living."

"That's not so, Mrs. Donahue. Jed only kills the outlaws to save his life or when he has no other option. Most of the time he brings his prisoners in alive."

"I'm glad to hear it."

"When you get to know him, you'll be proud of him as a son-in-law."

"Thank you, Mr. Olsen. Now, I think I'll go into the dining room and have some tea while I wait for Rafe." She almost chuckled. "I need to fortify myself for his temper when he realizes he's not going to find Amelia today."

* * * *

"Are you sure you want to give this up, Mr. Sawyer?" Amelia smiled at the sad old man who sat on the front porch with her.

"I'm sure, child. I sent a wire to my son in Chicago three months ago. I told him if he didn't want me to sell the ranch, to get in touch. I never heard a word."

"I think he made a mistake. It's a nice ranch."

"It was a good ranch when I had a wife and my children were all here, but it ain't no good to me now."

"And none of your other children are interested in the ranch?"

"No. My son, Will, might've wanted to be a rancher, but he was killed in the war. My son, Claude, as I said, is a banker in Chicago. My daughter is married to a man who got rich in the gold mines. They live on a spread near San Francisco and want me to come live with them." He glanced at Amelia. "How about you? Do you think you and your husband will like living on a ranch?"

"I was raised on a ranch. I can't imagine living anywhere else." She leaned back in the weathered rocking chair and looked out toward the mountains. "This is a pretty view."

"My wife always liked it. She'd sit out here about every evening and do some darning or knitting or something. As soon as I finished my chores I'd sit with her. When it'd get dark she'd put away her sewing and we'd enjoy sitting here 'til it was time to go to bed." He sighed.

"You miss her a lot, don't you, Mr. Sawyer?"

"Oh my, yes. We was together over fifty years." He shook his head. "It ain't the same with her gone."

"I'm sorry you lost her."

"I hope you and your husband get to share as many happy years as we did. Things will be hard sometimes, but if you love each other like me and my Minnie did, you'll get through them. Then you'll have good memories. My memories are what keeps me going."

Amelia didn't have the heart to tell the dear old man her marriage was only going to last six months. Neither could she tell him there was no love involved.

The sight of two riders coming in saved her from having to say anything.

"Looks like your husband and his friend are on the way back." He nodded. "Them two are young and strong. If they decide to buy my ranch, they'll make a good home for their families."

Jed reined up his red gelding, Devil, near the front porch and threw the reins around the hitching post. Curt followed with his big gray.

"Well, boys, what did you think?" Mr. Sawyer got up from the straight backed chair he had leaned against the wall.

"Not bad," Curt answered as they climbed the steps.

Jed went to a chair near Amelia and sat down. "There are several head of cattle on the open range. When did you last do a round-up?"

"I hired a crew and rounded up last year. I decided to sell my place when I didn't hear from Claude and didn't see a need to do a roundup this year. I thought whoever bought the ranch could go after the strays if they wanted to."

"Curt, why don't you rub down the horses? Mr. Sawyer could keep you company."

"I'd be glad to." He followed Curt down the steps.

When they were alone, Jed turned to Amelia. "What do you think?"

"I think it's more important what you and Curt think."

"I know, but I also know you understand a lot about ranching. The land looks good and there're a lot of cows out there. Since it's still early spring, we could probably get enough gathered to drive to market in the fall."

She smiled. "It sounds like you've made up your mind."

"It's not perfect, but I think I've decided. I only want to be sure you can live here for six months. What do you think of the house?"

"Mr. Sawyer showed me around and it's not a bad place. It's been neglected for a while, but with some hard work and a little loving care I think it can be made into a pleasant home."

"Want to show me through it?"

She stood. "Sure."

The last room they looked at was the largest bedroom on the second floor. Jed walked over to the window and looked out. He nodded. "This will be our room," he announced.

Amelia didn't tell him she'd had the same thought when she'd seen the room. "I thought you might like this one."

Jed was still looking out the window. "Looks like a wagon coming up the road."

She moved beside him and watched until the approaching vehicle pulled into the front yard. A boy about ten jumped out and a man came around and held up his hands to help a woman down. She had a baby in her arms.

Mr. Sawyer's excited voice could plainly be heard as he rushed into the yard. "Oh, my god. It's Claude."

"Hi, Grandpa," the little boy cried out. "We couldn't get here 'til Mama had the baby, but now we've come all the way from Chicago to live with you."

Chapter 6

Curt poured a cup of coffee from the pot setting on the campfire rocks. "Well, folks, how does it feel to lose the Sawyer Ranch to two grandsons and their parents?"

On the way back to Settlers Ridge they'd made camp at the same place where Amelia and Jed had camped three days earlier.

"It sure didn't take Mr. Sawyer long to change his mind about selling, did it?" Amelia smiled up at him. She'd liked Jed's friend the minute they'd been introduced. He was only an inch or two shorter than Jed and he had dusty blond hair which had recently been cut. Most important, he was kind and thoughtful and despite their opposite personalities he and Jed seemed as close as brothers.

"Guess we can't fault the man for changing his mind. It's too bad though. I'd already picked out our bedroom." Jed moved to sit between his wife and his friend as if he were staking his claim.

Amelia reached out and patted his arm. "Eventually we'll find a house with a bedroom as nice. The ranch is your dream and I feel honored you're bringing me along."

"I want you along."

"All right, you two, don't forget you have another party with you on this trip. You're going to have to postpone the honeymoon until you're alone."

"I don't see why. I could shoot you, you know. Then we'd be alone again." Jed cut his eyes at his friend, but they were full of mirth.

Amelia blushed and Curt laughed out loud. "I guess you could try, partner. On the other hand, I could shoot you, making your pretty little wife a widow. You know as your best friend, I'd have to comfort her for the loss of her husband."

Jed reached over, took Amelia's hand and stood. "Let's go for a walk before I have to beat up my friend and leave his body here for the wild varmints to devour."

Curt waved a hand at them. "Go on. Leave this old thirty-two-year-old bachelor sitting here listening to the coyotes and wishing I was married, too."

"Maybe Amelia can introduce you to a friend of hers when we get back to Settlers Ridge."

As Jed pulled Amelia to her feet, she said, "I certainly could. I know lots of available women."

"I'm sure none of your friends would want a cripple like me." He tossed the rest of his coffee into the campfire and turned his back to them.

Before she could answer, Jed led her away.

"Curt's a nice man. Why would he think nobody would want to marry him because of his limp?" she asked as soon as they were out of his earshot.

"He's sensitive about his leg. The best thing you can do is never mention it."

"I wouldn't say anything to…"

"I know, but…well, he can't believe I got married. I think he's still trying to get used to the idea. The two of us planned to buy a ranch and run cattle and round up horses to break and sell to the army. We never meant to have wives involved."

"And I've messed up your dream."

"I chose to marry you, Amelia. You only made the offer. If there was any messing up, I did it."

They reached the creek which was located below a little hill. Jed helped Amelia down and when they reached the stream she turned to him. "I'll be gone in six months and you can live your life any way you want."

He only looked at her for a long minute. Then without warning, he reached out and pulled her against him. His face moved over hers.

Her heart began to pound and she wondered if he was going to kiss her. She then wondered why she wanted him to. They were still strangers and theirs was a business arrangement. Though she'd agreed to share his bed, the marriage was still unconsummated. Her monthly flow began the day they reached Swanson and was still in progress. Yet, at this moment, she wanted him to kiss her more than she wanted anything else in the world.

Amelia wasn't sure when Jed's face moved near enough for her to feel his hot breath on her cheeks. She closed her eyes and moved her body a little closer to him. She felt his arms tighten around her then his lips touched hers. His mouth was soft—much softer than she'd imagined. She slipped her arms around his neck and though she didn't intend for it to, every inch of her body begin to surrender.

His kiss deepened and she felt his heart pounding against her chest. His kiss became more passionate and compelled her to respond just as passionately. Nothing like this had ever happened when she'd been kissed before. Of course, she'd never been kissed in this way. It was as if Jed had some magic power and his kiss was special and she was helpless to resist it. As the kiss grew deeper and he was rubbing his hands up and down her back a shot pierced the night and they jerked apart. Jed was instantly pulling his gun from his holster.

"What…" Amelia started to say.

Jed clamped his hand over her mouth. "Stay here and don't make a sound," he whispered.

"No. I'm coming with you," she whispered back.

"Then stay behind me and be quiet. I don't know what's happening, but I don't want to announce our arrival back at camp. Anything could be waiting for us." He started up the hill with her close behind him.

Amelia tried to be as quiet as Jed, but she couldn't. The big man moved through the wooded area without stepping on a twig or disturbing a limb. She wondered if it was his Indian blood.

They came in sight of the camp and Jed holstered his gun. "What the hell are you shooting at, Curt?" he demanded in a voice none too friendly.

"A blasted rattlesnake."

"Oh, no. I hate snakes." Amelia grabbed Jed's hand.

"It's okay, Amelia." Curt grinned at her. "I didn't let it get in your bedroll."

"Do you think there's another one around here?"

"There's probably hundreds in the area, ma'am."

"Is he telling the truth, Jed?" She looked up at him.

"There might be a few, but not hundreds. Relax."

"How can I relax if there are rattlesnakes in the area?"

Jed chuckled. "There are rattlesnakes all over Wyoming, Amelia."

"I know. We have them at the ranch, but I don't sleep with them. Do we have to stay here?"

"Don't worry. I'll see to it no snake gets you." Jed squeezed her hand and gave Curt a look she didn't understand.

She ignored it and asked, "Are you sure?"

"I wouldn't lie to you."

"I think I'll go check the horses and make sure no snakes have eaten them before we bed down." Curt nodded to them. "You two get settled in and I'll be back."

Jed spread out their bedrolls and insisted Amelia try to go to sleep. "We want you fresh and pretty when we reach Settlers Ridge. I don't want anyone saying my wife came back from her honeymoon worn out."

"I thought that's exactly how you'd want me to look. Wouldn't it be something you could brag about?"

Jed shook his head and lay down beside her. "It's for sure the men will be looking us over. Maybe I should let them think I've…"

"Hush, Jed. Curt might hear."

"I'm sure he's aware of everything we say."

"Please don't tell me that."

He pulled her against him. "All right, if you don't want him to hear what we're talking about, I'll whisper." He put his mouth close to her ear. "Are you well yet?" She stiffened and he laughed. "Got your attention, didn't I?"

"Jed, you're not supposed to ask such things."

"Why not? We're married and frankly, I'm ready to get this marriage going in the right direction."

"I'll be well soon."

"How soon?"

"Probably tomorrow."

"Probably tomorrow or for sure tomorrow?"

She took a deep breath and whispered, "Yes, tomorrow."

"Good. I was beginning to think I'd have to go see one of the girls at the saloon when we get to Settlers Ridge."

She turned over and faced him. "You promised you wouldn't."

"I know I did. I also know it was on the condition…"

"I know what the condition was."

"You're not going to back out are you?"

"No, Jed. I'm not going to back out. I can't help it if I'm a little frightened."

"I'm sure you can't." He reached up and brushed the loose hair off her cheek. "I guess I'm getting anxious."

Did she dare tell him she was still scared, but was getting a little anxious, too? Better not, she decided. Instead she cuddled closer to him. "Good night."

"Good night, Mrs. Wainwright."

There were several minutes of silence then she whispered, "Jed, do you think there are any other rattlesnakes around?"

He pulled her tighter. "I promised to protect you didn't I? I'm sure I can handle any old snake who thinks it's big enough to tackle you."

* * * *

"Is she asleep?' Curt asked when Jed walked up to him thirty minutes later.

"Yeah, but no thanks to you. Your snake tale got her keyed up and it was a while before she drifted off."

"It was the first thing I thought of, but even if it wasn't the smartest thing to say, I guess she swallowed the story?"

"She did believe you. Now, tell me what actually happened?"

"I was getting ready to throw out my bedroll when a man came sneaking up on foot. Pulled his gun on me and threatened to shoot me if I didn't tell him where the woman was. I didn't like that so I shot his pistol out of his hand and threatened to take his head off next time. Made him easy to talk to."

"What did he say?"

"Told me he came to get the woman you'd married and would split the money with me if I let her go with him. Said her daddy put the word out in Settlers Ridge he'd give any man who could bring his daughter home a thousand dollars in gold."

"Damn. I knew he wouldn't like the idea of her marrying me, but I didn't expect him to put a bounty on my head."

"I think this gives you a good hint her old man doesn't approve of you as a son-in-law."

"You're so right."

"What are you going to do about it?"

"Nothing, She's my wife and she's going to stay my wife unless she decides she doesn't want to be."

"So I guess I'm taking on the responsibility of her, too?"

"Of course. What are partners for?" Jed looked around. "What did you do with the man?"

"Gagged him and tied him to a tree the other side of the horses."

"I think I better go have a little talk with him. I want to know what's waiting for me in Settlers Ridge."

"Go ahead. I'll roll a smoke and keep an eye on your wife."

"An eye is all you better keep on her."

Curt chuckled. "Don't worry, my friend. I saw how you looked at her when you introduced us in Swanson. She might as well have 'Jed Wainwright's woman' stamped on her forehead." He chuckled again. "I feel sorry for any man who tries to take her away from you and that includes her daddy."

Jed didn't answer as he walked away frowning.

* * * *

It was late the next night when Jed looked inside the closed hotel lobby. Frank was behind the counter with a book spread out before him. Jed knocked on the front door.

Frank Olson's grin was genuine as he unlocked the door and ushered them in. "Mr. and Mrs. Wainwright, how good to see you. I hope you had a good trip."

Amelia gave the friendly man a big smile. "It was lovely, Mr. Olson."

"I'm glad. I guess you want room number four?" He eyed Jed.

"You're right, Frank."

"It's all ready for you. I knew you'd be back sometime soon and didn't rent it. Good thing I was going over the books when you got in tonight."

"Is there anyone else up?"

"Henrietta's in the kitchen. What do you need?"

"Amelia says she can't wait to get the grime of the trail off her. Could somebody set up a bath in our room for her?"

"It's practically on its way. How about you? You want a bath, too?"

"Yep. I'm grimier than she is."

"I'll get the water heated and the tubs will be right up. I'll also bring the things you left here, Mrs. Wainwright."

"Thank you," Amelia said.

"The man who left the message last week is taking the horses to the livery. Name's Curt Allison. He'll be coming in shortly. Rent him the room next to ours, will you?"

"Sure will, Jed. Reckon he'll want a bath?"

"You can tell him I recommend it." He took Amelia's arm. "By the way, I know it's almost ten o'clock, but we missed supper. Got anything left in the dining room?"

"I'll leave the front door open for your friend and go see about something for you. I'm sure it'll be no trouble."

"Tell Henrietta we appreciate it."

When they got in their room, Amelia said, "Look, Jed. The lace coverlet is still on the bed, even though it's been a week. I'm glad nobody has stayed in this room since our wedding."

"Me, too. After sleeping on the ground I'm looking forward to a nice soft bed."

There was a knock on the door.

Jed opened it.

"I'm what, sugar?"

"Naked," she whispered.

He laughed out loud. "I usually take my baths naked, don't you?" He stood.

"Oh!" Amelia wanted to grab her eyes, but she couldn't. She was fascinated by his perfect male form. He reminded her of one of those men she and her girlfriends had swooned over in boarding school art class, though those men were minus the scars adorning Jed's body and they were only drawings in a book.

He grinned and stepped out of the tub. Still looking at her, he picked up a linen towel and began to dry. He kept his eyes locked with hers, but he showed no shame or modesty. Only when he felt his member begin to swell, did he wrap the towel around his waist.

Walking over beside her tub, he dropped to his knees. "I'll help you wash your hair."

She didn't argue and Jed put his hand on the back of her neck. He leaned her head back enough to wet her hair, then he lathered it and gently began to rub it with his large hands.

The more he rubbed, the more relaxed Amelia became. It felt good to be pampered. "Close your eyes. I'm going to rinse the soap out now." She obeyed and he poured a pitcher of warm water over her head. "You have a lot of hair, so I'm going to do it again."

After the second rinse he wrapped her head in a linen towel. "I think it's time you got out of the water. You're going to wrinkle up like an old crone."

She gasped. "I don't have any clothes on."

Jed shook his head and stood. He reached for another towel and held it up in front of him. "I have this ready to wrap around you and I promise not to look."

Amelia stood and let Jed wrap the towel around her naked body. He assisted her out of the tub, led her to the bed and sat down beside her.

"Let's see if we can get some of this water out of your hair."

When it was dry enough to suit her, she reached for her nightgown. Her hand trembled.

"Don't put that on, Amelia." His voice was husky, but full of gentleness.

"But..."

"I agreed to go out of the room while you climbed into the tub. I agreed to keep my eyes to myself while you washed and when you got out. Now I'm ready to look at my wife."

Amelia could barely breathe. She squeezed her eyes together. "I understand."

"Do you really, Amelia?"

"I think so." She opened her eyes.

"We've been married over a week and the only time we've come anywhere near sharing passion is when I kissed you beside the creek. I thought by your reaction you didn't fear me any longer. Was I wrong?"

"I don't fear you, Jed. You've been nothing, but wonderful."

"Then what is it?"

"I'm scared about it," she managed to whisper.

He frowned. "It?"

"You know. Doing it."

"Do you mean about me making love to you?"

She nodded.

"Honey, you don't have to be afraid. What goes on between a man and a woman is beautiful and natural."

"I don't know about that. I've heard a man goes crazy and he doesn't care how much he hurts you." She looked at him with water pooling in her eyes.

"Oh, Amelia. Somebody has told you a pack of lies, and I'm going to prove it to you."

"How?"

"Like this." Jed took her in his arms and began to kiss her.

It wasn't long until Amanda realized he wasn't crazy and he didn't seem to be only concerned with his pleasure. The kisses Jed spread across her face and on the tips of her ears felt like brushes of butterfly wings.

"I'm going to remove your towel, sweetheart," Jed said against her lips.

Amelia moaned, but didn't resist when the towel fell from her body to the floor. Jed reached down and scooped her into his lap. His lips moved down her throat and landed on her shoulder. She felt as if she was on fire as his mouth moved back to her lips. She opened her mouth and his tongue plunged into the depths. With their lips locked and her in his arms, Jed stood and gently placed her on the turned down bed. Still kissing her, he threw his towel aside and stretched out beside her.

She stiffened and he whispered, "Still scared?"

"A little."

"Don't be afraid, Amelia."

She tensed and he kissed her deeply. Her body relaxed and he mumbled, "This will hurt for only a few seconds," he whispered. "It'll never hurt again."

As he entered her, there was a sharp pain and she let out a little cry.

She thought she heard him say the word, "mine," but she wasn't sure. In a few seconds the pain was gone and she lifted her hips to bring him closer.

When she thought she couldn't stand any more, she slipped over the edge and felt his warm seed fill her. He then collapsed on her chest, his body jerking. In minutes he rolled over and pulled her with him. His breath was coming in rasps and his eyes were closed.

"Oh, Amelia," he gasped, "I'm sorry if I hurt you. It'll be better next time."

"You didn't hurt me, Jed." She didn't think it could ever be any better, but she didn't tell him this.

After a moment's silence he asked, "Are you sure you're all right? I know it's uncomfortable for a woman the first time."

"I'm fine. I don't know why I was worried. I thought it was a terrible painful thing a woman had to endure because it's a man's right. I didn't think women were supposed to like it."

He pulled her against him. "Of course a woman can like it."

She was quiet a minute then she asked, "Am I a whore now, Jed?"

"What?" He looked down at her as if he couldn't believe she was asking such a question. "No, Amelia. You'll never be a whore."

"Miss Collier, at the school in Boston, said only whores enjoyed being with a man. Of course she called them women of loose morals, not whores." He chuckled and she went on. "She said ladies had to give themselves to their husbands, but it was a duty, not a pleasure."

"Miss Collier was an idiot. A lady can enjoy being with her man."

"Are you sure?"

"I'm positive."

"Good."

"Why do you say good?"

She mumbled something and he added, "I didn't understand."

"I said, I hope we'll do it again."

He pulled her closer. "You can bet your life we'll do it again, Amelia."

Not only did they do it again, but before the night was out, she enjoyed it as much, if not better than the first time.

Chapter 7

Jed awoke with Amelia still in his arms. He didn't understand why he felt so relaxed and fulfilled. He'd been with a lot of women since Marie's death, most of them whores, but he'd always tried to be kind to them. That was the way he'd started out with Amelia last night. There was no question about her being a lady, and though he was going to treat her as one, he fully intended to collect on her agreement to give herself to him. He knew she was an innocent, but he also knew she was at the age some man was going to take her. He figured it might as well be him. At least he'd made it good for her. Her reaction proved it had been.

But this morning he couldn't help feeling a little guilty. He'd only wanted to have her in his bed for the coming six months without any emotion or feelings other than relief of his physical need. Then he'd realized how pure she was. She knew so little about the human body. A woman's or a man's. Yet she'd trusted him completely and responded to his every touch. Then without resistance she'd given him the most precious gift a woman could give a man—her virginity.

At the time he thought it wouldn't bother him to take it, but when he heard her little scream, he knew something had happened to him. Somewhere a voice told him he'd now taken this woman as a part of him, not for six months, but forever. He vaguely remembered calling out the word "mine", an Indian custom his tribe followed when a man claimed his woman.

The same feeling that she was his forever filtered across his mind this morning, but he pushed it away. To keep it from settling into his soul he looked down to study her face. After only wanting women with dark hair and long voluminous bodies for so many years, why did he now think this tiny creature with wildflower blonde hair one of the most beautiful women he'd ever gazed upon?

She grunted, wiggled her head and snuggled against his chest. He watched for her to wake up, but she began breathing deeply. He didn't mind. It was pleasant lying here with her naked body in his arms.

A small smile twisted his lips as he took his free hand and lifted the covers to gaze on her beautiful form. He thought he'd be able to study it last night, but their passion got in the way. Oh, he hadn't completely ignored the shapely curves, but now he had time to see how lovely she was.

Her tiny soft and creamy body was pressed against his bonze muscled length. He studied the full breasts with their soft pale pink tips. Her legs were shapely and firm. Her feet were small and her stomach was flat below her tiny waist. He looked downward and his breath caught as he gazed at the triangle of soft golden hair which topped her secret place. Letting out his breath, he couldn't help comparing how it contrasted with the jet black mass circling his manhood.

"Jed, what are you doing?" Her sharp voice caused him to drop the sheet and meet her eyes. She was blushing.

"I was only admiring my beautiful wife's body."

She turned redder. "I don't think you should do that."

"Why not?"

"Well, I…uh…"

"I don't care if you raise the sheet and look at my body." When she didn't answer, he lifted it and said, "Here, look all you want to."

"Jed…" She reached up and pulled the sheet down. "You're terrible."

"Why? Because I like to look at you naked?" He put his hand under her chin and placed his lips on hers. "You didn't complain last night."

"But it's morning. The sun is shining."

"Making love is as much fun in the morning light."

She turned even more redder, but said nothing.

"Want me to prove it?" He threw the cover back and pulled himself above her.

Amelia stared up at him, then her eyes went to his groin and she gasped. "I don't think that'll fit."

"It fit perfectly last night and I'm going to show you how well it'll fit this morning."

He was right. It fit perfectly.

* * * *

"Where are you going, Rafe?" Elizabeth demanded.

"Amelia came back to Settlers Ridge last night. I'm going to get her."

"The food is on the table, dear. I think you should eat first."

"No, Elizabeth. The sooner I get to town, the sooner I get our daughter back where she belongs. I'm sure after a week with the savage, she'll be happy to see me."

"Mr. Olsen said she was happy. What if you're wrong and she doesn't want to come home?"

"I don't care what Olsen said or what she thinks she wants. She'll come home where she belongs." He crossed the dining room with his wife on his heels. "I've had enough of her foolishness. It's time she learned how to take orders."

"Rafe, Amelia is not one of your cowhands. She's your daughter. You don't give her orders."

"Orders are the only thing she understands."

When they reached his study, he went to his desk and picked up his gun.

"You're not going to wear a gun!"

"Oh, yes I am, Elizabeth. I don't intend to kill anyone, but if a gun is the only thing to bring our daughter back…"

Elizabeth gasped. "You wouldn't shoot Amelia!"

He laughed. "Don't be foolish, woman. Of course I'm not going to shoot Amelia, but I'm not sure who else I might have to shoot."

"Rafe Donahue, go in the dining room and eat with me. When we're through, have Vince hitch up the buggy. I'm going to town with you."

"Not this time, Elizabeth. Things could get sticky before I get her away from him. I don't want you in the middle of it."

"How do you know she's back in town?"

"Slim spent the night there last night. He said somebody told him Amelia and the breed were having breakfast at the hotel this morning." He shook his head. "It makes me sick to think of my little girl in a hotel room with him. No telling what he's done to her and I can't believe she's foolish enough to let him do it."

"I'm sure if Amelia didn't want to be with him, she'd come home."

"You're naïve, woman. Wainwright's a savage. Damn Indians don't know how to treat a woman. They use them and they don't care…" Seeing the fear on Elizabeth's face, he changed his speech. "Amelia has had no dealings with Indians."

"Now you've scared me, Rafe, and I'm going with you. I want to make sure my daughter is all right."

"Elizabeth, I said…"

"I know what you said and if you don't let me go, I'll follow after you leave. I don't intend to let you go into town alone."

"I'm not alone. Vince is going with me."

"Vince is not family. If you show up with him, Amelia will surely bolt. I'm her mother. I may be able to talk her into coming home, but not if Vince is there."

He seemed to think this over. "You could be right. She might listen to you. I can't believe she's being so hard-headed. For the first time in her life, I can't make our little girl listen to me."

Elizabeth didn't tell him she didn't think Amelia would listen to him now. Instead, she took his arm and led him to the dining room to eat his noon meal.

* * * *

It was almost eleven o'clock when Jed walked Amelia to Miss Purdy's dress shop. "Do you mind if I don't go in?" He gave her a pleading look.

"You don't have to go in. I only want to pick out a couple of things."

"How long do you think you'll be?"

"About thirty minutes."

"Good. I'll come back by for you and we'll go to the hotel and eat dinner."

"Why don't I meet you in the hotel dining room at noon?"

"I thought you wanted people to see me as an attentive husband."

"Attentive is fine, but you don't have to spend every minute with me." She smiled at him. "Now don't argue. I'll meet you there. It's only a few blocks from here."

"If you really want me to."

She nodded and went inside.

As Jed turned toward the street, he saw Curt coming in his direction. He waited.

Curt stopped beside him and eyed the dress shop. "You going to buy a fancy new hat or something?"

"No, I'm not buying a hat or anything else."

"Ah, I'm disappointed. I wanted to see you in a frilly one with pink feathers and red flowers."

Jed shook his head. "What are you doing this morning?"

"Actually I was looking for you. Happened to see you and Amelia here."

"What do you want?"

"There's something going on in the saloon I thought you needed to check out. If Amelia's going to be shopping for a little while, let's head there."

Jed walked beside his friend. "Isn't it a little early for the saloon to be having action?"

Curt shrugged. "There's a card game going on."

"Why do I need to check out a card game?"

"You don't. It's the four young men in there who seem to think taking you down and stealing your wife might be easy. They're drinking beer and talking loud. I'm a stranger so they didn't pay any attention to me. I heard your name mentioned a couple of times. Also heard them mention Donahue. I started listening and it looks like they want the reward her father has offered for her return."

They reached the swinging doors of the Wildcat Saloon. "Then I guess I'd better check those fellows out." Jed pulled his hat down and stepped inside. Curt followed.

When they entered, a silence fell over the room. Even the poker game stopped. Jed and Curt paid the small crowd no mind and headed to the bar.

The tired-looking bartender moved in front of them. "What can I get you fellows?"

"Beer," Curt said.

Jed nodded and laid money on the bar. Two mugs of beer appeared. From the corner of his eye he saw some movement to the left. There was the almost unnoticeable scuff of a boot. He was sure he heard a gun sliding from a holster. Jed whirled around and pointed his pistol at the young man before the boy's gun cleared leather.

"Unless you want to lose your hand, I'd move it away from your gun," Jed said.

The young man's eyes widened and he eased his hand away from his gun. "I wasn't going to draw on you, Mister."

"What's your name?" Jed's eyes didn't blink.

"Milt Gordon," the scared-looking guy said.

Jed guessed the guy to be about sixteen. In a gruff voice, he said as he holstered his gun, "Well, Milt Gordon, next time I won't give you a chance to change your mind and I guarantee you won't be able to ever pull your gun on anyone else."

"Why don't you fellows go on home? I don't want no trouble in here," the bartender said.

"We ain't causing no trouble," another young man said. "We got a right to be here."

Jed ignored him. He was still eying the guy who tried to draw, but he saw Curt shift. Jed looked at Milt's companions without moving his head. He saw one guy slipping a gun upward.

Without a word, Jed drew his gun and fired.

The young man cursed and grabbed his hand. "You shot me," he yelled.

"Be thankful I didn't kill you." He waved his gun toward them. "Anybody else want to see if I mean what I say?"

"We didn't mean nothing," Milt said. "All we wanted to do was tie you up so we could get the money."

"I think he's talking about the money Donahue said he'd give anyone who brought his daughter home." Curt took a sip of his beer.

"And what were you going to do, attack my wife?"

"No, sir. Mr. Donahue said she wouldn't fight because she'd want to go with us."

Curt laughed out loud and Jed sneered. "My wife has no intention of going with you or anyone else to Mr. Donahue's ranch, and if anyone tries to make her go they better have visited the undertaker for their coffin measurements."

Milt frowned. "What do you mean?"

"I mean I'll put a bullet in any man who touches my wife." Jed looked to the gamblers. "That doesn't only apply to these young hooligans. It goes for any man in town. If you don't believe me, ask Stumpy Deerman."

"What happened to Stumpy?" a man in his forties sitting at the poker table asked.

"I saw him this morning and he had his hand all bandaged up," another gambler said.

"It'll be a long time before he'll use a gun again." Jed nodded at Curt. "My friend here decided to let him live. If I had seen him creeping up to steal my wife he wouldn't be alive."

Jed turned around, picked up his beer and downed it. Without another word, he turned and walked out of the saloon. Curt followed.

* * * *

Grace came to the table and gave Amelia a fresh cup of tea then poured more coffee for Jed and Curt.

"The food was mighty good, miss," Curt said as he picked up his cup. "I wouldn't mind having a dinner like this every day."

"I'm glad you liked it, sir. Effie Vaughn is a wonderful cook and Mrs. Olsen is a great baker. She makes most of the desserts." She gave him a shy smile.

"No wonder Mr. Olsen is such a happy man." Jed looked at Amelia. "By the way, can you cook anything except what can be cooked at a campfire?"

She raised her eyebrow. "Would I dare marry a man like you if I couldn't cook?"

"I don't know. Would you?" he teased.

"I bet there are a lot of men who would have married you whether you can cook or not, Amelia. I don't see how he ever talked a lady like you into hooking up with him in the first place." Curt laughed.

"He promised me he'd buy a ranch and take me away from all this." She waved her hand toward the town.

"Aren't you going to live on the Double D, Amelia?" Grace asked.

"Jed and Curt want a ranch of their own and I'll live wherever they buy it."

"The problem is finding the right place," Jed said. "Don't happen to know of anything around for sale do you, Grace?"

"As a matter of fact, I do. John Lawson was in here the other day. He said he offered his place to Amelia's daddy, but Mr. Donahue put him off because he was trying to find Amelia."

"Do you think the place is still available?"

"Probably. I know Mrs. Lawson wants to go to Texas where she inherited a ranch from an uncle. I'm sure she wants to sell as soon as they can."

"This might be worth looking into, Curt." Jed nodded at him.

"Where is this place, Grace?" Curt asked.

"It's south of town. You know where the Lawson place is, don't you, Amelia?"

"Of course. Mrs. Lawson and Mother are friends. I've been there several times." She giggled. "Mrs. Lawson doesn't like me, though. She says I'm a bad influence on her daughter, Wilma."

Curt raised his eyebrow. "Why in the world would she say that?"

Amelia dropped her eyes, picked up her cup and took a sip.

Grace bit her lip and giggled.

"Okay. What's the story?" Jed asked.

"There wasn't much to it." Amelia looked at him and batted her eyes. "Some time back, Wilma and I wanted to see what you men find so attractive in a saloon so we decided to pay one a visit."

"Wilma and you?" Jed raised an eyebrow.

"Okay. I thought it up, but it didn't take long for Wilma and Grace to join me."

"So, you were in on it, too?" Curt looked at Grace and she turned red.

"They talked me into it."

"What I want to know is, did you discover anything surprising about the saloon?" Jed leaned toward Amelia.

"Not really. There was a woman in a short red dress trying to sing, but nobody was paying her any attention. A couple of other scantily-dressed women were hanging on some rough-looking cowboys and the place was stinky and nasty. We didn't get very far before Wilma's brother, Ralph, came in and made us leave. Of course, we couldn't have seen much more anyway. Smoke hovered over everything." She leaned closer to Jed. "I still don't see what the draw is to you men."

Jed reached out and touched her cheek. "Maybe it's the beer."

"Okay, you two," Curt said, "stop acting like newlyweds."

"We are newlyweds," Jed said.

"Well, now you know about your bride's sordid past; I want to hear more about this ranch Grace said might be for sale." Curt laughed and looked at Grace.

Jed leaned back. "I agree. It sounds like something we should check out right away."

Amelia looked at them. "Why don't we ride out there this afternoon and if it's still available, you can look it over?"

"Want to go, Curt?"

"Sounds fine to me, partner, but I'd like to get back here in time for supper. The food is good and the service is excellent." He grinned at Grace.

"I bet you won't get this waitress to serve you tonight."

"And why not, Mrs. Wainwright?"

"This is Grace's afternoon off. Sometimes we spend it together."

"Then, why don't you join us, Miss Grace?" Curt asked.

"I have some things…"

Amelia interrupted. "Come on, Grace. It'll be fun. While the men are looking over the Lawson ranch we can see how many times Mrs. Lawson wrings her hands wondering what kind of trouble we're thinking up to get Wilma into."

"And if that's not enough reason," Curt said, "I won't have to put up with the newlyweds ignoring me. I'd have you to talk to."

Grace finally agreed to go and after she and Amelia changed into riding outfits, the four of them headed toward the Lawson ranch.

* * * *

"Mr. Donahue, I'm sorry I don't know where your daughter is. She and her husband ate dinner in the dining room and left. Where they went, I don't know and I didn't ask."

"Damn it, man, don't you keep up with your guests?"

"Of course not, sir. Where they go is their business. I have no right to infringe on their privacy."

Elizabeth put her hand on her husband's arm. "Rafe, why don't we go in the restaurant and ask Grace Hunter?"

"Who's she?"

"You know her. Her parents were killed when their home burned to the ground. She's a friend of Amelia's and she works as a waitress here."

"Then let's go talk to her. Amelia might have said something to her."

"Excuse me, Mrs. Donahue, but Grace takes the afternoon off after she serves dinner on Wednesday. It's our slowest day and my wife and daughter serve supper."

"Hell and damnation. It looks like everything's conspiring to keep me from finding my daughter." Rafe jammed his hat on his head and strode out the door.

Elizabeth followed him and in a rough voice, he asked, "Got any more bright ideas, wife?"

She glared at him, but only said, "Let's go home."

"I'm staying right here until that bastard brings my daughter back. Then I'm going to…"

"What are you going to do, Rafe?" Elizabeth had regained her composure and her voice was soft. "Are you going to kill Amelia's husband right before her eyes?"

"It won't come to that."

"How do you know? He's a bounty hunter, Rafe. If you draw on him he'll probably kill you."

"If he does, at least Amelia wouldn't stay with him."

Elizabeth looked disgusted. "Listen to yourself. You're talking like a school boy who lost a fight on the playground. Why don't you give up and wait for Amelia to contact you. I'm sure she will soon."

He turned on her and his eyes blazed. "I'll be damned if I'll sit around while my daughter is giving her favors to the likes of Jed Wainwright."

"What are you going to do about it?"

"You're going to get in this buggy and go home and I'm going to the saloon to see if I can find out if anyone knows where they went." Without another word he turned from her and headed down the street.

Elizabeth couldn't understand what was going on in Rafe's mind. She used to be able to reason with him, but for some time now it'd been almost impossible to understand his moods. When her father died and he brought Amelia back from Boston, he'd changed. He ruled the ranch with an iron hand and the only person he listened to was Vince Callahan. Even with his hardnosed ways, he'd gotten over all the things Amelia had done, but she wasn't sure he'd be able to this time. He was determined to make his daughter bend to his will and marry Vince Callahan, no matter what Amelia wanted. Why he was so determined, she didn't know, but she didn't like it.

Knowing she couldn't do anything about the situation at the moment, she stepped into the hotel and went into the dining room. She'd have some tea and wait to see if Rafe would calm down and be reasonable. Though she doubted he would.

* * * *

Vince Callahan met Rafe on the sidewalk in front of Brown's Mercantile. "Where you headed, boss?"

"The Wildcat Saloon. That bastard took Amelia out of town again."

"I need to get my tobacco pouch refilled. I'll meet you there."

Rafe nodded and kept walking. "I'll wait for you."

Vince didn't answer, but stepped inside the store and looked around. "You alone, Andy?"

"Yeah. My brother, Stanley, and Papa have gone to Cheyenne to get supplies. Mama went to do some kind of church work. Ain't no customers been here for the last hour."

"Good." Vince tossed Andy his tobacco pouch. "Fill this up in case somebody walks in. Then we'll talk."

Andy filled the pouch and turned back.

Vince took the full pouch. "What do you have for me?"

"Not much, but I'm keeping my ears open like you paid me to do. Kemp Newton was in yesterday. He was half drunk and I got him to talking. I told him I'd like to find out if Wainwright and his bride were really married in the biblical sense. He asked what it was worth to find out and I said how about a dollar. Well, to Kemp, a dollar is a fortune. I didn't know how he planned to find out, but he showed up this morning to collect his money."

"What'd he do?"

"He saw the Wainwrights come back late last night and when he found the front door open and the lobby empty, he slipped in the hotel and hid until everything settled down. He then went into the hall and listened outside Wainwright and Miss Donahue's door." Andy grinned. "He said the bed springs squeaked a whole lot."

"Damn," Vince said. "Rafe tried to convince me their marriage was in name only and it'd be easy to make her annul it. Don't look like that's going to happen now."

"Ain't no man in his right mind would marry a woman as pretty as Amelia Donahue in name only."

"I guess the only way to get her is to get rid of him."

Shock crossed Andy's face. "Are you going to kill him?"

"I didn't say that, did I?" Vince's voice was rough.

"No. I was just wondering. I bet it'd be hard to kill Wainwright. Milt Gordon was in here earlier. He and some friends tried to take Wainwright in the saloon. Before they could get their guns out, the bounty hunter shot a gun out of one of their hands and Milt didn't get a chance to draw before Wainwright's pistol was pointed at him."

"Ain't a man been born yet who can't be killed, Andy. Jed Wainwright included."

"I guess you could set a trap for him."

Vince nodded. "Maybe I will."

"How are you going to do it?"

"I've not figured it out, but I'll come up with something. In the meantime, I'm going to see if I can convince Rafe that Amelia ain't gonna walk away from this man and get an annulment."

"So you're going to accept her marriage?"

"For the time being. It don't matter to me if I get her second hand.

She's still a pretty woman, but the important thing is getting the Double D. No matter what I have to do to get it."

"Do you think she'll turn to you if Wainwright is out of her life?"

"Her father will see she does. He wants her to marry me under any circumstances."

"Why does he think so much of you, Vince?"

Vince laughed. "I made myself indispensable to him. He thinks I'm the best hand he's ever had on the Double D. He also thinks I worship the ground he walks on."

"Do you?"

"Hell no, but to get the ranch, I'll let him keep thinking it."

"You're still going to give me a job on the Double D when you get it, ain't you?"

"I promised you I would, didn't I?"

"Yes and I take your word for it. I want to get away from this damn store. Papa has his head set on me and Stanley taking it over, but the last thing in the world I want to do is run a mercantile."

The bell over the door jangled.

"How much do I owe you for the tobacco, Andy?" Vince's voice carried across the store.

"Twenty cents."

Vince put some money on the counter and turned to leave.

"Hello, Mrs. Ellsworth. What can I do for you today?" Andy was saying as Vince went out the door.

Chapter 8

John Lawson and his son, Ralph, left to ride over the ranch with Curt and Jed. Grace and Amelia stayed at the house. The women sat with Gladys Lawson and her daughter, Wilma, in the big main room which went from the front entry to the back of the house. There was a large rock fireplace in the back wall with windows on each side. It looked out on a yard with a flower garden leading to the vegetable patch. Beyond the garden was the open pasture.

Amelia remembered the door to the left led into a large eat-in kitchen. Behind the kitchen were a couple of bedrooms the cook used.

Yes. The place is even nicer than I remembered. It will be easy to live here if Jed and Curt buy it.

"I must say, I was shocked when I heard you'd gotten married, Amelia." Gladys interrupted her thoughts. "How long have you known Jed Wainwright?"

"For some time. He has been bringing prisoners to Settlers Ridge for several years."

"Yes, my dear. I've heard of his reputation." Gladys stirred her tea. "What I mean, is how long have you been seeing him?"

"Not very long. In fact, we fell in love at first sight."

"Oh, how romantic," Wilma said.

"Pooh," Gladys said. "Only a fool would believe that. You can't fall in love that fast."

"In Amelia and Jed's case, it happened fast, Mrs. Lawson. She told me one evening at supper she was going to get married and low and behold, she got married that very night."

Wilma giggled and Amelia looked at Grace, hoping her eyes thanked her friend for her interjection.

"Stop laughing, Wilma," her mother said. "It's not the way a man and woman should keep company and get married. It just isn't proper."

Amelia wanted to stop Mrs. Lawson's criticism of Wilma. "It's probably not the usual way, but you know me, I never do things as others do. I do it all my own way."

"That's for sure," Gladys said. "How do your mother and father feel about your marriage?"

"My mother is visiting her sister in St. Louis, but I'm sure she'll be happy for me."

"What about your father?"

"You know how men are about their daughters. Daddy doesn't think there's any man good enough for me except Vince Callahan. He wanted me to marry him."

"Vince Callahan's an old man," Wilma said.

"He's sure too old for Amelia," Grace offered.

"I must say, I agree." Gladys put down her cup. "What is your father thinking? I don't know if I'd have chosen Jed Wainwright for you, but I do know I wouldn't choose Vince Callahan. He's not right for you at all."

"Daddy thought if I married Vince, I'd not embarrass him so often."

Gladys bit her lip. "From what I've heard about Mr. Wainwright, I have a feeling he's the type who can calm you down better than Vince Callahan ever could."

"I think we've talked enough about me. Why don't you tell me about your possible move?" Amelia didn't need Gladys's opinion of Jed.

"I'm so looking forward to it." Gladys grinned. "I hope your husband likes our place and will buy it. I want to move to Texas as soon as we can.

The ranch there is so much nicer than this one and I'm sure there will be lots of interesting people."

"I don't want to move," Wilma said.

"Of course you do, dear. There's a better chance for you in Texas. The ranch is not far from San Antonio. You're sure to find a suitable husband there. There's nobody in Settlers Ridge I want you to marry."

"I'm sure you'll like it once you get there, Wilma." Grace set her cup on the table.

"I keep telling her that, but she won't believe me." Gladys shook her head.

"When do you plan to move, Mrs. Lawson?" Amelia asked.

"John said when we sell, we'll move right away. He tried to approach your father about buying the ranch a week or so ago, but Rafe was so busy trying to find you he told my husband to come back in a month. I don't want to wait that long, so I hope your husband and his friend will buy our ranch today." She sighed. "I want to be away from here before the month is out."

Amelia sat her empty tea cup aside. "Would you mind showing me through the house, Mrs. Lawson? If Jed and Curt do buy the place, I'll need to know how my things will fit into the rooms."

"I don't mind." Gladys shifted her heavy frame. "I plan to leave the heavier furniture because our new ranch is furnished and the stuff is so much nicer. You can use whatever we don't take or give it to the needy."

"If they buy the place, I will, Mrs. Lawson." Amelia stood.

"Why don't you show your friends around, Wilma? I'll go make sure cook has started the vegetables to go with the roast for supper."

When the three younger women walked down the hall, Wilma said, "You've seen my room, Amelia, but I don't think you've seen the other bedrooms."

"No, I haven't."

"There are two bedrooms down here and two upstairs where my room is. Mother and Father used to have their room upstairs, but she got so heavy she has trouble climbing the steps, so they moved down here." She opened the door to her parents' room.

"It's nice," Grace muttered.

When they went upstairs, Wilma opened the door to a large bedroom. "As I said, they used to sleep here, but not anymore. I think it's the prettiest room in the house."

"Yes, it's lovely." Amelia walked to the window and looked out. There was a panoramic view of the rolling plains. The front yard was inviting with the white picket fence enclosing it. In the distance she saw riders coming in.

"I think you and Jed should use this room, Amelia," Grace suggested.

"Yes. I think he'd like this one."

"May I ask you something, Amelia?"

"Of course, Wilma."

"How do you like married life?"

Amelia colored a little. "It's better than I thought it could ever be."

"I've watched them, Wilma, and I can attest to the fact they have a hard time keeping their hands off of each other."

Wilma giggled. "I wish I could get married and not move to Texas. Ralph is excited about the move, but I want to stay here."

"Is a special man the reason you want to stay here?" Amelia eyed her.

Wilma dropped her head and looked at the floor. "There is and I'll tell you if you promise you won't tell Mother."

"Of course we won't tell her," Grace said. "Remember who you're talking to. We always keep each other's secrets."

Wilma whispered, "It's Stanley Brown."

Amelia was shocked. Everyone knew Stanley Brown was a tall, skinny, shy young man who hid behind his glasses and spent most of his time working on the financial end of his father's mercantile business. Nobody had ever seen him show an interest in a woman, unless you could call the nervousness he displayed when he waited on women as an interest.

"When did this happen?" Grace asked.

"Nothing has really happened, but he smiles at me when I go in the store and I always smile back."

"Then why…" Amelia started.

"I don't know why, Amelia. All I know is that I daydream all the time about working in the store with Stanley. I can see us married and having children someday." Tears came into her eyes. "I know if I move to Texas, I'll never see Stanley again and it breaks my heart."

"You could meet somebody in Texas who you'll like better than Stanley Brown," Grace offered.

"Grace's right. Somebody who'll not only smile at you, but will talk to you, too."

"Do you really think so?"

Grace and Amelia said almost in unison, "Of course."

Gladys Lawson's voice traveled up the stairs. "Hurry, girls. I think I see the men coming toward the house."

"We're about through, Mrs. Lawson," Amelia called. She then reached for Wilma's hand. "Don't give up. Sometimes when things look the darkest, something will happen to change it all."

Wilma nodded and wiped her eyes. "I try to believe Mother is right about somebody being in Texas for me, but I don't really think so. Stanley is the man I want."

"Have you told your mother this?" Amelia felt sorry for her friend.

"Yes, but she doesn't listen."

"Girls, are you coming?" Gladys called to them again.

"We'll be there in a moment, Mama."

They toured the rest of the house quickly and were descending the stairs as the men came in the front door.

Gladys rushed to meet them. "Well, what did you think, Mr. Wainwright?"

"I think it's a nice place and so does Curt."

"Are you going to buy it?"

Amelia saw Ralph and her father cringe, but Jed ignored her statement. He said, "If you'll excuse us a moment, I'd like to discuss it privately with my wife. After all, she'll be living here, too."

"Of course," Gladys Lawson muttered. "Would you like to see the house? Amelia looked it over."

"I'll see it when we get back." He reached for Amelia's hand. "Let's walk down to the corral, honey."

He held her hand all the way to the fence. She knew it was because the Lawsons were all on the porch watching and he wanted them to think the Wainwrights were a happily married couple. Still, she couldn't control the tingle running up her arm from the feel of his hand holding hers.

When they reached the corral, he dropped her hand and leaned one foot on the lower rail of the fence. The horses they all rode in on were prancing about the corral, but Jed was looking at Amelia. "It's a nice place. The brand is a fancy L. I guess because their name is Lawson. Of course we plan to change the brand."

"What do you plan to change it to?"

"When we made up our minds to buy a ranch, we decided the name would be the Circle 2. It represents the two of us in business together."

"I like it."

"I'm glad you like it, because we've already registered the brand and had irons made." His eyes twinkled when he looked at her. "For the cows with the Lawson brand, I guess we could say it stands for love."

She shook her head at him. "As if love had anything to do with it." He only lifted an eyebrow and she added, "It sounds like you and Curt have made up your minds to buy the place."

"Did you like the house?"

"I'd want to do some redecorating, but I like the arrangement of the rooms. And I think the main room is special."

"Does it have a nice bedroom for us?"

She laughed. "Jed, you're incorrigible. You would think of the bedroom instead of asking if it has a nice working kitchen."

"We can always cook over an open fire, but making love requires a special place of its own, and I discovered last night, I enjoy making love to you. I intend to take advantage of that liking for the next six months."

She looked away and changed the subject. "Are you going to buy it or not?"

"He made us a good deal. I was ready to go with it and Curt butted in. He offered him three thousand less. Told him it'd be a cash deal and he wouldn't have to hold a mortgage or anything."

"What happened then?"

"I figured he'd laugh at the offer, but he didn't. He reached out his hand to shake ours. 'You've got a deal, boys,' he said."

"Oh, Jed, how wonderful."

"I told him I had to talk it over with you, but I knew then we'd take it."

"Of course, you'll take it." She looked around. "What about the livestock?"

"We got it, as well as some of the equipment, included."

"I learned they're going to leave some of the furniture."

"Good. We can save some money there."

"When do we close the deal and move here?"

"Since you agree, we'll meet him at the Settlers Ridge Bank in the morning. He said his wife had packed a lot already, so he could be out in a couple of days. If we can get enough supplies to survive, we can move in over the weekend."

"I'm glad things worked out. Now I'm going to let them think I'm excited about it." She threw her arms around his neck, kissed him full on the mouth then grinned at the surprised look on his face. "Now let's go tell them to pack the rest of their belongings because we want to get ready to move to this ranch."

* * * *

"I can't imagine why he wanted to talk it over with her." Gladys frowned.

"I guess he values her opinion," John said.

"The way she kissed him, I guess she doesn't care that we're all watching them," Gladys muttered. "Must be more to this love at first sight than I thought,"

"See, Mama, I told you it was romantic."

"Romantic, or not, since it looks like they're going to buy the place, I think the neighborly thing to do is invite them to supper." She looked at Curt and Grace. "I had our cook put a big roast in the oven earlier. I'll get her to add some extra vegetables."

After the deal was sealed with another handshake, the Lawsons insisted the four of them spend the night. "We can go into town together tomorrow and sign everything legal-like," John said.

"I'm not sure we can stay the night." Curt looked at Grace. "Do you have to be at work in the morning?"

"I don't go in until noon."

"Then it's settled." Gladys took over. "Grace can sleep with Wilma, and you, Mr. Allison, can sleep in the bunkhouse with Mort." She looked at Amelia as if she was trying to make a decision. Finally she said, "Wilma, prepare the guest room for the Wainwrights."

"Putting me in the bunkhouse is a good idea, Mrs. Lawson. You're a smart woman," Curt said. "It'll give me a chance to talk with your ranch hand. If I like him and we get along we might want to keep him on to work for us."

Gladys looked flustered, but said, "I'm glad you like the idea. We send supper out there to him, but of course, you'll take supper with us in the main house, Mr. Allison."

"Thank you, ma'am. I love roast and I'd hate to miss out on it. I'm sure anything coming from your kitchen will be wonderful."

She actually giggled and took the arm Curt offered. Everyone followed them inside. Jed looked puzzled when he saw Amelia and her two friends hiding grins. His look only made them cover their mouths to keep from laughing out loud.

* * * *

The next morning was a busy one. Gladys insisted they have breakfast before going into town to sign the papers to transfer the ranch. As soon as they finished eating, she shooed them out and began barking orders at Wilma about sorting through the things they wanted to take to Texas.

Before they left, Amelia managed to whisper to Wilma, "Please write to me with your new address. I'll write back and keep you posted on what Stanley Brown is up to."

"Oh, thank you, Amelia. I'll write as soon as we get there."

There was no more time for conversation. The horses were saddled and brought to the front porch. They bid farewell to Gladys and Wilma and rode away.

At the bank things went smoothly. Though surprised, Charles Fielding, the manager, was efficient and business like and it didn't take long. When Mr. Lawson and his son headed back to the ranch it was almost noon.

The new ranch owners went to the hotel dining room and had the special. Fried chicken, potatoes, green beans and biscuits.

As they came out of the hotel Jed asked, "Are you sure you want to go out to your father's ranch today, Amelia?"

"I'm sure. We're into our second week of marriage. I think it's time my father met my husband."

Jed turned to Curt. "We'll be back later tonight even if I have to fight our way off the ranch."

Curt laughed. "I hope it don't come to that."

"Anyway, since Gladys Lawson said it was fine for you to come out there and stay in the bunkhouse, I'll see you in a day or so. I'm anxious to start rounding up all the stray cattle roaming around there."

"So am I, but I guess we should lay in some supplies. When the Lawsons leave why don't I bring the wagon into town? You and Amelia can gather up the supplies in the meantime and have them ready to load up. We'll then head to our new home and start work."

"Sounds good." Jed nodded. "If we can round up enough cattle in the next few weeks, we might have the makings of a fall drive. I hear the fort in Navaho country is paying top prices for beef. Horses, too if you have them."

"As I check on the cattle, I'll be checking out the wild horses." He laughed. "Now, don't let me have to come and console your widow. You stay away from her daddy's gun."

"No matter how much he wants to, I don't think Daddy will shoot Jed." Amelia chuckled.

"I sure don't plan on getting shot."

"I'll see you in a day or two." Curt headed to the livery stable.

"Is there anything you need to do before we go to your parents' ranch?" Jed looked at Amelia.

"I left our marriage certificate in our room. I want to take it in case Daddy doesn't believe we're married."

"Want me to come with you?"

"I can get it."

"Then, I'll have a smoke and wait here for you."

Amelia wasn't gone long. When she returned, Jed flipped his cheroot into the street and they headed toward the livery stable. A voice called out behind them, "Hey, Wainwright. Wait up."

They turned to see Sheriff Gentry headed in their direction. "What's up, Lance?" Jed asked when he caught up to them.

"I needed to let you know the judge is expected to be in town day after tomorrow. Will you be around?"

`"I plan to be."

"Also, I've still got your reward in the office for bringing in the McBride gang."

"I'm sure it's safe. I'll be by for it in a day or two."

Gentry laughed. "I understand why you've been too busy to come by." He grinned at Amelia and she dropped her eyes. "Congratulations."

"Thank you, Lance," she said.

Lance turned back to Jed. "Sure you don't want to come by now?"

"We're heading out to the Donahue ranch. I'll come by later."

"You're a braver man than I am."

"What do you mean?"

"I hear Rafe Donahue is out for your head. You might be better off facing outlaws again."

"Daddy's not going to kill, Jed," Amelia said. "He'd come closer to killing me."

"I know he's wanted to wring your neck a few times, but he's really mad this time, Amelia."

"I figured he would be, but he'll get over it."

"I hope so." Lance pushed his hat back on his head. "At least I heard how your husband put the fear of God into anyone who wanted to try for the reward your daddy offered."

"What do you mean?" Amelia frowned.

"Didn't you tell her about how you faced those men down in the saloon, Jed?"

"Haven't had a chance."

"What happened?" Amelia looked at him.

"I'll tell you later." Jed took her arm, and gave her a quick smile. He then turned to Lance. "As I said, I'll come by for the reward later."

"Come any time. If I'm not there Deputy Bryce will be. He knows where the reward money is locked up." Lance turned to Amelia. "I got a letter from Nelda the other day."

"How are things with her?"

"She's fine, but she sure is going to be surprised when I write and tell her you've settled down."

Jed laughed. "Who said Amelia has settled down? As a matter of fact, I doubt she ever does."

Lance slapped Jed's shoulder. "A truer word has never been spoken. You've got your hands full with her, my friend."

"All right, you two. It's not fair to gang up on me."

"Sorry, Amelia, but you must admit…well, at least you probably married the only man in the territory capable of settling you down."

"Lance Gentry—"

Lance interrupted. "Before I get in trouble with my friends, I've got to get to the office."

"See you later, Lance." Amelia shook a finger at him. "That is, if you don't keep besmirching my reputation."

"I wouldn't consider it." He pulled his hat down as he walked away and said, "Good luck with her, Jed. You're going to need it."

"Of all the nerve." Amelia put her hands on her hips and tried to look angry, but her eyes were filled with merriment.

Jed shook his head and took hold of her arm. "Shall we head to the Double D?"

She leaned her head to the side. "As soon as I hear about a showdown at the saloon."

"I promise I'll tell you on the ride."

As Amelia and Jed rode out of town they didn't say anything for several minutes. When they reached the edge of town and headed into the country, he pulled his horse up beside hers. "Curt met me outside the dress shop you went into yesterday. He wanted me to go to the saloon with him. A group of young men were there. They planned to tie me up and grab you so they could collect the reward your daddy offered."

"What did you do?"

"I convinced them you didn't want to go home to Daddy."

"You must have done something more."

"I scared them well enough that I don't think they'll try anything as foolish again."

"I'm glad."

They went for a long time without talking further. Finally Amelia broke the silence, saying, "Are you all right?"

He raised an eyebrow. "Of course. Why wouldn't I be?"

She glanced at him and saw the distant look in his eyes. She softened. "It's all right, Jed. You don't have to talk about it. I need to talk about something because I can't help being a little nervous. I know Daddy's going to be irate when we get to the ranch. I'm sure he'll make a scene and I dread it."

"Maybe it won't be as bad as you think."

"It would be better if Mother was home. She's been in St. Louis visiting her sister and I don't know if she's back or not."

"I forgot to mention it, but Frank told me she came to the hotel with your father looking for us."

She glanced at him. "Good. Though she won't buck Daddy openly, she'll be on my side."

"Don't worry. We'll be able to handle it if she's not."

"You'll back me up, won't you, Jed?"

He cocked an eyebrow at her. "Why wouldn't I?"

"Daddy may offer you a large amount of money to divorce me." When he didn't say anything, she went on. "I hope you won't be tempted."

He reached over and touched her arm. "I never go back on my word, Amelia. I made an agreement with you and I intend to stand by it for the next six months."

"Will you quit reminding me I had to buy a husband?" Her voice grew angry.

"I'm sorry, I didn't mean to upset you, but you know our arrangement."

She took a deep breath. "You're right, Jed. I'm acting like a silly child. I guess I'm more nervous than I want to admit. Daddy has always been able to make me feel guilty, even if I'm in the right."

He reached for her hand. "Remember, I'm here for you. Today will prove to you I'm worth the money you paid for me."

Hurt crossed her eyes, but she soon hid it. "Then, my dear husband, let's go let the folks know I've made my decision and there's nothing they can do to make me change my mind about who I marry."

"For six months anyway."

"Yes," she muttered. "For six months."

Chapter 9

Elizabeth Donahue looked across the dining table at her husband's somber face. "What's the matter, Rafe?"

"I'm thinking about taking the advice Vince gave me today."

"What advice could he possibly give you?"

"He said I should pretend to accept Amelia's marriage and it wouldn't surprise him if when I did she'd decide being married to the half-breed bounty hunter wasn't exciting any longer."

"From what people say, Amelia is happy with the man."

"I can't abide the thoughts of her being with someone like him, Elizabeth. Do you realize how many people he's killed or put in prison?"

"I'm sure they all deserved their fate."

"That's beside the point." Rafe threw down his napkin. "I know Amelia gets into things she shouldn't, but she's really got herself in a pickle this time. There's no way she can get out of it alone. As usual, I'll have to clean up her mess so life can get back to normal."

"I want to meet this man our daughter married."

Rafe glared at her. "Are you insane? Why in hell would you want to meet him? She's not going to be married to him long."

"Maybe not, but Amelia is my daughter. I'll not be separated from her because of who she's married to." She looked at him. "Nor will I be separated from her because you'll not accept her husband, Rafe Donahue."

He stood. "Damn it, Elizabeth, you're my wife. You'll do what I tell you to do."

She looked up at him and tears welled in her eyes. "I'm not one of your ranch hands. You will not order me around as if I were."

"I'm not ordering you, Elizabeth, but you're my wife and you're not to question any decision I make. After all, what I do is for your own good as well as mine and Amelia's. That's the way it has always been and how it will always be in the future."

Elizabeth folded her napkin and dropped it by her plate. "I'll do what's right for my relationship with my daughter. If it means accepting her marriage, I'll do it."

"No you won't."

She stood. "Rafe, I've told you before if you try to come between my daughter and me, you may find you've not only lost a daughter, but you've also lost a wife." Without another word she swept out of the dining room.

Rafe stared at the blue dress she wore as it disappeared through the door. How dare Elizabeth speak to him in this manner. She'd never defied him before. What gave her the right to do so now? He wouldn't have it. Women didn't defy men. Not men they depended on for their livelihood. Besides, he couldn't have her get this mad at him. She wouldn't dare leave him. He wouldn't allow it. It was the wrong time for anything like that. He had to get Amelia away from the bounty hunter and married to Vince. Then he and Elizabeth could take the trip to Europe. She would then calm down and know his decision was right all along.

The maid entered. "Would you like your coffee now, Mr. Donahue?"

"No! I don't want coffee, Delores. I need something stronger." He stomped out of the room and headed for his study where he kept his best bourbon.

Rafe was having his second glass when there was a knock on his door. He smiled to himself. "Come in, Elizabeth. I knew you'd come to your senses."

The door opened. "I'm not Elizabeth," Vince said.

"What are you doing here? I thought you were getting the herd ready to drive to market."

"The hands are working with the herd. I was up on the ridge where I thought I might get a glimpse of the rustlers who have been pestering us and I saw two riders coming in."

"Were they the rustlers?"

"Prepare yourself, Rafe. Amelia is coming in with a man. I presume it's her husband."

"I'll be damned." He sat his glass down. "I knew she'd come home."

"I'm not sure that's the case. She could be coming to get some of her belongings."

"She can have anything she wants as long as she leaves him and comes home, but she'll not take a damn thing out of my house if she insists on staying married to him. There's nothing around here I didn't buy, so it all belongs to me."

Vince grinned. "Sounds like a good incentive to me. I'm sure the bounty hunter can't give her all the things you can."

"Amelia has always had the best of everything, and I'm sure she won't want to live on what Wainright can provide for very long." Rafe stood. "I think I'd better go outside. I want to talk to my stubborn daughter before Elizabeth realizes she's here."

"I'll leave out the back way."

"No, Vince. I want you to…"

Elizabeth came down the stairs and glared at Vince. "What are you doing here?"

"I had some business to discuss with Rafe."

"I think you should leave. Amelia is coming up the road and I only want family here to greet her."

Rafe saw Vince work his jaw, but he tipped his hat to Elizabeth and stepped out the door.

"Wait, Vince. I want you to be here. After all, since Amelia will soon be your wife, you have an interest in how this meeting goes."

"I'm sorry, boss. I don't want to disobey one of your orders, but I think your wife's right this time. I'll check back later." Before Rafe could say anything else, Vince stepped off the porch and headed toward the barn.

Elizabeth glanced at her husband. "How could you?"

"What do you mean?"

"You know exactly what I mean. That man has no business here while we're greeting our daughter and her husband."

"I keep telling you, Amelia's not going to be married to that man long. She'll come home and marry Vince before you know it."

She shook her head and again tears came into her eyes. "I don't think I know you anymore, Rafe Donahue. You haven't been the same for some time, and since I've been back from St. Louis, you've become completely unreasonable."

"A hell of a lot has happened since you've been back from St. Louis. I don't think you understand what a serious problem our headstrong daughter has created this time. A problem I have to get worked out."

"I only know if there's a problem, you shouldn't think you have to handle it alone. We should face it together, but instead we're pulling apart."

"And whose fault is that?" he almost yelled.

Elizabeth turned her head and watched the two riders head their horses toward the house. She didn't want Rafe to see the hurt mixed with anger in her eyes.

* * * *

Amelia saw her parents waiting on the long, six-columned porch. She knew her home wasn't the typical ranch house, but her grandfather had fashioned it after the home his parents had in Virginia. "Plantation style is what I'll have," he'd proudly told anyone who asked why he didn't build out of logs or adobe like most ranchers. He'd always add, "I want my beautiful wife to have something of her former home. This house is for her."

Amelia's mother had been born and raised here as was Amelia. It was the only home she'd ever known and she loved it. It was as much a part of her as the rest of the ranch. It would be hard to leave it for six months, but if Jed said they had to live on the ranch he bought, she'd do it. Besides, to her surprise, she'd discovered a strange fact. She wasn't sure when it happened, but at this point she realized being with Jed was more important to her than any house would ever be. Even her beloved Double D.

As they came closer to the front, she could see a smile on her mother's face, but her father was scowling. She knew immediately her prediction would be right. They were in for a bad scene with him. Her heart began to pound. She probably shouldn't have come out here, but it was too late to change her mind now.

They ground hitched their horses and Jed dismounted quickly. He then reached up and lifted her off her horse. They strode toward the porch together.

"Oh, Amelia, darling. It's so good to see you." Her mother came down the steps and enveloped her daughter in her arms. "I've missed you so much."

"It's good to see you, Mother. I missed you, too. Did you have a good trip?"

"It was fine, but I think you have more news than I do." She looked at Jed.

"Yes, I do. I'd like to introduce my husband, Jed Wainwright. Jed, this is my mother, Elizabeth."

"Mrs. Donahue, I'm pleased to meet you." He removed his hat and took the hand she offered.

"I'm pleased to meet you, too." Elizabeth's smile was friendly.

"And this is my father, Rafe Don…"

Rafe butted in. "I'm sure the man knows who I am, Amelia. I know who he is, too." Her father folded his arms across his chest and ignored the hand Jed offered.

Jed dropped his hand. "Yes, sir, I know who you are."

Amelia saw neither man had any kindness in his eyes. She wasn't sure what she should do next. Her mother saved her from having to say anything.

Elizabeth said, "It's awfully warm here in the sun. Why don't you come in and I'll have Delores serve some lemonade. We had some for dinner and it was refreshing."

"That sounds wonderful." Amelia linked her arm with her mother's and they went up the steps.

Jed started to follow, but Rafe stepped in front of him, preventing him from reaching the porch.

"I'm glad you've decided to come home, Amelia," Rafe said without looking at her. "If you're ready to forget this frivolous marriage, then you're welcome to move back where you belong. But this half-breed bounty hunter is not welcome in my house. Not now and not ever."

There was no expression on Jed's face, but Amelia saw her mother looked as shocked as she felt.

"I don't believe you, Daddy."

"Rafe you can't say…"

"Be quiet, Elizabeth. This is between Amelia and me." He turned and glared at his daughter. "Are you ready to renounce this stupid marriage and act like you have some sense?"

"I have sense, Daddy. I'm married and there's nothing you can do to change it. I have the marriage certificate to prove it."

"Rafe, what are you trying to do?" Elizabeth wrung her hands and stared at her husband.

Rafe ignored his wife and grabbed Amelia's arm. "I'm saying you've been a damn fool, girl. You have everything here any woman could possibly want. This ranch, this house, will all be yours if you come to your senses and decide you want it more than you want some dirty half-breed."

"And marrying your precious Vince Callahan is part of the deal, I presume." Her eyes stared into her father's.

"Of course. You'll marry him, just as I told you to do in the first place. Things will then be like they should be around here."

Amelia jerked her arm away from her father. "I'm a married woman, Daddy. You can't tell me what to do."

"You're a damn fool child, Amelia. I ought to knock some sense into you…"

He raised his hand to slap her, but Jed jumped up the steps and caught Rafe's arm in mid-air. Though his black eyes were like ice, he said in a calm voice, "You are Amelia's father and I will respect you for that reason, but get one thing straight and get it straight now. If you ever strike my wife, you'll be sorry."

Rafe backed up a little. He looked startled. "She's my daughter," he muttered.

"Yes, she's your daughter by birth, but she's my wife. That puts her under my protection now, not yours." His eyes bored into Rafe's.

"Then she'll have to make the decision of who is more important to her, and she'll have to make it right now. She'll either be my daughter and come home where she belongs or she'll be your wife and leave with you." He turned to Amelia. "Come in the house and we'll discuss how you can rid yourself of this unsuitable man, and all is forgiven. You'll once again be the pampered and admired daughter of one of the largest ranchers in Wyoming." He took a breath. "Or leave with this half-breed and you'll no longer be my daughter."

Silence enveloped the porch. Even the birds stopped singing and the insects ceased to buzz around. Not a whisper of wind stirred in the trees.

Amelia broke the silence. "I'll get some of my things and…"

"You have nothing here. Everything in this house was bought by me and it belongs to me. If you choose to go with this bounty hunter, you'll take nothing from the Double D." Rafe stared at her. His eyes told everyone he didn't believe she wouldn't renounce her marriage and come home.

Amelia was stunned, but she managed to turn to her mother and hug her. "I'm sorry it's come to this, Mother."

"I can't believe this is happening, darling. There must be some way we can…"

"Get in the house, Elizabeth," Rafe yelled.

She glared at him and didn't move.

Amelia stumbled down the steps and Jed steadied her with his hand. As he helped her on her horse there were tears in her eyes, but she refused to break down in front of her father.

"By the way, drop that horse off at the barn on your way out. He belongs to this ranch." Rafe glared at her.

Before anyone could say anything Amelia snapped, "The hell he does. Grandpa gave me this horse. Rambler belongs to me and I'll not give him up to you or anyone else."

"I said…"

"It's her horse, Rafe." Elizabeth's voice was the sharpest Amelia had ever heard. "My father gave it to her and said nobody would ever own that horse, but his granddaughter. She owns it and she has a right to keep it."

"Then take the damn horse and get off my ranch, and don't come back for anything else. There's nothing here for you as long as you're married to that low-down Indian."

Without a word, Amelia turned her horse and headed toward the road. Jed followed her.

"I love you, Amelia. I'll see you soon," her mother called.

Amelia wouldn't turn around, but she did throw up her hand to let her mother know she'd heard her words.

When they were out of sight of the house, Jed asked, "Are you all right, Amelia?"

"I'll be fine," she said, though tears were streaming down her cheeks.

"Do you want to stop and cry it out?"

She shook her head. "Not on his property."

"I understand." Jed pulled Devil up beside Rambler. "We'll rest when we cross the river."

She only nodded because she knew she wasn't capable of saying anything else without breaking down.

* * * *

Jed hitched the horses to a cottonwood tree in a grassy area near the river. He removed the bed roll from behind his saddle, took a blanket from it and brought it over to where Amelia stood. Without saying anything he spread it out on the ground to make a comfortable place to sit. He then reached for her arm and motioned for her to move to the blanket.

She dropped down and he sat beside her. He still didn't speak, but he slipped his arm around her shoulder.

She leaned against him. "I knew my father would be infuriated, but I never dreamed he'd disown me, Jed. Not in a million years." New tears filled her eyes. "I thought he'd scream and holler and fuss at me, but not this."

Jed pulled her tighter to him. "I didn't think he'd be so cruel to you, either."

She looked up at him. "I'm sorry about those mean things he said to you."

"You have no reason to be sorry, Amelia. A lot of people don't like half-breeds."

"Jed, I know you're half Indian, but it doesn't matter. You're simply a man. A better man than a lot I know and much better than you think you are."

"I know it doesn't matter to you." He half-smiled at her. "If everyone in this world was as nice as you, this would be a better place."

She shrugged. "My daddy doesn't think I'm very nice. He wanted a son and he's never liked me. Now he hates me."

"Hate is a strong word, Amelia. I'm sure he'll see reason one day. In the meantime, your mother seems to think you're special." He tightened his arm around her.

"She only wants me to be happy. I was sure she'd accept our marriage."

Jed wasn't comfortable talking about their marriage. He changed the subject. "When we get back to town, I want you to try to relax. Since Curt is coming back soon with the wagon you could do some shopping and get a head start on the supplies for the ranch. Once we get there, you're going to be busy for the next few weeks."

"Busy enough to keep my mind off my family?"

"I hope so."

There was another silence then she said, "As I said, I knew it was going to be rough, but I didn't expect all this to happen when we got married." She sighed. "I knew my daddy would be furious and would give me a hard time. I even knew he wouldn't like you, but I never dreamed he'd be cruel to you or disown me. I'm sorry I got you into all of this."

"It doesn't matter, Amelia. I think when I warned him not to strike you, was what set him off today."

"What do you mean?"

"I think he realized no matter what, I'd never let you be pushed into marrying Vince Callahan."

"Do you mean you wouldn't let Daddy make me marry him?"

"Yes."

"Thank you, Jed. That means a lot to me."

Silence descended on them again, but it was a different silence. A comfortable silence.

Again Amelia broke it when she whispered, "Do you regret marrying me, Jed?"

Her question was one he didn't want to face. How could he tell her the days they'd been together had been some of the happiest he'd known in a long time. He couldn't give her false hope. This could never become a permanent arrangement. He wasn't the marrying forever kind. It wouldn't be fair to saddle her with a man who couldn't give her his whole heart and that he could never do. Most of his heart died ten years ago and was buried in Kansas with Marie and his child.

Before he could come up with an answer, a shot rang out. Amelia screamed and he felt a burning sensation on the top of his left shoulder. Realizing he'd been hit, he grabbed Amelia and forced her down the embankment where the river curved. Drawing his gun, he pushed her against the overhang and eased his head up to look around.

"Stay here," he commanded as he began to crawl back toward the blanket.

"I want to go…."

"Damn it, Amelia. I said stay here," he ordered.

She bit her lip and didn't say anything else as he moved forward in a crouch.

Another shot sounded and Jed slipped behind a tree. He was working his way to the horses so he could get his rifle. Reaching his goal, he jerked the rifle from the scabbard as another shout sounded. Jed raised the rifle and fired.

The shooter dropped his rifle and grabbed his arm. He whipped his horse around and took off in the direction of the Donahue ranch. Jed stood and started back toward Amelia.

She scrambled up the bank and ran to him. "Are you all right?"

He put his arm around her shoulder. "I'm fine."

"Did you kill him?"

"No. He rode off holding his arm."

"Are you going after him?"

"No. I can't leave you alone and besides he headed back toward your daddy's ranch." He grabbed the blanket and ushered her toward the horses. "I think we need to move on."

He was helping her on Rambler when she noticed the blood on his shirt. "Jed, you're hurt. Let me look at your shoulder. Why didn't you say something?"

"Calm down, Amelia. I'm fine. We'll take care of it when we get to town. Mount up and let's get out of here. We could still be in danger. He might have backup."

She didn't argue with him, but said, "Then let's hurry and get to town. I don't want you bleeding enough to pass out on me. I wouldn't know what to do."

He mounted and they turned their horses toward Settlers Ridge. Jed was surprised with everything going on; all he could think about was did he or did he not regret marrying Amelia Donahue?

* * * *

"What happened, Smithy?" Vince asked as he wrapped Smithy's hand with strips of a torn up bed sheet.

"I caught up with them as they crossed the river. I waited until they sat down on a blanket all nice and cozy. I crossed further up and worked my way down. I had him in my sight and pulled the trigger, but he moved. I got him on the shoulder, but I don't know how bad he was hurt. Before I could shoot again, he got her behind some rocks and came after me. He shot me before I could get him again."

"Damn. He's not going to be as easy to take down as I thought."

"He's a slick one for sure. I did my best, Vince."

"I know. If we'd had more time to plan, it might've been different."

"When they come back…"

"Rafe told her not to come back unless she got rid of him."

"Think she will?"

"No. She's as stubborn as Rafe." Vince tied off the bandage. "But don't worry. I'll get this ranch with or without her."

"Is there another way?"

"There's always another way, Smithy." Vince stood. "I'm going to make sure Rafe thinks you were shot by a stray bullet. We don't want anyone around here to get suspicious."

"I'm with you, boss."

"Thanks, Smithy." Vince went out the door cursing under his breath. He should've sent somebody other than Smithy to kill Wainwright. But the only other cowhand he trusted on the Double D was Herb Dinkins. Herb was working out on the range. Vince decided that next time he'd do it himself. It would've all been over if he'd gone to the river and waited until Amelia and Wainwright arrived. He wouldn't have missed the bounty hunter and then the ranch and Amelia would both be his.

Chapter 10

Jed's shoulder wound was like he said, only a scratch, but Amelia insisted she put a bandage on it and use some salve to prevent infection. "Now that I don't have a father, I have to be sure nothing happens to you," she teased him.

"You don't have to worry about that. I'll be here for you."

"For six months anyway?" She looked at him.

He smiled back at her. "Yes, Amelia. For six months."

When she finished doctoring him, Jed put on a clean shirt and smiled at her. "Thanks, honey."

"You're welcome." She put the pan of bloody water on the dresser and turned back to him. "Now I have something serious to talk about."

"What's that?"

"I was thinking as we were coming into town that I have some money in Settlers Ridge Bank. First thing in the morning, I need to go see Charles Fielding and make sure all my money is in my name. If I don't, I'm afraid Daddy will try to prevent me from getting it."

He raised an eyebrow at her. "How much money do you have, Amelia?"

"I'm not sure, but my grandfather left me some and when Daddy remembers it, he'll try to tie it up so I'll never get it. I can't let him do that."

"Then do what you think is best."

"Will you go with me?"

"It's not my business, Amelia. I don't want anyone saying I'm messing with your money."

"Nobody would know. You can trust Charles Fielding. Besides, after what happened today, I'm almost afraid to go out on the street alone."

He grinned at her. "Of course if you're afraid, I'll go with you."

* * * *

When they got to the bank at nine the next morning, Jed insisted he wait outside while she conducted her business. "As I said yesterday, I don't want anyone to think I'm pressuring you to do anything with your money."

She nodded and stepped inside as she watched him take out a cheroot and lean against a post.

"Well, Miss Don...I mean, Mrs. Wainwright. What can I do for you today?" the teller asked.

"I'd like to speak with Mr. Fielding, if he isn't busy, Mr. Blake."

"I'm sure he'll be able to see you." He motioned for her to come to the door beside the teller windows then he knocked on the office door. "Mr. Fielding, Mrs. Wainwright is here to see you."

For a moment Charles Fielding looked surprised, but he recovered. "Well, come on in, Mrs. Wainwright. I want to congratulate you again on your marriage."

"Thank you."

"I hope things are going well for you."

"Very well, thank you again."

"In that case, how can I help you today?"

When the door closed behind her, she moved to his desk. "I want to check on my money, Mr. Fielding."

He frowned. "What do you mean?"

"I mean the money my grandfather left me."

"Oh, yes. The trust fund. What would you like to know about it?"

"Is it really mine?"

He chuckled. "Of course it is. When you turn eighteen..."

"I turned eighteen last September, Mr. Fielding."

"Well, in that case, there's no problem. You can do whatever you want to do with the money. I only hope you'll decide to leave it here in the bank."

She nodded. "I'll leave it here if I can put the money in an account only I have access to."

"You don't want your father..."

"No. I don't want my mother or my father to be able to get to the money. I want it in my name only."

"What about your husband?"

"He doesn't want his name on it."

"Really?" Unbelief showed in Charles Fielding's eyes.

"Really. I do want to make an arrangement in the event something happens to me, my husband gets the money." She took a deep breath. "He'll probably fight it, but it'll be a done deal and there'll be nothing he can do about it."

"Very well, if that's what you want, let's get the paper work done."

"By the way, Mr. Fielding. How much money do I have?"

"I'll have to check to be sure, but I think it's around twenty-five or thirty thousand dollars."

Amelia had an inner struggle to keep from showing her surprise. She never dreamed it would be so much. Now she wouldn't have to worry about buying things for her new home.

* * * *

Rafe looked at Delores Rodriguez, their long time housekeeper, as she set a bowl of stew in front of him. "Why don't you wait and serve when Mrs. Donahue gets here?"

"She told me to go ahead and feed you. She isn't feeling well."

Rafe worked his jaw. Was she going to stay mad at him forever? After Amelia rode off yesterday, Elizabeth went to their room and closed the door. He expected her to cry a little and then come down for supper, but she'd sent word she didn't feel well and wasn't eating supper. When he went up to bed, she turned her back to him and pretended to be asleep. He decided to let her get over her pouting before he said anything to her. He knew she wanted him to apologize for his actions, and he had no intention of doing that. After all, he'd been right. Amelia was the one being unreasonable.

This morning when he got up, Elizabeth refused to get out of bed, saying she had a headache.

"Crying will do that to you," he'd said in a flippant way and went down to breakfast.

Now he was having his mid-day meal alone and he didn't like it. It was time for Elizabeth to straighten up and accept the fact Amelia would be home in a few days. She wouldn't like living the sparse life her bounty hunter could offer her. She was like all women. She wanted and needed pretty things in her life. A pretty new dress occasionally, a new fancy hat every few months, and a man who could provide those things were what it took to keep a woman happy. Since Amelia had never gone without anything she wanted, she wouldn't take lightly to giving them up. She was mad now, but she'd be back soon. There was no doubt in his mind about it.

Rafe finished his meal and pushed back his chair. He started out the door, but changed his mind. He turned and headed toward the stairs. He was going to make sure Elizabeth didn't spend the rest of the day in bed. He had no intention of eating supper alone.

Pushing the door open, he was surprised to see the bed made and his wife's clothes piled on it. He frowned and stepped inside. "What the hell is going on here?"

Elizabeth turned from the wardrobe and looked at him. She moved to the bed and laid down the clothes she had over her arm. "I'm packing," she said in a terse voice.

"Why?"

"I'm going on a trip."

Rafe frowned. "The hell you are."

She stared at him. "Are you refusing to let me go?"

"Damn right I am. You just got home from St. Louis and you're not leaving again. I want you here."

"Why, Rafe?"

He frowned again. "Because you're my wife and you belong here."

She turned back to her wardrobe. "You don't need me anymore."

"Elizabeth, what's got into you?" His voice grew irritated. "You've never acted like this in all the years we've been married."

She paused and gave him a weak smile. "Neither have you, Rafe."

"What do you mean?"

"I never thought I'd see the day you'd throw my daughter out of our house." Tears came to her eyes. "You were mean and cruel and I don't know what you'll do next. I'm afraid you might turn on me at any time."

"You're being ridiculous, woman. Amelia will soon see what a mistake she's made. She'll be home and marrying Vince before you know it. Why next year this time she and Vince will present us with our first grandchild. I'm sure of it."

Elizabeth shook her head. "No, Rafe. You're wrong. I looked into Amelia's eyes. She'll never come home."

"Oh yes she will. I'll see to it."

"Rafe, how can you be so obstinate? I don't know why, but I know you and Amelia have never had a good relationship. Now you've pushed her to the limit and there's no way to repair things between you." She shook her head. "Maybe you were jealous of how close she was to my father instead of you."

"That's a stupid thing to say."

"I don't think so. You've always thought of Amelia as another piece of your property, not as an intelligent person with feelings and opinions of her own. My father knew she was a smart human being with a good business head on her shoulders."

"That's ridiculous. Amelia's only a girl, Elizabeth. She needs my guidance."

"No, Rafe. She's not a girl. She's a grown woman now and she doesn't need your guidance. She needs your love."

"Of course…"

"No you don't. I'm not sure you know what love is or how to love anyone."

Rafe became angry. He stalked toward her. "How can you say that, woman? We've lived together for over twenty years and I've given you everything a wife could want."

"No you haven't."

He frowned. "Whatever else you want, buy it. I can afford it."

"What I want can't be bought with money. I want the same thing Amelia wants from you."

He looked confused. "What are you talking about?"

"I'm talking about respect and love, Rafe."

"For God's sake, Elizabeth. You're talking crazy. Of course I love you and believe it or not, I love her. Why, I'd give Amelia the world if she'd only use her head and do what I want her to do."

Elizabeth shook her head. "You think you love her, but you don't. You're like a lot of men. You have no idea of a woman's feelings or how to love her. You think possessions are what she wants, when that's far from her mind."

"If I'm so wrong, what has the last twenty years been about?"

"There were moments when you seemed to care. And of course, I had Amelia to love. Now you've taken her away from me and I have nothing."

"You're not making a damn bit of sense, Elizabeth. You have everything you've ever wanted. More, in fact. I'm probably the richest man in Wyoming. You can have anything you want." He shook his head. "Why don't you go into town and buy yourself the most expensive hat Mrs. Purdy has in her shop. A new hat always seems to make your problems go away."

"Oh, Rafe." She stared at him and tears ran down her cheeks. "You're such a fool."

"We'll discuss this when you can be more reasonable." With a bewildered look, Rafe turned and left the room, wondering if his wife had lost her mind as had his daughter. He knew Elizabeth was still crying, but he chose to ignore it.

* * * *

After they left the bank, Jed led Amelia into Brown's Mercantile. "I think we better get started on gathering the supplies we'll need. Curt may be here this afternoon or in the morning."

She knew he was trying to keep her busy so she wouldn't dwell on the incident at her father's ranch. She went along with him, because she did need a distraction and they needed supplies.

She was busy selecting linens and household items they'd want as soon as they got to the ranch when Jed walked up to her.

"I've picked out all the tools in here I'll need right away. I'm going to step out back with Stanley to look in the storage shed where he keeps the larger things."

"Fine. I'll be a while. I never dreamed we had to buy so much and I haven't even started on the food."

He nodded and went through the store to the back door.

Amelia carried the supplies she'd gathered to the counter. "Do you mind if I put these here, Andy? I still have more shopping to do."

"Please do, Miss Donahue."

"It's Mrs. Wainwright now. How about using my correct name?"

"I know you married him, but since he's not watching, would you like for me to help you escape?"

"Escape from what?" Amelia frowned at him.

"The half-breed, of course."

"Andy Brown, don't you dare refer to my husband in such a way. His name is Jed Wainwright." She slapped a pillow down on the counter.

"Oh, come on, Miss Donahue, your daddy said you'd be happy to get away from him."

"My daddy now knows differently. He found out when I chose my husband over coming back to the Double D to live."

Andy looked confused. "When Vince Callahan was in here he said you and him was going to get married as soon as you got away from the half...bounty hunter."

"He's a fool. Even if I wasn't married to Jed, I wouldn't marry Vince Callahan if he was the only single man in Settlers Ridge. I'd rather marry the town drunk."

Andy laughed.

"What's so funny?" Amelia stared at him.

"I'm sorry, Miss Donahue, but I can't picture you married to Kemp Newton."

"I told you to call me Mrs. Wainwright. If you call me Miss Donahue again, I'll dump all the supplies I've collected on the floor and insist my husband take me to another town to buy our supplies."

"No." Andy's eyes grew large. "Please, Miss...I mean, Mrs. Wainwright. If I let this big order...I mean Mama and Dad would kill me."

"Then you need to stop listening to people like my father and Vince Callahan. They have their own agendas, and believe me, they don't care who they step on to get their way."

"Are you saying you don't trust your father or Vince?"

"I used to trust my father, but I'm not sure I can anymore. I've never trusted Vince Callahan."

Andy still looked confused. "But you're going to marry him."

"Andy Brown, if you say that one more time, I'm going to hit you over the head with this curtain rod. I was never going to marry Vince Callahan, and I certainly will never marry him in the future. I can't stand the man."

"But how'll he get the ranch?"

"What?"

"Uh…nothing…Why don't you go on with your shopping, Miss…Mrs. Wainwright?"

"Andy Brown, what did you say about Vince getting the ranch?"

"Nothing. I figured he'd get it if he married you."

Amelia glared at him. "Has Vince talked to you about getting my father's ranch?"

"No. Of course not. He's the foreman, ain't he? I guess he thinks he can do things there." Andy was turning red and his brow was beginning to sweat.

She wasn't about to let him get away with what he said. "What things?"

"With you as his wife…"

"I told you there was no chance I'd ever marry that snake."

"Even if your husband was dead?"

Amelia leaned across the counter and took hold of Andy's shirt. "Does Vince Callahan plan to kill my husband?"

"I don't know." Andy looked as if he was going to cry. "All I know is I wanted a job working on the ranch and Vince said he'd give me one when you was married to him and he was running everything. That's all I know."

Amelia twisted the material of his shirt in her hand and said in a low voice, "You'd better tell me all you know because if something happens to my husband, I'll see to it you spend the rest of your sorry life in a dirty prison somewhere. Do you understand?"

He nodded and a tear appeared in his eye. "Yes, ma'am."

"Good." She let go of his shirt. "If you hear Vince say anything about my husband or me, you'd better let me know right away. If I find out later you don't…"

Jed and Stanley came back into the store and she turned toward them. "Oh, dear. You're faster than I am. I still have things to pick up."

"Do you need help?" Jed walked up to her.

"Sure. You can carry things to the counter."

Stanley spoke. "Andy, why don't you deliver Reverend Ellsworth's order? I put it on the shelf in the storeroom. I'll help Mr. and Mrs. Wainwright."

"Sure." Andy rushed toward the storeroom before anyone could say anything.

"I think he was in a hurry." Jed took hold of Amelia's arm.

"I know he was." She pulled Jed to the other side of the store. "I'll tell you about it later. Now, help me finish gathering the stuff we need."

As Amelia chose the things she wanted, Jed carried them to the counter for Stanley to begin adding. When they finished with the household items, she said, "I'll make a list of the food items we want and drop it by in the morning. I'm sure we can get it all together before Curt comes with the wagon."

"That'll be fine, Mrs. Wainwright," Stanley mumbled. "Or we could deliver it for you."

Jed shook his head. "I appreciate it, but we'll take what we can get in the wagon with us. If we need anything delivered, I'll let you know."

"I hope you're going to like ranching, Jed."

"I'm sure I will, Stanley. I never intended to be a bounty hunter all my life. Ranching was what I always wanted to do."

"I'm glad you were the one to buy the Lawson place."

"I think we'll like it there." Jed placed the last of the items Amelia had chosen on the counter.

"I was surprised to hear the Lawsons left so quickly." He glanced at Amelia then turned his head back to Jed. "They all went didn't they?"

"Yes," Amelia said. "Wilma didn't want to go, but she had no choice."

"She didn't want to go?" Stanley looked surprised and turned a little pink.

"No, but her mother insisted she go with them. It wouldn't surprise me if she came back, especially if someone gave her a reason to return to Settlers Ridge. A reason Gladys wouldn't fight."

Stanley blushed and Jed looked confused, but he didn't say anything.

* * * *

Vince Callahan was riding into town when he saw Andy Brown leaving Preacher Ellsworth's house. Andy was waving frantically to him.

"What the hell does that kid want?" Vince muttered and turned his horse toward the mercantile wagon. Reining in, he pushed his hat back. "I don't have much time. I've got to send a wire to some cattle buyers for Donahue and then get back to roundup."

"I wanted to let you know Mrs. Wainwright came in the store today to…"

"Hold it. Why are you calling her Mrs. Wainwright?"

"She made me."

He shook his head. "Go on."

"She said she wasn't ever going to marry you."

"She's dead wrong." Vince's eyes grew cold. "I'll get her one of these days."

"She said she'd never leave her husband."

"She won't have a choice if he's dead."

"She asked me if you planned to kill him."

Damn kid. Why did he have to start running his mouth? I shouldn't have trusted him. Aloud he asked, "What'd you say?"

"I told her you'd never kill anybody."

"What else did she want to know?"

"She wanted to know if you wanted her daddy's ranch."

Vince frowned. "Did you tell her I did?"

"No. Her husband came back in and Stanley told me to deliver the preacher's order, so I got out of there."

"Are they still at the store?"

"I don't know. They had a lot of shopping to do."

"Why?"

"I guess they're setting up a household or something."

Vince frowned. So they were getting ready to settle somewhere. He wondered where. At least he knew it wasn't on the Double D. Rafe had made it clear he wouldn't allow them to live there.

"Do you know where they're settling?"

"She didn't say, but she bought a lot of bed clothes and some household items."

"Like what?"

"Pots, dishes, curtains, that sort of thing."

"Anything else you can tell me?"

"That's about it."

Vince straightened his hat and picked up the reins. "Go back to the store and find out anything you can about them. If they're not there, ask somebody."

"I'll do it, Vince. I'll get word to you when…"

"I'll come to you. I don't want people seeing you talk to me. Now, head out and if anyone asks, I saw you leaving the preacher's house and stopped to ask if you got the new branding iron I ordered."

"I didn't know you ordered a brand…"

"Damn it, Andy. Don't be a fool. I didn't order anything, but who has to know? That's just something to cover up what we were really talking about."

Andy swallowed. "I'm sorry, I thought…"

"Don't think. Do what I tell you to do. You want to work on the Double D when I get it, don't you?"

"Sure, Vince. That's why I'm telling you this."

"Then get back to the store and I'll see you in a couple of days."

Vince rode off muttering, "That kid's gonna be trouble. I'll have to get rid of him as soon as he's no more use to me."

Chapter 11

The next morning Jed left Amelia at the hotel when he went to testify against the McBride gang. Mrs. Olsen said the cook, Effie Vaughn, had everything under control in the kitchen and suggested Amelia and Grace spend some time together since the Wainwrights were moving to the ranch that afternoon.

The girls were delighted and spent the morning shopping mostly at Miss Purdy's shop for some personal things Amelia wanted.

At noon, Jed came to the hotel and told her the trial was over and the prisoners were on their way to Cheyenne. He asked if she was ready to head for home. With a promise to get together again soon she and Grace said goodbye. Amelia left with her husband and Grace returned to help out with the hotel dining room evening meal.

It was after three o'clock when Amelia and Jed led their horses into the barn at their new ranch. He dismounted and held out his hand to assist her. "Well, Mrs. Wainwright, we're home."

"I'm glad to be here, Mr. Wainwright."

"Really?" He looked surprised.

"Yes, Jed, really. The Olsens have been wonderful, but I was ready to leave. I wanted to get out where I could ride Rambler and check fences and look at cows again."

He began unsaddling his horse. "I was ready to leave, too. It'll be good to get out here and work with the cows instead of looking at them like you do."

Before she could reply an older man with a scraggly beard and a floppy brown hat stepped into the barn. "Hello, boss." He looked at Amelia. "Ma'am, I'm Mort Godfrey. Mr. Curt said you'd be here today. I'm glad you made it."

"Thank you."

"We're glad to be here," Jed said.

"I'll cool your horses down and turn them into the corral for you."

"Thank you, Mort." Jed took their saddle bags and turned to her. "Let's go see what needs doing in the house before Curt gets here with the supplies."

They went inside through the back door. Amelia moved to the large wooden kitchen table and waited for Jed to lay their saddlebags down. "It's not too bad, is it?"

"I know it's not what you're used to, Amelia, but…"

She frowned. "I wasn't comparing it to my daddy's house, Jed. I meant the kitchen wasn't too dirty."

He gave her a sheepish grin. "Then, you're right. It isn't bad."

She put her hat on the rack beside the door. "Mort is kind of old for a hired hand, isn't he?"

"He is and I don't think he'll be much help rounding up horses and cows, but Curt said he kept things in pretty good working order around the house and the barn."

Amelia nodded. "Why don't we check out the rest of the house so I can see what I need to do to make us comfortable?"

They ended the tour in the upstairs bedroom she liked. "I thought we'd use this room if it's all right with you."

"I think it's fine." He moved to the window. "I like the fact it looks out toward the front, but the furniture isn't great."

"I know. I bought some things to make it look better."

"We'll buy a new bed, too. I still have some money left and I haven't touched the five thousand you gave me."

"I want you to use that money to build up the ranch, Jed."

"The house is part of the ranch."

"I know, but it wouldn't be fair to Curt if we started spending money on things only we would use."

"He might want a new bed, too."

Amelia laughed. "All right, if he wants a new bed, you'll both get new ones."

"I'm a little hungry. Think we might find something in the pantry to hold us until Curt gets here with the food?"

She reached for his hand. "Let's go see."

When they looked in the pantry, Amelia had to laugh. "Gladys left some furniture, but she sure took all the food. There's not a smidgen to eat. Only an old bucket and a worn scrub brush."

"I could go out and scare up a rabbit or something."

"How would we cook it? She took the pots, too."

He shook his finger at her. "If I recall correctly, you're pretty good at making a meal over a campfire."

"So you bought a ranch, but I still have to cook over an open fire?" she teased him.

Before he could answer there was a shuffling on the back porch.

"It could be Curt." Jed moved to open the door.

"I come to see if you and the missus would like a cup of coffee or something. I know Miz Lawson cleaned everything out cause she only left me and Curt enough food to get by for a couple of days."

"Coffee would be great, Mort. You're right about Ms. Lawson. We checked the pantry, but couldn't find a thing." Jed turned to Amelia. "Let's go have a cup of coffee."

"I'll bring it to you. The bunkhouse ain't no fit place for a lady like Miz Wainwright."

"I understand." Jed grinned. "I'll walk with you and bring her back a cup."

When Amelia was alone in the kitchen, she looked around again. Jed was right. This place was nothing like the big house she'd grown up in, but she'd never let Jed know she'd made the comparison. It would hurt his feelings and she knew he'd had enough of that in his lifetime.

Lifting a burner lid, she decided the stove was clean, but the kitchen table was another matter. It was caked with grease and probably ground in food. It would never do.

Moving back to the pantry, she looked at the bucket with a worn scrub brush left in it. She picked it up and returned to the kitchen. She filled it with water from the pump over the sink and grinned as she dumped the hunk of lye soap she found on the window sill into the water. Wouldn't her daddy gloat if he could see her getting ready to do the work only the cook and maids did at the Double D? She'd show him. She was a woman and she could make this place as clean and livable as his fancy house. Without another thought of Rafe Donahue, she plunged the brush into the soapy water and began scrubbing the table.

* * * *

Two weeks after Amelia's visit, Rafe Donahue lit a cigar, puffed deeply, sat back in his leather chair and glanced out the window. His wife was cutting flowers from the rose garden. Thank God he'd managed to calm Elizabeth down. It took promising her he'd try to make peace with Amelia by accepting her husband. It didn't matter if it was a lie. She didn't know the difference and by the time she learned he'd never accept the half-breed as Amelia's husband, she'd come around to his way of thinking. Probably Amelia would, too. He still couldn't see his spoiled little girl living the way she'd have to with Jed Wainwright. Why he wouldn't put it past the man to make his daughter live in a cave or a tent or something worse. Indians had no feelings about where they made their women live. He knew for sure the man couldn't continue to live at Olsen's hotel with Amelia. Being a bounty hunter didn't pay enough to live like that long. He'd seen the wanted posters. He knew most of them offered one hundred dollars for a man's capture. It wouldn't take long for that amount of money to get gone when you lived in a hotel and ate in a restaurant all the time.

So now was the time to relax and let Amelia realize what a mistake she'd made. It wouldn't be long until she'd be begging to come back home. And of course he'd let her. After all, he wanted her and Vince to have those grandsons for him.

In the meantime, Rafe decided he'd get back to taking care of the ranch as it should be taken care of. He'd talked with Vince a few days ago and laid out his plan of how he intended to buy two more ranches. The Lawson place butted up to a corner of his land and though the Garcia ranch was small, it was situated in such a way it squared off the land between the Double D and Lawson.

"I'll probably have them both by the time you get back from the cattle drive," he'd jovially told Vince.

"I'm sure you will, boss. I'll look forward to bringing them under the Double D brand." Vince grinned. "If there's any way I can help you speed up the purchases, let me know."

"I will."

Rafe knew there wouldn't be a problem getting the Lawson place. Gladys was eager to get to Texas and though he put John off the other week, Gladys would now push him to sell at a bargain price. Rafe liked bargaining. He'd acquired a lot of his land at a rock bottom price by making his offers at the right time.

Roberto Garcia might be a little harder to deal with, but the man had no idea Rafe knew he was behind on his mortgage payments and was about to lose the place. Garcia was proud of his ranch and he worked hard, though rustlers kept stealing his cows. He'd even accused Rafe of letting his cowhands take the young calves and putting the Double D brand on them. Rafe knew this wasn't the case. Vince would never permit this to happen.

Vince was an honest man and Rafe trusted him more than anyone else on the ranch. He let his mind wander back to when his foreman had earned that trust. It was soon after he'd come to work at the Double D. Rafe was complaining about there not being enough profit for the amount of work they did and the number of cattle they sold. Vince told him to slip the books to him and he'd see what was going on. He'd told Rafe he'd been a bookkeeper in Georgia. Rafe did get the books to him and it wasn't long until Vince pointed out how old man Downey was trying to cheat his son-in-law out of part of the ranch profits. Of course there was no way he could tell Elizabeth about this. Downey was her father. She'd never believe he was trying to run Rafe off the place so Elizabeth could marry a man he liked better. Though a name was never mentioned, he and Vince together figured out that man was probably Charles Fielding since he was one of Elizabeth's suitors before Rafe came along.

Rafe pulled his thoughts back to the idea of buying the neighboring ranches. He knew another problem Garcia had been facing was the fact that his hired hands kept leaving after only a few weeks. Rafe didn't know why nobody seemed to want to work for him. Of course the fact he was Mexican could have something to do with it. Though the Garcia place was smaller than most, there was no way he and his eight-year-old son could run it without help.

Rafe decided he'd pay a fair price for their land even if Roberto was about to lose it. He'd make sure there was enough for the family to relocate or maybe he could talk them into working for him. Since Garcia's wife was related to Delores, he might be able to. He could always use another cowhand and the wife would make a good maid. Lula, one of their present maids, was getting old and would have to be replaced soon. The Garcia woman was in her late twenties or early thirties, so she'd be able to work hard for several years.

Bringing his thoughts back to the present, he took his gold watch out of his pocket and glanced at it. Six o'clock.

A knock sounded on his study door. He grinned and muttered, "Charles Fielding is right on time. I always look forward to his visits. Not only does he envy me all my money, he can't hide the fact he still worships the ground my wife walks on. Even after all these years, I like seeing him jealous because I'm the one who got the girl and he never will."

* * * *

Wilma Lawson sat back in the stagecoach as it got ready to pull out of the way station. It had taken her a while to talk her father into letting her return to Settlers Ridge. Of course she knew it never would've happened if her mother hadn't said she couldn't stand riding any further in the wagon and had decided to take the train from Denver to Texas. Wilma didn't know what her mother would say when her father and brother arrived at the Texas ranch without her, but she'd worry about it later. Now all she wanted to do was get back to Settlers Ridge, but what she'd do when she got there she wasn't sure. She no longer had a home, which didn't bother her much. Wilma didn't like ranch life. All she wanted to do was move to town and marry Stanley Brown and work in his store.

Of course when she got back to town, she'd have to stay at the hotel. Maybe she could get a job from the Olsens. Grace liked working for them and they might need somebody else to work there. She sure had enough experience in the kitchen, cleaning rooms and making beds. Since Gladys Lawson gained so much weight, she couldn't get around as she did when Wilma and her brother were younger. In the past couple of years all the household chores fell to Wilma. She was even a good cook.

Wilma smiled to herself. These were things she'd gladly share with Stanley when she was able to convince him to overcome his shyness and notice her. That wasn't going to be easy, but she knew she'd do it one way or another.

Since she was the only passenger, Wilma was settling back to take a nap when the stagecoach door opened. She jumped and let out a little gasp.

"Don't worry, ma'am. We're only picking up a woman and her kids. They just got to the station," the burly driver said.

A woman climbed inside followed by two children. The boy looked to be about eight and the girl looked like she was probably ten. The mother sat on the seat facing Wilma and the children sat on either side of her. "Good afternoon, miss," she said. "My name's Esther Venable and these are my two children, Benita and Joel."

"Hello. I'm Wilma Lawson."

As the stage lurched forward, Wilma saw a sadness in Esther's eyes. She was probably in her mid-thirties, tall and thin with soft brown hair. Her expressive dark brown eyes and the sadness in them were somewhat hidden by the spectacles she wore. Yet, Wilma thought there was something striking about the woman.

"I'm hungry, Mama," the boy announced.

"We'll get something at the next way station, Joel. In the meantime you may have an apple from the sack we brought with us."

"I'm tired of eating apples, Mama. That's all you ever give us."

"Don't complain, son. Apples are a wonderful food and are very good for you. They've been a favorite of mine since I was a child."

"May I have one, too, Mama?"

"Of course, Benita."

She handed the children their apples and glanced at Wilma.

Wilma shook her head. "Thank you, anyway."

"Are you on your way to Settlers Ridge?" Esther put the sack away and looked intently at the young woman on the seat in front of her.

"Yes, ma'am."

"I'm going there, too. I hope it's a nice town."

"It is. I was born and raised on a ranch near there."

"So, are you headed home for a visit or something?"

"Yes." Wilma didn't want to go into detail of why she was headed home so she asked, "How about you, Mrs. Venable? Are you going to Settlers Ridge to visit someone?"

"No. I'm taking a job there. I'm a nurse and I'll be working for a Doctor Sheldon Wagner. Do you know him?"

"Yes, I know Dr. Wagner. He's a nice man. I'm sure you'll like working with him."

"I hope so," she mumbled and brushed some dust from her gray skirt. "Is it always this dusty and hot in Wyoming?"

"On the prairie it is this time of year." Wilma smiled. "You're not from around here are you, Mrs. Venable."

"We're from Nashville, North Carolina," Benita spoke up. "And I want to go back home. I don't like it here."

"Mama said we couldn't go back home," Joel said.

"But I want to." Benita puckered her mouth as if she was going to cry.

"Children, please," Esther said. "You must calm down. I'm sure Miss Lawson doesn't want to hear you argue."

Wilma didn't say anything and Esther went on, saying, "This change has been a shock to all of us. I lost my parents suddenly and we were forced to come west. When I saw Dr. Wagner's advertisement for a nurse, I decided this is where we should come."

"I'm sure you'll learn to like Settlers Ridge. It's a nice town and there are always exciting things happening."

"Are there any Indians?" Joel asked.

"There are a few."

"Will they scalp us?" Benita's eyes got big.

"No." Wilma smiled at her. "Most of the Indians are out on the plains. The ones in town stay mostly to themselves."

"Why?" Joel looked at her.

Wilma shrugged. "I guess they don't want to be with white people."

Esther spoke. "The only Indians my children hear about are the ones who are written up in the newspapers. It says they raid ranches and scalp and kill everyone there, and that's what has them scared about coming here."

"I don't think there has been an Indian raid for a long time in or around Settlers Ridge."

"Do you know any Indians?" Joel asked.

"I know a man who is half Indian."

"Really?" Joel's eyes got big. "Do half Indians kill people?"

Wilma couldn't help smiling. "This half Indian wouldn't kill anyone except maybe an outlaw. He recently married a friend of mine and they bought a ranch to live on about two weeks ago."

"Is she a half Indian, too?" Joel asked.

"No. She's a white woman."

"Does she live on a ranch with him?"

"Don't be a dummy, little brother," Benita butted in. "Of course his wife lives where he does. Married people live together."

"Not Mama and Daddy," Joel argued.

Esther broke in this time. "You've asked enough questions, children. I think you should stop bothering Miss Lawson."

"They're fine," Wilma said.

"It's time they took a nap anyway. I'm sure we have a long ride before we get to the next way station."

In a little while, the children drifted off and Esther had her eyes closed.

Wilma felt the woman was as unhappy as the children were about coming to Wyoming. She wondered about her situation. If Joel was right about her and her husband not living together, was she separated from him because she wanted to be or was she forced to come west without him? Wilma knew there was no way of knowing the answers, but she wished there was some way she could make the move easier for Esther Venable, though she doubted there was.

Esther opened her eyes and glanced at her children, then at Wilma. "I'm sorry they were so inquisitive about Indians, Miss Lawson."

"I didn't mind, and I wish you'd call me Wilma. We'll probably be seeing each other in town."

"Then you must call me Esther."

"I will."

"If you don't mind, would you please tell me about some of the people in Settlers Ridge? You could start with your friend and her half-Indian husband."

"Of course, I'll tell you all I can. Everyone in town was shocked when Amelia Donahue married Jed Wainright. She's the daughter of the richest rancher in the area and Jed was a former bounty hunter. I was surprised myself, but when I met him, I could understand why she could fall in love with him."

"What did her parents think about the marriage?"

"Her father was furious and I haven't heard how her mother felt."

"So, he's a bounty hunter turned rancher?"

"Yes. He wanted to settle down."

"I guess the bounty hunting life got to be too much for him."

"It must have." She gave Esther a small smile. "Or he came up against Amelia and she decided she wanted him. Amelia Donahue always gets what she wants."

They fell into a conversation with Wilma telling her many things about Settlers Ridge, the Donahue ranch, her friend Grace and about the happenings of the town.

Finally Ester asked, "Would you tell me about Doctor Wagner?"

"He was married until last year. His wife was his nurse and everybody liked her almost as much as they did the doctor."

"What happened?"

"One day, she was hurrying across the street in the rain. There was a big crack of thunder and a horse broke loose from a hitching post. It went racing down the street and ran over Mrs. Wagner. She died a little while later."

"How tragic."

"Yes. We were all sad about it." Wilma shook her head. "They had no children and the doctor was lost for a while. He seems to be doing all right now."

"I hope my services will be a help to him."

"I'm sure they will."

Before they could talk any more, the stage started slowing. Wilma looked out the window. "It looks like we're at the next way station."

"Thank you for talking with me, Wilma. It has certainly helped the afternoon pass quickly." She then turned and began waking her children.

* * * *

"When the hell did Lawson sell his place?" Rafe glared at Charles Fielding.

"A couple of weeks ago." Charles grew uncomfortable.

"Whatever possessed him to do such a thing? He knew I was going to buy it."

Charles shrugged and took a drink of the bourbon from the heavy crystal glass Rafe had served him. He wasn't sure what to tell his friend.

"Who bought it? Do you think I could give him a little profit and still get it?"

"I'm surprised you don't know who the new owner is."

Rafe frowned. "How would I know?"

Charles decided to be straight forward with Rafe. He'd find out who the owner was anyway. "Jed Wainwright and his partner, Curt Allison, bought it."

Rafe's eyes filled with fury. "How the hell did a man like him have enough money to buy the place?"

"He's been putting his money in the Settlers Ridge Bank for some time now. I think it has always been his plan to quit hunting outlaws and settle on a ranch."

"Hell and damnation! The last person in the world I want settling anywhere near me is the son-of-a-bitch who stole my daughter." Rafe grabbed the crystal decanter and poured himself another drink. "Did the bastard use any of my daughter's money to buy the place?"

Since the total of Jed's savings added to his partner's was enough to pay for the ranch, Charles could honestly say, "All the money for the ranch came out of his account and from what his partner brought with him."

"I suppose his partner is another lowdown bounty hunter?"

Charles was glad Rafe hadn't pursued asking about Wainwright's account. "Said he'd been working on a ranch somewhere in New Mexico. Previously he was a US Marshall until he got hurt."

"And you believe him?"

"Have no reason not to. He has the limp to prove he'd been wounded."

"Probably got it when a bank robbery went wrong." Rafe sneered.

"You are cynical, Donahue, my friend."

"I have every right to be." He took a swallow of the drink. "What would you do if your daughter was with a man like Jed Wainwright?"

"You know damn good and well I'm not married and I don't have a daughter."

"Well, if you did, what would you do?"

Before Charles could answer there was a tap on the door.

"Come in." Rafe's voice came out almost as a growl.

Elizabeth opened the door. "Supper is ready, gentlemen."

"Thank you, Elizabeth." Charles stood and walked to the door. "May I have the honor of escorting you?"

She took his extended arm. "I'd be delighted, Mr. Fielding."

Rafe downed the rest of his bourbon and followed them to the dining room with a scowl on his face.

Charles noticed, but ignored the look. He knew, even after all the years, her husband was still jealous because Elizabeth and he had been sweethearts before Rafe came into her life. Every time Charles saw her, though he didn't particularly want to irritate Rafe, it made him feel good to know that the powerful Rafe Donahue thought he was a threat. He also couldn't help remembering he had planned on asking Elizabeth to marry him until she informed him she'd fallen in love with Rafe. There were still times when he wondered if Elizabeth regretted choosing Rafe over him. But no matter how much he liked being with the woman he still cared for, Charles knew he was going to be happy when this evening was over.

Chapter 12

After rearranging the furniture in the parlor the way she wanted it for the fourth time in two weeks, Amelia decided to start supper. She knew Jed and Curt would come in from the range hungry because they always did. She sliced ham, cooked some dried apples, stewed potatoes, cooked green peas and cut up tomatoes. Knowing the men would want bread, she made biscuits and put them in the oven. Since she still had time, she decided to make fritters with the stewed apples.

At six-thirty Jed came into the kitchen. "Something smells good."

"I'm not the best cook in the West, but I think it's edible."

"So far, nobody has complained."

"Good." She took the biscuits from the oven. "It's ready. Tell everyone to wash up."

"Mort wanted me to ask you if you still want him to come in. I don't think he can get used to having his meals in the house."

"It's hard enough to keep you and Curt full. I don't intend to cook and start carrying plates around. Which means Mort eats with us or he doesn't eat."

Jed chuckled. "I'm sure he'll choose to continue to come inside over starving."

Mort still seemed to be a little uncomfortable at the table, but he ate well and thanked Amelia profusely, telling her it was one of the best meals he'd had in a long time which was the same thing he said every evening. After a second cup of coffee with the apple fritter, he thanked her again and hurried out the back door.

"Well, Amelia," Curt said, "I think you're winning over our hired hand and I certainly understand why. It was delicious."

"Thank you."

"If Jed hadn't already snagged you, I'd be there fighting for your hand."

"Sorry, my friend." Jed laughed. "Amelia's hands are taken."

For six months anyway, she thought. Aloud, she said, "I appreciate the thought, Curt. Even an old married woman likes to be flattered. Now would you fellows like another fritter?"

"I would like another one." Jed winked at her and added with a grin, "And I don't appreciate you calling my wife old."

Amelia blushed.

"Since you twisted my arm, I guess I'll have one, too." Curt gave her a sheepish grin.

She poured them more coffee and served the fritters. As they ate she began stacking the dishes.

"Have coffee with us, Amelia." Jed took hold of her arm. "I'll help you clean up when we finish."

She gave him a surprised look. "Don't tell me you wash dishes."

"I've washed a good many of them in creeks throughout the West. I figure it won't be much different in a kitchen."

"He's right, Amelia. I don't expect you to wait on us. Me especially." Curt cut into his fritter. "You're Jed's wife, not mine."

"You guys are working hard rounding up those cows to brand. I don't mind doing my share." Amelia sat beside Jed.

He patted her knee. "I know you don't, and don't get me wrong. I appreciate this wonderful meal, but I don't intend for you to become a servant to me or anyone else on this ranch."

"Thank you, but cooking a meal isn't all that hard, Jed."

"I know you're willing, honey, but while I was out on the range this afternoon, I was thinking that it's not fair to ask you to do all the cooking and cleaning around here. Keeping this house going is a job within itself and I know you enjoy getting out on the range with

Rambler."

She smiled. "I do like riding my horse. But when it comes time, don't ask me to take part in the branding or castrating, though. I feel sorry for those poor cows."

Jed chuckled. "Don't worry. You won't have to do any branding or castrating."

"Good."

"What I'm getting at is, I think we should hire somebody to help with the cooking and cleaning around here."

"That's sweet of you, Jed, but don't think you have to do it."

"I agree with Jed, Amelia. Since I own part of this place, it gives me a vote, too."

"You know we're going to have to look for a couple of hands soon and your work will increase, especially in the kitchen."

Curt nodded. "He's right, you know."

Amelia shook her head and smiled at them. "I can't fight the both of you. If you think we should have a cook, then we'll look for one, but let's not rush into it. I want the right person, not just anybody."

"Sounds good to me." Jed threw her a smile. "Do you suppose if I had a third fritter it'd keep me awake tonight?"

She chuckled then got up and got both him and Curt another fritter.

* * * *

"Hello, Mr. Olsen. My name's Wilma Lawson and I'd like a room, please," Wilma said as she walked up to the front desk in Olsen's Hotel.

"I recognize you, Miss Lawson, but I thought your whole family left for Texas."

"We did, but I decided I didn't want to live in Texas. Papa let me come back to Settlers Ridge because he knew I'd only be happy here. I came in on the evening stage."

"What about your mama?"

Wilma laughed. "Mama couldn't handle the ride to Texas in our wagon so she caught a train in Denver. She'll probably have a fit when Papa shows up without me, but it'll be too late then."

"I understand." Frank handed her a key. "Room three is at the top of the steps. Is there anything else you need tonight?"

"I haven't eaten. Is the dining room still open?"

"It is. Go on in and have your supper. I'll get Teddy to take your bag to your room."

"Thank you, Mr. Olsen."

As Wilma headed to the dining room the front door opened and Mrs. Venable and her children came in.

"Good evening, Ma'am. Could I help you?"

"I need a room for my children and me."

"Certainly. Sign in and I'll fix you up. A week will be five dollars or it's a dollar a day."

"I want it for a week." Esther signed the register and handed Frank a five dollar gold piece.

Frank glanced at the name the woman had written down. "It's room eight, Mrs. Venable, and it has a big bed and a small bed. It's at the end of the hall on the right. If you haven't eaten, the dining room will be open another hour and I'll get your belongings to the room."

"Thank you very much. We do need to eat something." Esther took the key and pointed the children toward the dining room.

* * * *

It was after midnight when a sound from outside filtered through the open window of the Wainwright's upstairs bedroom. Jed frowned and listened. He heard it again. Without waking her, he eased Amelia's head from his right shoulder. Slipping his feet to the floor, he soundlessly stepped into his pants. Looking out the window, he saw a glow near the barn.

Cursing silently, he grabbed his gun and left the room. At the bottom of the steps he called toward the downstairs bedroom his partner had chosen as his. "Curt! The barn's on fire."

As Jed reached the porch, a shot rang out and he jumped behind the railing, firing as he took cover. There was a curse from a man and the sound of a horse disappearing into the darkness.

"He's gone," Jed yelled as he headed toward the barn. "I don't think the fire has done much damage, but let's get the horses out."

"I'm right behind you." Curt was on his heels.

Amelia came onto the porch and followed them across the yard "Rambler. I've got to get Rambler." She sounded as if she was about to panic.

Mort ran up. "Let the men get the horses, Miz Wainwright. Me and you need to fill the water buckets so they can put out the fire."

"But…"

"Come on. We don't want to waste time."

When she saw Jed come out of the barn leading a scared and rearing Rambler along with a frightened Devil, she nodded. "There's a bucket beside the pump. Start filling it and I'll grab another one from the porch."

Mort pumped the water and she carried the buckets toward the barn. Curt met her and as soon as Jed had the horses in the corral he joined them. In relay fashion, they passed full buckets of water to douse the fire. When she saw Mort was slowing at the pump, she told him to carry the buckets and let her take his job.

It didn't take as long as anyone thought it would to quash the fire and get the horses settled. Jed came up and put his hand on Mort's shoulder. "Thanks for your help. Everything seems to be under control. I think we can all go back to bed now."

"I'm glad it weren't no worse, Mr. Jed. It could've been awful if you hadn't a woke up."

"I was lucky to hear the horse and rider come into the yard."

"Who'd want to do somethin' this awful?"

"I don't know, but when it gets light, I'll see if I can pick up the horse's tracks." Jed looked down as Amelia walked up beside him. He put his arm around her shoulder. "You did a great job, honey."

"I'm glad it didn't burn the barn any worse and I'm especially happy the horses are safe."

Curt joined them. "Now that everything's taken care of, do you think we could get a cup of coffee, Amelia?"

"I don't see why not. Let's go inside." She smiled at Mort. "Would you like some coffee, too, Mort?"

"Thank you, Ma'am, but I think I'll go lay my head down and get a little more sleep."

He nodded to the men and headed toward the bunkhouse.

Jed built up the banked fire to heat the coffee, then joined Amelia and Curt at the table. "I'll have to say we were lucky."

"Yeah. Lucky you woke up."

"I didn't hear a thing until you called to me about the fire. What woke you, Jed?" Curt asked.

"The man's horse snorted a couple of times. I knew it wasn't one of ours."

Curt shook his head. "All damn horses sound the same to me, but of course you'd know the difference."

Jed nodded. "When I was a boy I learned all horses have their own distinct sound."

Amelia butted into their conversation. "Do you think Daddy is responsible for this?'

Jed touched her arm. "I don't want to think your father would do this. Not when there would be a danger to you."

"I'm sure Jed's right. No man would want to do something to hurt his daughter."

She shook her head. "I don't know about that. My father hates me now."

Curt frowned. "I've never asked, but what went on when you went to your father's ranch?"

"He disowned me."

"I'm sure if you'd agree to divorce me, he'd welcome you back." Before either of them could say anything, Jed went on, saying, "If you'll keep your eye on things here, I'll go to town tomorrow and report this to the sheriff. I know there's nothing he can do without a suspect, but in case it happens again, I want this incident on record."

The coffee bubbled and Amelia got up to fill their cups. "Do you want me to go to town with you?"

"If you like."

"I'll think about it. I have a lot of work here, but I do need to pick up some more ranch clothes. You know Daddy wouldn't let me take any of my clothes from his house." She sat down beside him.

She saw a look pass between Curt and Jed. Before she could ask about it, Curt said, "You should go with him, Amelia."

"Why? Is there some reason you don't want me to stay here?" She looked from one to the other.

Jed took her hand. "Honey, I'm not sure who tried to burn our barn tonight. I think it best if you don't stay alone until we find out who did it."

"But…"

"Besides, I want you there to help me ask around for some woman to work in the house with you. You know the people in Settlers Ridge better than I do."

"Are you sure that's the reason?"

"Of course. What else could there be?" Jed stood and drained his coffee. "Now, I think we should get a couple more hours of sleep before daylight."

* * * *

It was mid-morning and they had ridden in silence for a couple of miles since leaving the ranch. Amelia glanced at Jed. His mouth was set in a hard line and he had a frown on his face. She nudged Rambler a little closer to Devil, and asked, "What are you thinking so hard about, Jed?"

"I see someone coming."

"Who?" She looked confused.

"I don't know but there's a big cloud of dust to our right. Somebody's coming up fast." He nodded toward a shallow ravine surrounded by a grove of mesquite. "Ride over there until we determine who it is and what they want."

Amelia started to protest, but knew it would do no good. She turned Rambler to the ravine. Jed followed her.

Once hidden, she turned to him. "What's going on, Jed?"

"I'm not sure. After the incident last night, all I know is somebody is out to get you or me or both of us. We need to stay on guard all the time."

When he didn't elaborate she asked, "Do you think it's Daddy?"

"Your father might hate me and want me dead, but I don't think he'd condone anyone hurting you. He may have disowned you, but he's still your father."

"Do you think he might send one of his men to kidnap me?" Amelia still looked worried.

Jed raised an eyebrow. "You know him better than I do, Amelia. Do you think he'd send one of his men to get you?"

"A month ago, I would've said no, but now, I don't know. My father has always been hard-headed and had a fierce temper and he yelled and screamed a lot, but until you and I went to the ranch, I'd never seen his cruel side. I don't know what to think about him now."

Jed didn't comment about her father, but nodded toward the side road. "Looks like a wagon. I don't think anyone after us would use a wagon. We might as well find out what the rush is." He walked his horse toward the road.

Amelia nudged Rambler forward and stopped beside him.

The wagon pulled up to where they waited.

"What's going on, young man?" Jed asked the young boy driving.

"I got to get Doctor Wagner for my poppa."

Amelia recognized the boy. "Miguel, what has happened?"

"They beat Poppa bad, Miss Amelia. I'm afraid he's gonna die."

"Who beat your poppa?" Jed asked.

"Some bad men and they made me watch. I've got to go…"

"Where is your father?" Jed looked at the boy.

"At home."

Amelia put in. "The Garcias have a small ranch. It joins Daddy's on one corner and yours at the north pasture."

Jed nodded. "I've run into Roberto a time or two when we were working on the north end. Why don't you go home with Miguel and see if you can help there? I'll get the doctor."

"But Mama said…"

"He's right, Miguel. His horse is faster than your wagon." She turned to Jed. "If you follow this side road Miguel is using and cut across the back section of our ranch, you'll come to Garcia's place quicker."

"I'll be back as soon as I can. You and Miguel be careful."

"We will. Thank you, Jed."

He galloped off toward town and Amelia turned to Miguel. "Let's head back to your house. I'll see if I can be of any help to your mother and father."

"Yes, Miss Amelia."

She turned Rambler toward the Garcia ranch. She didn't want Miguel to know she saw the tears in his eyes.

* * * *

Wilma Lawson picked up a white cotton nightgown on the table in Brown's Mercantile. She turned to Grace. "Do you think Amelia would like this?"

"I think we might find something she'd like better at Miss Purdy's shop."

"You're right. Something in silk or lace is what she probably wears for her husband." Wilma giggled.

"She's sure crazy about him, isn't she?"

"I picked up on that when all of you came to buy the ranch."

The bell over the door jangled, interrupting their conversation. The woman who was on the stage with Wilma and her children came in. She smiled. "Hello, Wilma."

"Hello, Esther." Wilma moved to the other side of the rack of cloths. "I'd like to introduce you to a friend of mine, Grace Hunter."

The two women greeted each other.

"Is she the one married to the half Indian?" Joel blurted.

Grace frowned.

Wilma laughed. "No, Joel. This lady works at the hotel dining room, but she wasn't working when we came in the other night."

"Wilma told me you're Doctor Wagner's new nurse." Grace smiled at Esther.

"That's correct. I start work tomorrow and I came in to get some things to entertain the children while I'm busy."

"Then come with me, Esther." Wilma took her arm and walked up to the counter. "Stanley, this is Esther Venable and her children, Benita and Joel. She's Doctor Wagner's new nurse and needs to find some things for the children," she announced without her usual self-consciousness when she was forced to talk to Stanley Brown.

"I'll be glad to help. How about some books?" Stanley put the kerchief he was folding in a box and looked at it as if he was avoiding Wilma's eyes.

Grace walked up beside her friend. "Why don't I help Esther and the children look for books while you and Stanley get reacquainted?"

Esther and Grace walked away.

Wilma blushed and so did Stanley.

* * * *

When they reached the Garcia ranch Miguel said, "I'll take care of our horses, Miss Amelia."

"Thanks, Miguel." She ran up the steps and into the small cabin calling, "Juanita, where are you?"

"In the bedroom," Juanita answered.

Amelia hurried to a door on the side of the parlor and kitchen combination and entered the room. "When we ran into Miguel, my husband went for Doc Wagner because we knew his horse was faster than Miguel's wagon. I came back with him to see if I could help you."

Juanita sat by her husband's bedside and looked up with tears in her beautiful dark eyes. "I don't understand it, Amelia. We don't bother people and we try to keep our stock close to home. Why would anyone be so mean and attack Roberto like this?"

Amelia moved beside the grieving woman and put her hand on Juanita's shoulder. "I don't understand it either, but there are some mean people in this world."

"There sure are."

"Do you know what happened to Roberto?"

"Not really. He went out to work on some down fences while I was cooking dinner. The next thing I knew, Miguel came running in and said three men had attacked his poppa and left him in the field to die. We got him to the house and I sent Miguel for the doctor."

"How bad is he hurt?"

"I think some ribs are broken and probably some other bones. The place on his head keeps bleeding. I've tried to stop it, but so far nothing has worked."

"Was he shot?"

"No. They have beaten him badly."

"They didn't hurt Miguel, did they?"

Juanita looked away. "No. They only warned him."

Amelia frowned. "Warned him about what?"

"I don't want to talk about it anymore."

Amelia continued to frown. She had a feeling Juanita didn't want to tell her something. Probably something important, but she didn't push it. "Where was your hired hand, Juanita?"

"He quit yesterday."

"Why?"

Juanita shook her head. "I don't know. All he would say was since we were moving he'd have to look for work someplace else. Roberto told him we had no intention of moving, but…" Her voice trailed off.

"But, what?"

"Amelia, we've been friends ever since I came to your father's ranch to visit my Aunt Delores."

"I know, Juanita. In fact, if you remember I'm the one who introduced you to Roberto."

She smiled a sad smile. "I remember how I thought he was the most handsome man in the world and wanted to marry him right away, but he was so sad because he'd lost his wife and was left with a baby son."

"But you worked through it and now you're a happy family."

"Yes. Miguel is my son as much as if I'd given him birth."

Miguel came into the room. "How's Poppa?"

"He's still unconscious." Juanita held out her hand to him. "Please try not to worry, Miguel. We have to pray and believe your poppa will be well soon."

"They said Poppa would die and I'd be next if we didn't…"

"That's enough, Miguel!"

"Why can't I tell? We'll have to tell the sheriff."

"No. Poppa will get well and we'll…"

"What, Mama? Sell our ranch to Mr. Donahue and move away like they said?"

"What does my father have to do with this?" Amelia demanded.

Roberto moaned. Juanita ignored her and turned toward him. "It'll be all right, Roberto. The doctor will be here soon and you're going to be fine."

Amelia could tell the woman was fighting to keep the fear from her voice.

When Roberto grew quiet Juanita took hold of his hand and whispered, "Please, dear God, don't take my husband from me. Miguel and I need him and love him so much."

Miguel began to cry. "I don't want Poppa to die."

Amelia touched Miguel's arm. "Why don't you and I go make your mama some tea? She looks like she could use some."

He followed Amelia out of the room.

When they got to the kitchen she asked, "Are you hungry, Miguel?"

"A little."

"Let's see what your mama cooked." She turned to the stove and noticed Juanita had pushed the food to the back of the stove so it wouldn't burn. "She made Chili Verde."

"I like the way Mama cooks pork."

"It has finished cooking. All I have to do is serve it." Amelia took a plate, dipped some rice and beans on to it then added the pork in green sauce. She put the prepared corn tortillas on the side. "Here you go, Miguel. Enjoy."

Miguel began to eat as Amelia made a cup of tea. "I'll take this to your mother and I'll be right back."

Miguel had eaten half of what was on his plate when she returned. He glanced up at her and had tears in his eyes. "I shouldn't be eating with Poppa sick, should I?"

"Of course you should eat, Miguel. Your poppa would want you to. You have to keep up your strength so you can help your mama."

He gave her a half grin and ate another bite.

"Tell me what happened, Miguel."

He dropped his head. "There were three men. One said Poppa shouldn't bother with the fence because as soon as Mr. Donahue bought the ranch he'd pull down all the fences so the cows could run free." When she said nothing, he went on. "Poppa said Mr. Donahue wasn't going to buy our ranch because he wasn't selling it. The big man laughed and said Poppa should think it over."

"And then what happened," Amelia prodded after Miguel paused.

"Poppa said he didn't have to think. Then the man said if Poppa didn't sell they'd burn us out. Poppa reached for his rifle, but the big man rode his horse up beside him and kicked him in the chest. The others laughed. I started to run to Poppa, but the big man threw a rope around me and held me tight. He told me to watch what happened to people who didn't do what Mr. Donahue wanted them to do. The other two men got off their horses and one held Poppa while one began to beat him. He tried to fight back, but one hit him in the head with his gun. Even after Poppa was unconscious on the ground, they kept beating him and kicking him. I thought they'd killed him for sure."

"Oh, Miguel. I'm so sorry."

It was as if Miguel had to get the whole story out now that he'd started telling it. He continued, "I figured they were going to kill me, too, but the big man said, 'See what happens to people who don't cooperate with Mr. Donahue, boy?' Then the big man told his men to quit beating Poppa. They didn't want to, but they kicked him a few more times and got back on their horses. The big man took the rope off me and told me he knew Mama wasn't my real mama."

"She may not have given you birth, Miguel, but Juanita thinks of you as her real son."

He nodded. "I think of her as my mother and I love her. I never knew my real mama. She died when I was a baby."

"I know. Juanita has been a wonderful mother to you. She loves you just as much as you love her."

He nodded and took another bite of food.

Amelia watched him finish his meal and push his plate back. Taking a breath, she asked, "Did the man say anything else?"

"Yes. He said if I didn't convince Mama to sell to Mr. Donahue the evening after Poppa's funeral the same thing would happen to me and her."

Amelia moved beside Miguel and put her arm around his shoulder. "I'm sorry this happened. Those men need to be put in jail. Do you know who they were?"

"They work for your Poppa. I think the big one was the foreman. He came over the other night and said Mr. Donahue wanted our ranch, but Poppa told him no. He told Poppa he'd be sorry if he didn't change his mind." He looked up at her with tears running down his cheeks. "How could your poppa do that to mine, Miss Amelia? How could he be so mean?"

Amelia was asking herself the same question.

Chapter 13

Jed hurried to Doctor Wagner's office as soon as he reached town. Sheldon came to the door after the first knock.

"Hello, Wainwright. How can I help you?"

"Roberto Garcia has been hurt. I ran into his boy coming into town and told him I'd come get you because my horse was faster than the one he had pulling his wagon."

"What happened to Garcia?"

"His son said some men beat him and left him for dead. Amelia has gone to see if she can help until you get there."

"I'll leave a note for my new nurse and go right out." He began writing on the slate which lay beside on the desk.

"Thanks, Doc. I need to see Sheriff Gentry then I'll be there."

The doctor propped the slate on the desk and picked up his bag. "You'll probably catch me. If your horse is faster than Garcia's wagon, it has to be faster than my buggy."

The doctor headed toward the buggy parked in front of his small white house and Jed headed to the sheriff's office.

When Jed entered the sheriff's office he saw Lance Gentry sitting behind his pine desk with a cup of strong coffee and a stack of papers in front of him. "Hello, Jed. I knew you'd eventually come by to collect your reward." He opened a desk drawer and took out a stack of bills. "There were four of them at two hundred each." He counted out eight hundred dollars.

Jed nodded and put the money in his pocket. "Actually I came by to report a couple of things."

"Oh?"

"On the way into town, Amelia and I ran into the Garcia boy. Somebody beat up his daddy this morning. I sent Amelia to their ranch with the kid and came for the doctor."

"Has Doc headed out there?"

"He was getting in his buggy when I left to come here."

"Good. What else do you have to report?"

"Someone tried to burn my barn last night."

"Damn, I hate to hear that. Did it do much damage?"

"No. I caught it in time."

"Any idea who it was?"

"I have my suspicions, but it was too dark to see." Jed pushed back his hat.

Lance frowned. "Do you think the two incidents are connected?"

"Could be. I found some tracks around my barn. I'm going to Garcia's ranch to see if the hoof prints there are the same as the ones at my place."

Deputy Bryce Langston strode in the door. He nodded to Jed. "Everything seems to be quiet in town. Anything going on?"

Lance shoved the stack of papers in his desk. "Somebody attacked Roberto Garcia. I'll ride out there with Jed and see what I can find out. You keep things under control here."

"I'll do it."

Jed nodded at Bryce, pulled his hat down and headed for the door. Lance followed.

* * * *

Rafe sat back in his leather desk chair and looked at Vince Callahan. "So, you think Garcia is thinking about selling?"

"I'm sure of it. He and his son were working on a fence near your ranch when a couple of hands and I ran into them this morning. Of course, we stopped to talk and I mentioned you were interested in buying his place. He said he'd consider it." Vince took the cigar Rafe offered.

"Since I lost the Lawson place I don't intend to lose Garcia's. Did you mention a price to him?"

"No, Rafe. I thought it was your place to talk money."

Rafe nodded. "If I could figure out a way to get the Lawson ranch…" His voice trailed off.

"Well, you never know. Something could happen."

There was a short silence then Rafe asked, "What are you thinking?"

"I'm thinking there are probably ways to make the bounty hunter give up his ranch."

"Such as?"

"He could meet with an accident and not be able to do any ranching. It's happened to better men than him."

"I guess an accident could work, but I wouldn't be upset if the son-of-a-bitch was dead. Of course I'd be the first person they'd look at if anything happened to him. It's no secret I hate his guts because of all he's done to me."

"Wainwright could get hurt so bad out on the range that he doesn't get over it." Vince gave his boss an evil grin.

"Wouldn't his partner continue to run the ranch?" Rafe raised an eyebrow and puffed the expensive cigar.

"The partner's a cripple. He's not able to run a ranch alone. I'm sure he'd sell out in a hurry if something happened to Wainwright."

"An accident would have to be well planned and would need to take place away from the house. Though I'm still mad at her, I don't want anything to happen to Amelia."

"Nothing will happen to her. She'll come home, safe as the day she left. I know there's no way she'd want to stay there if…well, let's say…she'd have no reason to stay there without him." He grinned again. "Of course we'd both welcome her back even if she has been with the dirty bounty hunter."

Rafe nodded. "You're right, and I'm glad you still feel that way about her. As a matter of fact, I'm surprised she hasn't tired of him and come home already. I thought she'd get over being mad at me by now."

"I think she probably wants to come home, but he has some kind of hold on her." Vince puffed his cigar. "Of course, I'm waiting for her to realize what a mistake she made by taking up with him, and to turn to me for comfort."

"That's good, Vince. You know I want to meet Elizabeth's rich relatives in England and who better to leave my ranch to than you with Amelia at your side. I know the two of you will make a good team."

"I'm going to make sure you'll be able to take that trip sooner than you think, Rafe."

Rafe nodded and stood. "Let's hope we can have everything in place by the time you get back from the cattle drive."

"We plan to pull out at dawn." Vince stood, too. "Now, don't you worry about a thing. As soon as we get the cows to the train, I'll pay the boys and they'll go into town to celebrate and I'll head back here. Amelia may even be home by then. If she isn't, I assure you it won't be long until she is."

"I hope she comes to her senses by then, but if not, I know you'll be able to handle it." Rafe walked to the door with Vince. "I'll come out to see you and the boys off in the morning."

"You know you don't have to, boss, but I'm sure the hands will appreciate it."

"I have to thank you, Vince. You've proven to me, more than one time, what a fine foreman you are and what a good husband you'll be for Amelia." Rafe chuckled and patted him on the shoulder. "Now, I have to go have dinner with my wife. I'm trying to keep her calm until everything is settled. She still thinks I'm going to accept

Amelia's marriage. Of course, you know damn good and well I'll never do it, but it was the only way I could keep Elizabeth happy."

"Women are easy to fool sometimes."

"When you and Amelia are married, you'll learn there are many things you'll have to keep from her. Women think they have more control over you than they do. They even think they're as smart as men and you and I both know no woman is."

Vince didn't answer, but he did laugh as he went out the door.

* * * *

Amelia stood on the Garcias' front porch with Jed and the sheriff.

"We're getting ready to ride out to where Miguel told you the incident took place," Jed said.

"Miguel also told me the men who attacked his father worked for Daddy." There was sadness in Amelia's voice.

Lance frowned. "Did he know their names?"

"The way Miguel described them, I know one of them was Vince Callahan."

"How could you be sure?" Jed looked down at her.

"Miguel said he had blond hair to his shoulders and he was a big man who wore a brown hat. That doesn't describe anybody on the Double D except Vince."

"You don't suppose Garcia was doing something to make the men attack him, do you?"

"Lance, you know Roberto wouldn't do anything to antagonize anyone." Amelia stared at him. "Vince, on the other hand, wouldn't think twice about attacking the man for no reason."

Lance put his hand on her arm. "Do you think it would be too much to ask Miguel to ride out and show us the area where his father was attacked? We wouldn't have to spend time searching for the exact spot."

"I'm not sure. You'd have to ask Miguel."

"Ask me what?" Miguel came out the door.

"Son, could you describe to me what happened to your father?" Lance looked at the young boy.

"Yes, sir."

"Before you talk to the sheriff, Miguel, tell us if the doctor is still with your father."

"Yes, Miz Amelia, he is."

"Has he told you anything?" Jed asked.

"No. He told me to leave, but Mama is still in there with them."

"I'm sure Doc will tell you something soon." Lance pushed his hat back. "Now could we have that talk?"

"I told Miz Amelia everything I know."

"It would be helpful if you'd tell me."

Miguel nodded and told Lance the same story he told Amelia.

"And that was it?"

"Yes, sir."

Lance rubbed his forehead with the back of his hand. "I appreciate the information, son. Wainwright and I'll go out and see if we can find the place where this all took place."

Miguel asked, "Do you want me to go with you?"

Lance glanced at Jed and Jed said, "We'd appreciate it, but don't feel you have to, Miguel. I'm sure we'll be able to find the right place."

"I don't mind going. I want to help."

"Then why don't you double with me on Devil? He doesn't mind carrying two people."

"I'd like to ride your horse, Mr. Jed." He turned to Amelia. "Do you think it's all right for me to go with them with Poppa being so sick?"

"Of course it is, Miguel," Amelia said. "I'm sure the doctor will be with your father a while and if there's any news you need to hear right away, I'll ride out and get you."

He nodded. "Then I'll go with you."

"Good. Why don't you go make friends with Devil and I'll be there in a minute."

Miguel nodded and went down the steps.

Amelia looked up at Jed. Her voice was almost a whisper when she said, "I'm afraid."

"Of what, honey?"

"I helped Juanita dress some of Roberto's wounds. He's in bad shape, Jed. It'll be a miracle if he lives. If he does, I don't know what kind of shape he'll be in."

Jed slipped his arm around her shoulder. "Then, we'll have to help the Garcias."

"Of course we will."

"I'll be back soon, but if you need Miguel or me back sooner, fire a gun in the air two times."

"I'll fire it twice if the news is good."

He nodded. "And if I need to prepare Miguel for the worst, fire it three times."

Amelia would have said more, but the doctor stepped out on the porch. His gray moustache didn't hide the gloomy set of his mouth.

"How's my Poppa?" Miguel asked.

"Why don't you go back in and see your poppa, sonny. He's talking a little and I'm sure your mother would want you in there." Sheldon Wagner took out his handkerchief and wiped his brow.

Without a word, Miguel came back on the porch and ran into the house.

"How is Garcia, really, Doc?" Lance asked.

Doc Wagner shook his head. "I did everything I could, but I'm afraid he's hurt on the inside. His ribs are broken and without cutting him open there's no way to know for sure whether or not some of his vital organs aren't damaged beyond repair. He's just too weak for an operation like that."

"Is he going to…" Amelia couldn't finish.

"I don't know, Amelia. We'll have to wait and see. It's up to a higher power than me." He gave her a weak smile. "Do you think I could get a cup of coffee?"

"Sure. I'll be right back." She went into the house.

"I didn't want to say this in front of her, Jed, but there's little hope for Garcia. I don't think I've ever seen a man beaten as bad. If he makes it through the day, I'll be surprised."

"I thought you said he was talking."

"He is, but I don't foresee him getting better."

"The sheriff and I are going out to the site and see what we can find. Miguel was going with us, but I don't know if he'll want to now. Either way, maybe you should tell Amelia there's little hope so she can be prepared as well as help prepare the boy."

Sheldon nodded and turned to Lance. "Mrs. Garcia said her son told her one of Donahue's men did this to Roberto. Do you believe it, Sheriff?"

"We'll know more after we take a look, but I have no reason to doubt the boy."

"How about you, Wainwright?"

Jed shrugged. "I know Donahue hates Indians enough to want to beat them to death. I'm not sure how he feels about Mexicans."

Doctor Wagner lifted an eyebrow. "From personal experience, I presume."

"You're right about that."

Amelia came back on the porch with two cups of coffee. She handed one to the doctor and glanced at Jed and Lance. "If I knew you'd still be here, I would've brought you both a cup."

"Thanks, Amelia, but we'll be leaving as soon as we find out if Miguel is going to go with us. You can have a cup ready for us when we get back." Lance turned to his horse.

Miguel returned to the porch. "Mama said I was to go with you. She doesn't want you to miss anything out there."

"Then let's get going so you can get back to your father soon, Miguel." Jed headed toward his horse. He threw Amelia a quick smile and mounted, pulling Miguel up behind him. As soon as Lance was on his horse, the three of them rode off.

* * * *

A faint line of pink raked across the Eastern sky as Amelia and Jed climbed the steps to their bedroom.

"I'm thankful Roberto regained consciousness and was able to tell us Vince Callahan was the one who ordered two men to beat him as he held Miguel." Jed began unbuttoning his shirt.

"It's still hard for me to believe Daddy would condone this." Amelia was on the verge of tears. "How could I live with him for over eighteen years and not see what kind of man my father is?"

"Maybe your father didn't know what Vince was up to, honey. His foreman could be doing this on his own."

Amelia shook her head. "I don't think anything ever happens on the Double D that my father doesn't know about. He always brags that he knows what each and every one of his men are doing at any given time."

"I hope you're wrong this time."

"So do I, but I doubt that I am."

Neither said anything else as they undressed and climbed into bed. Amelia thought she was tired enough to fall immediately asleep, but she was unable to. All she could think about was how Roberto Garcia had been so brutally beaten. It angered her to think the man who orchestrated this crime was the man her father wanted her to marry.

How could he not see what an evil man Vince was? Or was her daddy as evil?

Without warning, Amelia burst into sobs.

Jed turned over and put his arm around her. "What is it, sweetheart?"

She pressed her face into his chest and said through her tears, "How could my father want me to marry a man who could do this awful thing?"

"I'm sure your father doesn't realize how terrible Vince is."

"I'm so thankful you decided to marry me. If you hadn't, I could've ended up living with that evil man."

"Don't even think about that. You were able to thwart that plan and we are married."

"I know."

"Try to relax."

She said nothing, but after a few minutes, her sobs began to subside. Finally she muttered, "I know one thing."

"What, honey?"

"After this terrible incident, I know I'll never reconcile with my father. Thinking he knew what was going to happen to Roberto means I could never look him in the face again. When he disowned me, he might have thought it was temporary, but it wasn't. It was forever." She put her arm around his waist and pulled herself closer to him.

Jed tightened his arms around her. "Try to put it out of your mind, Amelia. You need to get some rest. We may have to go back to the Garcias' place later today."

"I don't know how not to think about it, Jed."

He moved his hand to her chin and tilted it upward. "Try to think of something else," he whispered as he kissed her.

It wasn't long until their lovemaking drove everything out of her mind except the fact that she was in Jed's arms and she was his. If not forever, at least at this moment and he cared what happened to her. She knew there was no way he could be as kind and gentle if he didn't care at all.

* * * *

Three hours after going to bed, Amelia and Jed were awakened by a sharp rap on the front door. Amelia grunted and sat up and Jed got out of bed and slipped into his pants. "Go back to sleep. I'll see who it is."

Amelia nodded and dropped back to the feather pillow.

In a matter of minutes, Jed was sitting on the side of the bed patting her face gently. "Amelia, I know you want to sleep, but you need to wake up."

"Why?" She didn't open her eyes and her voice was so low, he could hardly hear her.

"Miguel was at the door. His father died a little while ago and his mother wants Curt and us to come. I told him we'd be there as soon as we could get dressed."

Amelia sat up and threw her legs over the side of the bed. "Then we need to get ready and go. Do we have time for coffee?"

"I don't think so. Maybe Juanita will have some."

A short time later, Curt brought their horses to the door, saddled and ready to ride. The three of them mounted and rode off toward the Garcia ranch. When they arrived, Amelia was surprised to see Doctor Wagner, Sheriff Lance Gentry, Charles Fielding and Father Dellrio of the Catholic Mission, sitting on the porch. She wondered why there were no neighbor ranch women to console and support Juanita and Miguel in their time of grief.

They hitched their horses to the rail and dismounted. Jed said, "Miguel wanted us to come as quickly as we could. Are we too early?"

"No, Jed," Lance said. "We're all here at the request of Roberto Garcia."

Jed frowned. "But Miguel said his father was dead."

"He is," Sheldon Wagner said. "He died about four o'clock this morning."

"Juanita had sent for me so I was here to give him the last rites and to honor his funeral requests," Father Dellrio said.

"Then where are their friends and neighbors?" Amelia looked puzzled. "I'm surprised none of them are here."

"They don't know Garcia's dead," Lance said. "Juanita doesn't want to tell them yet."

"Why not?" Amelia frowned.

"Roberto made a list of the people he wanted to be here to take care of some business before anyone else knew of his death," the sheriff explained.

"Are you sure we should be here?" Curt asked.

"Absolutely. She wouldn't have sent Miguel for you if he hadn't wanted you to come." Charles Fielding stood. "I'll inform Mrs. Garcia you've arrived."

Before he could go inside, the door opened and Juanita stepped out. Everyone could tell she'd been crying. "I heard them arrive, Mr. Fielding."

Amelia walked to her and took her hand. "We wanted to come."

Juanita gave her a weak smile and looked around at the others. "Please, everyone, come inside. I've cooked breakfast."

"You shouldn't have troubled yourself, Mrs. Garcia," Lance said.

"I had to do something." Still holding Amelia's hand, she added, "Will you come and help me serve?"

"Of course." Amelia followed her into the house.

The others walked in behind them.

After everyone had been seated and served, Juanita sat beside her son. "Miguel and I had a talk with Roberto before he passed away this morning. Doctor Wagner was here and Roberto asked him to go for Father Dellrio. Father sent someone for the sheriff and the banker. Miguel came for you." She nodded at Amelia and went on, saying, "Roberto told us exactly what he wanted done after his passing. Everyone, with the exception of the Wainwrights and Mr. Allison, was here in time to witness what my husband said."

Everyone nodded as Juanita paused and wiped the corner of her eye with a napkin.

"If you want to tell us later, Juanita, we don't mind." Amelia patted the woman's arm.

"No, Amelia. I must tell you now. That's what Roberto wanted." She took a deep breath. "The funeral will take place as soon as we finish up the business here. We will then bury my Roberto. Though it's unusual for things to happen this fast, Father Dellrio has given his permission for the burial. He has someone preparing a grave at the chapel."

"So soon?" Amelia frowned.

"It was the way Roberto wanted it done, Mrs. Wainwright," Father Dellrio said. "Under the circumstances as he explained them, I have no objections to doing it his way."

Juanita looked again at Amelia. "I know it must upset you to know your father's ranch hands were responsible for my husband's death, but I don't hold anything against you. You've been a wonderful friend. Not just since Roberto's beating, but from the time we met."

"I don't know how much my father knew about the beating, Juanita, but I want Lance to investigate every aspect of it. If my father was involved, he should answer for his crime, just like anyone else."

"Mr. Donahue was not with them, but his foreman was." Miguel spoke for the first time.

"He sat on his horse and held me with a rope. He made me watch, but I didn't know the two men who kept hitting and kicking Poppa."

"Don't worry, Miguel. The guilty parties will pay. I'll see to that." Lance lifted his coffee cup and drank.

Juanita nodded. "Now, to get to the business my husband wanted me to handle this morning. Since Mr. Donahue's man told Miguel they would be taking over the ranch as soon as my husband was dead, Roberto came up with a plan to keep him from getting any of our land and Miguel and I agree with his plan."

Jed said, "Mrs. Garcia, Curt and I will do anything we can to help you keep your ranch."

"We sure will," Curt said. "Roberto and I would often talk when we met at the edge of our property. He had plans for his place."

"Yes, he wanted to build a big ranch someday, but even if we wanted to keep this place, there's no way Miguel and I can carry out those dreams. There's too much owed on the ranch and there is no way we could ever pay it off. There are other bills, too. Also, there's too much work for the two of us." She paused. "As I said, Miguel and I had a talk and we're going to do things just the way Roberto told us to. That way we'll be safe and know we honored his last request."

Curt asked, "What did he want you to do, Juanita?"

Juanita smiled at him. "To carry out my husband's plan is the reason Mr. Fielding is here, Mr. Allison. Roberto signed all the proper papers to make everything legal. Now to conclude the deal, all that is needed is for you and Mr. Wainwright to sign them and this ranch will be yours."

Chapter 14

"Come in, Sheriff." Rafe stood and held out his hand as Elizabeth showed the lawman to Rafe's study.

"Hello, Donahue." Lance took the outstretched hand.

"Could I bring you gentlemen some coffee?' Elizabeth asked.

"No, thank you." He smiled at the woman.

"Then, I'll leave you alone." She went out and closed the door.

"Well, Sheriff, now she's gone would you like something a little stronger than coffee?"

Though Lance would have liked to have a glass of Rafe's expensive liquor, he decided he didn't want to move this meeting away from the business at hand. "This isn't a social call, Donahue."

Rafe raised an eyebrow. "What kind of business could you possibly have with me? Has that dirty bounty hunter done something to my daughter?"

"Of course not. The business I have is with your foreman. Would you send for him, please?"

"That's impossible."

Lance frowned. Was Donahue going to cover for Callahan? If not, why was he refusing to bring him into the house? "Why can't I speak with him?"

"The simple reason is that Vince left on the cattle drive before dawn this morning. He'll be back in a week or so. Whatever you need to see him about will have to wait." Rafe narrowed his eyes. "What business could you have with Vince anyway?"

Lance ignored the question. "Was he at the ranch yesterday?"

"Of course. He was getting things ready for the drive."

"Could he have left for a while?"

Rafe's voice became hard. "I told you he was here getting the cattle ready to move. Why are you so interested in where my foreman was yesterday, Lance Gentry?"

Lance twisted the gray Stetson in his hand. He had a feeling Rafe was lying. "I want to talk to him about a murder."

"What the hell do you mean? I'm sure Vince doesn't know anything about a murder."

Rafe's defense of his foreman wasn't convincing Lance. "I was told differently."

"Well, whoever told you differently was lying. I'd trust Vince with my life."

The Sheriff eyed Rafe. He could tell the man was angry. He decided he had nothing to lose. He was going to push him as far as he could. "I'm sure you would trust him with your life, Donahue. After all, you trusted him enough to try to push your daughter into marrying him."

"Damn it, Lance Gentry. Who I intend for my daughter to marry is none of your damn business."

"Not unless you force her to be a bigamist."

"How dare you. When she finally tires of that Indian bastard, I'll see this frivolous marriage of hers is annulled and she'll marry Vince."

"From what I've seen of the Wainwrights, there's no way there can ever be an annulment of that marriage." He chuckled. "Those two are so in love they can't keep their hands off each other."

Rafe's face turned red as he jumped from his chair. "Get out of my house."

"Please, calm down, Rafe," Lance said in a calm voice. "I apologize. I guess I was concerned about why you'd rather your daughter marry a murderer than a decent man like Jed Wainwright."

"There's nothing decent about Wainwright and I know damn well Vince Callahan didn't murder anybody."

"How do you know, Rafe? Were you with him all day yesterday?"

"I know the man. He wouldn't hurt anyone." Rafe still looked mad, but he settled back in his chair. "He's the best hand I've ever had and someday soon he'll be my son-in-law."

"You're dreaming, Rafe. Amelia will never marry Vince Callahan. She hates the man."

"She only thinks she hates him. She'll come to her senses."

Lance knew he wasn't going to convince Rafe, so he leaned toward the huge carved desk and spoke slowly. "Why haven't you asked me who was killed, Rafe? One would think you were more interested in covering for your foreman's actions yesterday than who lost their life."

"I don't give a damn who died. I only know Vince didn't do it. He's not that kind of man."

"As I said, someone saw him and two of your men commit the murder."

"That's it." Rafe jumped up again. "Get out."

"I'm going, but don't think this is the end. Your foreman committed murder and I intend to see him and those who helped him hang for it." Lance stood and put on his hat. Looking directly into Rafe's eyes, he said, "And if you ordered the killing, I'll see to it you pay for it, too."

"What do you mean, if I ordered it? That makes no sense."

"It makes sense to me." Lance opened the door. "Everyone knows how bad you want Garcia's ranch."

"What does Garcia have to do with it?"

Lance watched for Donahue's shocked reaction when he said, "He has everything to do with it. Roberto Garcia is the man Callahan and his cronies killed."

* * * *

Astride Rambler, Amelia rode beside Jed as they headed toward Settlers Ridge. She was thinking what a busy day they'd had yesterday. After the shock at breakfast, they agreed to take over the Garcia place then they attended Roberto's funeral. Afterward they returned to the Garcia cabin to eat the dinner Juanita insisted on cooking. They then left Curt at the ranch to protect Juanita and Miguel and headed home. By the time they took care of a few of their ranch chores, night fell and they were exhausted. They fell into bed and slept soundly.

When they awoke, she made breakfast and they ate. Jed hurried out to work until noon. She cleaned the kitchen, fixed a small dinner and straightened the house, including Curt's room.

With the increase in the size of the ranch Jed and Curt had decided yesterday they needed to hire at least three extra cowhands to work on both places. Jed insisted he do the hiring. Amelia was surprised until he told her, "Honey, a lot of men will refuse to work for a man with Indian blood. I don't want them coming to the ranch, then riding off because of who my mother was." Though she thought it unfair, she understood his reasoning.

Now it was early afternoon and they had ridden the last mile toward Settlers Ridge in silence. It seemed there was little else to say. Amelia was still thinking about what had happened and in such a short period of time. When the thought struck her, she looked over at Jed and said, "Didn't you tell me Lance said he was going out to the Double D either yesterday afternoon or this morning?"

"That's what he said."

"I wonder how he made out there."

"I'm sure Callahan will deny being involved, but that won't faze Lance. He'll bring him in and make him name his partners in the crime."

"I wonder if Daddy will deny it."

Jed gave her a quick smile. "Amelia, please don't dwell on it. I'll check with Lance while we're in town. I'm sure he'll talk with your father, too."

"It's hard not to dwell on it."

"I know it is." He reached over and touched her arm.

She nodded and didn't say anything for a little while. Then she again broke the silence. "I'm sorry I got you into all this, Jed. I never dreamed when we got married it would turn into so much trouble."

"I'm used to trouble and this time, I'm not dodging bullets and fighting rattlesnakes or cougars."

"If Vince gets away from Lance, you may have to dodge those bullets, yet." She gave him a weak smile.

"At least you avoided marrying the man."

"Thanks to you."

He raised an eyebrow at her. "And I'm reaping the benefits."

"I guess you have gotten the ranch you wanted out of it."

He chuckled. "I wasn't thinking about the ranch or the money."

Amelia knew exactly what he was talking about and couldn't help blushing.

Jed laughed out loud and winked at her.

She didn't say anything else.

When they reached Settlers Ridge, Jed reined his horse up in front of the hotel. "Why don't you go in and visit with Grace. I'll see if there's any men around we can hire. After I talk with the sheriff, I'll join you here for supper."

"Sounds good." Amelia dismounted and watched him ride down the street and stop his horse in front of Brown's Mercantile. Her heart fluttered. She frowned because her heart had been doing this a lot whenever she looked at Jed. Shaking her head, she entered the hotel. Waving at Frank Olsen, who was busy with a customer, she went directly to the dining room.

As she entered, Grace motioned her toward a table near the window. "I'll be right with you."

Amelia nodded and sat down.

Grace set plates before two cowboys then hurried over to Amelia's table. "I think it's time you finally came to town. How's married life?"

"It's fine." Amelia waved to the chair in front of her. "Won't you join me?"

"Let me serve you first."

"I'll just have tea for now. Jed is taking care of some business and he'll join me for supper in a little while."

"I'll get your tea and be back in a minute."

While she was waiting for Grace, Amelia was surprised to see Wilma coming down the plank sidewalk. Tapping on the window, she motioned for her friend to come inside.

Minutes later the three friends gathered around the table. "I told Mrs. Olsen you both were here and she said it would be all right for me to join you if I'd watch for customers coming in."

"Great," Wilma said and turned to Amelia. "I guess you're still happily married?"

Amelia nodded. "I am, but right now I want to know what you're doing here. How in the world did you talk your mother into letting you come back to Settlers Ridge?"

"My mother had nothing to do with it."

"Oh?" Amelia looked confused.

Wilma explained how she talked her daddy into letting her come back and it wasn't long until the friends were chatting as if there had been no changes whatsoever in their lives.

There was a pause in the conversation and Grace said, "Would you two excuse me for a minute? There's something in my room I need to get."

"Sure, but hurry back," Wilma said.

When Grace left, Amelia turned to Wilma. "Now, tell me. Have you seen Stanley Brown?"

"Yes, I have. I actually talked to him a few days ago. Grace brought Dr. Wagner's new nurse in the general store. I took her up to Stanley and explained to him how he should help her."

"That's a start, Wilma."

"I know. I think seeing you marry a man like Jed Wainwright has given me courage. If you can handle a strong tough man like him, surely I can handle someone as sweet and gentle as Stanley."

"I'm sure you can, but let me assure you, Jed's not as tough as some people thinks he is. He's really very sweet and kind, and gentle, too."

Before Wilma could answer Grace returned and handed Amelia a wrapped package. "Since we didn't have the chance to get you a wedding present, Wilma and I thought you might be able to use this."

"And we thought Jed would like it, too," Wilma added.

"Oh how sweet of you both." Amelia took the gift and tore into the wrapping. She couldn't help blushing when she pulled out a lacy light blue nightgown. "Oh, my goodness. It's beautiful. I love it."

"Do you think Jed will like it?" Wilma cocked an eye at her.

"I don't have to think. I know he will," Amelia said and blushed again.

Wilma and Grace had big smiles and Amelia knew they were delighted with her reaction.

* * * *

Andy Brown looked up when the bell over the door of the mercantile jangled. "What can I do for you?" he asked when Jed entered.

"I'm looking to hire some hands. Thought your pa might have an idea of some men looking for work. Is he around?"

"He's sick. Ma made him stay home today." Andy bit his lip. "You looking for somebody to work on your ranch?"

"I am. You happen to know anyone who'd be interested?"

"I'm interested."

Jed raised an eyebrow. "How could you work for a man who you think took Vince Callahan's woman away from him?"

"I'm not so sure about Vince anymore."

"May I ask why?"

"Well…" Andy stammered then went on. "Grace and Wilma have been talking to me."

"What have they been saying to you?"

"They said Amelia never loved or wanted to marry Vince. They said she loves you and she's happy being your wife."

Jed's expression didn't change, but his spine tightened. It was the first time somebody had said the word "love" to him. He wasn't sure how he felt about it, but he'd have to decide later. "And you believe them?"

"Yeah. Besides, my brother Stanley says Vince can't be trusted. He's seen him pocket some things when he was filling the Double D supply order. I know it weren't very valuable, but stealing is stealing ain't it?"

"It is to me." Jed looked at him carefully. "Are those the only reasons you've decided you can't trust Callahan?"

Andy shook his head. "I think he's lied to me."

"What about?"

He shook his head again. "I don't want to say."

Jed watched him for a minute then drawled, "Then, I don't think I'd be interested in hiring you."

Andy looked puzzled. "Why not?"

"When I ask a man a question, I expect an answer. If he can't be honest with me, I don't want him on my ranch."

"All right, I'll tell you." Andy seemed nervous, but he went on. "I hate this damn store. I don't want to work here. I want to be a cowboy. I love to be around horses and cows, not shut up in this place waiting on grumpy people all the time, but my pa wants me and Stanley to run this blasted store. A couple of months ago I asked Vince for a job on the Double D. He told me when he married Miss Donahue he'd give me one."

"And now you know he'll never marry Amelia?"

"I realized she cared about you the day you came in and bought the stuff for your ranch. She told me if I ever called her Miss Donahue again she'd make my life miserable. I knew right away she didn't like me calling her Miss. I was confused because Vince was telling me that he was going to marry her as soon as she left you. At the time I wasn't sure what to believe so when you came back in, I left to deliver the preacher's order. I saw Vince when I was leaving the preacher's place and he acted like he didn't want to talk to me. He came in here one time since and he said he didn't know if he'd hire me or not 'cause I weren't reliable since I couldn't tell him nothing about you and your wife. I ain't seen him since. I guess it was then I realized he don't intend to ever give me a job."

"Thanks for telling me all this, Andy. Why don't you talk it over with your pa? If he's willing for you to leave the store, come see me. I think I could find work for you."

"Oh, thank you, Mr. Wainwright. I'll do you a good job. I promise you and I'll never call Amelia Miss Donahue again."

Jed suppressed a grin. "In the meantime, could you give me more names of men who might be interested in work?"

"Sure. I know one man. Ward Kyler was in here the other day. He used to work for Donahue, but when he got hurt busting a mustang

Vince fired him. He's well now and needs work. I don't know nobody else. You might check with Stanley or Pa later."

"I will." Jed pushed his hat down and started out the door. "I'll be looking for you out at the ranch in a few weeks."

"I'll get there as soon as I can convince Pa."

Jed couldn't help smiling as he stepped outside and headed toward the jail. He didn't expect Andy to come to the ranch. He felt sure Walter Brown was going to keep both his sons behind the counter of his mercantile for as long as he could.

"You look happy, Jed." A voice said as he stepped onto the plank sidewalk.

"Hello, Charles. Andy Brown said something funny."

"He often says amusing things." Charles Fielding changed the subject. "How do you think things will work out with the new ranch?"

"I think it'll be fine as soon as I hire more help."

"I'm sure you'll need it. And the Garcias? Are they doing all right?"

"Curt spent the night there to be sure they were safe. I haven't seen them today."

"I'm glad Curt stayed. I noticed the boy seemed to take to him when we were there."

"I noticed the same thing. I'm sure Curt will be patient with him. His son would have been about Miguel's age if he'd lived."

"I didn't know Curt was married."

"Was married are the right words. His wife and son died of some kind of illness eight or nine years ago."

"I'm sorry." Charles moved toward the bank. "Guess I better get things closed down for the day."

"And I have to make a stop at the saloon to see if I can hire some hands before I meet Amelia for supper."

The men nodded at each other and headed in opposite directions.

* * * *

Rafe rode his horse toward the back of his ranch. He felt if he got out on the range he'd be able to think through some of the questions going through his mind. He also wanted to get away from the house before Elizabeth started asking questions. She was sure to wonder what the sheriff wanted and he had no intention of telling her. It seemed to him she was sticking her nose into things at the ranch more than ever lately. Why did she have to try to be a part of a man's world? He saw to it she had everything she wanted. Since her father was dead, why couldn't she accept the fact that her place was in the house and in his bed? His place was running the ranch any way he saw fit and he needed to do it without her input.

When he married her, he didn't expect her to become so difficult. He'd been a good husband. He'd denied her nothing, and he'd made sure she had no reason to suspect he'd not been faithful. Not once in their twenty years together had he visited any of the women in Settlers Ridge or the house of pleasure at the saloon. The few times he'd been with other women were when he was in Cheyenne or some other city. He was careful so Elizabeth would never be embarrassed by his actions. His only request of her was to give him a son, and she'd failed to do it. He couldn't understand why the doctors said she shouldn't have any more children, but he'd had little to say about it. Her father told the doctor to make sure she'd never bear another child.

There was no recourse. He was stuck with Amelia. Not only did she have to be born a girl, she'd always tried to take part in ranching matters even more than her mother did. While her grandfather Downey was still living, much to Rafe's displeasure, he encouraged the girl to take part in everything on the ranch. Though Rafe had put out a lot of money for her to attend a fancy school in Boston, it hadn't made Amelia any more interested in womanly things. Rafe still had to deal with her stubborn ways, but he had no intention of giving up. As soon as he got her back home he intended to see her settled for the rest of her life. She could fight him all she wanted, but he knew he'd win in the end no matter what she or her mother said.

Now Lance Gentry had the ridiculous notion that Vince Callahan had killed Roberto Garcia. Rafe wondered how the sheriff came to such a stupid conclusion. Vince was a hardworking hand. He did everything the way Rafe wanted it done. Since Vince now had the authority to do some things on his own, he'd shown he could make good decisions. There was no way the man was a cold-blooded killer. Rafe was so sure of Vince's innocence he'd even lied to Lance. He knew Vince had met up with Garcia on the day in question because he'd admitted it. But that meant nothing. He was sure Lance Gentry was going to feel like a fool when he realized how preposterous it was to try to charge Vince with a crime somebody else committed.

Rounding a group of Aspen trees, Rafe's thoughts came to an abrupt halt when he noticed two of his hands trying to pull a cow out of the muddy stream. He rode to them and dismounted. "What happened here, Wayne?"

"This dumb old cow has gone and got herself stuck in the mud," Wayne Rivers said as he looked up at his boss from the mud he was standing in almost to his knees.

"Yeah," the other hand, Smithy, said. "We been trying to pull her out for over half an hour. I don't think we're going to be able to do it."

Rafe walked to the stream, being careful not to get in the mud. "She's an ugly old heifer. She sure doesn't look like a cow from my good stock."

"She's probably a milk cow from a neighboring ranch, boss. I don't see a brand," Wayne said.

Knowing if the cow had wandered over from the Garcia place, he'd never keep such a critter when he bought the ranch. Might as well get rid of her now. Without hesitation, Rafe ordered, "Well quit wasting time. Either leave her here to die or shoot her. Then get back to work."

"Sir, I don't want to shoot the poor helpless thing," Wayne said.

Rafe raised an eyebrow. "Got a reason why, Rivers?"

"I don't like shooting anything helpless unless it's in pain."

Before Rafe could say anything, Smithy said, "I'll do it. I'm tired of messing with her." He left the creek and grabbed the rifle.

"Why don't we…" Wayne's protest went unheeded as Smithy raised the rifle to his shoulder and shot the cow between the eyes.

* * * *

The next morning as she washed the breakfast dishes, Amelia heard the sound of horses. She glanced out the window and saw Jed coming out of the barn. Three men dismounted and shook hands with her husband. As she watched them remove small bundles from behind their saddles and throw them over their shoulders, she thought one of them looked familiar. Removing the saddles, they put them on the fence and turned their horses into the corral.

She watched Mort amble toward them and shake their hands. He motioned for them to follow him to the bunkhouse. Jed came toward the house. She wondered if the men had eaten and if she'd be expected to cook breakfast for them. Mentally, she thought there was plenty of bacon and she could make gravy and biscuits. There were no eggs, and she decided she should tell Jed they needed to buy some chickens.

Jed opened the back door. "The new hands have arrived."

"Have they eaten?"

"They said they had."

There was the sound of more horses in the front yard. Jed crossed the kitchen and headed to the front door. "I'll see who it is."

Amelia followed him to the porch and was surprised to see Juanita Garcia and Miguel in the small wagon she and Miguel always drove. Curt was beside her on his horse.

Curt dismounted and said, "When I told Juanita you went to town to hire hands yesterday, she insisted on coming here to help."

"I know Amelia is not used to cooking for so many men," Juanita said to Curt, then turned to Miguel. "Start bringing in the supplies."

"Juanita, I appreciate the offer, but I don't mind cooking. It's my place to help Jed and Curt until we can hire someone to help."

"I want to return the favor for all you people have done for Miguel and me and you can stop looking for someone to help you." She took the hand Curt offered and stepped from the wagon. "I need to get away from the cabin. I don't feel at home there, since Roberto is gone."

"Come inside. We'll discuss your helping me later." Amelia took the woman's arm.

* * * *

Jed came down the steps and walked over to Curt. "What's going on?"

Curt shrugged. "I'm not sure, but from my bed on the couch I heard Juanita and Miguel talking into the night last night. They were in the only bedroom in the cabin and I couldn't tell what they said, but thought they were only talking about what had happened. I guess I was wrong, because this morning she informed me she and Miguel had made plans. She said she was going to move here and become our housekeeper."

"I don't think that's a good idea."

"Neither do I and I told her so."

"What did she say?"

"Said there wouldn't be much money left when she paid off what was owed at Brown's Mercantile and the feed store. She told me she was going to have to work somewhere and there was nowhere better for her to work than here."

"I don't mind her staying here a few days, but I'm not sure about her working here. Amelia might balk at having a friend as an employee."

"If Juanita is set on it, I think it could be the answer for Amelia. When the new men you went to hire get here, it's going to double her work."

"They've already arrived. Mort took them to the bunkhouse to choose their beds and put their things away."

"Good. I'll go meet them." Curt shifted his bad leg. "What happened with Vince Callahan?"

"I saw Lance yesterday. He said Callahan left on a cattle drive the morning after the beating. He was going to try to catch up with it today, but I told him I didn't think it would hurt to wait until Donahue's men came back. There's no way Vince Callahan won't return. He still has aspirations of marrying Amelia and getting his hands on the Double D."

Miguel came out of the house and ran down the steps. "I got everything inside. Should I put the wagon in the barn, Mr. Curt?"

"Fine, Miguel. Come along and I'll take care of my horse at the same time, then we'll go meet the new men who are going to be working here."

Jed and Curt headed across the side yard with Miguel trailing behind them.

* * * *

"Juanita, are you sure you want to do this?"

"I'm positive, Amelia. Curt told me you were going to hire someone to help you. I have nowhere to go and I need a job. Nothing could work out better for both of us."

"You don't have to move out of your house. I'm sure Jed and Curt..."

Juanita interrupted. "I understand. But, let's face it. You have a wonderful big house with much room. My house is a simple two-room cabin. We had a small bedroom and Miguel had a bed in the loft over the kitchen. Besides, you now have a large ranch to run. I feel guilty because Curt said he would sleep at the cabin to protect Miguel and me. It's best if I come here and become your housekeeper and cook."

Amelia gave up and decided Juanita was right. "If you're sure, then let me show you the rooms behind the kitchen. There's a large one with a connecting smaller one, which I assume was meant to be used for storage or for a bath area. It might work well for Miguel. Of course, if you don't like those rooms, we have four bedrooms in the other part of the house."

They stepped through the door and Juanita let out a little gasp. "Oh, Amelia, it's perfect. I never dreamed there would be so much room. It's bigger than our whole cabin."

Before Amelia could answer a voice called, "Mama, where are you?"

Juanita went to the door. "Here, Miguel. Come see the rooms where we'll be staying. They're wonderful and you get a room to yourself."

Miguel came in and looked around. When he spied the adjoining room, his eyes got big. "Do you mean I can have that room?"

"Yes, Miguel. Miz Amelia says these will be our rooms if we want them. What do you think?"

"I want this room. I can put my bed in the corner and have room for other things."

"Then it's settled. You and I will move in here." She turned to Amelia. "Do you think one of the men could go to the cabin and bring our beds and maybe a few other things?"

"Of course. I'll go talk to Jed about it."

"Good. Do you mind if I bring my chickens and my milk cows?"

"I think that'd be wonderful. I was going to ask Jed if I could get some chickens so we'd have eggs. Milk cows will be wonderful, too. I'm sure Jed will pay you for them."

"No he won't. He actually owns them now anyway."

"I'm not so sure about that."

"Well, I'm sure." Juanita smiled. "Now, go see if you can find someone to help us move and I'll start cooking. I'm sure the men will be hungry for a mid-day meal."

Amelia nodded and started to the back porch. Jed was coming in the door at the same time. "There you are, Amelia. Would you come out here and meet our new hands?"

"First, let me ask you something. Juanita wants to move into the rooms behind the kitchen. Will you send someone to her cabin to bring the beds and her animals?"

"Animals?"

"Yes. She has chickens and milk cows."

He nodded. "I think we can handle it, but I think she should go along so she can tell us what to bring."

"I agree." She followed Jed out the door.

Three men were standing around the steps. Amelia looked from one to the other then her face lit up. "Ward Kyler. I thought I recognized you. What in the world are you doing here?"

He grinned. "I got fired from the Double D and needed a job. Your husband needed a ranch hand and it worked out for both of us. It's a pleasure to see you, Miss Amelia...uh...Miz Amelia."

"I'm glad he hired you, Ward. I know what a hard worker you are."

"Thank you, Ma'am."

She looked at the other two men.

"I'm Elton Bowler, Ma'am," a man in his mid-thirties said as he tipped his hat to her.

"And I'm Darrel Reid," said a short man with a neat beard and graying hair pulled back in a braid behind his neck. He looked as if he might have some Indian blood. He was holding his floppy hat in his hand. "I'm pleased to meet you, Miz Wainwright."

"I'd like to welcome all of you to the Circle 2."

They mumbled their thanks and Jed spoke up. "Men, you're not the only ones moving in today. Curt and I have acquired the adjoining ranch and we need to move some of the things from there to here. I need a couple of you to go with Mrs. Garcia to the cabin to see what she wants moved."

"Shall we go now, boss?" Ward asked.

"Yes. I think that will be good. You can take her wagon and also the one we have in the barn."

"I'll tell Juanita you want to go now." Amelia looked up at him. "She'll be ready by the time you get the wagons hitched up."

Chapter 15

When there was a rap on his study door, Rafe Donahue looked up from the books he was working on. "Yes," he grunted.

Delores opened it and said, "There's a woman here who says she wants to see Vince Callahan."

"A woman?" Rafe frowned. "What else did she say?"

"Nothing, sir."

"Then, I guess I'll see her. Show her in, Delores."

"Yes, sir."

Rafe closed his ledger and slipped it into the drawer. He turned as the lean, well-dressed lady came into the study and held out her hand. "Esther Venable, Mr. Donahue."

Rafe couldn't help noticing her southern drawl as he shook her hand. "I understand you want to talk to my foreman."

"Yes, sir."

Rafe wrinkled his brow. "How did you know Vince Callahan worked for me?"

"I knew he was in this area and I asked at the mercantile. They told me he worked here."

"I see." Rafe eyed the young woman. "Why do you want to see him?"

"It's a personal matter, Mr. Donahue."

"Well, Miss Venable, you're going to have to wait to see him. Vince Callahan is on a cattle drive and won't be back for a week or so."

Esther stood. "Then I won't take any more of your time, Mr. Donahue."

"Is there some message I can give Vince?"

"No."

"You don't want me to tell him you came by."

"It doesn't matter. He'll say he doesn't know me."

Rafe frowned. "Then why would you want to see him?"

"I said he'd say he didn't know me, Mr. Donahue, but he does. He knows me very well."

* * * *

"Who is the woman in the study with Rafe, Delores?"

"I don't know, Miz Elizabeth. She came to the door and said she wanted to talk to Vince Callahan. Since I knew he was gone, I sent her to see Mr. Donahue."

Elizabeth frowned. "What did she want to talk to Vince about?"

"I don't know. That was all she'd say to me."

Rafe came into the dining room. "I'm sorry I held up dinner, my dear. I had some business to attend to."

"Who was that woman, Rafe?"

"I haven't the foggiest idea. She said her name was Esther Venable."

"What did she want with Vince?"

"Elizabeth, when in the world did you become interested in strangers who come around here asking about my ranch hands?" Rafe gave a nervous chuckle. "I'm getting hungry. Let's eat."

She glared at him. "I'm interested in what goes on here, Rafe. After all, my daddy taught me to take a part in some of the ranch business. I think it's time I started paying attention to what's going on."

"This had nothing to do with the ranch." Rafe's voice was a little irritated. "Miss Venable said it was something personal she had to discuss with Vince."

"I wish you would have found out more. She could know things about Vince Callahan we don't. I've never trusted him."

Rafe moved behind her to pull out her chair so she didn't see the fury on his face. Finally he said, "Vince Callahan's a wonderful man, Elizabeth, and I trust him completely. I don't see why you can't believe me when I tell you this."

"I didn't say he wasn't nice. I only said I wasn't sure we should trust him as much as you do. You act sometimes like he's your son instead of a middle-aged ranch hand."

"Elizabeth, Vince has done nothing but help me. If it wasn't for him, we wouldn't be as rich as we are today. I hope someday to leave this ranch to him and our daughter."

Elizabeth glared at him. "You said you were going to keep an open mind about Amelia's marriage to Jed Wainwright. Were you lying to me, Rafe?"

"Of course, I'm going to give Amelia's marriage a chance, but I can't help it if I believe it's doomed to failure. Amelia is too smart for the likes of Wainwright."

"If you plan to give Jed a chance, when are you going to take the time to find out where he and Amelia are living?"

Rafe could not hide his surprise when he said, "What are you talking about, my dear?"

"It's been some time since she came to visit us and we had the terrible scene. Since you promised to accept her husband, I think you should use your influence to find them so we can pay them a visit. I want to see my daughter."

He cleared his throat. "I'm sure they're busy getting settled. I think a visit from us would be a distraction."

"You're being ridiculous. A visit from us wouldn't interfere. I'm sure Amelia would welcome a visit from us."

Delores entered with a platter of chicken. She added it to the table where vegetables already sat. When she left, Elizabeth went on, saying, "So, shall we plan a trip to town tomorrow to find out where Amelia and her husband live?"

"No!"

"But…"

Delores came back into the dining room. "Mr. Donahue, Wayne Rivers is at the back door. He says it's important he speak to you right away."

"Can't it wait until after dinner?" Elizabeth looked at her husband. "You and I haven't finished out discussion about a visit to Amelia."

Rafe dropped his napkin beside his plate. "Something critical may have happened. I'll be back shortly. Go ahead and eat."

* * * *

Later in the afternoon, Elizabeth guided the horse pulling her buggy with one hand, then reached over and patted Delores's arm with her other. "I'm sure Juanita will be happy to see you, dear."

"I don't know, Miz Elizabeth. Why didn't she let me know Roberto was dead? It looks like she'd want her only relative in the area to know." Delores wiped her eyes. "When Pablo came to the kitchen door and told me that Roberto was dead and buried, I could hardly believe it."

"Well, we won't be too long getting there now. The Garcia ranch is only a couple of miles away."

"I appreciate you bringing me, Miz Elizabeth. I hope Mr. Donahue won't mind."

"If he'd come back after Wayne Rivers came to get him, he'd be with us. Since he wasn't back, we had no choice except to leave him behind."

"I don't want you to get into trouble."

"Don't worry. I won't." Elizabeth glanced at Delores. "I'm sorry Mr. Donahue has been so difficult lately, but he's been awfully upset about Amelia's marriage. He's not taking it well at all."

"I don't mind, Ma'am. I know he's been mad about Miz Amelia running away, but he hasn't been hard on me."

Elizabeth didn't say anything for a minute then she took a deep breath and asked, "Delores, I was in St. Louis visiting my sister when Amelia got married. Though he was as stubborn and hard headed as always when I left, it seems like everything changed when I returned home. He's not only stubborn, but now he's unreasonable about things, especially Amelia. I don't know when he decided she was going to marry Vince Callahan. He hadn't said anything about it before I left. I was stunned when I got his wire telling me to come home to plan the wedding."

"I know, Miz Elizabeth. I was shocked when he told me she was going to marry Mr. Callahan, too. I didn't think…" She closed her mouth.

"Didn't think what, Delores?"

"I didn't think Miz Amelia liked Vince Callahan very much."

"Did you talk to Amelia about it?"

"Only in passing, Ma'am. I mentioned it to her one morning at breakfast and she told me she thought her father had lost his mind. She said she'd never marry an old man like Vince Callahan and her father might as well accept it. Then in a few days, she said she was going into Settlers Ridge to have a wedding dress made. I was surprised she'd changed her mind, but I didn't feel it was my place to question her."

"Of course, we now know she had no intention of getting a wedding dress made. She went into town to marry Jed Wainwright." When Delores said nothing, Elizabeth went on, saying, "Did Amelia tell you anything about her intentions to marry Mr. Wainwright?"

"Nothing at all. I was as shocked as everyone else when I heard she'd married the bounty hunter. I didn't even know she knew him."

"I see." Elizabeth sighed. "I know you heard the fight she had with her father when she came to the ranch a little while back."

"Yes, Ma'am."

"Rafe says he's going to try to accept her husband, but so far I've seen no signs of acceptance. I want to see my daughter, Delores, but I don't know where she lives. Do you have any idea where she and her husband have settled?"

Delores looked surprised. "You don't know?"

Elizabeth shook her head. "No. If I did, I'd visit her."

"Miz Elizabeth, I thought you knew Amelia's husband bought the Lawson ranch."

Elizabeth reined the horse to a stop and turned to look at Delores. "Did my husband know Wainwright had bought the Lawson's place?"

"I think…I don't…I'm not sure."

"Delores, we've always been honest with each other. Tell me the truth. Did Rafe know Amelia and her husband were living on the Lawson Ranch?"

Delores dropped her head and muttered something.

"I didn't hear you."

"I'm sorry, Miz Elizabeth, I don't want Mr. Donahue to fire me."

"Mr. Donahue is not going to fire you. You work for me, not him. Now answer me."

Delores nodded. "I didn't mean to overhear, but I was in the hall when I heard Mr. Donahue and Mr. Fielding talking that night several weeks ago when he came to supper. Mr. Fielding told him about them buying the ranch then. Mr. Donahue yelled and cursed and threatened…"

Elizabeth dropped her head and a tear rolled down her cheek. "My daughter has been this close to me all the time and Rafe didn't tell me."

"Maybe he thought…"

"No, Delores. There's no excuse. He knew how I was longing to see Amelia. He didn't care how I felt because he purposely kept the information from me."

"I'm sorry, Miz Elizabeth."

"So am I." Elizabeth shook the reins and the horse began to trot forward. "If we had time, I'd go see Amelia today, but tomorrow will be soon enough. I need to confront Rafe about this. He has no business treating me this way." There was a determined look on her face.

* * * *

Rafe raced his horse toward the Garcia ranch. *What is Elizabeth thinking? Doesn't she know better than to take off to visit Juanita Garcia with only Delores along? Stupid women out alone in this area isn't safe. That woman has been almost impossible to control since she came back from St. Louis. Damn city people. I don't know what they put in my wife's head, but I sure wish she'd get it out. Things are going to have to change. I can't put up with her actions much longer. First Amelia turns into a stubborn child and now Elizabeth is doing the same thing. I don't know what the hell to do with the two of them. It may take a good lashing to put them back in their place.*

His mind continued to mull over his problems as he rode along. He should have asked the stable boy what time the women left. Now he wasn't sure he could catch his wife before she got to the Garcia place. He sure hoped he could, though. He didn't want somebody there spewing the ridiculous notion that Vince had killed Roberto. It would be like Elizabeth to believe them and he'd again have a fight on his hands. And with the mood she'd been in lately, it could get nasty.

Why couldn't she wait till I came back in? I would've taken her to the funeral and we'd have paid our respects as neighbors should. He grinned as thoughts continued to enter his mind. *Then I'd have sent a man to help Juanita out and in a few days I'd come talk to her about buying the ranch. Of course, she'll sell it to me. Though the place is small, there's no way she and her little boy could run it. They might miss it, but if they don't want to work for me, I'll help them move into town or even to Mexico if they want. Even if some people think so, I'm not a heartless man.*

Rafe knew he wasn't going to catch his wife when he turned his horse down the road leading to the ranch. It wasn't long until the small cabin came in site. There were two wagons sitting in front of the house and Elizabeth's buggy sat off to the side under a tree.

Pulling back on the reins to stop his horse, Rafe frowned. What was going on? It looked like some men were loading the wagons with things from the house. Was the Garcia woman leaving so soon? No. There hadn't been a funeral and no woman would leave before burying her husband.

Spurring his horse, Rafe could distinguish more of the scene the closer he came. He saw Elizabeth sitting on the bench under a shade tree in the side yard several yards from her buggy. Two women sat in chairs near her. They looked as if they were drinking tea or coffee. He headed in their direction.

Climbing from the saddle and ground hitching his horse, he walked up to them. "Ladies," he said, tipping his hat.

"What are you doing here, Rafe?" Elizabeth looked up at him.

"I was concerned because you came all this way on your own, my dear." He turned to Juanita. "I'm sorry about your husband, Mrs. Garcia."

Juanita nodded, but didn't speak.

"I know this is a hard time for you. If I can relieve some of your worry, I'd be happy to send a couple of my men over to help you until you can decide what you want to do with your ranch."

"That won't be necessary," she said.

Ignoring the fact Elizabeth and Delores said nothing, Rafe continued. "I'm sure you think so, but there's no way a woman and a young boy can keep this place up without help."

Elizabeth broke in. "I don't think this is the time to bring such a thing up, Rafe."

"Now, my dear, I know how women are. At a time like this, a man's clear head is needed. Women aren't capable of making decisions because their emotions have them almost paralyzed. They rely too much on their hearts and aren't thinking clearly."

"It wouldn't hurt you to rely a little more on your heart." Elizabeth's voice was sharp.

Rafe bit his lip to control his anger. He was smart enough not to show ire toward his wife in front of these women, even if one was his housekeeper. "You're probably right, but right now, I'd like to be of assistance to Mrs. Garcia in a practical way. I'm sure she needs it and will appreciate it in the long run."

Nobody answered and a minute of silence followed. Rafe broke it. "I can't help noticing you're moving things out of the house, Mrs. Garcia. May I ask why you're in such a rush to get away? Don't you think you'll need some of these things when the neighbors come to give their condolences?"

"I know what I'm doing, Mr. Donahue."

Rafe shook his head and turned to look at the man coming around the cabin with a crate. It was filled with chickens. He frowned. "What in the world are you doing with your stock, Mrs. Garcia?"

Before she could answer, Elizabeth stood and took hold of Rafe's arm. "Let's walk over here. I want—"

"No, Elizabeth…I want—"

"I insist, Rafe. Come with me." Her voice was firm and she tugged at his arm.

He took a deep breath and followed her. When they were several feet away, he stopped. "Now, tell me what the hell is going on. Has she already dug a hole and thrown Roberto in it?"

"You can be so irritating." Elizabeth looked up at him. "The Catholic church allowed Juanita to bury Roberto in the church yard yesterday."

He looked stunned. "I'm surprised she did it so quickly, but I guess Catholics do things differently."

"Juanita buried her husband the way he requested and the priest agreed to do it for her."

"Then, it might be time to talk with her about buying this ranch."

"I don't think so, Rafe. She said she was going to stay with a friend and she'd be making decisions later this week."

"But…if—"

"Rafe, please. Put off talking with her about it today."

He hesitated then finally took a deep breath. "I won't say anything to her today, but rest assured, I won't put off talking to her for very long. I want this ranch."

"I know you do, Rafe. You seem to want a lot of things lately." Elizabeth sounded disgusted.

"What do you mean?"

"Never mind, dear. Now, why don't you go on home? Delores and I will be along soon."

"There's no way in hell I'm going to let you keep running about this country all alone. It's not safe."

"Then, let me collect Delores and say goodbye to Juanita. We'll leave shortly."

Rafe nodded and turned to watch the men loading a bedstead. He recognized Ward Kyler. How in the world did he end up moving Mrs. Garcia's belongings?

He walked back to Juanita, again gave her his condolences, and headed toward the men. He wanted to find out why his former employee was helping this woman move out of her cabin.

When he saw Ward come out of the house, he spoke. "Hello, Ward."

Ward nodded and placed the stack of blankets he was carrying in the Buckboard. Without speaking, he turned and started back into the house.

"Wait a minute," Rafe said. "I want to talk to you."

Ward paused and looked at him. "We don't have anything to say to each other."

"I want to know what's going on here. Why is this woman moving out of her home and why are you helping her do it?"

Ward pushed his hat back and wiped his brow with the back of his sleeve. "I don't see that's any of your business, Donahue."

"It's not, but for all the time you spent working on my ranch, I thought you might give me the courtesy of answering my questions."

"Look, Donahue. I don't owe you a damn thing. I gave you five good years of hard work as foreman and how do you repay me? As soon as your wife's daddy died, you demote me and handed the foremanship over to a man who had only been on the ranch a short time. I held my tongue and still gave you a good day's work for my pay and as soon as I have an accident, you fire me without giving me a chance to do other jobs while I heal."

"Look, Kyler. I had no choice. Vince said you didn't want to do anything but lay around in the bunk house and…"

"I don't give a damn what Callahan said, I was working my tail off. He wanted to get rid of me because I was onto him. He was afraid I'd eventually make you see what he was up to."

"You're wrong about Vince. He's been…"

"Forget it, Donahue. Nobody can make a stupid man see what's right in front of his face."

Rafe couldn't believe what he'd heard. How dare a ranch hand talk to him this way.

He couldn't help saying, "Well, since you're whole again, I was going to offer you your job back, but with your attitude—"

"Rafe Donahue, I wouldn't take a job back on your ranch if you doubled my wages. I'm working for an honest man now."

"Who?"

"As I said before, it's none of your damn business. Now, get out of my way. I have work to do."

* * * *

On the way home, Elizabeth ignored Rafe as he rode his horse alongside her buggy. She and Delores talked some, but their voices were low and he wasn't able to understand a thing they said. Why had she been so aloof with him? She should have been happy he'd tried to show his sympathy to the Garcia widow. Instead, she rushed away as soon as he arrived. He didn't even have time to find out if the woman was going to sell her place. Of course, she could be upset because Delores was. After all, Juanita was Delores's niece or some kind of kin and the woman had a right to be weepy. He only hoped the housekeeper would be able to cook supper when they got home. He'd had a rough day and he was hungry. He wanted more than a sandwich or a bowl of soup.

When they got home, Delores headed into the kitchen and Elizabeth went directly to her room to freshen up. Still puzzled by his wife's actions, Rafe went to his study and poured himself a glass of whiskey. He decided he'd keep his mouth shut and wait until she was ready to tell him what was going on in her head. That was, if she didn't take too long to let him in on her thinking. If she did, he'd have to find out in his own way.

In less than an hour, Delores put supper on the table and it wasn't a sandwich. She had ham, beans and corn as well as a peach pie for dessert. Rafe was glad, but he didn't tell her how this pleased him.

He and Elizabeth ate the meal in silence then Delores served coffee and dessert. Stirring cream in her coffee slowly, Elizabeth looked at him. "Why didn't you tell me Amelia's husband bought the Lawson ranch?"

Surprised, he muttered, "How did you find out?"

"It doesn't matter. What matters is why you didn't tell me."

"I didn't think the time was right."

Elizabeth stared at him. "And when was the time going to be right?"

"My dear, I think you're making too much of this. I knew you would eventually find out."

Glancing down at her pie, she said, "You've lied to me, Rafe Donahue, and I don't like that."

He frowned. "I've never lied to you."

"Have you forgiven Amelia for marrying Jed Wainwright?"

His jaw worked as he searched his brain for an answer to satisfy her. "Elizabeth, I—"

"A yes or no will be the correct answer, Rafe. Don't try to pull the wool over my eyes about it."

"It's not that simple, my dear. You know I still think Amelia should have married Vince. I wouldn't be surprised if she doesn't already regret her marriage to the half-breed."

"Juanita told me Jed and his partner have been wonderful neighbors. She's seen Amelia and says our daughter is happy with her husband and loves being a ranch wife."

"So you'll take the word of a Mexican peasant over my opinion of the situation?" He was becoming angry.

She took a small bite of pie and sipped her coffee before answering. "Yes. Especially when she's right and you're wrong."

"Be reasonable, Elizabeth. Amelia has to come to her senses sometime. When she does, she and Vince will be married and…"

"My daughter will never marry Vince Callahan." She raised her head and looked him directly in the eyes. "I'll see to it my daddy's will excludes Vince Callahan from ever owning an inch of this ranch."

"I'm stunned. Why wouldn't you want…"

"Vince isn't the man you think he is. Not only is he a cheat and a liar, he's a murderer."

"You're wrong. He's—"

"I don't want to hear any more of your praises about your saint Vince tonight. You'll know how wrong you are when you see him hanged for his crime. I want to see the look on your face when you finally have to face the truth about the man." Elizabeth pushed her pie away and stood. "I will be sleeping in the guest room tonight, Rafe. Please don't disturb me."

"I'll be damned. You'll do no such thing." He shoved his chair backward and stood.

"What are you going to do? Force your way into the room?" She dropped her napkin and walked toward the door.

Rafe caught her at the end of the long polished table. "You're acting like a fool, Elizabeth. You're my wife and you'll not leave my bedroom."

"I will not share a bed with a man who is trying to force my daughter to marry a murderer."

Rafe was too shocked at her determined look to say anything. He needed time to decide how to stop her from running off to visit Amelia, though there was no doubt in his mind she intended to do just that. Thinking it was best to let her go to the room, he dropped his grip on her arm and watched her march out of the dining room and up the steps. He'd give her a little while to settle down, then he'd take her a glass of wine to settle her nerves. Elizabeth sometimes liked a glass of wine before she went to sleep.

Chapter 16

"I'm a little tired, are you?" Amelia asked as she stretched out in Jed's arms. Feeling his nearness, a thrill ran down her spine. She wasn't sure why, but this had been happening a lot lately. Seems every time he touched her it gave her a thrill. She was going to have to watch these emotions. Jed would be out of her life when their arrangement was up and she didn't want to start caring too much for the man.

"I'm a little tired, too, but we got a lot done today."

"Yes. I think it's going to work out well with Juanita and Miguel here. They're happy with their rooms. Especially Miguel. He thought it was wonderful to have his own room and not have to sleep in a loft over the kitchen."

"Our kitchen doesn't have a loft."

She nudged him gently. "Of course it doesn't. I was only making a statement."

"Speaking of statements, let me make one. The two of you cooked a good supper tonight."

"Thank you, but I think you're saying that because you want to change the subject."

"That could be a true statement."

She felt his warm breath on the side of her face. "Whatever, you sure ate like you enjoyed the supper anyway."

He hugged her close to him. "I'm a big man. I have to eat a lot."

Amelia couldn't help herself. She began running her fingers through the dark hair on his chest and tracing some of the scars. He'd never told her what caused them and she couldn't help wondering about them sometimes. She was also wondering if her nearness meant anything more to him than a release of his manly needs. She had to get such things off her mind and changed the subject. "May I ask you something, Jed?"

"Sure."

"I thought Indians didn't have much hair on their bodies, but you have a thick beard and have to shave every morning. Then there's all this hair on your chest. How did it happen?"

He laughed out loud. "You ask some of the weirdest questions sometimes, but if you must know, I inherited my coloring from my mother. I suppose you can blame my hairy Scottish father for my body hair."

"Tell me about your parents, Jed."

"Not much to tell. My father was a trapper. He had a good relationship with the Indian tribes in the area and visited their camps often. My mother was a Lakota Indian maiden, but she'd been injured in a raid by the soldiers and had a deep scar on her face and was blind in one eye. It didn't matter to my father. The minute he met her he thought she was the most beautiful woman in the world. I thought she was, too."

"Both of them must have been good looking to have a handsome son like you."

He chuckled. "Thank you, Ma'am."

"Are they still living?'

"No. They're both dead."

"What happened to them, Jed?"

"My mother died when I was nine. My dad couldn't stand being around the Indian camp without her, so we went to live with his friend in Colorado. Though I loved it, Dad didn't take to ranch life and went back to the mountains to pursue his trapping. He was killed in a fight with a bear a few months later."

"Did you grow up in Colorado?"

"No. After his death, I was shipped off to live with my dad's sister in Kansas. She was a nice lady, but I wasn't very well accepted by her friends and their children. She decided I might fit in better if I had an education, so she sent me to a school in the east. Though it surprises people when this half-breed can read and write, it didn't make a lot of difference with Aunt Prudence's friends. It wasn't long after graduating that I gave up the idea of living in Kansas. I came back to my mother's people and stayed there for a while."

"Is your aunt still living?"

"Yes. I write to her every few months. She threatens to visit me when I settle down, so I haven't told her I bought a ranch, but I'll tell her one of these days." He pulled her closer to him. "Enough of my life story."

"But it's not all. You haven't told me about getting married or becoming a Marshall or where all your scars came from or—"

"Some other time. Right now I want to do something else and to do it I'm going to rid you of this fancy gown your friends gave you." His hand was pushing her nightgown off her shoulders. "I'm glad you told them I'd like their thoughtful gift because I do, but it just gets in the way sometimes."

She knew exactly what he was talking about, but she asked anyway. "Why does it get in your way, Jed?"

"It slows me down in what I plan to do."

"What do you plan to do?"

"Do I have to explain it to you?" He began kissing her forehead and moved to her ear.

She giggled and nibbled his chin. "How about showing me instead of explaining?"

Jed moved over her as his mouth captured hers. "I'd be happy to show you, Ma'am."

In seconds she was oblivious to anything except the feel of Jed's hands on her body and his tenderness as he claimed her as his own once again.

* * * *

Delores turned as Rafe came into the kitchen. "Good morning, sir."

"Good morning, Delores. Mrs. Donahue is sleeping in late this morning. I'll be having breakfast alone then I'm going into Settlers Ridge to take care of some business."

"Yes, sir. I'll bring your breakfast right in."

"Please don't disturb Mrs. Donahue for a while. She was rather upset when we went to bed and needs her rest." Rafe didn't want the maid waking Elizabeth up too soon. He knew his wife would probably still be in a mad snit and go running off to see Amelia.

"Yes, Sir."

Rafe turned back into the dining room. Pulling out his chair at the head of the table, he sat down. *If Delores knew anything about Elizabeth's plan to visit Amelia, she certainly is keeping it well hidden. Personally, I don't think the woman is capable of hiding her feelings. If she suspected anything, she'd show it. I'm not worried that Elizabeth will be able to get away before I come back from town.*

He twisted his mouth into a sneer. *As I've always known, women are easy to fool. Our faithful housekeeper is a simple Mexican peasant. There's no problem there, and even with her fancy Eastern education, my wife is no match for me. I'm still in control of what happens on this ranch and I intend to stay in control.*

He straightened and gave Delores a slight smile as she set a plate filled with fluffy eggs, a slice of ham, and fried potatoes in front of him. She followed it with steaming coffee, freshly baked biscuits and an assortment of jellies.

"Thank you, Delores. It looks good." He began to eat.

"I hope you enjoy it, Sir." She left the room before he could speak again.

After Rafe finished eating, he pushed back his plate and headed to the barn. As he entered, Richard came out of the tack room.

"Can I saddle your horse for you, Mr. Donahue?"

"I can saddle it myself, Richard. I'm sure you have work to do."

"I was working on some saddles and bridles. They were getting stiff and I was oiling them up."

"Good. We never know when we'll need the equipment."

"Yes, Sir."

"By the way, Richard, Mrs. Donahue isn't feeling well, but you know how women are. She may come down and want you to hitch up her buggy. I don't want her leaving the ranch. I'm afraid it would make her sicker."

Richard looked scared. "What should I do if she does want to leave, Sir?"

"You're a bright boy. You can think of something to keep her here. Now, get back to your work. I'll be home later this afternoon."

* * * *

Amelia and Mort were shooing the chickens Juanita had brought into the coop Mort had constructed for the wayward flock when she saw a rider headed for the ranch. She latched the coop's gate and placed her left hand above her brows to shield her eyes from the mid-morning sun. She still couldn't tell who the rider was.

"Looks like company's coming, Miz Wainwright."

"Yes it does, Mort. I can't see who it is yet."

"It's a lone man."

"I'm sure it's someone wanting to see Jed or Curt." She smiled at the ranch hand. "Now that we've got the chickens in their new home, why don't you go work on the stall in the barn for the cow?"

"Miz Garcia told me she had two cows. Do you think we'll find the other one?"

"I don't know, Mort. The men are keeping an eye out for her and if she turns up, you can fix up another stall." She glanced back toward the approaching rider. "Since I have to get chicken feed and Jed doesn't want me going to town alone, I'll get ready and we'll leave as soon as you're finished."

"I'll get to the barn whenever I make sure ain't somebody coming who's up to no good, Ma'am."

"I appreciate the concern, Mort, but I'm sure it's probably somebody we know."

"Probably, but there's no harm in making sure."

Amelia wrinkled her brow. "Did my husband tell you to watch me, Mort?"

"Not exactly, Miz Wainwright."

"Well, what exactly did he tell you?"

"He told me to make sure you and Miz Garcia was not bothered."

"I understand, Mort. After what happened to the Garcias, he's protective of me." She turned and again looked toward the rider. "I know him. It's Andy Brown."

"Do you trust him?"

"Of course. I've known his family all my life. They own the mercantile in Settlers Ridge."

"Then I'll be headin' to the barn."

Amelia nodded and started toward the front yard.

It wasn't long until Andy reined up. "Howdy, Miz Wainwright."

She couldn't help smiling. "Thank you, Andy. At least you got my name right this time."

"Yes, Ma'am. I won't make the mistake of calling you Miss Donahue again. I've learned my lesson."

"Good for you. Now, what brings you out here to the Circle 2?"

Andy climbed down from his horse and threw the reins around the hitching post. "I came to talk to your husband about a job. Can I see him?"

"He's out on the range, Andy." She turned toward the house. "Why don't you come inside, have a cup of coffee and tell me what this is all about?"

"I'll be glad to." He followed her.

When they reached the kitchen, she asked, "Do you know Mrs. Garcia?"

"Yes, Ma'am. She comes in the store." He nodded to the woman at the stove. "Hello, Ma'am."

"Hello, Andy." She took two cups from the cupboard. "Do you drink your coffee black?"

"Yes, Ma'am."

Amelia moved to the shelf where a pan of water was kept. "I've been chasing chickens this morning, so as soon as I get my hands clean, I'll see if I can find some of the apple cobbler Juanita made for supper last night."

"I love apple cobbler." He dropped to a straight back chair.

Juanita moved to the back door. "I'm going to build a fire under the wash pot, Amelia."

"Good. As soon as I finish with Andy, I'll gather up the dirty clothes and bring them out there."

Amelia dried her hands, got him a serving of pie and sat down across the table. "Now, Andy, tell me why you're here looking for work? Did you do something at the mercantile which caused your father to let you go?"

"Oh, no, Miz Ame...I mean, Miz Wainwright."

"I don't mind if you call me Miz Amelia, Andy. I only want you to know who I'm married to, and accept it."

"I accept it, Ma'am," he said with his mouth full of pie. "As a matter of fact, I think you're better off with Mr. Wainwright than you would be with Vince Callahan."

"I'm glad you finally understand that, Andy." He nodded and she went on, saying, "Now that we've settled my wedded status, tell me why you're here."

He took a breath. "When Mr. Wainwright came into the store and asked if I knew anybody who might want a job, I told him about Ward Kyler then I told him I'd like a job. He told me to talk it over with my dad and if he said I could work for the Circle 2 it was all right for me to come see him, so I have come to get the job."

"And your father said it was all right?"

"Not at first. He said he didn't have anybody to work in my place in the store. I was so upset I talked to Miss Grace about it. She told me to hang in there and things would probably work out. The next thing I knew Stanley talked to Pa and he said if he could find somebody to work at the store I could try being a cowboy. So here I am."

"Then he found someone to work at the store in your place?"

"Yes, Ma'am." He pushed his cobbler dish back. "That was good."

"You can tell Juanita on the way out that you liked it." He gave her a blank look and Amelia chuckled and went on. "You'll find Jed if you ride out across the pasture behind the barn. They're branding out there over the ridge."

"Thank you, Miss Amelia." He jumped up, slapped his hat on his head and headed out the door.

Amelia shook her head and decided not to mention that, in his excitement, he'd forgotten to address her as a married woman.

* * * *

"Miz Elizabeth, please try to wake up." Delores sounded concerned. "It's after nine. I know you've slept enough. It's time for you to get up."

Elizabeth half way opened her eyes. "Let me sleep." She slurred her words.

"You've slept enough, Ma'am. Please open your eyes." Delores took hold of Elizabeth's shoulders and sat her up in the bed.

"Please, a little longer," Elizabeth whispered.

Delores let her employer slide back to the pillows and stood. Taking a deep breath, she moved to the windows and opened the heavy velvet curtains. Looking out on the vast lawn, she wondered how it would be to own something so grand. No wonder Miz Elizabeth had put up with her husband's ornery ways for all these years. Of course, when Mr. Downey was alive and Miss Amelia was home, it was easier for all of them. After her father's death, Miz Elizabeth and Miss Amelia seemed to make life happy for each other and together they were able to keep themselves separate from all the unpleasant things going on at the ranch, including Mr. Donahue's temper. Since Mr. Downey's death, Mr. Donahue was left to run things any way he wanted to. Of course, he always had his faithful foreman, Vince Callahan, to help him.

It seemed to Delores it was then things began to change between Mr. and Mrs. Donahue. He didn't hide his temper as well and he became more demanding and less able for her to reason with, even over minor situations. Then Vince Callahan's importance on the ranch grew and Mr. Donahue treated him almost like a member of the family. Elizabeth began to act more aloof and spent more and more time visiting her sister in St. Louis. Amelia had been their only common ground and now that she'd moved away, things were getting worse. Delores had heard them arguing last night, and she couldn't help wondering how much longer it could go on before there was a big blow up between them and something drastic happened.

This morning she wasn't sure it hadn't happened already. She knew Miz Elizabeth confronted her husband about Amelia and her husband buying the Lawson place, but she now wondered if Mrs. Donahue hadn't let it slip that they'd learned yesterday about the Wainwrights and Mr. Allison buying the Garcia Ranch. If she had, she knew her boss man would be livid. She wasn't sure what he'd do when he found this out.

A moan came from the bed and interrupted Delores's thoughts. She turned to see Mrs. Donahue tossing her head from side to side.

Delores moved to the bed to hear a slurred mutter, "No, Rafe. I don't want to drink it. Take it away. No, Rafe. I…"

Delores frowned and reached for Elizabeth's hand. "What are you saying, Ma'am? Drink what?" When there was no answer, Delores went on. "Did Mr. Donahue make you drink something?" Still silence. "Please, Miz Elizabeth, talk to me."

None of Delores's attempts brought Elizabeth to consciousness. She gave up and stared at the elaborately decorated master bedroom. Did Mr. Donahue make his wife drink something? Was that why she was having such a hard time waking up? Was he trying to make her sick or was he trying to kill her?

Afraid of what the answers might be, she moved to the brocaded fainting couch on the other side of the room and sat. She wasn't leaving this room until her mistress awoke enough to tell her what was going on and if the woman didn't wake up soon, Delores knew she was going to send for the doctor.

* * * *

"Well, Miz Amelia, when your husband hired me, I didn't expect my first job to be going into Settlers Ridge to pick up chicken feed at the feed store and supplies at the mercantile."

From her seat on the wagon bench, Amelia couldn't help smiling. "There are many jobs on a ranch besides working with cattle, Andy. Everyone has to do a lot of different things."

"Yeah, I guess."

"Don't worry. I'm sure Jed will have you out on the range soon."

"Are you sure?"

"Of course, I'm sure. We don't go into town every day."

"I hope you're right. Going into town for supplies seems like I'm still working for the store. Only I'm doing it backward."

"Backward?"

"Yeah. I'm just going to get things instead of delivering them."

"I see." She chuckled. "You know, this could be a test that Jed is giving you."

He frowned. "What kind of test?"

"Jed could want to see how well you follow orders. Remember how clear he was when he said you were to go to the feed store while I got the supplies at your father's store."

"He did tell me not to go to the feed store until you were safe inside the mercantile. It was like he was trusting me to look after you."

"Jed is sometimes over protective of me. He doesn't think I can take care of myself."

Andy grinned. "I'm sure it's because he loves you so much."

Surprised at his words, Amelia muttered, "Think so?"

"Sure. Any fool can see he's crazy about you."

Amelia didn't say anything further, but she couldn't help hoping Andy was right. It would make it so much easier to face the fact she was falling in love with her husband if he had feelings for her. On the other hand, she was sure at times that he did care, but at this point in their marriage she thought the word "love" was still too strong to use about their relationship. At least it was on his part.

It was a busy day in Settlers Ridge. Wagons and horses filled the dusty dirt street. The young boys and girls were playing games of tag with each other while their older brothers were eyeing the girls who were on the brink of their teen years. Women were walking up and down the plank sidewalk, some with babies in their arms or leading toddlers. Several of them waved at Amelia and she waved back.

She couldn't help wondering if she would ever have a child. If she did, would Jed be happy to be a father? *Oh, my Lord, where did that idea come from? The last thing Jed would want is a baby. We'd be tied to each other for more than six months. Or would we? Would he send me away instantly if there was a child? Children are something we've never discussed and now I feel it's too late to bring them up.*

Before she could think any more, Andy pulled the wagon to a stop in front of Brown's Mercantile and said, "I'll be back as soon as I get the feed, Miz Amelia. You wait for me right in front here. Don't you go nowhere else."

"I'll wait for you right here, Andy. Don't worry." She climbed down from the wagon and started inside the store. A voice stopped her.

"Hello there, Mrs. Wainwright. I haven't seen you since the wedding. How are you?"

Amelia turned and smiled. "Mrs. Ellsworth. How good to see you. Has your daughter-in-law had her baby yet?"

"No, but it's due any day now."

"I'm sure she's anxious for it to arrive."

"Yes. We all are getting a little excited." The tiny older lady poked a finger toward Amelia's midsection. "Do you have any good news for me yet?"

"What do you mean?"

"You know I'm waiting to hear there's going to be a little Wainwright coming along."

Amelia blushed. "No, Mrs. Ellsworth. Not yet."

Gertrude Ellsworth raised an eyebrow. "I'm not so sure. Maybe you haven't had the signs yet."

Before Amelia could answer, Margo came out of the mercantile. "There you are, Mother Ellsworth. I declare you can get away from me in a matter of seconds."

"I needed some air. I was tired of hearing all you gossipy women in there. You'd think there was nothing to talk about in this town except each other."

Margo shook her head. "Hello, Amelia. It's good to see you."

"Nice to see you, too. Mrs. Ellsworth tells me everyone in your household is getting excited about the baby."

"We sure are. I know it'll come when it's ready, but I do wish it would hurry."

"I'm sure you do."

"I'd like to chat, Amelia, but I've got to get my mother-in-law home before I have to send out a posse." Margo chuckled.

"I understand. Maybe we'll see each other again soon." Amelia reached for the door to the store then realized Andy was still sitting in the wagon. He was serious about taking his order to make sure she was safely inside the mercantile before he left. She turned, waved at him and stepped inside.

Several customers were in the store and Amelia spoke to those she recognized. Then she spied the woman behind the counter and could hardly believe her eyes. Wearing a modest blue print dress, with her hair braided and twisted on top of her head, stood Wilma Lawson adding up a rancher's order.

Chapter 17

Rafe Donahue stared across the desk at Charles Fielding. "The Garcia woman was abandoning the place when we were there. I know they were having trouble paying their mortgage, so I guess the place can be bought cheaply and I want to—"

"Before you go on, Rafe, I have to tell you the Garcia Ranch has been sold."

"Have you lost your mind? How could the ranch be sold? The man died a couple of days ago."

"I know, but I'm telling you the truth. Everything is paid off and the property has been transferred to the new owner."

"Damn it!" Rafe hit Fielding's walnut desk with his fist so hard a couple of papers flew to the floor. "I want the Garcia place. I'll not be deprived of it. How do I get in touch with the new owner?"

"Calm down, Rafe. I knew you'd be upset, but Mrs. Garcia was determined you not buy the ranch. She approached another rancher and offered it to him."

"Why the hell didn't she want to sell it to me?"

Charles looked at him for a long minute. Finally he said, "She said she'd never sell the ranch to the man who had her husband killed."

Rafe was stunned. "What the hell did she mean? I never had anybody killed."

"Her husband told her before he died your foreman and two of your men were the ones who attacked him."

"That's a damn lie. Vince wouldn't do such a thing."

"I'm only telling you what Mrs. Garcia told me."

"Who bought the place?"

Charles had already decided the answer because he knew Rafe would ask this question. "Curt Allison and his partner."

"I've never heard of him so he can't be from around here."

"I think he's kind of new."

"I still don't know him and I know all the ranchers between here and Swanson." He eyed Charles.

Charles swallowed and prepared himself for the explosion. "His partner is Jed Wainwright."

Rafe stood and flung his chair backward. "That bastard! I'll see him in hell for this. Nobody makes a fool of Rafe Donahue twice and gets away with it."

"Calm down, Rafe. Wainwright nor his partner had any idea Mrs. Garcia wanted to sell her ranch to them until she asked them to buy it."

"I don't believe you. They're probably the ones who killed Garcia and tried to blame it on my men." Rafe was still furious.

"No. They were unaware of the whole thing until after his death."

Rafe frowned. "How do you know all of this, Charles Fielding?"

"I was there."

"You what?"

"Mrs. Garcia sent for me. She offered the ranch to them in my presence."

"So, you're a turncoat, too, you bastard?"

"Of course not. I've always been your friend, Rafe. You know that."

Rafe shook his fist at him. "You've pretended to be my friend, though Elizabeth married me instead of you."

"What are you saying?"

"I'm saying you're only friends with me so you can be near my wife. You've always wanted her, but let me tell you, you'll never get her. I'll kill you and her both before I'll see the two of you get together." Rafe became red in the face. "I see how you act when you come to the ranch.

You fawn over her like a school boy. No wonder she's always so glad to see you. She likes the way you flatter her."

Charles stood and pushed back his chair. "I think it's time you left, Rafe. You're talking foolishness."

"Foolish, am I? I'll…I'll…"

There was a knock on the office door. "Is something wrong, Mr. Fielding?"

"Everything's fine," he called back. "Mr. Donahue is leaving."

"You're damn right, I'm leaving, but I'll be back. As soon as I make Elizabeth sign some papers, you'll be ruined. I'll be putting all my money in another bank. I won't do business with a man who stabs me in the back." With that, he turned and stormed out the door.

"Are you sure everything's all right, Mr. Fielding?" His teller came to the door Rafe left open.

"It's fine, Mr. Drake. Mr. Donahue was just upset because he didn't get to buy the Garcia place."

The teller chuckled. "I guess you expected that."

"I sure did. Of course, I didn't expect him to threaten to take his money out of my bank though."

"Will he do it?"

Charles shook his head. "He can't. His wife has to sign before he can, and I don't think she'll ever do that."

* * * *

On the sidewalk, Rafe took a deep breath. Damn Charles Fielding. Damn Juanita Garcia. Most of all, damn the low-down bounty hunter. Not only had the man stolen two ranches from him, he'd also taken his daughter. It was too much for any man to bear. There was no way Rafe Donahue would be shamed like this. He'd get the damn half-breed if he had to kill him himself.

Starting for his horse, Rafe came to a quick stop. Were his eyes playing tricks on him? Was it really Amelia coming out of Brown's Mercantile?

He watched as Stanley Brown followed Amelia with a box of supplies and put them in the back of the wagon driven by the younger Brown boy. Where was her husband? Was he actually making Amelia come into town for supplies? Didn't the fool know that was a job for ranch hands? What the hell was happening? Amelia wasn't used to this kind of thing. She needed to be back at home where she could be loved and pampered like her mother. There was no way she would last with this kind of treatment. He had to save her.

He watched Amelia as she hugged the woman beside Stanley, then climbed upon the wagon seat beside the younger Brown boy. They drove off toward the end of town.

Rafe decided to go to the store and see what he could find out before heading out to catch up with Amelia. Now was the perfect time to get his daughter and take her home where she belonged.

* * * *

"But, Delores, Mr. Donahue said not to let Mrs. Donahue leave the ranch." Richard looked exasperated.

"I don't care what Mr. Donahue said. Get the buggy ready."

"But he'll fire me and I need this job. Mama doesn't make enough money to feed all of us taking in washings."

"Don't worry, Richard. I'll see you keep your job. Now do like I say. Hitch up Mrs. Donahue's buggy and bring it to the front door."

"But—"

"Do it, Richard. If you don't, I'll personally see that you do get fired."

"You wouldn't—"

"Oh, yes I would. Now are you going to do what I tell you to do?"

"Yes, Ma'am. I'll hitch up the buggy."

"Thank you." Delores turned and headed back to the house.

* * * *

Smithy knelt on the knoll at the bend of the road on the way to the Circle 2 Ranch. He saw the wagon approaching and his heart beat a little faster. It was going to work this time. He'd watched as the boy and Wainwright's woman went into town, but thought it best to make his move when they came back. Then people who saw them in town wouldn't be able to say she never reached Settlers Ridge.

Checking his rifle, he started to mount his horse, but paused. There was a cloud of dust some distance behind the wagon. Damn, he didn't need a witness. Was he going to have to adjust his plan? Vince would kill him if he screwed up the way he had when he only nicked Wainwright's shoulder. Now he had a chance to redeem himself. He'd promised Vince he'd grab the woman if he got a chance. It seemed to be the right chance, but now somebody was going to mess him up again.

He watched as the wagon passed below, then glanced back down the road. The dust cloud was still a distance away. Yet, the rider could get to her before he was able to get the woman away from the kid and get to the prearranged hiding place.

Putting his rifle back in the scabbard, he climbed on his horse and eased it down the knoll on the other side. He'd get rid of this lone rider and then he'd still have time to catch the wagon and grab Wainwright's woman. It didn't matter that he'd have to kill the kid to do it. Nobody would probably even miss a young ranch hand like him.

When he was sure the sounds of his horse wouldn't be heard by the people in the wagon, he gigged his mount into a gallop. In minutes he was close enough to the rider for a good shot. He drew his pistol, but hesitated. There was something familiar about the man on the black stallion. Frowning, he slowed his horse and waited.

As soon as the rider was close enough, he bellowed, "Mr. Donahue. What the hell are you doing here?"

"I'm going after my daughter, Smithy. Why are you out here?"

"Well, all you've done is mess up my plans, boss. I would've had your daughter home tonight if you hadn't come along."

Rafe stared at him. "What do you have to do with my daughter coming home?"

"I had it all fixed with Callahan."

Rafe frowned. "How could you fix anything with Vince? He's gone on the cattle drive."

"Damn it, boss. I wish you hadn't followed your daughter. Before he went on the drive, Vince and I set things up. He told me to watch their ranch and to grab her the first chance I got. I was to bring her home so she'd be there when he got back."

Rafe slumped. "Why didn't somebody tell me?"

"I guess Vince wanted to surprise you."

"Well, I don't need you now. I'm going—"

"I don't mean to be rude, Sir, but how long do you think you'd been able to keep her? I was ready to make sure the widow Wainwright stayed at home with her rightful family. How were you going to keep the kid from telling everyone you'd abducted your daughter? Did you have guts enough to kill him?"

"I don't think it would come to that."

"Vince said you were too nice to kill anybody, but it wouldn't have bothered me at all. In fact, I had my gun trained on the kid's head and was ready to pull the trigger when you showed up. I would've gone ahead and shot, but I didn't need a witness riding up."

"I didn't know—"

"Go home, Mr. Donahue, and let me handle things." He shook his head. "I might be able to catch them yet, but you can't be anywhere around when I do."

Rafe nodded, but it was lost on Smithy. He'd already turned his horse and was riding toward the wagon.

* * * *

Lance Gentry was walking out of the hotel when Delores pulled the buggy up to the front. "Sheriff," she yelled. "I need help."

Lance hurried to the carriage and noticed Elizabeth Donahue slumped in the seat. "What's going on?"

"Mrs. Donahue's sick and she needs a doctor." Delores was climbing out of the carriage.

"Let's get her inside." Lance swept the woman into his arms as Delores ran to open the hotel's front door for him.

"Mr. Olsen, Mrs. Donahue is sick. Please get a room for her and send for the doctor." Delores didn't care if she did sound demanding. All that was important now was to get help for Mrs. Elizabeth.

"Yes, Ma'am. Follow me." He turned to his son, who was sitting on a stool behind the counter. "Teddy, go get Doc Wagner."

The boy shot out the door. Mr. Olsen grabbed a key and led the way up the stairs. Delores and the sheriff followed. He unlocked the first door they came to. "Bring her in here."

Delores darted around him. "I'll turn down the bed."

Lance gently placed Elizabeth on the bed. "What happened to her?"

"I'm not sure." Delores began unbuttoning the jacket and taking it off her mistress. When she finished she took off Elizabeth's shoes. "I only knew she needed a doctor when I couldn't get her to stay awake."

"Where's Rafe? Shouldn't someone should go for him?" Lance asked.

"No!"

Lance frowned. "Why not, Delores? He has a right to know."

"No he don't, and I'll explain everything to you both as soon as the doctor gets here."

There was a noise in the hall and Doctor Wagner entered the room. He moved directly to the bed and sat his black bag on the floor. "What happened?"

"I'm not sure, Doctor," Delores said. "Mrs. Donahue couldn't seem to wake up this morning. She said she drank something last night…"

Sheldon began to examine Elizabeth. "Did she tell you what she drank, Delores?"

"She said it was wine. Mr. Donahue gave it to her."

"When did she drink it?"

"Last night. After she got ready for bed, I guess. She went straight up to bed after supper. I didn't know anything was wrong until she couldn't get up this morning. Mr. Donahue said to let her sleep and not try to wake her up. But it got late and I was worried so I went to check on her. When I finally got her to talk a little she told me about the wine."

"Where is Donahue?"

"He came to town early this morning. I haven't seen him since."

The doctor nodded and glanced at Lance and Frank. "Would you fellows step outside for a minute, please?"

"Sure," they said almost in unison.

Delores hovered as the doctor continued his examination. When he finished, he looked up at her. "When Amelia got married I gave Rafe some drops to help his wife relax and sleep. I think she may have taken too much of it last night. Was she upset about something?"

Delores hesitated.

"Please, Delores. You must tell me everything. I don't want to give Mrs. Donahue the wrong thing. It could be fatal."

"Mr. and Mrs. Donahue had a misunderstanding. She was upset because he hadn't told her Miss Amelia was living nearby on the Lawson place. She planned to go visit her daughter today and I'm sure Mr. Donahue didn't want her to. I think he gave her something so she wouldn't be awake enough to go."

"I see." The doctor looked back at Elizabeth. "Then we need to make sure Mr. Donahue doesn't upset her anymore."

"I agree, Sir. Will you tell the sheriff not to send for him? He wanted to."

"I sure will." Dr. Wagner turned back to Elizabeth and put his hand on her cheek. He patted it firmly. "Elizabeth, you need to wake up. Come on. You've slept enough."

She stirred.

"Delores, go see if you can get some strong black coffee brought up here."

"Mrs. Donahue likes tea better than coffee."

"This time I want her to have coffee. It'll be better for her in this case."

"Yes, Sir."

"And, Delores."

"Yes."

"I think you should tell the sheriff exactly what you told me and let Mr. Olsen know I said Mrs. Donahue is to have no visitors, including her husband. If they question you, tell them to see me."

"Thank you, Dr. Wagner. I'll tell them right now." She stepped into the hall.

"How is she?" Lance asked.

"Dr. Wagner said he wants me to get some strong black coffee. He also told me to tell you and Mr. Olsen that she's not to have any visitors, including her husband."

"I'll see she's not disturbed," Frank said. "I'll also go send up a pot of coffee. You don't have to go get it, Delores."

"Thank you, Sir."

Lance asked, "Does the doctor think Rafe gave Elizabeth something?"

"I know he did, Sir. She kept mumbling, 'I don't want to drink the wine, Rafe' so I know he gave her wine. The doctor said it looks like she's had too much sleeping powder."

"Damn. I never dreamed Rafe Donahue would hurt his wife."

Mrs. Olsen came into the hall with a steaming pot of coffee and a cup. "Frank said you needed this."

"Where's he?" Lance asked.

"He stayed downstairs in case anybody tried to come up here."

"I see."

Delores opened the door. "Take the coffee in here, Mrs. Olsen."

In a minute the doctor came out. "Thanks for waiting, Lance."

"I needed to see what's going on."

"I think the woman's been given too much sleeping medicine. I can't prove Rafe gave it to her, but she keeps saying she doesn't want to drink the wine."

"Should I arrest him?"

"Not yet. Wait until she comes around. We'll get a clearer story then."

"So, she's going to be all right?"

"She's going to be weak and sluggish for a while, but with the proper care, I think she'll pull through."

"Is there anything I can do? Should I go tell Amelia?"

"Let's wait, Lance. I've got Mrs. Olsen and Delores pouring black coffee in her. I hope that will help flush out the medicine. I don't want to alarm Amelia if there's no reason to."

"I understand. The woman has enough trouble with her father as it is. I sure don't want to tell her that her father tried to kill her mother."

* * * *

Amelia heard something shift in the bed of the wagon and turned around to be sure everything was secure. It was then she saw the rider coming up behind them.

"Andy, somebody is following us. Maybe you should speed up."

"Who is it?"

"I don't know, but he's riding hard." She leaned forward and took the rifle from under the bench. "I have a feeling he's up to no good."

"You can't shoot him, Miz Amelia."

"I don't intend to shoot him, Andy. I'm only going to be ready just in case he is trouble for us."

"Do you know how to shoot a gun?"

"I sure do. My grandfather taught me a long time ago, but I won't shoot at him unless he fires first."

"Oh, my lord. Mr. Wainwright will kill me if anything happens to you. If anybody gets shot, please let it be me."

"Let's hope nobody gets shot. We're close enough to the ranch that a gunshot can be heard. I'm going to let Jed know what's happening." Amelia raised the gun and fired two shots into the air, the signal to anyone who could hear she needed help.

Andy glanced around and said, "He's pulling back, but he's not leaving."

"You drive. I'll keep an eye on him."

"Yes, Ma'am." He slapped the reins over the horses and they sped up.

They went for several minutes and Amelia watched the rider. The man raced his horse forward and she saw him take his gun from his scabbard.

"Duck, Andy. He's raising his gun," Amelia shouted and turned the rifle toward the rider. Without a second thought she pulled the trigger.

The rider jerked his horse around and grabbed his shoulder. He'd been hit, but she could tell he was hesitating as if he still wanted to come after them. Eventually, he turned his horse and headed in the other direction.

Amelia turned back and faced the front. "I think I nicked him and he's given up, but don't slow down yet."

"I'm not going to." Andy's voice was shaking.

They rode in silence for several minutes then Amelia said, "I think you can slow down now. He's not following us."

"I want to get you back to the ranch as quick as I can. Lord, I don't want anything to happen to you. Mr. Wainwright would kill me for sure."

"Jed's not going to kill you, Andy, and you don't need to wear the horses out. I'll keep watching behind us and if he appears again I'll let you know. You can then speed up again."

Andy slowed the horses. "Maybe going for supplies can be as exciting as branding cattle."

"Yes, it can. I guess… Look, Andy. Somebody's coming in the other direction."

"Better get the gun again, Miz Amelia."

"I have it across my lap, but I don't think I'll need it this time. Jed's on one horse, and one of the hands is on the other."

Andy stopped the team and Jed reined Devil up on Amelia's side of the wagon. "What's going on?"

Before she could answer, Andy's shaky voice blurted, "A man was chasing us on a horse aways back and Miz Amelia shot the signal in the air. Then he kept coming and when he started to shoot us, she shot him before he had a chance to pull the trigger, but she didn't kill him and she kept watching to make sure he didn't come back after us. She's very brave."

Jed dismounted, came up to the side of the wagon and took her hands. "Are you all right?"

"I'm fine. As Andy said, after I shot at him, he turned and went in the other direction."

"Did you know him, Amelia?"

"I'm sure it was one of Daddy's hands. The one who's always with Vince."

"I wonder what he wanted with us." Andy frowned.

"He was up to no good, I'm sure," Jed said.

"It was probably the hand we called Smithy," Ward Kyler spoke for the first time. "He and Vince Callahan were always tight."

Jed frowned. "We'll escort you back to the ranch, honey."

"Thank you," Amelia whispered.

Jed squeezed her hands, then climbed back in his saddle and dropped back as the wagon pulled away. He began a conversation with Ward as they rode behind the wagon.

* * * *

Rafe Donahue glared at Richard. "What do you mean you let Delores leave with Mrs. Donahue? I told you not to let Mrs. Donahue leave this ranch."

"I couldn't stop Delores, Mr. Donahue. She said Mrs. Donahue was sick and she had to take her to the doctor. I don't know what she would've done if I hadn't let them leave."

"If Mrs. Donahue was sick, why didn't she send you for the doctor?"

"I told her I'd go get the doctor, but she said there wasn't time."

Rafe frowned. "What was wrong with Mrs. Donahue?"

"I don't know, Sir. All I know is when I brought the buggy to the front of the house, Delores had to almost carry Mrs. Donahue down the steps."

Rafe continued to frown. "This horse needs rest. Saddle me a fresh one and bring him up to the house in fifteen minutes. Cool this one down and turn him in the corral." Without giving Richard a chance to answer, he turned and stalked out of the barn.

When he reached the house, Rafe went directly to the kitchen.

Of course there was no fire in the cook stove. He looked in the warming oven over the stove. Though they were cold, there were three biscuits on a plate beside two pieces of cooked ham. He grabbed a biscuit, cut it open, slapped a slice of ham in it and began to eat. Since the coffee was cold and he didn't want to make a fire to heat it up, he filled a glass with water.

"One hell of a meal," he muttered. "What good is it to have a cook if she doesn't cook for you?"

Gobbling down the last bite and drinking the last of the water, he sat the glass on the kitchen table and headed to his study. Unlocking the bottom drawer, he took out the bottle of sleeping drops. He had asked the doctor for the drug when Amelia married the bounty hunter. He thought Elizabeth would be so upset she'd need the drops. Nobody could have been more surprised than he was when Elizabeth didn't swoon over the news.

When she said she was moving out of their bedroom last night, he remembered the drug and decided he'd show her she wouldn't desert him. He put some in her wine and brought it to the guest room. She didn't want it, but he finally convinced her to drink it. When he was sure she was asleep, he'd then picked her up, carried her to their room and dumped her in the bed. He only wanted to show her she couldn't disobey him by leaving their room. He thought she'd wake up this morning and see how foolish she'd been.

Now he wondered if he'd done something wrong. He was sure the doctor said to give Elizabeth two or three drops when she became agitated. He figured it would take five or six drops to knock her out. Of course, it had put her to sleep, but was it too much? Yes, she was still sound asleep when he left, but he expected her to get up in an hour or so. Did he give her so much she couldn't wake up? No, he couldn't have. She hadn't changed her will the way he asked her to. He couldn't let her die. Things would be a mess if she did. Of course he didn't want her to die, but if something were to happen to her, it had to be at a later date. After the will had been changed.

Damn women. Why couldn't they know their place and stay in it? Now he had to go back to town and straighten things out with Elizabeth and bring her home. When were things going to get back to normal? He'd envisioned a time when he could sit back and let Vince take on more responsibility of running the ranch. He wanted to spend time training the grandsons he expected Amelia to have. But it could never be if something unforeseen happened to Elizabeth. Why hadn't he made her change the damn will before now?

Slamming the desk drawer shut, he locked it, stood and stalked out the door. This was not the way he planned to spend this afternoon, but he had no choice. He only hoped to get Elizabeth home in time for Delores to cook a good supper. The biscuit and ham was the worst mid-day meal he'd had in ages.

Chapter 18

Amelia walked into the back yard as Juanita pinned the last sheet to the line. "I got the men off to the branding pit and came out to help, but it doesn't look like you need me."

"It's all done for the week." Juanita smiled at her. "I saw the young fellow who took you to town ride off with the rest of the men."

"Jed said he felt Andy earned a chance to work on the range. He did a good job of protecting me when the rider tried to stop us."

"Who do you think is after you, Amelia?"

"I thought I recognized him and Ward Kyler confirmed my suspicion. It was one of Daddy's men. Even though he's disowned me, I'm sure my father thinks he can have me kidnapped and brought home where he believes I'll become his sweet little happy daughter. You and I both know he's wrong. That will never happen. This is my home now." She glanced around.

"You have a wonderful home, Amelia. I know you're happy here. It shows on your face." She smiled. "We've been so busy since I've been here that I haven't even told you about your mother visiting me at the cabin."

"How wonderful. How is she?"

"She was upset to learn you'd bought this ranch and her husband hadn't told her where you were."

"Daddy knew?"

"I guess so. I'm sure your mother will be here to visit soon."

"I hope so. I'm ready to see her."

"Now, I think I better go start supper."

"I've already peeled the potatoes and I put a roast in the oven."

Juanita shook her head. "You didn't have to do that. I would have cooked everything."

"I know you would, but I want to help." Amelia changed the subject. "Where's Miguel?"

"He wanted to help with the branding and Curt said he'd keep an eye on him."

"I'm sure he will. Curt is a dependable man. I think Miguel likes him."

Juanita nodded. "Miguel more than likes him. He thinks Curt is the smartest man in the world."

Amelia chuckled. "He's smart, but I'm sure he's not the smartest man in the world."

"Miguel would argue with you."

"I'm glad Curt is taking him under his wing. It'll help Miguel accept what happened to his father."

Juanita nodded. "When I get it on my mind, I can't believe your papa...never mind. Let's go inside and finish supper. Those men will probably all come in hungry."

"I'm sure they will." She was glad Juanita changed the subject. She didn't want to think about her daddy having a hand in killing Roberto. Amelia turned to go inside, but paused when she glanced down the road leading to the ranch. "Looks like a buggy coming this way."

"I do declare. I spent months at my cabin and didn't have a guest. I've been here only a few days and somebody has showed up almost every day."

"I can't imagine who's coming, but I don't think it's anyone who means us harm."

Juanita laughed. "I don't know many bad men who drive buggies."

Mort came from around the barn where he was working on the cow's stall "You sure have a lot of company, Miz. Amelia. I thought I'd check on who's visiting now," he said.

"Thanks, Mort. Juanita was just saying the same thing." Amelia wrinkled her forehead. "That looks like my mother's buggy."

When she realized it was her mother, Amelia walked to the front yard. It was then she saw Delores driving.

Delores reined up in front of the porch. "Miz Amelia, will you help me get your mother down. She's feeling poorly."

"Of course." Amelia took her mother's arm.

"Hello, darling," Elizabeth said. Her voice sounded sleepy.

"Mother, what's wrong."

"Let's get her inside and I'll explain," Delores said.

"Can I help?" Mort asked.

"We'll be here a while so you can take care of the horse and buggy," Delores said.

"Yes, Ma'am." He took the reins and headed to the barn.

Juanita ran to the front door and opened it. The women helped Elizabeth inside and sat her on the sofa. Amelia dropped to her knees in front of her mother.

"You don't look well, Mother. Have you seen the doctor?"

"Yes, honey." Elizabeth reached out and touched Amelia's cheek. "I'll be fine."

"I'll make some tea." Juanita headed for the kitchen.

Amelia nodded and looked at Delores. "Tell me what happened."

"When I saw your mother wasn't well yesterday morning, I took her to Settlers Ridge to see the doctor. He said she'd had too much of the sleeping drops he'd given her and it would take some time for it to get out of her system."

Wrinkling her brow, Amelia asked, "Why were you taking sleeping drops, Mother?"

"I wasn't, dear."

"I'm confused. How…"

"Your father and I had an argument last night. He hadn't told me you were living close enough that I could visit and I was furious with him. I was going to sleep in the guest room, and it made him angry. After I was settling in the extra room, he brought me a glass of wine as a peace offering. I didn't want it, but he insisted I drink it. I did, but told him I was still sleeping away from him."

"Then how did you get the drops?"

Elizabeth looked at Delores and her maid said, "Mr. Donahue must have put the drops in the wine."

"Do you really think so?"

Both Elizabeth and Delores nodded. Elizabeth went on, saying, "There was no other way I could have gotten them, honey."

"What in the world has come over Daddy?"

"He has certainly changed." Elizabeth leaned back into the cushion of the sofa. "After I went to sleep, your father must have carried me to our room because Delores found me there."

"Found you?"

"When Mr. Donahue came down for breakfast, he said to let Mrs. Donahue sleep, but I got worried and went up to check on her. I didn't like what I saw. She was so groggy she couldn't hold her head up and she kept muttering something about not wanting to drink the wine. I was afraid to let her keep going on like that so I got her dressed and took her to the doctor."

"Where was Daddy?"

"He went to town after breakfast and said he'd be back later," Delores explained.

"What did the doctor say?"

"Like your mother said, he told her to rest and drink a lot of coffee, tea and water so the sleeping drug would get out of her system."

"This is almost unbelievable." Amelia held onto her mother's hand.

There was a moment's silence. Elizabeth broke it. "I hope you don't mind me coming to you, dear. I was afraid to go home. I didn't know what kind of mood your father would be in."

"I'm glad you came, Mother. You must know how much I've wanted to see you, but you surely understand why I couldn't come to the ranch."

"I do understand." She looked sad. "Your father has always been hard on you, but he's acting completely unreasonable about your marriage."

"I've thought a lot about it, Mother. I wonder if Daddy has always been like he is now and we only ignored his outbursts. I know I went on with my life and said he'd get over it when he would march around the house cursing and yelling."

"I think I did the same thing, because he would calm down and things would get back to normal." Elizabeth smiled when Juanita came in with a tray of tea. "If you could say living with a dictator was normal."

"I'm going to finish supper, Amelia," Juanita said after serving them.

"I'll help." Delores stood.

"Before you cook, Juanita, will you please set up the extra bedroom upstairs for my mother?"

"Of course."

A knock on the back door interrupted. Juanita hurried to open it. In minutes she came back with two valises in her hand. One was expensive looking, the other was slightly tattered. "Mort said these were in the buggy."

"I thought we'd be at the hotel for a while so I packed us a few clothes. When the doctor said Mrs. Donahue would be all right to come here, I decided it would be better to be with you, Miz Amelia."

"I'm glad you both came, Delores." Amelia smiled at her.

"I asked Mort to ride out and tell Mr. Wainwright your mother was here,"

"Thank you, Juanita."

"I hope your husband won't mind if we stay the night."

"He won't mind at all, Mother. You can stay as long as you like."

Juanita and Delores headed for the kitchen, leaving mother and daughter alone.

Elizabeth reached for Amelia's hand. "I'm sorry your father has treated you so mean. I want you to know, I never thought Vince Callahan was right for you, but for some reason your father couldn't understand why I felt that way."

"I don't see how Daddy can think he'd be a good husband for me. I couldn't stand the thought of marrying him. He's too old and I know he wants the Double D. I also know he was behind Roberto Garcia's death."

"I think the same thing, but Rafe won't listen to any criticism of the man. It's as if he thinks Vince is perfect. I don't understand it."

"Neither do I."

"Now," Elizabeth took a sip of her tea, "that's enough about your father and Vince. Tell me about you and your husband. Are you happy, Amelia?"

Amelia blushed. "I never dreamed I'd be as happy as I am, Mother."

"I'm so glad. Like everyone else in town, I've heard tales about Jed Wainwright. He's sometimes called the nefarious bounty hunter and I have to admit, when I first heard you'd married him, I was concerned for your safety."

"Jed's nothing like people say. He's the kindest, gentlest man in the world. No woman could ask more of her husband."

"I'm so glad. A happy marriage is all I ever wanted for my daughter."

"So it doesn't bother you that Jed is half Lakota Indian?"

"No, dear. It doesn't bother me." Elizabeth dabbed her mouth with a napkin and smiled. "In fact, I think he's rather handsome. You and he should make me some beautiful grandchildren."

Amelia blushed again, but she didn't have to say anything. The sound of boots coming into the room caused them to look up.

"Mrs. Donahue," Jed smiled at her, "I'm glad you've come to visit."

"Thank you, Jed." She reached out a trembling hand to him. "But this isn't exactly a visit. I'm looking for a sanctuary for a day or so."

"What's happened?"

Amelia explained and Jed nodded. When she finished, he said, "You're welcome to stay here as long as you wish, Mrs. Donahue. We feel honored that you came to us."

"Thank you, Jed, but I do have one request." He raised an eyebrow and she went on, saying, "Please call me Elizabeth."

"I'd be happy to."

She turned to Amelia. "Honey, I feel a little shaky. Would you mind if I lie down for a little while."

"Of course not. Juanita has your room ready, I'm sure. I'll show you to it."

Elizabeth stood, but was unsteady and had to grab the arm of the chair.

"Here. Let me help." Without waiting for permission, Jed picked her up and followed Amelia up the stairs.

When they reached the room, Amelia turned down the bed and Jed put Elizabeth down gently. "Thank you, son," she whispered.

"You're welcome and when you're ready to get up, call out. We don't want you falling down the stairs."

"I'll take off your shoes, Mother." When she finished, Amelia put the light quilt over her mother. "If you need anything, I'll be downstairs. As Jed said, don't try to come down on your own."

"Thank you, children." She smiled, but her eyes were closed. "I feel safe now."

* * * *

Rafe stopped his horse in front of Doctor Sheldon Wagner's neat white house. He dismounted and threw the reins around the hitching post. He walked up the five steps to the front door and went inside without knocking.

Esther Venable looked up from the desk in the entry way. "Hello, Mr. Donahue. How can I help you?"

"What the hell are you doing here?"

"I'm Doctor Wagner's new nurse and as I asked, how can I help you?"

Rafe ignored her question. "Where's Sheldon?"

"I'm not sure. He went out late this morning and he hasn't come back."

"What did he do with my wife?"

Esther looked confused. "Your wife?"

"That's what I said." His voice was sharp.

"I haven't seen your wife, Mr. Donahue."

"Our housekeeper brought her to town to see the doctor. Did he see her or not?"

"Mrs. Donahue didn't see him at the office. She might have...." She didn't finish her sentence because Rafe Donahue had walked out the door.

With a curse, Rafe grabbed the reins and swung up into the saddle. *If they didn't come to the doctor's house, where could they have gone?*

Somebody at Brown's Mercantile might know. Or the hotel. If neither of them know, I'll try the sheriff's office. Lance Gentry seems to always know what is going on in Settlers Ridge.

Turning onto the main street, Rafe headed for the mercantile. Before reaching it, he saw the sheriff heading into the hotel. He decided to talk with Lance Gentry first. After hitching his horse in front of the hotel, he stepped inside.

Frank Olsen's daughter was behind the counter. Rafe tried to keep his voice civil when he asked, "Is Mrs. Donahue here?"

"I think she left sometime before Daddy asked me to watch the desk."

"When was that?"

"About an hour ago."

Rafe nodded. He knew there was no need to question the little girl any further. "Did the sheriff come in here?"

"Yes, Sir. He came in to eat just a minute ago."

Rafe nodded again and headed into the dining room. He paused at the door and looked around. Lance Gentry sat at a table near the back. He was laughing at something the waitress said.

Walking up to the table, he said, "I need to talk to you, Sheriff."

"Have a seat, Mr. Donahue. How can I help you?"

Rafe sat in the chair facing Lance. "Our housekeeper brought my wife to see the doctor, but she wasn't at his office. I'm concerned about her."

"She was here when the doctor saw her."

"What did he say?"

"He said she'd had too much sleeping medicine and almost died. He said the tiniest amount more and he couldn't do anything for her."

Rafe tried to hide his shock. "I'm sure she only misjudged the dosage."

"It's possible."

Grace arrived with the sheriff's plate of food. As she sat it before him, she asked, "Could I get something for you, Mr. Donahue?"

Though Rafe was hungry, he wasn't in the mood to eat. "I'll have some coffee."

Grace smiled at him. "I'll be right back with it.

Rafe put his hat on the empty chair. "Where's my wife, Gentry?"

"How would I know? As I said, she was here in the hotel earlier."

"Don't try to pull the wool over my eyes. You know everything that goes on in this town."

"Most everything, I guess."

Grace set a cup of coffee in front of Rafe. "If you decide you want something else, let me know."

Rafe ignored her and asked again, "I said, where's my wife, Sheriff?"

Lance cut a slice of roast beef. "I'll say it again. She was in a room upstairs when I last saw her. Is she not there now?"

"You know damn good and well she's not."

The sheriff grinned. "I guess I did know that."

"Damn it, Gentry. I want to know where Elizabeth is. I need to get her and take her home."

"I don't think it'll happen, Donahue."

"What do you mean?" Rafe squinted at the sheriff.

"When the doctor said he thought she'd be all right as soon as the sleeping drops were out of her system, she said she was going to visit a friend of hers."

"What friend?"

"I'm not sure. All I'm sure of is that Elizabeth made it clear she didn't want to go home."

Rafe gritted his teeth. It was all he could do to hold his anger inside. "Why would she say that?"

"I think you'd know more about why she wouldn't want to come home with you than I would, Mr. Donahue."

"You're talking in circles, Lance Gentry. Why won't you answer my questions?"

"Let me ask you a question. Were you trying to kill your wife when you put too many sleeping drops in the wine you served her last night?" Lance's eyes bored into Rafe's.

"How dare you ask me that!" Rafe slammed his cup so hard on the table it sloshed coffee on the checkered cloth. "I love Elizabeth. I'd never hurt her."

"Undoubtedly, she thinks you might. She says she's afraid of you and has asked everyone to keep you away from her."

"This is ridiculous. She has no reason to be afraid of me."

"I only know what she told me. When she feels better, I'll talk with her again and see what's causing her fear." He put a fork full of potatoes in his mouth. "Of course, by putting those drops in her drink, she may have reason to be afraid. She almost died."

"Damn you. If you think I tried to kill my wife, why don't you arrest me?"

"I wanted to, but Mrs. Donahue asked me not to. She said she couldn't prove you caused her illness, though she was sure you did."

Rafe stood and shoved back his chair. "I'll not stay here and listen to any more of this. If you won't tell me where Elizabeth is, I'm sure somebody in town will."

Without speaking to anyone, Rafe went out on the dusty street. Looking in all directions, he wondered where he should look next. Noticing the church, he wondered if Elizabeth could have gone to her friend, Margo Ellsworth. He decided it was worth a try and headed in that direction.

* * * *

Smithy picked up the coffee pot from the potbellied stove in the cabin on the secluded section of the Double D Ranch. He poured a half cup then filled the rest from the whisky bottle sitting on the table. Though his wound was only a scratch, it hurt like hell. He almost grinned as he thought of how Amelia Wainwright, or should he call her Donahue, had raised the gun and shot him without a second thought.

She must be some woman. Most of the women he knew didn't know which end of the gun to point at someone. They were only interested in what they could get from a man, and that usually meant money. Of course he had to admit the women he was familiar with worked in dance halls and bordellos and were willing to do anything a man wanted for a dollar or so. Then there were the promiscuous wives and daughters whose husbands and parents tried to make slaves of them on farms and small ranches. These women were different. All they wanted was a man to appreciate them enough to make them feel beautiful, even if they looked worse than the back end of the mules they owned. Of course, a man could luck up and find a pretty one now and then. It was a special treat when he did.

He took a sip of the coffee he'd poured and stirred the stew. His mind remembered the pretty raven-haired fifteen-year-old daughter of that mean old devil in Colorado. The bastard was determined his daughter would stay pure and untouched until he could get her married to one of their neighbor boys.

Smithy laughed out loud as he remembered how he'd found the pretty little thing in the barn while her daddy had gone to town for supplies. She was crying because he wouldn't let her go with him and of course Smithy had to comfort her. He comforted her too long, because the old man came home and caught them naked in the hayloft. Her old man was irate and demanded they get married. Of course, Smithy agreed, but after everyone was in bed, he slipped away in the middle of the night. He kind of hated to leave because she sure was a sweet little thing and she learned fast what it took to please a man. Too bad he didn't remember her name.

Taking the pot from the stove, Smithy sat at the rough wooden table and un-wrapped the bread he'd made earlier. *Pretty good meal, but when I get that pretty Amelia here she'll make me some fancy food. Of course, if I thought I could get away with it, cooking is not the only thing I'd get from her.* He chuckled. *I better quit thinking like that. Vince would kill me if I touched the woman. He says that's all going to belong to him when he gets here.*

He took a bite of the stew and burned his tongue. "Damn," he muttered and pushed the pot back to cool a little.

Yep. When I kidnap Mrs. Wainwright and Vince gets back, things are going to get a lot hotter around here. He said he was going to keep her here until she begged him to marry her and take her home to daddy. Of course, the way Vince has it planned Jed Wainwright will be slapped in jail for killing Miss Amelia. After his hanging, Vince will bring her home and be the hero of the whole state of Wyoming. The Donahues will head for Europe and Vince will take complete control of the ranch and I'll be the new foreman. Life couldn't get any better than that.

He smiled to himself and decided to give his shoulder another day or so to heal, then he'd make his move. He'd spy on their ranch again tomorrow and it would tell him when he needed to act.

Reaching for his pot again, he took a bite of stew and found it the right temperature.

Smacking his lips, he muttered, "Yep, old Donahue will be surprised when I don't bring his baby girl to him, but he'll never know Vince and I are the ones who made her disappear."

He laughed out loud and spoke once more into the air, saying, "Not bad for a couple of guys who are wanted in three states for rape and murder."

* * * *

Amelia came into their room and smiled at Jed, who was already in bed. "Mother's tucked in."

"Is she feeling better?"

"I think so." She took off her robe and placed it on a chair.

Jed lifted the covers and she slipped in beside him. "I hope she knows I mean it when I say she's welcome to stay here as long as she wants to."

"I think she does. You sure charmed her at supper. I could tell she likes you."

"I like her, too." Jed put his arm around Amelia. "You're a lot like her."

"Thank you. I consider that a compliment because I think my mother is wonderful."

"It was meant as a compliment."

There was a slight pause then Amelia snuggled closer to him. "It upsets me knowing Daddy gave her so much sleeping medicine, Jed. She could have died."

"Maybe he didn't mean to."

"Or maybe he intended to kill her."

"You don't really think he'd try to kill her, do you?"

"I don't want to think it, but right now I wouldn't bet against it. My father has done too many things I didn't think he'd ever do."

"Do you think he'll come here looking for her?"

"Oh, my lord. I hadn't thought of that. What will we do if he does?"

Jed slid his hand up and down her arm. "I'm sorry. I didn't mean to upset you."

"I'm not upset. I was a little surprised because it never entered my mind that he'd come here." She took a deep breath. "I guess I'd better plan what to do in case he shows up."

"There's really nothing we can do about it tonight."

"I'm the one who's sorry now. I'm rattling on and you want to go to sleep."

"I'm not so sleepy. And you're right. We should have a plan."

"You're not humoring me, are you?"

"I'll humor my wife if I want to."

She put her arm around him and kissed his cheek. "Thank you."

"Now, stop that or I might take advantage of you and we won't get around to making a plan."

She giggled. "I won't complain. We could plan later."

"All right, Mrs. Wainwright. Get serious. We'll start with the fact your mother made it clear she didn't want to see Donahue. I feel we should honor her wishes."

"Of course. She can stay in the house if he comes."

"If he insists on coming inside…"

"No. I won't allow him inside. He wouldn't let my husband in his house. Therefore, he's not welcome in mine."

"But he's your father."

"That doesn't matter." She snuggled against him. "Don't you know that anywhere you're not welcome, I'm not welcome either?"

"Amelia, I'm used to being snubbed, ignored and called names because of my heritage. You're not and I don't want you to think you have to defend me. I've been handling such treatment most of my life. It doesn't even bother me anymore."

"Well, it bothers me and now I'm here to handle it all with you. As long as we're married, I intend to take my vows seriously. I'll be there through sickness and health and through name calling and being snubbed or any other thing people do to you."

He was silent, but he did pull her closer.

"You've already shown you'll be there for me, Jed. You defended me from my father, you had a showdown in the saloon over me and now you're helping protect my mother. It's my turn to be there for you. I hope you…" Her voice trailed off.

"I appreciate it, honey, but I can't help being a little surprised you want to be there for me."

"Well, I do."

He kissed the top of her head. "If you're not careful, you're going to mess around and make me fall in love with you."

She muttered something against his chest and he said, "I didn't understand what you said, Amelia. Say it again."

"It's probably better you didn't understand."

He frowned into the night. "Why? Don't I have a right to know?"

"If you insist on knowing, I said, I wish you would start falling in love with me because I'm already falling in love with you."

His body tensed beside her and she felt him pull away. "Please don't fall in love with me, Amelia. It would never work out between us. You know that."

Amelia felt a pain shoot through her heart. "Why not, Jed?"

"When my wife died I lost the capacity to love. There's nothing left in me to share. As wonderful as you are, there's no way I could ever love you the way you deserve to be loved."

Though Jed had made his position clear from the beginning, Amelia was crushed by his words. She felt everything in her wanting to cry. It was at that moment that she knew she loved Jed as deeply as any woman could love a man. If she didn't, it wouldn't hurt so much. She knew, too, though she would never have him as her own, she'd love him until the day she died and there was nothing he could do to make her stop feeling this way.

"Amelia," he said after a long pause, "I'm sorry. I'm only being honest with you."

"I know. You've been honest with me from the first day we met."

"Shall we get back to making a plan to…"

Biting back tears, she said, "Let's talk about it in the morning. I think I want to go to sleep."

"Are you sure?"

"Yes. Good night."

"Good night, Amelia," he said, but he didn't remove his arms from around her.

She said nothing else, but tears pooled in her eyes as she cried silently. She wasn't conscious of the fact Jed felt her wet lashes against his chest.

Chapter 19

Jed watched Amelia slip out of bed at dawn. She removed her gown and washed herself with the water bowl on the dresser. She dressed quickly, brushed and braided her long blonde hair and turned to leave the room.

He sat up. "Good morning," he muttered.

"Good morning. Breakfast will be ready by the time you get to the kitchen." Her voice showed no emotion and she didn't smile at him as she usually did. She slipped out of the room without waiting for him to answer.

Jed moved to the basin, washed himself and dressed in the same clothes he wore the day before. He would be branding today and there was no need to mess up clean clothes. Amelia had to wash his things and he didn't want to put more work on her. As he sat to pull on his boots, he noticed her brush lying beside the water pitcher.

Why it attracted him, he didn't know, but he reached over and picked it up. Though he'd watched her pull the loose hair from it and throw it in the trash can beside the dresser, there were a few long blonde hair strands still in the bristles. He pulled them free and ran them through his fingers. As he realized what he'd done, he tossed the brush on the dresser, rubbed his hand on his ankle and finished putting on his boots.

He opened the door to the hall and the smell of bacon hit his nose. He closed the bedroom door and headed downstairs.

Curt was at the table.

Jed pulled out a chair and sat. "Where is everyone this morning?"

"They ate early." Curt laughed. "Mort said after supper last night, they thought there were too many fancy women at the table for them, so Juanita fed them and got them out the door. I guess they were talking about Amelia and her mother."

Amelia handed Jed a cup of coffee. Juanita placed a platter of bacon on the table and followed it with a bowl of eggs and a basket of biscuits.

"Mother hasn't come down yet. She's used to sleeping later." Amelia took the chair beside Jed and sipped her coffee.

"We'll see she eats when she wakes up." Juanita took a seat. "Miguel was excited last night because you let him help out with the branding yesterday, Curt. He had a hard time going to sleep so I thought it would be all right to let him stay in bed a little longer this morning."

"It's fine, Juanita." Curt smiled at her. "The boy did a good job yesterday and he deserves to rest."

Jed dipped eggs onto his plate and passed them to Amelia. He then picked up the bacon. "I think we'll let Miguel or Andy help out around the house this morning. We won't be far away, but I want someone here to come for me if Donahue happens to show up."

"I think that's a good idea." Curt filled his plate.

"I don't think it's necessary," Amelia said in a flat voice.

Jed frowned. "Why not?"

"I'm going to have to get used to taking care of my problems without your help, and I might as well start today."

Everyone looked at her. Curt broke the tension which settled on the group. "I don't see why you say that, Amelia. Jed will always back you up."

Jed didn't say anything. He was waiting to see what she'd say.

She looked at Curt. "You're getting the herd ready to drive to market. I figure it'll take the both of you away for a few weeks. Miguel and Juanita will be my only back up then, and things won't have changed between my father and me."

Jed knew she wasn't talking about the cattle drive. She was thinking of when their six months were up, but he still didn't say anything.

Again Curt spoke. "I'm not sure it'll take both of us for the drive. What do you think, Jed?"

"One of us could handle it with no problem. I think one of us should stay here. After Juanita and Miguel's experience, I wouldn't feel right leaving the women alone."

Without warning, Amelia jumped up and pushed her chair backward. She ran out the back door.

"What in the world?" Curt looked confused.

Jed and Juanita stood at the same time, but she spoke first. "Let me go, Jed."

He nodded and sat down.

When they were alone, Curt said, "Looks like you may have had your first disagreement, my friend."

"I wouldn't call it that." Jed wasn't about to tell Curt why Amelia was upset. "We need to hurry and join the men at the branding pit."

"Aren't you going to wait and check on your wife?"

"I'll see her as we leave." He took another biscuit and refused to be drawn into a conversation about Amelia.

"I'm about ready, but I have to say one thing before we go." When Jed ignored him, he went on. "I'm one of the few people who knows what you went through when you lost Marie, but that's all in the past now. You now have a chance to be happy again with Amelia. The woman is crazy about you and you know everybody doesn't get a second chance in this life. I don't want to see you blow it."

Ignoring Curt's statement, Jed put down his fork. "Let's head out."

"Did you hear what I said or are you ignoring it?"

"My marriage to Amelia is none of your business, Curt. I don't appreciate you interfering so drop it." Jed stood. "We have cows to brand."

Curt shook his head. "Man, there's times when I don't understand you at all. I loved my wife, too, but if I had a chance with someone like Amelia, I'd jump at it."

When Jed said nothing, Curt shrugged and followed him out the door without saying anything else.

Jed saw Amelia and Juanita walking back from the privy. It was possible his wife wasn't mad. She could have had an emergency and had to hurry out. He walked toward them.

"Are you all right?"

"I'm fine. I'm sorry I ran out so quickly."

He smiled at her. "As I said, we'll be close. I want to help if your father shows up."

"I know you do and I appreciate it." She returned his smile though hers was a weak one.

He leaned down and kissed her cheek. He whispered, "Things will work out."

She nodded. "I know."

He then turned and mounted one of the horses Mort brought from the barn.

* * * *

Amelia watched until he was out of sight, then she turned and began throwing up. She didn't know how she'd kept from letting him know she was sick. She was upchucking for the third time and she wondered how much more could be in her stomach. She'd been sick before, but never like this.

Juanita wasn't helping. She simply stood beside her and grinned. Amelia wanted to smack her, but of course she didn't.

Finally, her stomach seemed to settle and she looked at Juanita. "I'm sorry I ruined your nice breakfast, but I couldn't help it. I don't know why I got so sick. It was sudden and unexpected. I hope nobody else catches it."

Juanita laughed. "Amelia, nobody is going to catch it because I think I know exactly what your problem is."

"What?"

"I bet you're pregnant."

Amelia looked stunned. "No. I can't be."

"Are you sure?"

"I don't…of course we… Oh, my goodness… What will I do… I mean…"

"My friend, you'll do what women have been doing for thousands of years. You'll have a beautiful baby and make your husband proud."

"I can't let Jed know."

"Why not? He'll be excited, I'm sure. Most husbands look forward to their first child."

"No, Juanita. You can't tell him. I want to be sure and…"

"I wouldn't presume to take it on myself to tell him, Amelia. That's your job and if you want to wait, I understand. I can keep my mouth shut if I have to."

"I don't want anyone to know, Juanita. Not yet. You have to keep my secret from everyone."

"Even your mother?"

"Yes. Especially my mother."

Juanita frowned. "I don't understand why, but I'll keep your secret if you're sure you want me to."

"I'm sure and thank you."

A voice came from the back porch. "Mama, where are you?" He sounded scared.

"I'm here, Miguel."

They reached the porch.

"I came into the kitchen and didn't see you. I was sc… I mean, I didn't know where you were."

"Miz Amelia wasn't feeling well and I took a little walk with her. I'm sorry I wasn't there when you got up. I'll get your breakfast now."

"Are you feeling better, Miz Amelia?"

"Yes, Miguel. Thank you for asking."

"I think she should lie down for a while. She'll be fine by this afternoon if she'll get a little rest."

Amelia nodded. "I'm sorry to leave you with all the work this morning, but I think I will go to my room for a little while."

"Don't let it worry you. I'll be fine. Miguel will help me, won't you, son?"

"Sure."

Amelia nodded and headed up the stairs. She stretched out on the bed, stared at the ceiling and let the questions enter her mind. Of course, Juanita was right. She was pregnant. She'd wondered why she hadn't had her monthly for a couple of months, but she figured it was the hard work and the stress of her situation. But the upchucking confirmed the fact that she was with child. What in the world was she going to do now? There were two more months left in the marriage contract. Could she hide the fact there was a baby for two months? If she let Jed know she was going to have a child, would he end the marriage or would he force her to leave? She didn't think he'd make her leave, but did she want him to stay with her because of the baby? She knew the answer to that was "no". If he didn't want to stay with her without a baby, she didn't want him to stay with her because she was going to have one. Then she wondered if he'd be upset if she didn't tell him. She closed her eyes and thought. When they popped open, she had her answer. She would keep the secret until the marriage ended. Then, she'd go visit her aunt in St. Louis. When she came back, she would introduce Jed to her baby. That way if he wanted to be in the child's life he could be.

With it settled in her mind, she turned over and hugged the pillow to her chest. She smelled Jed's scent. It was comforting and she drifted off.

* * * *

Jed let one cow get away before it was branded and Curt had to rope it and get it back in line. Jed cursed and tried to shift his mind back to his work, but he found it wasn't easy. He could still see Amelia's haunted eyes when she said she might as well get used to handling her own problems. Though she covered well by talking about the cattle drive, he knew the drive had nothing to do with it. She meant she'd have to handle her problems when they were no longer living together. Of course, he knew she'd be fine. The sheriff knew Vince Callahan was behind Roberto Garcia's killing and Amelia no longer had to worry about being forced to marry him. Rafe would probably have to go to jail for his part in everything, and Amelia was capable of running the Double D as well as her father, especially since he and Curt would be close by to help her.

In fact, there was no reason to stay married now that the problem of the forced nuptials was no longer an issue. They could end the marriage today if they desired, but he'd agreed to stay married to her for six months and he would honor the agreement unless she decided there was no need to stay together. Maybe he'd ask her tonight what she wanted to do.

"Watch it, boss." Elton Bowler's voice cut into his thoughts. "Damn, if you didn't almost brand my hand."

"Sorry," Jed muttered and pulled his thoughts away from Amelia. "Take over here, Ward."

"Sure."

Jed backed away and headed for the pasture. No matter how many times Amelia invaded his thoughts he figured he couldn't make a mistake if he ran the cows into the branding pen. Any fool could do that.

* * * *

Vince Callahan could've made it back to the Double D a day earlier, but the little redhead in the house of pleasure had been worth the extra day. He felt satisfied as he rode his horse southward and who was to know he'd dallied a day. It was a man's right, whether he was single or married. It wasn't natural to be faithful to one woman. Of course after he married Amelia, he'd be like Rafe. He'd use women away from Settlers Ridge for variety and not embarrass his wife. Until after she gave him a child or two anyway. After that it wouldn't matter. She'd be stuck.

As he neared the turnoff, he thought about going into town for a bath and shave before heading for the ranch, but he changed his mind. He was anxious to see if Rafe had been able to get Amelia to come home or if Smithy was able to get her to the cabin. It was vital to his plan for one or the other to have taken place. Getting her away from Wainwright was the key for the rest of his life. Of course, it would be fun to whip her into line, but the main thing was to marry her so the ranch would be left to her, and through the union, be his. It didn't matter that she'd been sleeping with the damn half-breed bounty hunter. He'd heard rumors of how the Indian was capable of making a woman beg him for more of his loving. Amelia would soon learn he could satisfy her in a way Wainwright never could.

Of course, Rafe was fool enough to think he was going to be gentle and loving to his precious child, not demand she bend to his will. But she would end up bending any way he desired. That was what a wife was for. After all, he'd already had one who wouldn't do what he wanted her to. That's why she wasn't his wife any longer.

As for the ranch, there was no way he'd go on as the foreman after the marriage, though Rafe expected him to. What the fool didn't know was he'd be sole owner of this ranch. Though they didn't suspect a thing, Rafe and the snooty Elizabeth would never see these things come about. The couple would leave on the long-intended trip to Europe, but they'd never come home. If all went as planned, they'd never get out of this country. Several types of accidents could befall them, before they left Wyoming. Vince was already working on the plan to get rid of them.

Rounding a curve, the majestic main house on the Double D came into Vince's view. He grinned. He couldn't wait to make his home in that place. He and Amelia would sleep in the largest and most elaborate bedroom. He'd probably keep Delores on as housekeeper. The woman was a damn good cook. Vince did like a good meal after a hard day's work and a good breakfast after a night of hard loving. Of course, his cowhands would be doing most of the work on the ranch. He'd do like Rafe does now. He'd sit in his study, drink expensive whisky, count his money and when he was in the mood, he'd demand Amelia come to him and submit to his every whim.

His thoughts were interrupted when he saw Rafe walking across the back yard toward the barn. He sped his horse up and watched as Rafe paused and looked in his direction. He reined up beside him. "Where you headed, boss?"

"It's a long story. Give your horse to Richard and let him rub him down, then come in the house and let me catch you up on what's happened around here."

Vince nodded. After turning his horse over to the stable boy, he hurried toward the house thinking maybe Amelia had come home. Rafe was waiting for him on the porch. "Come on in the study. Want a drink?"

"Sure do. I could use one of Delores's good meals, too."

"That's not going to happen today." There was a snarl in Rafe's voice.

Vince frowned as they crossed the dining room. He was surprised to see dirty dishes and a couple of open jars left on the table, but he didn't ask any questions. He felt Rafe would tell him everything.

After Rafe finished his story, Vince cursed then said, "So, your wife has deserted you and I'm a wanted man."

"That's about it."

Vince took a swallow of his liquor. "I had nothing to do with that damn Mexican's death. You believe me, don't you?"

"Of course, I do. I told Lance Gentry as much."

"Thanks. I knew you'd always stand behind me."

"You know I will, Vince. After all, you were the one who kept me from losing everything when old man Downey was alive. If it wasn't for you, the bastard would have eventually run me off this ranch."

"We couldn't have that could we, boss? You'd worked too hard and sacrificed too much to be put out."

"You're damn right. When I married Elizabeth, I married this ranch, too. It was part of the bargain I made with myself."

"I understand that." He sipped his whisky. "Could I get a refill?"

"Sure." Raft stood and brought the crystal decanter to his desk. He refilled Vince's glass. Then his own. "There's one more thing I need to tell you about, Vince."

"What's that?"

"A woman came by here to see you. Said her name was Esther Venable. Know her?"

Vince arched an eyebrow. "Never heard of her. What did she say?"

"Said she'd see you when you returned. I figured she was some woman who had you mixed up with someone else." Rafe drank the rest of the whiskey in his glass and stood. "Now you know everything and I'm going to get Elizabeth. Can you believe she's staying with that half-breed and Amelia?"

"I'm surprised, but I'm not sure it's a good idea for you to go running down there to get her."

Rafe frowned. "Why not? I want her to come home."

"If you go to Wainwright's ranch, there's a good chance Elizabeth won't come home with you, Rafe. You said yourself she can be stubborn at times."

"That's true, but she'll come home this time. I'll make her."

"And how's that going to look to the sheriff? You said he suspected you tried to kill her when you gave her the sleeping medicine."

"But I didn't. I only wanted to make her sleep late so she wouldn't go traipsing off to find Amelia."

"Is the sheriff going to believe that?"

Rafe paused. "Why wouldn't he? It's the truth."

"Think about it, Rafe. He thinks I murdered the Mexican. Now your wife almost dies. He's going to put things together and think you were behind both."

"Damn it, Vince. I wasn't behind anything."

"I know that and you know that, but others might think differently."

"Then what the hell should I do?" Rafe dropped back in his chair.

Vince took a long drink of his whiskey. "Write her a letter. Apologize several times. Say all those things women like to hear whether they're true or not. Tell her you love her and you can't live without her, but you're afraid to come for her because the bastard bounty hunter might shoot you. Of course, leave out the bastard part."

Rafe almost smiled. "Then what?"

"Ask her to come home and add something like you'll have a candle-lit dinner waiting." He thought a minute. "Tell her you want her to accompany Richard back to you."

Rafe frowned. "Richard?"

"Yeah. You're going to have him take the letter to Elizabeth."

"Do you really think it'll work?"

"What have you got to lose?"

"I guess you're right."

"While you're busy wooing Elizabeth, I'll make plans to bring Amelia home."

Rafe's face lit up. "How?"

"Leave that to me. I'll clue you in later."

"I knew I could count on you, Vince."

"If you only knew how much, Rafe." Vince grinned and held his glass up in a salute. Inside he could hardly believe how gullible the man was. He'd been leading him around by the nose for over four years and the fool didn't suspect a thing.

When Rafe finished writing the letter he handed it to Vince. "I sure hope this works. Believe it or not, I miss Elizabeth. Something is not right around here when she's gone."

"I hope I feel that way when I'm married to Amelia." Vince headed for the door. "I'll send Richard to you so you can tell him what to do."

"Thanks, Vince." Rafe picked up the decanter and poured himself another drink.

Richard was confused when he arrived at the study and Rafe told him to take one of the good horses and deliver the letter to Elizabeth at the Lawson place. "Be sure to tell them all I want is my wife to come home."

"Yes, sir. I'll do it."

Vince walked Richard to the front door and waited until he saw him ride out. He then returned to the study. Taking the refilled drink Rafe offered, he said, "There's one more thing. I hate to ask you this, boss, but I put your money from the cattle sale in the bank and I need a little to run on until we get our plans worked out."

"Sure. That's no problem. How much do you need?" Rafe moved to the safe in the corner of his study.

"Make it fifty."

The safe swung open and Rafe took out a stack of bills. He turned to face the barrel of Vince's pistol. "What the hell?"

"I'll take it all, boss."

Still confused, Rafe gasped, "I don't understand, Vince?"

Vince snarled. "Rafe, you're such a fool. Now I'm wanted by the sheriff, I need the money to get away."

"But you didn't—"

"Of course, I did. I had Garcia beat up. Hell, I thought the wetback was dead. I intended to add his ranch to this one so I'd have the biggest ranch in Wyoming when I take over the Double D. I now know I should have killed the kid."

"But, I thought—"

"Damn, Rafe, I know what you thought. You wanted me to marry your prissy little daughter and be your flunky until you and your fancy wife decided to die. Well, that would've taken too long. I had other plans. They would've worked out if Amelia hadn't married Wainwright. Now I've got to adjust my plans."

"I can't believe I could've been so wrong about a man." Rafe looked devastated.

Vince laughed. "You're the easiest man to bamboozle I've ever met, Rafe Donahue. I planted all those suspicions in your mind about your father-in-law. The man never had any intention of taking this ranch from you. All he wanted was for his daughter and granddaughter to be happy. Then after old man Downey died, all I had to do was to make myself indispensable to you. That way I came off as your right-hand man. At first, all I wanted was to get my hands on a wad of your money. I was headed to California because I knew they'd never catch up with me there, but as I saw how you rich folks lived, I decided to stick around to see how I could live the same way, too."

"Who was trying to catch up with you?"

"Hell, I might as well tell you. Esther Venable is my ex-wife. She divorced me after she caught me with her cousin. She might have forgiven me, but I had to kill her brother over the cousin. Esther vowed she'd find me someday and make me pay." He let a wide grin cross his face. "Of course I never thought she'd have the guts to come after me. Sad situation. Me and that little cousin of hers had a blast all the way from North Carolina to Kansas, where I had to drop her. She got it in her head she wanted to marry me and start raising a brood of kids. Hell, I already had two kids by Esther. I never intended to have any more, except maybe a couple out of pretty Amelia. A kid would keep her busy after her ma and pa's untimely death."

Rafe gasped and Vince laughed again.

"Ain't you sorry you didn't listen to your father-in-law about not keeping me around? Good thing he died when he did. He could have screwed everything up if you'd started listening to him."

Rafe felt his whole world collapsing. "You didn't kill him, did you?"

"I would have, but I didn't get a chance. Nature took him with his weak heart." Vince shrugged. "Now you know enough. Put everything in the safe in one of those bags you have folded there. Me and Amelia's got to have something to live on."

"You're not taking Amelia."

"Of course, I am. Didn't you always want me and her to be together?" He was enjoying watching the reaction on Rafe's face. "Can't wait to get my hands on that pretty little body of hers."

"I'll hunt you down…"

Vince shook his head. "You don't even know my real name."

"I assume it's Venable."

"Oh, yeah. The bitch told you." He waved the gun. "Get the sack loaded. I've got plans for your money. I figure I'll set us up in a nice little whore house in California and get rich. Amelia will be quiet a draw, don't you think."

"Why, you dirty bastard." Rafe leapt toward Vince, but he was too late.

Vince fired and Rafe fell backward, hitting his head on the corner of the fireplace.

Once outside, it didn't take Vince long to set fire at the corner of the house. He'd decided to burn the place, but he didn't have time to make sure it was completely destroyed. With luck, it would catch. Richard was away and he knew Wayne Rivers and the other hand that had stayed here from the cattle drive were working out on the range. Too bad the snooty Elizabeth was away. He'd like to know she died in the fire, too.

Chapter 20

Amelia and her mother were sitting on the front porch having a cup of tea and chatting about the beautiful day when the front door opened. Jed stepped out. "Hello, Elizabeth."

"Hello, Jed. I'm sorry I didn't see you at breakfast. I must confess, as I get older, I like sleeping late."

"You have a right to sleep as late as you want."

"Is something wrong at the branding site?" Amelia looked at him.

"Everything's fine. The men were taking a break to eat the meal Juanita and Delores packed for them. I took advantage of the time to come check on you. I knew you weren't feeling well this morning."

"How sweet of you, son," Elizabeth said.

"Yes, it was thoughtful, but as I said I'm, fine. You didn't have to sacrifice your work time." Amelia couldn't keep the coolness out of her voice.

"Well, if you two will excuse me, I think I'll go see if Delores has the soup ready the doctor wanted me to have. I didn't eat much breakfast and I'm a little hungry." Elizabeth stood.

"You don't have to go, Mother."

"I know, dear, but I'm sure Jed didn't come to see me." She smiled at Amelia then slipped through the door.

"It looks like you and your mother are enjoying her visit."

"Yes. We've been talking about going to St. Louis to visit her sister. I haven't seen my Aunt Josephine in a long time."

"When are you planning to go?"

"Why are you interested? It looks like your duty to me is over."

Amelia's voice went up an octave.

Jed moved beside her chair and took her arm. "If you're going to yell your answers, let's take a walk."

"I don't want to go for a walk."

"Well, you're going." His grip was firm and she knew he meant what he was saying.

She let him lead her off the porch and toward the sycamore tree in the corner of the yard.

"I think we're far enough away from the house. You can yell back at me if you like."

"I don't want to yell at you, Amelia. I'm here because I was concerned about you."

"Why, Jed?" A tear came in her eye.

He was quiet a moment, then he reached for her and pulled her against him. "Because looking after you has become a habit."

"You now know I want to be more than a habit to you."

"I do know, but I explained to you, why it would never work. I—"

She jerked away from him. "I only know one thing. You want to get rid of me. So be it. I'll pack my clothes tonight, and Mother and I will head for St. Louis tomorrow."

"Amelia, you don't have to go. We can—"

"We can what, Jed? Stay together two more months so you can get your next five thousand dollars. Well, don't worry. I'll put it in your account before I leave town."

"I don't want your damn money."

"Then what do you want?"

"I want you to relax and take care of your mother. We'll discuss all this when she goes home."

"She doesn't want to go home. She wants to go see her sister and I want to go with her."

"Then, wait until—"

"Until what? Until you decide you'll be happy with your whores again?"

"I'm not interested in whores."

"Then what are you interested in, Jed? Tell me. I want to know."

"Right now, all I want is for you to calm down."

Amelia gritted her teeth. "I will not calm down. I want to scream and yell. I want to hit you in the head with the first thing I get my hands on. I want to stop loving you and at the same time I want to make you love me back. But I can't and I have to live with that. So don't worry your handsome head about it. I'll go to St. Louis and get a job as a school teacher or something. You won't have to worry about ever seeing me again."

"Amelia, you'll meet somebody someday and get married and be happy. I know you will."

"You don't know a damn thing about it. You spend too much of your time living with the ghost of Marie. When that gets too lonely for you, you run to the whores." She let out a coarse laugh. "Maybe I should get a job in a bordello. You could visit me then."

He grabbed her shoulders and stared into her eyes. "You're talking foolish, and I don't want to hear words like that come from your mouth ever again."

She tried to jerk away, but he had a firm grip on her. "Why not? A whore is what I am."

He shook her. "You know damn good and well that's not so."

"Let's face it. You bought my body for six months with your name and now that you're through with me, you're going to start handing out money when you want your pleasure in bed. You paid me with your name, and you'll pay them with money. That makes us all whores. I don't see a difference, do you?"

"For God's sake, Amelia, you're being ridiculous. I'm going back to work and we'll talk about this later. In the state you're in, there's no reasoning with you."

"Go on back to your branding. When you come in tonight, don't worry if I'm not here. You can sleep with the ghost of your precious Marie." She did jerk away this time. Shaking her hair over her shoulder, she turned and marched toward the house.

"If you're still acting this way when I come in, I don't give a damn whether you're here or not."

Amelia didn't think she could be hurt any more, but those stinging words cut into her soul. She heard Jed walk in the other direction, but she was too hurt to turn around. As she entered the house, her mother met her at the door.

"Honey, what's wrong?"

"Nothing."

"Don't say that, Amelia. I'm your mother. I know when something is wrong with my child."

Amelia burst into tears. "Jed and I had a fight."

"Oh, honey." Elizabeth put her arms around her daughter. "Was it your first?"

"I guess. We had some words last night and today we fought. We said some really mean things to each other."

"That's normal, dear. He'll come in tonight all apologetic and you'll forgive him. Your love will be stronger than ever."

Amelia shook her head. "No, it won't, Mother. Jed doesn't love me."

"Of course he loves you, darling. All anyone has to do is watch the way he looks at you."

"He has everyone fooled."

"How can you say that, Amelia?"

"I can say it because he told me last night he didn't love me. He also said he never would."

"I can't believe that."

"It's the truth, Mother. I wish it wasn't, but it is." Amelia clung to her mother's neck and began to sob. "The saddest part of it all is I love him with all my heart and I know I always will."

Elizabeth held her daughter and let her cry. At this point there was nothing else she could do.

* * * *

Jed was holding a calf for Curt to brand. He was still angry with Amelia and had been trying not to show it for the last two hours. Couldn't the woman see he did care for her? Not in the way she wanted, but he wasn't heartless, though she'd made him feel like he was. Didn't she know she'd be better off without him? Once Vince Callahan swung from a rope, she'd have her pick of any man in Settlers Ridge. Why in the world would she want to tie herself to a half-breed? Didn't she know being with him hurt her chances of ever being invited to the big social events in town? Being Rafe Donahue's daughter wouldn't change things. Even if he did love her, he'd never let her tie herself to him for the rest of her life. It wouldn't be fair and in the end, she'd probably hate him.

Curt landed the brand. The cow bellowed and Jed let it go. He reached for the next one.

"Man, you haven't said two words since you came back. Is everything all right at the house?"

"It's fine."

"Uh oh. That means something's wrong. What is it?"

Jed frowned at him. "If you must know, Amelia and I had an argument."

"I figured as much. She acted strange at breakfast."

"It'll be all right."

"Sure it will. All you have to do is get down on your knees and beg her forgiveness."

"I'm not going to do that and you know it."

"I know it'd be hard for you to say you're wrong. You've never wanted to admit it, but in this case you probably are."

"What the hell do you mean?"

"I know sweet Amelia couldn't…."

His words were cut off when two shots rang in the air.

Jed let the calf go and Curt dropped the branding iron. "Something's wrong at the house," Curt said and headed toward his horse.

"Take over, Ward," Jed yelled as he followed.

When they reached the house, both men jumped from their saddles and ran toward Delores, who was hovered over a form on the ground. Juanita was holding Miguel by the shoulders. She and her son were crying.

Jed wasn't sure his knees were going to hold him. Amelia's angry, hurt face flashed before his eyes as his heart fell to his stomach. She had told him she loved him and he'd flung it back in her face. How could he have hurt her so?

"What happened?" Curt asked.

Delores was holding Elizabeth's head off the ground and was cleaning blood from her face. "He hit her with his gun," Delores said.

"Who hit her?" Jed went to his knees and held his mother-in-law as Delores bandaged her head.

"Vince Callahan," Elizabeth muttered.

"It was the man who held me so they could kill Poppa," Miguel cried.

Jed's heart thumped. "Where's Amelia?"

"He took her." With Jed's help, Elizabeth got to her feet. "They…"

A horse came into the yard. Both Curt and Jed pulled their guns.

"Don't shoot me," the boy cried. "I came to bring something to Miz

Elizabeth."

Jed holstered his gun. "I think Elizabeth will be all right. I'm going after Amelia."

"Wait." Curt took his arm. "Maybe this has something to do with Amelia."

Jed hesitated and turned toward Richard. "Give it to me, boy."

"It's for Miz Elizabeth." The scared boy looked down from his horse at her. "Are you all right, Ma'am?"

"Give it to Jed, Richard."

Jed scanned the letter. "Nothing here." He handed the letter to Elizabeth. "Your husband wants you to come home."

Elizabeth was leaning on Delores. "I should go see what's going on."

Jed didn't answer, but headed for his horse.

Again Curt stopped him. "Use your head, Jed. Treat this as one of your chases. If you go running off without knowing where you're going…"

"You're right." Though his heart was pounding and he wanted to run after Amelia as fast as the horse would take him, he knew he had to be smart. He'd get her back faster. He turned toward Elizabeth. "Where was Amelia when he took her?"

She showed him and in few minutes, he had the tracks picked out. He was glad Curt had stopped him. He would've headed down the road toward town, but after finding the tracks left in the yard he saw they headed toward the back of the ranch which connected it to the Double D.

"Get two or three of the men, Curt. I don't have time to go for Lance Gentry. We're forming our own posse." He straightened up. "Delores, we'll send the others back to watch out here."

"I'm going to go home, Jed."

He frowned. "Why, Elizabeth?"

"I want to know if Rafe is behind this and I intend to find out."

"But…"

"Don't argue with me. I'll be fine."

"If you go, at least let one of the men go with you."

"All right, I will, but you forget about me. All I want is for you to go find my daughter for me."

Jed leaned over and kissed her cheek. "I'll find her for both of us."

Ward, Andy and Elton rode up with Curt and the four men headed out across the yard behind Jed.

* * * *

Mort stayed with Juanita and Miguel. Darrel Reed, Richard, and Delores struck out to the Double D with Elizabeth. They were still some distance away when they saw smoke coming from the vicinity of the ranch.

Elizabeth grabbed her throat. "Oh, Lord, he must have burned my house."

"It could be something else, Ma'am," Darrel suggested. "We have to burn lots of things on ranches."

"The men are on a cattle drive. I don't think the few left would burn anything that would create that much smoke."

She turned to Delores with tears in her eyes. "Everything I own is in the house."

Delores patted her hand. "Maybe we'll get there in time to put it out."

It was as if Elizabeth didn't hear Delores. She placed her hands over her face and began to sob. "My daughter has been kidnapped and my home is burning, and only God knows what has happened to my husband."

Delores held Elizabeth's hand tightly. "You're a strong woman, Miz Elizabeth. You can handle anything this old world throws at you. Please dry your tears and try to be strong. We don't know what'll be facing us at your house, but we know Mr. Jed is going to bring Miz Amelia home to us and we have to be brave for her. She's going to need our support when Mr. Jed gets her away from that terrible man."

Elizabeth rubbed her eyes with the back of her hand. "Of course, you're right, Delores. I have to be strong for the others. Thank God I have you to remind me of it sometimes."

They were silent until the house came into view. There was still smoldering smoke, but it looked like the fire was out. The house was blackened on the side and one of the columns on the front porch had fallen. "Oh, my Lord, I hope nobody was hurt." Elizabeth moaned. "Drive faster, Darrel."

"Yes, Ma'am." He slapped the horse's rear with the reins.

"I'll take care of the horses, Miz Elizabeth," Richard said when Darrel pulled her buggy to a stop in front of the scarred mansion.

"Thank you, young man."

Darrel jumped down and turned to help the women from the buggy. As soon as Elizabeth's feet touched ground, she started to run toward the house. Darrel grabbed her arm. "Wait. You better not get too close, Ma'am. It could be dangerous. It looks like that porch roof could collapse at any moment.'"

"I've got to see if Rafe is all right." Elizabeth looked at Darrel. "He could be hurt."

Wayne Rivers appeared at the door. "I heard the buggy pull up. Hello, Mrs. Donahue."

"Where's Rafe, Wayne? Is he inside?" She pulled her arm from Darrel's hand and headed toward the porch.

Delores followed her.

"Yes, Ma'am. He's been hurt so I put him in the back room. It seems to be safe in there." He met her at the top of the steps. "Be careful coming in. There are some loose boards on the porch."

Elizabeth took the hand he offered and stepped carefully across the porch and inside the entry. Without saying anything, she headed to the first floor bedroom. The others followed her. As soon as she opened the door and entered the room, she let out a gasp and ran to her husband.

He looked awfully white and there was blood all over his chest where the shirt had been ripped away. His eyes were closed and she knelt beside him and asked no one in particular, "Is he dead?"

Darrel moved next to the bed, reached down and touched Rafe's wrist then his throat. "He's alive, Ma'am, but barely. Looks like he's been shot and needs a doctor immediately."

"Yes, yes. Get the doctor, someone," Elizabeth cried. "Delores, get…"

"As soon as we got the fire out, I sent for the doc, Miz Elizabeth," Wayne Rivers said. "He should be here anytime now."

Delores put her hand on Elizabeth's shoulder. "Let me see if I can help him, Ma'am. I might be able to help stop some of this bleeding."

Elizabeth moved over and Delores knelt beside her.

Rafe's eyes flickered. "Elizabeth…"

"I'm here, Rafe." She bit her lip to hold back tears. "Can you tell us what happened?"

"Elizabeth…" His voice trailed off.

"Don't try to talk, Rafe. You can tell us what happened later. You need to save your strength now." She squeezed his hand and looked at Wayne. "Do you know what transpired here?"

"Cal and me was working down by the creek. He happened to see the smoke and we got here as fast as we could. The fire was pretty bad and it took us a little while, but we managed to get it out. Then I thought I better check inside. I found the boss trying to crawl out. If Cal hadn't seen the smoke, it would have burned down with the boss inside."

"I'm thankful you got here in time." She looked back at her husband. "Did he say anything?"

"He said the name Vince."

"Do you think Callahan did this?" Darrel asked.

"There's not a doubt in my mind that he did it." Wayne Rivers looked determined. "That fool is capable of anything."

Elizabeth looked up at Wayne and tears ran down her cheeks. "If Vince Callahan tried to kill Rafe, what will that evil man do to my daughter?"

"Don't worry, Miz Donahue. Jed won't let anything happen to her," Darrel said.

"What if he's too late?"

"He won't be. When it comes to tracking a man, ain't nobody better than Jed Wainwright." He glanced back at Wayne Rivers. "Why don't we leave these ladies here to look after Mr. Donahue until the Doctor arrives? We should check the damage the fire did and see if there's a way we can shore up the porch so it won't be a danger."

Wayne nodded.

Darrel turned to Delores. "Come get us if you need anything."

Delores nodded. "Thank you, Darrel."

The men left and Elizabeth looked at Rafe with tears in her eyes. "Oh, you foolish man. I guess you now realize you trusted Vince Callahan too far, don't you, Rafe?"

"Do you really think Vince Callahan did this?" Delores was removing the crude bandage Wayne had put on Rafe.

"I know he did. I'm sure he sent Richard to get me so he could sneak in the back way and steal Amelia. Vince is an evil man,

Delores. I think I've always known, but there was no convincing Rafe the man had any faults."

"Now, he knows."

"But is it too late for him to rectify his mistake and make up with his daughter?"

"If the doctor doesn't get here soon, it may be." Delores sighed. "Now we have to get busy. I need some hot water and a slew of bandages. Tear up a sheet if you have to. In the meantime I'm going to use his shirt to hold the wound together."

"I'll get the rest for you." Elizabeth stood, brushed back tears and scurried out of the room. She didn't mind taking instructions from her maid. At least Delores seemed to know what she was doing. Elizabeth sure didn't. She'd never had to deal with a gunshot wound before and having something to do kept her from falling apart about all that was happening to those in her family at this moment.

* * * *

When Amelia opened her eyes, it took her a minute to realize where she was. Then it came back. Vince had hit her mother with the butt of his rifle and when she tried to rescue her mother, he had roughly grabbed her and threw her in front of him on his horse. When she tried to fight him and get off the animal, he'd hit her in the mouth with his fist. She didn't remember anything else until they arrived at this cabin. She recognized it as one of the line shacks on the back of her father's ranch. When Vince pushed her inside, she fought him again and he'd hit her in the mouth once more with his fist. Everything then went black. He must have thrown her on this rough cot. Her head was turned to the wall and he didn't know she was conscious. He was talking with somebody, so to keep him from knowing she'd regained consciousness, she closed her eyes and listened, hoping she'd pick up some kind of clue on how to escape.

"Don't you think we should head on out of here, Vince?"

"Not yet. There's one more thing I need to do."

"What's that?"

"I'm going to kill the breed before I go."

"Think he'll come alone to rescue her?"

"Absolutely. Indians ain't that smart. He'll be so mad he'll not think to get back-up."

"What if you don't kill him when he gets here?"

"Damn it, Smithy, I'm not the bad shot you are. I'll kill him on the first try."

"I'm not a bad shot."

"The hell you're not. You missed him the day they came to the ranch and he shot you in the arm. Now you tell me you missed the man driving the wagon and Amelia shot you in the shoulder. You've messed up twice. I don't know why I don't get rid of you for all the help you've been to me."

"I would've got 'em if they hadn't been too far away. Besides, I beat the hell out of that Mexican for you."

"Yeah. Are you going to try to make me pay you for that like Herb Dinkins did?" Vince's voice had a sneer in it.

"What'd Dinkins do?"

"The damn fool wanted me to pay him double for working the cattle drive or he threatened to tell everyone I was behind the wetback's murder."

"How'd you convince him not to tell?"

"Got him in the middle of the herd and shoved him off his horse." Vince laughed his vicious laugh. "Wasn't a sign of him after five thousand cattle took a stroll over his body. And the best part was nobody knew what happened. They decided he must have run off because the work was too hard."

"I ain't gonna tell nobody nothing." Smithy's voice sounded scared.

"That's smart of you. Now, give me a cup of coffee. It should be done by now."

"Want somethin' to eat, boss? I heated the stew and it's pretty good."

"Give me a bowl."

"When's your gal gonna wake up? She could probably cook somethin' good."

"Go check on her."

Feet moved across the bare floor. Amelia kept her eyes closed.

"Sleeping like a baby."

"Then get me some stew. She'll eventually wake up."

The feet moved away.

"She's such a pretty little thing, I'm surprised you ain't took her yet, boss."

"All in good time, Smithy. I want her to be wide awake and I want the bounty hunter tied up in a chair right over there watching when I show her and him both what a real man can do."

Smithy laughed. "You sure do know how to get revenge."

"Damn right I do. If it hadn't been for that bastard, I'd be married to the bitch and be the sole owner of the Double D by now. Instead, all I got is the money I took from Donahue's safe and the daughter he planned to give me anyway."

"You gonna marry her now?"

"Hell no. Got no reason to. All I wanted from that marriage was a couple of kids and the title to the Double D Ranch. Since that's not going to happen I've decided as soon as I get to California with her, she's going to start making up for the money I've lost."

"How's she gonna do that?"

"Look at her, Smithy. As you said, she's beautiful. Those California men will pay a good price to get between those legs."

Smithy laughed again. "If I save up my money, can I get a turn?"

"Your money is as good as anybody's."

There was a pause.

"Why did you get so quiet, Smithy?"

"I think I heard something outside."

"Check and see if it's him." A chair scraped and a gun cocked. "If he's found us, it's time for the fun to begin."

Amelia felt her heart leap into her throat. She hoped Jed had used his head and brought someone with him.

Chapter 21

Jed crept to where Curt was squatted behind a mass of twisted bushes. "There are two horses stabled in a shed. There's another window in the back of the cabin, but it's covered. Elton and Andy are there to make sure nobody leaves the back way. Ward's off to your right. I think I made enough noise to get one of them to come out and check."

"How many do you think are there?"

Jed shook his head. "If we go by the horses, there are only two."

"Then this should be easy."

"We have to make sure Amelia doesn't get hurt."

"That goes without saying, my friend."

The cabin door opened a crack and the barrel of a rifle came out. A raspy voice asked, "Is that you, bounty hunter?"

Jed nodded to Curt and then to Ward. He stepped forward, but shielded himself behind a tree. "Where's my wife?" he shouted, letting the anger show in his voice.

"You ain't got no wife now, red man. She belongs to Vince just like it was always meant to be."

Before he could reply, Amelia screamed.

Jed had the urge to rush forward to rescue her, but he managed to control himself. He gritted his teeth. "If either of you bastards touch her, this red man will make you sorry you ever heard the name Amelia Donahue."

"What you gonna do about it, Injun?"

"I'll skin you alive and I mean that literally. My people are specialists at it and they taught me well."

A shot whizzed by Jed's head.

He fired back and the door slammed shut. Jed took advantage of it and darted closer to the cabin.

Glass broke in the small window in front and the gun barrel came out. It fired, but was way off the mark.

Jed fired and the rifle fell from the window. "Come on out and face me like a man, Callahan."

"If you think you're so tough, come on in and save your wife, breed." It was Vince's voice this time.

There was the sound of ripping cloth, then Amelia screamed again.

Knowing Vince had torn her dress, Jed gritted his teeth and darted to the next tree.

"Come on, Wainwright. I want you to see what a real man can do with pretty Amelia."

"Don't come in, Jed," Amelia cried. "They're going to kill…"

"Shut up, bitch."

There was the sound of a slap then Vince yelled, "Gag her, Smithy."

Jed darted again, dropped to the ground and rolled to the edge of the side wall of the cabin. In a fluid motion, he was on his feet and pressed near the door. He looked back and saw Curt and Ward easing forward.

"Check outside, Smithy. He's too quiet."

"I want to watch you take her clothes off, Vince."

"Damn it, fool. Look outside. I want him in here when I rape his wife."

Smithy cracked the door and peered around. "Don't see him. Maybe he left."

"Left, hell. He's out there. Start shooting."

Smithy stuck his pistol out, but before he could get off a shot, the door slammed against him. He fell backward, shooting toward the roof as he fell.

"What the…" Vince whirled around, putting Amelia in front of him. "Now you're here, the party can begin." He grabbed Amelia's right breast and she tried to cry out, but the gag stopped the sound.

Smithy was scrambling to his feet, but Jed kicked him in the groin and he crumpled, screaming in pain as he fell.

Jed started to spring toward Vince, but Callahan raised his pistol and placed it on Amelia's temple. "Come a step closer and I'll blow her head off. Wouldn't you like to see her pretty little brain scattered all over this room?"

Amelia looked at Jed with pleading eyes. It broke his heart, but at the moment, Callahan had the advantage. If he could get to Callahan without hurting Amelia, he'd rip the man apart with his hands. It was the first time he'd felt such rage since Marie's death. A rage he'd thought he'd never feel again, but he did. He felt it deep in his soul.

He knew Amelia must have seen his turmoil because she tried to smile at him through her tears and behind the bandana across her mouth. When he saw the smile in her eyes, it calmed him a little.

"Now I have you where I want you, Wainwright, and I'm going to put on a little show for you. You've had the pleasure of this beautiful woman for several months and now it's my turn."

"Touch her and you'll die."

"Oh, you mean touch her like this." Vince grabbed her breast again and twisted it.

Amelia withered in pain.

"You bastard."

Vince laughed. "If you think she has it bad now, wait until I start selling her body in California. Might start at the gold fields. Those miners will gladly pay a hefty price for something this pretty."

"I'll see you in hell first."

Vince laughed again, but stopped abruptly when Amelia slumped in his arm. He was caught off guard and stumbled trying to hold her. Jed went for his gun, but didn't get a chance to fire. Shots came through the door and Amelia was free. She staggered toward Jed as Vince fell backward. There was a bullet hole in his chest and one between his eyes.

Ward and Curt entered. One shoved Smithy, who was trying to get up, back to the floor. Elton and Andy ran in as Amelia fell into Jed's arms.

He took the gag off her mouth and whispered, "It's all right, honey. I'm here now. You're safe."

"Oh, Jed," was all she could manage to say.

Holding her exposed breast against his chest to prevent her embarrassment, he said, "Let's get out of here. The guys can handle it from here." He picked her up and headed out the door.

He didn't stop until he reached his horse. He only let her go long enough to remove his shirt and put it around her. He mounted then he reached down and lifted her into his lap and turned Devil toward their ranch.

Amelia put both arms around his waist and buried her face against his bare chest. He could feel her tears on his skin. "Jed, I never wanted any man to touch me except you."

"They never will, Amelia." He pulled her closer with his right arm.

It wasn't long until the others caught up with them. Smithy was riding with his hands tied and Ward was leading his horse. Vince was tied in a tarp across the horse Curt led.

Curt said, "We'll go to town and turn this vermin over to the sheriff. I'm sure he'll hang as soon as the circuit judge comes through. The town will take care of burying Callahan."

Jed nodded. "While Curt and Ward take care of things in town,

Andy, you and Elton go by Donahue's place and tell him what's happened. He has a right to know. Amelia and I'll see all of you back at the ranch later."

They nodded and rode away.

When they were out of sight, Jed said, "They're gone, honey. It's just you and me now."

"I knew you'd save me, Jed."

"I'm glad I was able to. I couldn't stand the thought of that man touching you."

"He said he was going to rape me in front of you."

"Thank God, he didn't get that chance."

They rode a little way in silence. Jed knew she needed to relax and he was trying to decide if he could tell her what he knew he should. Finally he broke the silence. "Do you feel like talking?"

"I don't know anything else to tell you."

There was a short pause. He then said, "Amelia, I swore if I found you before Callahan hurt you I'd confess to you why I've been so adamant about our relationship not lasting longer than the six months we agreed on."

"You don't have to, Jed."

"Yes I do. Curt says I'll never accept what happened to me if I don't share it with you. I'm beginning to believe he's right." He took a deep breath and continued. "I thought Marie's death left me unable to love again, but almost losing you made me realize that's not true. Still, I want you to know why I didn't think I could love another woman."

When she didn't reply, he went on. "Marie and I were kids when we fell in love and got married. I was eighteen and fresh from school in the east. Marie was only seventeen, but we were very much in love. Aunt Prudence bought us a small farm in Kansas. We built a cabin and began tilling the fields. We wanted to be farmers because we knew it was a good and honorable life. Our baby girl was born within a year of our marriage. She was a pretty little thing and we loved her very much. We named her Lily.

"Lily was a few weeks old when the tragedy happened. It was in the spring and we'd just eaten supper. I went out to do the chores in the barn while she fed the baby. Four rough-looking men rode up. I knew we were facing trouble and started running to the house, but I didn't make it. A bullet caught me in the side and I fell. The men dismounted and began laughing and cursing. They said things like, they had a half-breed cornered and how I thought I was living the life of a white man. One of them brandished a whisky bottle and asked if I had a wife who might need some company. I started for him and was shot again. One of them went into the house. I was screaming and cursing at them, but it did no good."

Amelia shuddered, but didn't say anything.

Jed's voice was filled with sorrow as he continued to speak. "He came out, dragging Marie. She was holding the baby to her breast, but they didn't care. They kept saying how she was nothing but a breed, too, and she should be honored to be with a white man. I tried again, to get to her, but they shot me a few more times and began beating me until I was in a semiconscious state. I was barely awake and close to death when one of them grabbed Lily and said they should rid the world of one more Indian by using it for target practice."

He swallowed and his voice got shaky when he said, "He tossed the baby in the air and they began shooting it. By this time Marie was hysterical, but that didn't matter. They began pawing at her and ripping off her clothes. When she was naked, they took turns raping her. That went on for a long time. They'd make a trip in the house, get something to eat, then come out and take turns on her again. I was in and out of consciousness, but somehow I memorized every one of their faces. I vowed those men would die for what they'd done to my family.

"Before they left, they set fire to the cabin. The leader looked down at me trying to crawl to my wife. I can still hear his ugly laugh as he shot me a couple of more times, then rode off."

"Oh, Jed." Amelia held him tighter. She wanted him to know she was feeling his pain with him. "The physical and mental pain must have been excruciating for you."

He responded by drawing her closer to him. "When I came to, twelve days had passed. My wife and child had been buried. When I realized I wasn't going to die, I let the hate and revenge fill my soul. I knew I'd never be satisfied until I caught those men. At first I thought being a U.S. Marshall was the answer, but the law moves too slow. I quit and became a bounty hunter. It took me five years, but I caught every one of those bastards and put them six feet under."

"That explains all those scars on your body." Amelia was crying as she held Jed. "I'm so sorry for all you've suffered."

"I've been filled with hate so long I didn't think I knew how to love."

"I think you can't help but love, Jed. You're a good man who has had a terrible past."

"No, Amelia. I'm jaded and…"

"I believe you care more than you admit. If not, why were you determined to get me away from Vince?"

"When I got to the house and found he'd taken you, everything in me screamed with the same pain I felt ten years ago. Though I have no right, I've known for some time that I love you, Amelia, but I wouldn't admit it, even to myself. Then when Vince kidnapped you, I knew I couldn't stand the thought of losing another wife."

"I'll be here as long as you want me, Jed."

"We have two months to work something out. Is that all right with you?"

"Yes, darling. Two months will give us all the time we need."

* * * *

After hot baths and supper, Amelia and Jed went to bed. They were exhausted and went to sleep with their arms wrapped around each other.

Curt was waiting for them when they came down for breakfast the next morning. After they were served, he broke the news about the Donahue ranch.

Tears came into Amelia's eyes. "How's Mother?"

"She's a strong woman and she's looking after your father. Wayne Rivers is keeping the ranch running."

"Did she want me to come?"

"Yes."

She looked at Jed and he said, "We'll go right away."

"Thank you," she whispered and squeezed his hand.

It was midday when they got to the Double D. Amelia's heart sank when she looked at the charred house where two men were working. The Wainwrights left their horses with Richard and Jed put his arm around her shoulder as they walked to the house.

Delores came out to meet them. "Oh, Miz Amelia, I'm so thankful you're all right. Your men came by and told us all about your rescue."

"I'm thankful to be away from that horrible man, Delores."

"We all are thankful." She looked at Jed. "You're Miz Elizabeth's hero, Mr. Jed. She said she'd love you like a son forever since you saved her girl."

"I appreciate that, but I would've tried to save Amelia if it was only for myself."

"I know that. Ain't a doubt in my mind how much you love your wife."

They reached the house and Delores said, "Your parents are in the downstairs bedroom, Miz Amelia."

"I think it's best if I wait in the kitchen with Delores," Jed said. "I could use another cup of coffee anyway."

"Are you sure?"

"Yes. You know how your daddy feels about me."

"I won't be long." She kissed his cheek quickly and headed down the hall.

Tapping on the bedroom door, Amelia didn't know what to expect. Would her Daddy greet her or would he turn her away? She prepared herself for either.

The door opened and Elizabeth threw her arms around Amelia. "Oh, darling, I'm so glad to see you. Jed told me he'd bring you back safe and he did. How are you feeling?"

"I'm fine, but how are you, Mother? You must be devastated about the house."

"I'm not as upset as you'd think. I have my daughter back and your father is beginning to see the light at last."

"How is he?"

"Come see. He's awake."

"Will he want me to come in?"

Elizabeth took her arm. "Yes, dear. He's been expecting you."

Amelia moved to the bed and almost gasped. Rafe looked sick and hollow-eyed. His hand shook as he reached for hers. "I'm glad you came."

"I'm sorry you were hurt, Daddy."

"I'll be all right. I'm the one who is sorry for what I almost did to you. I was a blind fool, Amelia. Can you ever forgive me?"

Amelia knew she was telling the truth when she said without hesitating, "Yes, Daddy."

"Your mother told me what happened. Did Callahan harm you in anyway?"

"No. Jed got there in time to save me."

Rafe nodded. "Amelia, I want to ask you something and there have been enough lies between us. I want you to tell me the truth about this."

"All right."

"Did you marry Wainwright to keep from marrying Vince or do you love the man?"

Amelia decided she would tell him the truth. Maybe he would listen this time. "A little bit of both." He frowned and she went on, saying, "I didn't want to marry Vince, so I made a play for Jed, but it wasn't long until I realized he was the only man I'd ever love. I want to give him children and grow old with him."

"Does he love you?"

She smiled. "Yes, he loves me."

"I want to talk to him, but I'm a little tired right now. It will have to be later."

"Why don't you take a nap, dear? Amelia and Jed will eat dinner then you can talk with him this afternoon."

"Will he come to see me?" Her daddy looked at her.

"If I ask him to, he will." Amelia smiled at him.

"Good. I'm glad he respects you that much." He closed his eyes. "Why don't you go eat with them, Elizabeth? You need to get out of here for a while."

"I'll do that." She straightened his covers. "Sheldon said he or his nurse would be back to check on you after dinner."

Amelia leaned over and kissed his cheek. "I'm sorry Vince shot you, Daddy. I've never trusted him, but I never dreamed he'd do that."

"I did trust him, honey and he shot me anyway, but the important thing is he didn't hurt you."

Amelia patted his hand and went out the door with her mother.

* * * *

After a special dinner Delores served them, Jed and Amelia stood with Elizabeth around Rafe's bed. He was saying, "Now that I've admitted what a fool I've been and apologized to Wainwright for my actions toward him, I'd like for you ladies to leave the room. I need to talk to him alone."

"But Rafe, shouldn't we…" Elizabeth started.

"Don't worry, dear. He's the only one wearing a gun."

Jed winked at Amelia.

She smiled back at him and turned to her mother. "I think they'll be fine. Let's go see how the men are doing with the repairs on the house."

Jed watched the door close behind Elizabeth and Amelia. He couldn't understand why Rafe Donahue wanted to talk to him alone, but he'd go along with it. He waited for Rafe to break the silence.

"There are some things going on I don't want my wife and daughter to know right now," Rafe said.

"I don't like keeping things from Amelia."

"Humor me. It won't be long until she knows all about it." Jed nodded and Rafe went on. "I'm not long for this world, Wainwright."

"Why do you say that?"

"The doctor told me I'm dying. I asked him not to tell Elizabeth for a few days. I want to make things right for her and I need your help."

Jed couldn't hide his surprise. "I'll do what I can."

"Then let's see if we can come up with a plan we both can agree on."

* * * *

"Mother, they've been talking for almost two hours. What in the world could they be saying?"

"I don't know, honey, but I haven't heard any yelling."

"They won't be talking or yelling much longer. I see the doctor coming."

The doctor climbed out of his buggy and helped his nurse down. He introduced Esther to Amelia, then Elizabeth led the two of them down the hall to Rafe's bedroom.

In a matter of minutes, Jed joined Amelia on the porch.

"I'm glad to see you alive. I hope Daddy is." She looked at him with a laugh.

Jed chuckled. "We're both fine." He reached for her hand. "Come on. Let's take a ride. I want you to show me this ranch."

Richard saddled Rambler while Jed saddled Devil. Soon they were headed across the land. Jed had very little to say and Amelia concentrated on pointing out different sections of the ranch. She knew it would take several days to show him all of it, but she had special places she wanted him to see on this first time out.

Two hours later, they dismounted and tied their horses in a hidden glade near a stream with a small rocky waterfall. "This has always been one of my favorite spots. When I was little, I'd come here and play. As I grew older, I'd come here to pout when I didn't get my way. As an adult, I'd come here to reflect and think."

"Let's sit awhile." He took a blanket from his horse and spread it under a cottonwood tree.

She sat beside him in silence. She knew he wanted to talk with her, but she wouldn't ask questions. She wanted the lead to come from him.

Sitting with his back against the tree, he put his arm around her and pulled her close to him. Without preamble, he said, "Your father wants me to take over the Double D Ranch."

Shocked, Amelia looked up at him. "Really?" When he only nodded, she added, "What did you say?"

"We haven't worked out the details." She frowned and he said, "What do you think?"

"I want you to do whatever makes you happy. I'll support you."

"So if I turn it down, you'd be satisfied to live at the Circle 2?"

"Yes, Jed. As long as you want me with you, I'll live anywhere you choose."

"About that," he said as he pulled her closer to him, "I don't have five thousand dollars in my pocket, but I haven't spent a dime of the money you gave me. Next time I go to town, I'll get it out of the bank. Would you be willing to take it and extend our time together?"

"For another six months?" She looked at him.

He smiled as he looked into her eyes. "I was thinking more like forever."

She trembled. "Oh, Jed. Are you sure?"

"I've never been more sure of anything. I love you, Amelia. I've known all along I was falling in love with you, but was too stubborn to admit it. Yesterday I realized I didn't want to live without you. I know I'm asking a lot of you to tie yourself to a half-Lakota Indian, but I want us to be together for the rest of our lives. I'm even going to write Aunt Prudence and invite her to visit."

"Oh, Jed." She flung her arms around his neck and kissed him hungrily.

Within minutes they were undressed and making love as a cool breeze filtered across their bodies. Amelia knew she'd never love this man more than she did as she surrendered not only her body, but the rest of her life to him.

Their passion spent, she lay in his arms with a contentment she never dreamed she'd feel. There was only one thing she felt she had to do. Running her fingers through the hair on his chest and fingering the scars there, she said, "I need to tell you something, and I'm not sure how you'll feel about it."

"What is it, Sweetheart?"

She decided the best way was to be blunt. "I'm pregnant, Jed."

He chuckled. "I think it's time you told me."

She sat up and looked down at him. "How did you know?"

He pulled her closer. "I didn't know for sure until today."

She frowned and he went on, saying, "Amelia, we've made love enough times that I know every inch of your body. When I held you today, how could I miss the fact that you were getting a little thick in the middle? Not to mention the throwing up. It had made me wonder."

"Why hadn't you said anything?"

"I was afraid you didn't want to have my child."

She sat up and glared at him. "How could I not want the child of the man I love?"

"A lot of women wouldn't want to have a child fathered by a man like me. You know this baby will be part Indian."

"Of course it will and how dare you think I wouldn't want it."

He pulled her down on his chest. "I'm happy you want our child, Amelia. I want it, too."

"You're not just staying with me because I'm pregnant, are you, Jed?"

"No, Amelia. I love you and I want us to be together always. I'm sorry I ever doubted you'd want our baby."

"We made this baby together and it'll be half of each of us." She kissed his chin. "I hope it's a boy with beautiful black hair and bronze skin, like his father."

He smiled and pulled her tighter to him. "A beautiful little girl would be nice, too, but I don't want her running off at eighteen and marrying a strange man like her mother did."

"If this stranger turned out to be as wonderful as her father, I wouldn't mind too much."

"Whatever it is, let's hope we can keep it here on the ranch to grow and thrive until he or she is a responsible adult."

Her forehead wrinkled. "Are you saying we're going to move to the Double D?"

"If we can work out a few more details. I still have to clear some things with your father and there're things I have to work out with Curt."

"As I said, as long as I'm with the man I love, it doesn't matter to me where we live."

They lingered in each other's arms for a while longer, then dressed and headed back to the house, both knowing with the love they shared, they could work through anything.

Epilogue

Rafe Donahue died three weeks after Jed and Amelia moved into the master suite of the huge house. He was pleased to learn he was going to be a grandfather and was content knowing life would go on through this child. Elizabeth spent most of her days sewing baby clothes and making sure Amelia and her man had the best of care. Delores was about as bad. One would have thought she was going to be a grandmother, too.

Amelia's now large protruding stomach announced to the world it would only be a short time before there was an heir to the former Double D Ranch. It took a while for everyone to accept the ranch was now part of the huge Circle 2 spread. Renaming the ranch was one of the details Jed worked out with Rafe. It wasn't easy for the older man to give in, but he did and now everyone was beginning to accept the new name. For the present, Jed and Amelia owned three fourths of the ranch, but there were papers drawn up saying Curt would be buying the original Circle 2, where he lived and where Juanita had stayed as his housekeeper. Another agreement that Jed and Rafe had was that both ranches would be combined as one but would carry the names of Jed Wainwright and Curt Allison and their families as owners of the enormous Circle 2. It surprised Jed when Elizabeth had to sign for everything to be legal which she did gladly. He never dreamed she was the one with all the real power in the Donahue family.

Only two of Rafe's cowhands refused to work for an Indian and left when Jed took over. The others seemed to come to life and were proud of the work they did, now they were out from under Vince Callahan's demanding ways. Because of his hard work, Ward Kyler was promoted to head foreman and worked between the two sections of the ranch. His assistants were Wayne Rivers at Jed's place and Darrel Reid at Curt's.

Jed wrote his Aunt Prudence in Kansas and told her about his marriage and his coming child. It wasn't long until she wrote back and told him she was thrilled and she'd be visiting as soon as she could pack her bags and buy her ticket.

When her letter reached them, they had two days to get ready for the visit. Delores scurried around and set up a special guest room for her. Elizabeth managed to find out from Jed some of the woman's favorite foods and plans were made to throw a party to introduce Jed's aunt to the rest of Settlers Ridge.

The two days slipped by quickly and on the morning Prudence Wainwright was to arrive, Amelia announced at breakfast that Jed should be the one to pick her up. "You haven't seen her in several years, honey," Amelia explained. "It would be best if yours was the first face she saw when she got off the stagecoach."

"But I don't want to leave you. It's getting awfully close to the time our baby will be born."

"I'll be fine. This baby will come when it decides to come. We can't make arrange…" She suddenly dropped her fork and her eyes got big as she bent over and grabbed her stomach. "Oh! It hurts," she screamed.

Jed didn't wait. He threw down his napkin and grabbed Amelia up in his arms. "I'm putting you to bed. Send Richard for the doctor, Delores."

"I'll do it." Delores set the coffee pot on the table and ran toward the back door.

Elizabeth jumped up and followed Jed up the stairs.

In their room, Jed put his gasping wife on the bed. "Amelia, I love you," was all he could think of to say.

"I love you, too, Jed, but I want my mother."

"I'm right here, honey." She turned to Jed. "Go downstairs and make sure Delores puts on lots of hot water then go get your aunt."

"I'll tell Delores, but I'm not leaving. I want to make…"

Amelia let out another scream.

"Then send someone to get Prudence. Now scoot. I'll get Amelia undressed."

"I'll send Ward." Jed ran to the door.

"He's excited, isn't he, Mother?"

"Very excited, dear, but I'll try to keep him under control."

Amelia laughed then grimaced and let out a groan.

If he didn't know better, Jed would've sworn the day was a week long. Amelia kept crying out and he wouldn't leave her side. "I swear I'll never put you through this again," he promised her over and over.

When the doctor arrived, he shooed Jed from the room. Since Esther came with him, Elizabeth was able to go downstairs and try to calm her son-in-law. She didn't have much luck.

Six hours later, tall, sophisticated Aunt Prudence walked through the front door and Jed started forward to welcome her. A baby's cry stopped him and without speaking to anyone, he turned and took the stairs two at a time.

"Why, land of Goshen, that boy hasn't changed a whit. He's still scattered in all directions," Prudence said.

"Please come in, Miss Wainwright. I'm afraid my son-in-law isn't quite himself today."

Before Prudence could answer, Jed appeared at the top of the steps with a big grin on his face. "I have a son, everybody, but they won't let me see Amelia yet."

With a smile, Elizabeth said, "Don't worry, honey. They'll let you see her soon."

An hour later, Elizabeth and Prudence entered the bedroom. Amelia looked tired, but beautiful, propped on the feather pillows and Jed looked comfortable sitting in the rocking chair beside the bed with his son in his arms. He was still grinning.

"Our son has his father's black hair and dark eyes. He's beautiful, Mother." Amelia reached for her mother's hand.

"I knew he would be." Elizabeth kissed her daughter's forehead, introduced Prudence then turned to view her grandson.

"Well, young lady, if my nephew here doesn't treat you and the little one right, you let me know. His Aunt Prudence could always handle him."

Amelia laughed. "I'll do that, but so far he's been a wonderful husband. I know he'll be a great Daddy."

"Come see your great-nephew, Aunt Prudence."

Elizabeth and Prudence cooed over the baby.

"Have you chosen a name?" Prudence asked.

"We have." Jed looked down at Amelia. "He's Aaron after my father and Rafe after Amelia's."

Tears filled Elizabeth's eyes. "Thank you."

Jed stood and held the baby out to his mother-in-law. "Would you like to hold him, Grandmother?"

"Oh yes." She took the chair and Jed gave her the baby. Prudence came to stand by her shoulder.

After the baby went to sleep, Elizabeth placed it in the crib beside the bed. She and Prudence kissed the happy couple and left the room.

Jed moved to the edge of the bed and took Amelia's hand. Leaning over to kiss her, he whispered, "Thank you for my wonderful son."

"Next time I'll try to give you a daughter."

"I promised you I wouldn't put you through this again."

She laughed. "Give me six months and I'll change your mind, Jed Wainwright."

He shook his head. "Who would've ever thought that when a tiny blonde knocked on my hotel room door, my six-foot-four frame would become her slave for life?"

"I decided that six-foot-four frame could do anything with me it wanted the minute he dropped the towel, and I saw the first naked man I'd ever seen."

He grinned. "He better be the only one you ever see."

"Don't worry. No other man could ever measure up to you."

He kissed her. "No woman will ever compare to you either, my love. Not only have you made me a happy man, you've given me a chance to love again. You're my life, Amelia. You always will be."

Neither needed to say anything else. The love in their eyes said it all.

About the Author

Agnes Alexander knew she'd one day write western novels when she made her first trip west. Other vacations in the area fueled this flame and her first western novel, *Fiona's Journey,* was published in 2012. Since then, she's had seven other books published and *Amelia's Marriage* will be her eighth. When she's not writing, she loves spending time with her family, making jewelry, playing board games and hanging out with other writers. She lives in her home state of North Carolina and loves hearing from her readers. Contact her at www.Agnesalexander.com

For your reading pleasure, we invite you to visit our web bookstore

WHISKEY CREEK PRESS

www.whiskeycreekpress.com

Made in the USA
Columbia, SC
18 April 2022

59153901R00174